MRS. WOODBINE'S PREJUDICES

ABOUT THE AUTHOR

Michael Ladner was born in Princeton, N.J., where his Viennese father was a medieval historian at the Institute for Advanced Study, alongside fellow academics Robert Oppenheimer and Albert Einstein. Having been patted on the head approvingly by the latter, Michael went on to take a B.A. from Harvard, an M.A. from New York University, and a Ph.D. in Philosophy from Claremont Graduate University, with further studies at the San Francisco Art Institute and School of Visual Arts. He has taught American and European History, Art History, Psychology and English, and has lived mostly in Brooklyn and Manhattan. In 2006, he and his wife moved to California. In this, his third novel, he draws on his father's and grandfather's forced exile from Austria, following the Nazi *Anschluss*.

Mrs. Woodbine's Prejudices

Michael Ladner

Published 2024 in Great Britain and the USA by EnvelopeBooks
12 Wellfield Avenue, London N10 2EA
116 West 73rd Street, New York, NY 10023
www.envelopebooks.co.uk
A New Premises venture in association with Booklaunch

Cover design by Stephen Games | Booklaunch

A CIP catalogue record for this title is available from the British Library and the Library of Congress Cataloging-in-Publication Data

Edited and designed by Booklaunch
EnvelopeBooks 21
ISBN 9781915023490

To the real Adrian and Val

The Age of Ike

TEN YEAR-OLD Marcus Lash brought his bicycle to a standstill next to his mother and father, pushed his eyeglasses up on his nose, and searched for his big brother among the troops gathered in formation at the opposite end of Running Brook Park. Yes, there was Adrian, wearing a uniform and supporting a heavy flag against his shoulder. Marcus especially admired his brother's flat-brimmed, high-crowned hat; it reminded him of a picture in a textbook: volunteers charging up a hill with fixed bayonets; the future president mounted on a horse, waving a pistol. Adrian was almost too old for the Boy Scouts, Marcus thought, but not too young to have enlisted in the Spanish-American War.

"Having a good time? Thank heavens it's nice weather!" Joyce Lash's voice, anxious on her youngest son's behalf, banished the Rough Riders. "We didn't have much fun last Fourth of July, did we? Not with all that rain."

Marcus knew he was his mother's favorite. Her purpose in life was to make him happy. But what if he'd never been born? Who would have been her favorite then? He felt an urge to do something she wouldn't like: pull his T-shirt up over his round stomach and skinny chest. The shirt snagged on his eyeglasses before he managed to yank it over his head.

"The sun's going to get covered up by those clouds," Joyce said. "Aren't you going to be cold?"

"I don't think so. It's at least eighty degrees."

"Oh, Marcus! It can't be more than the seventies!"

Marcus glanced sideways at his father, a great believer in the outdoors. His father would approve. Boys needed toughening! But his father was distracted by a group of veterans who were laughing uproariously. He shook his head disapprovingly, as if their fun were out of place. Then he bent down and ruffled the hair on the back of Marcus's neck.

"Tail feathers!" said Professor Lash, fingering his own hair. "I could stand a trim myself. We'll go on Saturday. We won't be too busy, will we Joyce?"

"Just packing up a thousand things."

"I thought that's why you sent for Mrs. Woodbine. But if you want me to stay home all weekend, I won't leave the house."

"Just tell Mario not too short. Tell him to make it look like a crew-cut growing out."

"Mario knows what he's doing."

Marcus let out an exaggerated sigh. "Do I have to go?"

"Daddy's right. You should look nice when you see your grandfather."

"I don't see why there's always a problem with the boys' haircuts," Professor Lash said."

The problem, Marcus wanted to say, was that Mario's clippers left his neck and ears looking scalped. Besides, the magazines in the barber's shop were months, even years old. He practically knew by heart a story about a family leaving a hubcap out overnight to collect moisture so they wouldn't die of thirst in the desert. On the magazine's back cover there was an advertisement for whisky, featuring pictures of explorers, with captions that explained what was going on. *Tracking Grizzlies to their Lair Was the Easy Part. The Hard Part Was Getting Out Alive!* When it was all over, the men rewarded themselves with Canadian Club. Marcus liked that his own father drank Canadian Club, even though he didn't go on any dangerous adventures.

"When I was two years old," Professor Lash was saying, "the mothers wanted their boys to look like *Little Lord Fauntleroy*. Long curls! *Muttersöhnchenen,* my father called it. Mama's Boys!"

"I'm not a Mama's Boy."

"Of course not, darling!"

"I hate Mario's."

Mario's wall calendar for the year 1960, with a picture of Miss Rheingold above the days of the month, for some reason put him in a bad mood. So did the jar of blue disinfectant that held scissors and combs. Then there were the uncanny reflections in the wall mirrors facing and behind the barber's chair. Finally, after it was all over, he had to tip the elderly black man who swept up the customers' fallen tufts.

"Val's hair's longer than mine. Mr. d'Ambrosio hardly takes off any. Can't I go to the Kleencut?"

Professor Lash chuckled. "You're not Val. You wouldn't like it if we treated all three of you alike, would you?" He patted Marcus on the back.

Marcus thought he *would* like it. That way he would be entitled to the same freedoms that his two older brothers enjoyed. There was a time when he'd envied Val and Adrian's spankings, which were a mark of being old enough to get into trouble. But those spankings, which didn't seem to hurt all that much, came to an end after his mother read a book about raising children without corporal punishment.

"If I were you," his mother was saying, "I'd be much happier at Mario's. It's where all the kids go. Hardly anybody goes to the Kleencut."

Marcus knew perfectly well why his brother was sent to the town's only other barber shop; it was because he'd once said something rude to Mario. The "flaxen prince" walked out of the Kleencut looking as handsome as when he'd walked in. Mr. d'Ambrosio, whose hands were abnormally long and white, joked that Val had a future in Hollywood. The barber wasn't the only one. When the family dined out, powdery old ladies whispered compliments. *Those eyes!*

"Do I *have* to go?"

But Professor Lash had already forgotten about haircuts. He was watching some women arrange food on a picnic table.

"The usual. Hot dogs, hamburgers, potato chips, Coca-Cola. The Great American Diet."

"I hope it's safe," Joyce said. "All that raw food sitting out in the heat, with flies buzzing around."

"I haven't heard," Arthur said, "of anyone getting food poisoning."

Marcus sighed and shaded his eyes against the sun's bright glare. At the far boundary of Running Brook Park, he could make out the town's historic cemetery, where the bones of a certain slave-owning Jacob Van Planck lay buried. Closer in, an Uncle Sam on stilts bowed and waved to the crowd. Children rode past on bikes decorated with colored streamers. A dog chased a tennis ball. All but a few stubborn clouds had disappeared. Marcus felt the sun beating down on his exposed flesh. He thought back to last year's Fourth of July. He and his mother had taken shelter from a downpour. An older boy had run out from under the canvas, let his baseball cap fill up with water and spilled it over his head. Then he'd run around in the warm rain, laughing. Marcus remembered feeling sick with envy. But it was useless; his mother wouldn't want him getting drenched, with nothing dry to change into.

Loudspeakers announced the national anthem. Everyone faced in the same direction. Professor Lash placed his hand on his chest; it was important to show loyalty to his adopted country. There were three patriotic songs in all, followed by the Pledge of Allegiance. When it was over, people sighed, stretched and looked around. Marcus dismounted and rested his bicycle on its kickstand. He sat down on the grass and stretched his legs out.

"Adrian looks handsome in his uniform," Joyce was saying. "I'm sorry it's his last year. If he'd tried harder he could have made Eagle Scout."

"When I was a Boy Scout," Arthur said, "things were different. We climbed the Alps, slept in huts, lived on bread and cheese."

"You should volunteer, once Marcus is old enough."

"*Ach!* I can't change how they do things in this country. I don't blame Val for quitting. Marching around the football field in the rain!"

"Val's troop had a different hat," Marcus said. "Like the one Uncle Philip wore in the army. I'll only join if I can wear a hat like Adrian's."

His mother and father both laughed and then began talking in lowered voices. It seemed to Marcus, not for the first time, that they were different from other parents. Wasn't there something special about them? He had always thought so. Four years ago, everyone else's parents wore *I Like Ike* pins, whereas the Lashes went *All the Way with Adlai*. His father made fun of American politics and customs. He had a special word for things like plastic furniture covers and lace doilies—*Dubrova*, he called them, after the janitor who'd lived on the lowest level of his childhood home. Another word, *Cat-Fat*, stood for American snacks loaded with artificial cream, sweeteners, flavors, coloring. None of the other fathers knew more than one language, spoke English with an accent or had relatives living overseas.

And in a week, the whole family, even the dog, were going to cross the ocean to visit Granddaddy, who wouldn't last many more years, even if his new wife pretended he was as young as she was.

Marcus stretched out on the grass, crossed his arms behind his head and faced the sun with his eyes shut. The aching brightness penetrated his eyelids. He turned his head to the side and watched his mother, still talking about something she didn't want him to overhear. Wasn't she special too? She wasn't foreign but she was beautiful in a framed photo that stood on her bureau, taken before her marriage. In the picture, her hair fell in soft wings and a string of pearls formed a semicircle against her expensive sweater. Marcus doubted that the other mothers in Garnet had ever looked that nice. But today she was wearing an ordinary blouse and skirt, and she looked middle-aged. Well, she *was* almost middle-aged, forty-two in another month.

Joyce noticed that her son was staring. "What's on your mind, darling? You look lost in thought."

"Nothing."

"His name's Marcus," Professor Lash interjected. "*Darling* is for babies and little dogs."

"Forgive me, Arthur; I'll remember to call him Marcus next time."

"Your mother's getting forgetful. Just wait until she's my age! Fifty, for God's sake! She won't remember where she left the car keys." Arthur leaned over and kissed his wife on the cheek.

It seemed to Marcus that his mother and father had been married a long time. Long enough to have three children anyway. For years he'd pictured them in a doctor's office, lying flat on their backs on a table while something was transferred from male to female. But then last summer, Kathleen Billet told him about her first visit from a "Mr. X". Kathleen lived opposite St. Thomas the Apostle, where the Lashes went to Sunday mass. She wouldn't explain who Mr. X was but she kept teasing Marcus for not knowing, and finally he went home and asked. His mother had informed him that from now on Kathleen would bleed from a certain place in her body, at a certain time of the month. It wasn't at all dangerous, but simply a sign that she was old enough to make a baby. *Intercourse*, his mother went on to explain, was something married people liked to do with certain parts of their body because they loved each other, even when making a baby was the farthest thing from their minds. A couple could avoid having a child, if they didn't want one, by practicing the rhythm method. There were other, less natural methods that Catholics weren't allowed. The Davidsons must have used no method. The Davidsons were friends who lived in Buffalo. There were eleven of them including the mother and father, and when a large chunk of the family came to visit it was hard finding places for everyone to sleep.

Marcus felt wiser once he understood who Mr. X was but he didn't see what was so enjoyable about intercourse. Young people, his mother said, sometimes got carried away, but it was better to wait, otherwise a girl might feel taken advantage of. Besides, risking an unwanted baby was asking for trouble. Marcus had wanted to ask her why they got carried away in the first place. He didn't see the point of kissing a girl you weren't even related to, or the other things teenagers supposedly did at parties with the lights turned off. He wondered if Adrian thought about intercourse very often. It wasn't something they'd ever discussed. He vaguely remembered touching himself when he was a very small boy, when his "thing" felt hard and tingly, until his mother caught him doing it and told him to stop. Another time he'd opened her gown while she was holding him in her arms and tried to peek at her breasts. One day, maybe, he would find himself attracted to the opposite sex, in the same way iron filings were attracted to a magnet. In the meantime, it was mysterious and even a little frightening. A few weeks ago, his mother had sat on the edge of his bed, just before he was supposed to go to sleep. A man, she said, had been caught somewhere in town. It had come up at a PTA meeting. Parents were advised to speak frankly to their children. Marcus mustn't ever go off with a stranger, who might want to *do things*. She didn't want to frighten him but it was best to be on the safe side.

He'd had trouble falling asleep afterwards, imagining a man in baggy trousers jumping out from behind some bushes and grabbing his arm. Suppose the man tried to pull his pants down? He would run for help. There were bound to be adults around: a policeman maybe, or one of the grown-ups in Running Brook Park, waiting patiently for their hamburgers and hot dogs. Most had children of their own. None of them wanted to pull his pants down.

"I hope Horace is all right," Joyce was saying. "It's a long time to leave him alone."

Marcus suddenly remembered that he was supposed to have put out a water dish for Horace, left behind in his fenced enclosure. Absorbed in decorating his bike, he'd forgotten. A dog could die of thirst on a hot day. He ought to ride home and fill Horace's dish from the garden hose. But there was a smell of charcoal and frying meat in the air, the Coca-Cola bottles sparkled in their tubs of ice, and if he went, all the food would have been eaten up by the time he got back. Horace could wait another half-hour.

"Horace is fine," Professor Lash said. "But where's Val gone to?"

"He probably went somewhere with Curtis Blow." Marcus didn't say that Val and his friend were probably making little fires out of twigs and leaves. Curtis Blow was a firebug.

"Val is getting harder to keep track of every day. Like Sputnik!"

Marcus snickered at his father's joke. He knew what lay behind it. Lately Val had taken to keeping his distance and insisting on his rights. The previous week he'd insisted on wearing his engineer boots to eighth-grade graduation. The boots, made of dull black leather with buckled straps, were a fad; all the boys at Van Planck Middle School owned a pair. Marcus recalled sitting on the staircase, listening to his father and Val shout at each other in the living room. Did Val want people thinking he was a *Strassenbube?* But then his father had laughed in spite of himself and translated the word into *street boy,* although it was more like *juvenile delinquent.* In the end, as a concession, Val was allowed to wear his blue nylon bomber jacket, at least until the graduation ceremony got underway.

After graduation, Val had wanted to go off with some of his friends, but there was a special lunch waiting at home, with cake and a present. In the car driving home, Val had leaned his head against the glass on his side of the back seat and sulked. His eyes were closed. Marcus had thought his brother might be holding back tears. It was hot in the car; his father hated drafts, even in summer, so all the windows were shut, except for a small triangular one next to his mother, who was driving. His father liked to repeat a story from his childhood: how, flushed and sweating from over-exertion, he sat too close to an open window and afterwards felt strangely shivery and weak. The next day he'd come down with whooping cough. The doctor, a grey-bearded gentleman in a long coat, prescribed two weeks in a darkened bedroom. He might have perished!

"If Val's not back in five minutes," Professor Lash was saying, "we'll have to start our picnic without him."

Val wouldn't have cared. His eating habits were strange. What everyone else liked left him cold. Shredded cereal soaking in milk and sugar was his favorite. Why were they even discussing it? Everybody, Marcus thought, ought to be used to him by now.

Mrs. Woodbine

THE WEEK FOLLOWING July Fourth was taken up with travel preparations. Mrs. Woodbine came to help pack and close up the house. She was a widow in her fifties, originally from the rural South. Two or three times a year she traveled up from her home near what she liked to call "the nation's capital". Almost the first thing she did when the taxi left her off at the Lashes' was to change into sensible shoes and a house dress that shifted back and forth across her frame. She was not fat, only very big. Her large hands rested in her lap when she sat in the kitchen and talked at length about her grown-up children, John-Wesley and Arlene, her son-in-law Woody, and her two grandchildren, Junior and Harlan. Mrs. Woodbine also had an aged mother and numerous brothers and sisters as well as cousins who suffered from strange-sounding ailments—one had a collapsed womb and another had something that sounded like *tick doolaroo*—or else they were down on their luck in some other way.

Ruby Woodbine and Marcus had once been best friends. She'd laughed at his clever sayings and delighted in his crayon drawings; given him his bath; even comforted him when they were out for a walk and he was gripped by a terrific cramp and had to let everything go. At the Lashes' summer cottage, she lay next to him on the bed when he took his nap with the windows open and a fan blowing. If he couldn't fall asleep, Mrs. Woodbine told him about her childhood: how she could make a hen go to sleep by adjusting its wings, and how she'd slept on a straw mattress and walked miles to school, traveling always in a group, in case anyone was lying in wait with jeers—or worse.

Mrs. Woodbine did not play cards, nor drank, nor danced. Her Daddy had made her promise that she would not do these things, and Mrs. Woodbine thought a promise made to a parent was no different than a promise made to God and therefore binding forever. She made an exception for Go-Fish, and on occasion she took a sip of wine at the dinner table. When this happened, Professor Lash congratulated her on her courage and, in revenge, Mrs. Woodbine put on an ironic smile as she watched the family get ready for Sunday mass. She knew all about incense, holy water and other sorts of idolatry; her own church had swept such nonsense away long ago. "All those monks messing around," she told Marcus behind his parents' back. "Never an honest day's work!"

Mrs. Woodbine would like to have accompanied the Lashes across the ocean, to see for herself a part of the world that hadn't reformed yet. The family, she understood, would be making a side trip from Vienna to Italy. That aroused Mrs. Woodbine's curiosity. She'd seen pictures in a magazine of a Roman fountain with water spouting from the mouths of Neptune and his minions. She would like to have seen it all just once, so that she could tell her brothers and sisters and children and grandchildren. But, of course, no one thought of taking her along.

The week of travel preparations passed quickly. On a Tuesday morning, the Lash family rose early and took a train and then a taxi to their point of embarkation. Mrs. Woodbine tagged along; she insisted on seeing them off before she headed back to Pennsylvania Station and caught her train home. Professor Lash said it was a wonder all their luggage fit into the taxi; Mrs. Woodbine's suitcase, he muttered to Joyce, took up practically the whole trunk. This was an exaggeration but it was true that everyone had to keep a bag or suitcase on their lap.

The departure shed was already crowded when the Lashes arrived. There were separate lines for the two classes. The Lashes were traveling "tourist". Arthur had declined his father's offer to pay for first class; they would all be perfectly comfortable, he said, with less luxurious accommodations. Joyce had felt momentarily disappointed, but after all it wasn't her father's money and she had no right to object.

The S.S. *Columbus* was supposed to embark at noon, with boarding to commence well in advance. By eleven o'clock there were still no signs of departure. The Lashes began to feel very restless. Marcus wondered if somebody had discovered a gash in the hull; in that case, they would have to go home. More likely, he decided, it was a routine delay, no different from waiting for hours in the pediatrician's office. In the meantime, children sat on suitcases and folded-up coats; two boys were playing tag. A porter elbowed past, shouting something. Marcus felt nauseous from the stuffy air. His father had insisted on dress shirts and ties, and his mother had made everyone bring trench coats in case of rain. Val hadn't been allowed to take his bomber jacket and engineer boots. What would Granddaddy say? Hermann Lasch drew an inflexible line between respectable boys and *Strassenbuben.*

"They're bound to start boarding any minute. Someone needs to find Val." Joyce checked her wristwatch. "We shouldn't have let him wander off."

"Adrian, go look for him." Professor Lash folded down a corner of a page in his paperback and shoved it into his jacket pocket. "Or do I have to go myself?"

"We should have put him in the crate with Horace," Adrian said.

"Just go, Adrian. And don't dawdle."

Marcus imagined Val locked up in Horace's crate. He wouldn't fit. Even Horace barely squeezed in. His parents had meant to board Horace, but then his mother read a newspaper article about dogs getting sick and even dying in boarding kennels, and none of their friends was willing to adopt a dog for six whole weeks. Horace, Joyce said, would enjoy a change of scenery. The dog was going to be a nuisance, Arthur said, but he was too excited about the trip to argue.

Over an hour earlier, a porter had wheeled Horace away. Watching him go, Joyce began to worry. For the next several days, the dog would have to make do with dry food instead of his usual ground beef. Suppose he refused to eat? He would lose weight. He might get seasick. Why couldn't they have flown? They had all seen a photograph of the president boarding a commercial jetliner. *IKE'S HISTORIC FLIGHT,* the caption read. But Professor Lash said that jet airplanes hadn't been thoroughly tested. Marcus thought his father was right: the passengers might survive a crash in an inflatable raft, but Horace, thrown from the aircraft along with the other baggage, wouldn't stand a chance.

"I keep thinking about poor Horace," Joyce said. "All alone for four days."

"It was your idea," Arthur reminded her.

"I'll have to see if I can take him for a walk on deck, even if I have to bribe an officer."

Marcus had studied the ship's brochure and seen the picture of officers in white uniforms and braided caps. You could probably be arrested for trying to bribe one of them. Another picture showed a crew member, also in white, serving bouillon to a woman stretched out on a deck chair. According to the brochure, there would be dancing to a live band, betting on wooden horses and a club with a nautical theme for teenagers. Joyce said it would be a good opportunity for Adrian and Val to mingle.

"Val's going to make us miss the boat," Professor Lash was saying. "We'll have to leave him behind—" But then he stopped short, startled by the rapid approach of a tall, big-boned woman. Mrs. Woodbine! Hadn't she already said her good-byes and kissed each of the boys on the cheek? Shouldn't she be on her train by now?

"I never knew I had it on me," Mrs. Woodbine said between breaths, "not until I was on the train!" In one hand she held a sack containing Horace's blanket, bowl, toys and biscuits. In her other hand she gripped her big suitcase.

"What's she doing here?" said Val, who had returned with Adrian just in time to witness Mrs. Woodbine's arrival. He sounded disgusted, as if she were a stranger asking for change.

"She's brought us Horace's blanket. Really, she shouldn't have bothered … ." Joyce's words trailed off. She looked as if she was standing at the scene of an accident.

"Awfully kind of you, Mrs. Woodbine," Professor Lash said. "We're always forgetting things, right boys?"

"Awful kind, my foot!" Mrs. Woodbine took a deep breath. "There I was, the train rarin' to go. I said, 'Ruby, you've got a-hold of Horace's things!' I knew that dog wouldn't get a wink of sleep without his blanket to lay himself across. I had a feeling the boat wouldn't leave on time and you all hadn't boarded yet." Mrs. Woodbine gave Marcus a conspiratorial wink. "Slowpokes!"

"I don't know why," Joyce said, "I always have to think of everything."

"I reckon it's a *sign*."

Adrian whispered in Marcus's ear: "*A sign*. She's getting up the nerve to say she wants to come with us. Maybe she already bought a ticket."

Marcus giggled. It was all so funny! Of course, Adrian was kidding. Mrs. Woodbine would have let them talk her into it, but she wouldn't dare buy a ticket on her own, and at the last minute, would she?

"My mouth sure gets dry. Anyone want a Life Saver?" Mrs. Woodbine rummaged in her pocketbook and gave a little cry.

"You'd never guess I had *this* on me!" She withdrew a booklet stamped with the seal of the United States of America. "I always keep it on me, just in case." Mrs. Woodbine looked sheepish, as if she realized the Lashes knew she was fibbing, and then added, "I don't have a driver's license. Suppose somebody asks me to prove I'm me?" She winked at Marcus again and lowered her voice to a whisper. "One of those fellas from the F.B.I."

People were observing the Lashes with amused, curious faces. A woman in line ahead of them turned around and grinned at the comedy. Mrs. Woodbine fell silent. A strange look passed over her features, as if she had been caught red-handed. It reminded Marcus of a story she'd once told him: how she'd played hooky and her Daddy had come after her with a switch, and she'd managed to wheedle her way out of being punished.

Mrs. Woodbine cleared her throat and straightened her shoulders.

"Dr. Lash, there's something I'm meaning to say. I haven't been truthful, and it's now or never."

"Is she going with us?" Val had an evil look on his face.

"Sure I'm coming, Val, if you all want me to." Mrs. Woodbine had recovered her confidence. She drew an envelope from her pocketbook. "Isn't it a wonder? There's a travel agency right there in the railroad station. They're generally booked awful far in advance, the fella said, but it's all airplanes these days. And shipwrecks! Suppose there aren't enough lifeboats and the crew skedaddles before the passengers even get a chance?"

"Mrs. Woodbine, what a thing to say!" Joyce said. "The *Titanic* was a long time ago. I'm sure … ."

"She means the *Andrea Doria*," Val interrupted.

"Four years ago, wasn't it?" Professor Lash was suddenly interested in the *Andrea Doria's* fate. "They say the crew didn't behave very well. Still, a modern ocean liner is safer than a jet plane. I thought we all agreed … ."

"*I'm* not scared!" Mrs. Woodbine cut him off. "I handed over my money, cash on the barrelhead, and I guess they'll give me a refund if you all don't want me to come." She took a deep breath. "I expect you'll want some help though; the boys sick to their stomachs and old Horace a-whoopin' and a-hollerin'."

Professor Lash forced himself to put on a serious expression. "It's good of you to offer, Mrs. Woodbine, but the boys will be fine. There's nothing wrong with the food over there." The others all knew what he was thinking; he'd been talking about it for weeks: *Schnitzl, Sacher Torte, Palascinta* and *Kompott* made from cherries that grew on trees in Granddaddy's back yard. "Thanks to you," he continued, "Horace has all his things. We're very grateful. You've done more than enough." He hesitated. "It's not so cheap over there as people think. I can't accept the responsibility. If you should run short of money … ." He gave Mrs. Woodbine a look that meant: *Don't expect to be paid!*

Marcus thought he was a poor match for Mrs. Woodbine.

"I've turned it over in my mind, Dr. Lash. I expect I'll manage." Mrs. Woodbine put her passport and ticket back in her pocketbook. She hadn't forgotten the Life Savers; she unwrapped a roll and offered one to Marcus and then took one for herself.

"John-Wesley's over there in the service. He writes me a letter or a postcard every week. Says he turned on a faucet in some awful broke-down place and not a drop came out, and if it had done, he wouldn't have drunk it anyway because of the typhoid they got over there." Mrs. Woodbine wagged her head. "It's all Communists and dope fiends, John-Wesley says. Or else it's youngsters pestering you for a quarter." She stopped herself, conscious that she was weakening her case. "John-Wesley says they're not all bad. There's good, honest ones too. It's just they don't have all our advantages." She threw her arms up. Her eyes gleamed. She appeared to be calling upon Heaven to witness her in all her reckless glory.

"Won't we have a bushel of fun?"

She Looks Like a Giraffe

THE FIRST NIGHT'S meal on board the S.S. *Columbus* was served buffet style. Standing in line, Joyce Lash planted her feet against the rolling and groaning below decks. The ship had encountered a "swell". She felt dizzy, on the verge of seasick. The babble of voices, the bright lights and the artificial ventilation didn't help. She was already tired of the *Columbus*. It reminded her of a mediocre hotel. The dining room's columns were fake; the heavy draperies, stenciled with seagulls, blocked out most of the natural light. And there was something unappetizing about so much food. She hadn't expected such abundance. Apparently, management was spoiling the passengers for fear of losing them to the airlines. But Arthur would be disappointed if she picked at her food. Recalling an article in the *Reader's Digest* about mercury contamination, she wondered whether the seafood was safe. Risk it! She picked up a pair of tongs sturdy enough to deliver a baby and lifted a lobster tail and a couple of shrimps from their beds of ice.

"Not bad, eh, Joyce?" Arthur stood next to her, filling his plate. Behind him, the boys were filling theirs. "What do you think? Shall we order champagne?"

"The boys will want to try it."

"My poor mother was the same way; always afraid Philip and I would get too accustomed to the good things in life." Arthur chuckled. "'*Gut gevoynt*', she called it. One of her few Jewish expressions. But my father liked to spread himself."

Joyce was reminded of other ways in which Hermann Lasch spread himself. In his heyday he'd collected expensive, second-rate paintings and furniture; there had been something called an "elephant table" in the living room. Business trips to Paris meant introductions to actresses and intimate suppers in what Hermann, reminiscing, liked to call *chambres separées*. Not exactly a model husband! It didn't matter now. Arthur's mother was a remote figure, dead from cancer long ago. The no-nonsense woman Hermann had married in his old age, Anna-Maria, needn't worry. At nearly eighty, Hermann was happily

16

dependent on her. He felt he had a right to a tranquil, comfortable life. Joyce smiled. Like father, like son! Arthur didn't like to dwell on the painful past. And tonight he was in an expansive mood. He'd already drunk a Manhattan cocktail in the lounge, after removing the cherry and handing it to Marcus with an air of bestowing a royal favor.

"My father used to say, alcohol and salt water don't mix," Joyce said.

"A shame he didn't practice what he preached."

"You don't need to remind me."

Her father had been something between a social drinker and an alcoholic. The rounds of whiskeys and bourbons made him gregarious, then boisterous, and at last gloomy. Drinking and smoking had hardened his arteries. Dead from a heart attack at fifty-six! It gave Joyce a pang—half pitying and half angry—to think of it. Henry Michelson had intermittently slept and thrashed around for two days before succumbing. "I don't want to die!" A fox terrier at the foot of the bed flattened its ears and let out a whimper. Her mother had fled the room.

Joyce glanced over at a table where the Lashes' first and last names were written on white place cards. *Mrs. Arthur Lash.* As if she hadn't a given name of her own! In Vienna she'd have a borrowed title, *Frau Professor Lash*—or *Lasch*, like Arthur's father—assuming people still clung to the old formalities.

The boys had finished with the buffet and were taking their seats. Beside the places set for the Lashes and Mrs. Woodbine there were three more for a middle-aged couple and a girl in her early teens. The girl's glossy hair fell over the back of her sleeveless blouse and her arms were covered with a light down. Joyce watched her touch a string of pearls, adjust her cloth napkin and pass her tongue over her lips. When the mother made a remark, the girl rolled her eyes and glanced at Adrian.

"Have you seen who's at our table?" Joyce whispered.

They looked round.

"The mother looks like a giraffe."

"The girl's pretty. I see the parents have ordered wine."

Joyce sighed. Arthur would make the waiter bring over a bottle as good as whatever the others were drinking. After he'd sniffed it and rolled it on his tongue, he would fill their glasses. She would make Marcus top his off with water; she didn't want him to get a headache. She herself would take just a few sips. She disliked Arthur's favorite, Pinot Noir. *Red ink!*

"Where's Mrs. Woodbine?" Arthur asked. "I'm going to make her tipsy for once in her life."

"I told her to meet us here at seven. The purser wasn't happy about making a last-minute change in the seating arrangements."

"I hope she's not seasick. She can't say we didn't give her fair warning."

"The boat isn't as thinly booked as she made out. She's sharing a cabin with a woman from Atlanta. I'm sure they must be friends by now." Joyce lowered her voice. "They've probably agreed that the Blacks are getting ahead of themselves."

Arthur chuckled. "It's how she grew up. Besides, it's not as if we have any colored friends. Even if we did, they wouldn't be allowed on the golf course unless they were carrying someone's clubs. For that matter, does a single, solitary Jew belong?"

"I haven't any idea."

In fact, Joyce was certain no Jews belonged to the Garnet Hills Country Club. Probably none had ever applied. Why risk a refusal? She herself wouldn't object to sipping iced tea on the club terrace while the boys took tennis lessons. It wasn't as if Arthur had to announce his ancestry to the world. If anyone inquired, he was Catholic, and Catholics were popular lately on account of the new pope. No one would have to know about his Semitic origins. Yes, she would like to join! Did that make her a hypocrite?

"None of the members would care. Not Sandra Van Riper."

Marcus was in the same grade as Skip Van Riper; their mothers chatted when they ran into each other in town. Sandra's husband, Jody Van Riper, came from an old Garnet family; his home was two-hundred-years old; the oaks and elms on the property were even more ancient.

"Sandra's surprisingly up to date," Joyce went on. "She's seeing a psychoanalyst."

"I wonder," Arthur said, "whether she isn't Jewish herself."

"Anyway, you were wrong about my mother."

"She surprised me. She had no objection to my forebears. But going over to the Catholics! Unforgivable. Besides, Frieda thought all continental husbands beat their wives."

"I suppose quite a few do. Besides, my mother has a right to her prejudices. All that rigmarole, sinners roasting on spits and boiling in cauldrons, and babies waiting around in limbo."

Arthur shrugged. "You have to expect a certain amount of folklore. You have only to read the *Inferno.*"

"The truth is you only converted because you thought it would make life easier."

"Do you blame me? My family weren't religious. We had a Christmas tree when I was a child."

"It's not as if converting made you safe."

"It turned out a Jew was a Jew. I ought to have known."

"You could have dropped the whole thing, once you were over here."

"And remained *Artur Asch*? I might never have gotten a decent job. We should thank the Jesuits."

"At least you might have left me out of it. I was a perfectly happy lukewarm Protestant." She was conscious of the resentment in her voice. But really it was her own fault. She shouldn't have let him influence her. He'd insisted that a mixed marriage would be confusing for their children. But what harm would it have done? She should have stuck to the beautiful Anglican prayers. *We have done those things we ought not to have done … .*

"The funny thing," Arthur was saying, "is that I got used to it. It's a link with the past. Two thousand years of art, music, learning. You can't look at a Gothic cathedral and not be impressed. Besides, so much of Catholicism is Plato and the Stoics."

"So you've told me. And the Orphic Mysteries. You left that out."

"True enough: Orpheus sacrificed and raised from the dead."

They neared the end of the buffet table where there were desserts, trays of fresh fruit, cheeses and a platter of dried figs, each one dressed up with coconut shavings and a shelled walnut in the center.

"*Ach,* Joyce!" Arthur took pineapple to go with his ham. "Don't ask me to defend a crazy world. The Church is no exception. As if saving one's soul hinged on avoiding dirty books and movies! But I like the idea of our children growing up believing in God. It hasn't done my brother any good, having no religion at all. Everything reduced to atoms and numbers!" He thought of his brother's mood swings. "Numbers haven't made Phil happy."

"It's not too late, you know. We can leave the Catholics and join the Unitarians. Keep God in the picture and not bother with all the rest."

Arthur smiled. "Perhaps we should take our cue from Mrs. Woodbine. I always forget whether she's a Baptist or a Methodist."

"She switches back and forth, depending on the preacher."

"I've been thinking. We'll have to pay her something, won't we? It wouldn't be fair not to. I suppose she might turn out to be helpful. It's given me an idea. We can leave her with the boys and go somewhere, just the two of us. Venice! What do you think?"

"Anna-Maria's perfectly capable of looking after the boys. But I wouldn't mind seeing Venice again. It must be twenty-five years."

"We'll put Mrs. Woodbine in charge of Horace. I doubt if Anna-Maria wants to bother with his mealtimes." Arthur grinned. "I can't wait to see my father's face when I introduce Ruby Woodbine. I'll say she's a sort of governess."

"Anna-Maria won't like having her around at all hours, interfering."

"Perhaps they'll get along. Both of them were raised in the country."

They walked over to their table and exchanged introductions with their table mates. The Eigers were from the town of Rushton, in western Connecticut.

"I was about to ask these young men where you're from and where you're headed," Helen Eiger said. Her long neck and prominent features, Joyce thought, really made it impossible not to think of a giraffe. Her husband, Hank Eiger, was slender and wore wire-rimmed eyeglasses. He might, Joyce thought, be another academic. Maybe that was why they were seated together.

"Garnet," Arthur was saying. "Thirty minutes from Grand Central, except when there's a delay. Which happens all too often. It seems they can't get the trains to run on time." He laughed. "Perhaps that's just as well."

"Oh, we *know*," Helen Eiger exclaimed. "It's the same problem getting in from Rushton. And if there's snow it can take hours."

Arthur laughed again. "I was referring to *Il Duce*. Punctuality was Mussolini's proudest accomplishment."

Mrs. Eiger looked puzzled for an instant and then her face cleared. "Of course! We read that somewhere, didn't we, Hank?"

"It was in the newspapers," her husband said. Joyce studied his sardonic expression. Was he subtly mocking his wife?

"We'll be visiting my father in Vienna," Arthur continued. "Afterwards we'll spend a week on Lake Como." He gave Joyce a look. "My wife and I might run off to Venice for a few days, just the two of us."

"That sounds wonderful!"

Helen Eiger announced that her family were going to be touring several countries—six in all. They planned to stay in a lot of different hotels, so that Helen, who owned her own travel agency, would know which ones to recommend to her clients. It turned out that Hank Eiger wasn't an academic after all; he ran a company that supplied schools with sports equipment. Helen alluded to her husband's fondness for birds; Hank had packed binoculars and ornithological guides. Julie Eiger looked down at her plate and frowned, as if there were something ridiculous about her father's hobby. Or else it was her mother who embarrassed her. At any rate, the girl was blushing.

Helen Eiger turned her attention to Arthur.

"Are you in the medical field, Dr. Lash? Let me guess. Surgeon!"

"I'd say optometry," Hank Eiger put in. "He doesn't look the type to stand the sight of blood."

"I'm afraid I won't be of any use if you break a bone or need an eye exam." Arthur smiled. "The awful truth is that I teach philosophy. You may have heard of Seven Sacraments College? It's in Cromer, the next town over from Garnet." He decided to try a well-worn joke. "Our best students major in Penance."

The quip met with blank looks. Now it was Joyce's turn to blush. Helen and Hank Eiger were obviously unfamiliar with the Catholic sacraments, and they had never heard of Arthur's third-rate institution. But Arthur was lucky to have his tenured professorship; he'd published very little. He was a teacher, he liked to say, not a scribbler.

"Philosophy!" Helen Eiger placed a hand on her husband's arm. "Hank and I would love a real talk. The meaning of life!"

Arthur laughed. "I'm afraid we philosophers haven't made much headway in that regard." He turned to face Julie Eiger. "What about you, Julie? What are you interested in? Don't tell me it's the Existentialists!"

There was a painful silence. Arthur kept his eyes on the roll he was buttering. The three boys were staring. Julie's mother looked hopeful. Hank Eiger cut his roast beef into bite-sized pieces. It was as if everyone was waiting for a dumb animal to speak. Joyce sympathized with the girl. It was wrong of Arthur to put her on the spot, simply because he wanted to avoid a "real talk" with the Eigers. People who professed an interest in philosophy, he liked to complain, were apt to want to discuss their horoscopes.

"I guess I don't have any interests," the girl said finally. Joyce wondered if she was being sarcastic. But no, she followed it up with: "I know it's a terrible thing to say. I guess I'll pick some up when I go to college."

"Why, Julie!" The mother let out a ringing laugh. She faced Joyce and Arthur. "Young people! Of course, they have their own lives. Julie has so many friends this year, I can't keep up. And then the horses take up a great deal of her time."

Joyce was taken aback. Horses! The Eigers did well for themselves.

"What are the horses' names?" Marcus asked.

"There's Fairy, who's the mare," Julie answered, relieved to be on safe ground, "Buck, who's the gelding, and Lord Randall, the pony."

"I'd like a horse," Marcus said. "I'd go galloping over the prairie."

Arthur laughed. "You'll have to wait until I rob a bank. Feeding three boys costs enough—" He stopped abruptly. Best not to mention money around strangers.

"Horses don't cost that much to feed," Julie said, with perfect seriousness. "It's hay and oats mostly." Marcus snickered. Val smiled sarcastically.

"Adrian," Arthur said, "eats enough for three."

"It makes up for Val," Adrian said.

"I have one son who's fussy and another who's a glutton."

"They look fine to me. I'm sure they're fine," Mrs. Eiger said.

"I'm fine," Marcus said. "I eat just the right amount. Not too little and not too much. Like *Goldilocks and the Three Bears*."

"It's *not too cold and not too hot*. Stupid!"

Joyce put down her fork and knife. "Val! Don't speak to your brother like that or you'll have to leave the table."

"Okay with me. The food is no good anyway."

"*Val!*" Joyce would have liked to muffle her child with a table napkin. Taunting her in front of these people! Better let it drop. Marcus meanwhile was rubbing his midsection, where his seersucker jacket was unbuttoned.

"Are you feeling okay, darling?"

"*Mom!*" Marcus whispered fiercely. "You promised!"

Arthur shook his head ruefully. "He eats too fast," he told the Eigers. "The food doesn't have time to digest. It's why he's got a bit of a football stomach."

The Eigers glanced at each other. *Football stomach!* Joyce felt her face redden. What was Arthur thinking? He claimed that looks weren't so important, but really, they were. He stared at his own reflection after his shower, in the mirror on the closet door in the bedroom; pulled at his flesh; twisted around to check the condition of his buttocks. There were tufts of hair on his chest. Joyce couldn't help being repulsed by the growth. There had been a time when she had clung to him in bed and called him her "brown bear," kissed him in places that now felt alien. Nowadays the wild urges she had once felt were a distant memory. For his part, Arthur seemed as interested as ever. It didn't matter to him that she had begun to droop.

She was ashamed of her waning desire. But what could she do? She would have been content to be touched only on those unpredictable occasions when she felt a sudden tenderness. Even then, Art spoiled things by overdoing it, crushing her, making sounds like a soul in torment, when all she'd wanted were gentle caresses, and then very quietly and gently to be brought to her own pleasure. Did other women in their forties feel the same? She really had no idea. With whom could she discuss it? She had no sister. Sandra Van Riper would recoil like a frightened deer and refer her to her Dr. Spielman in the city. Dorothy Davidson? Dorothy, glowing with vitality despite her nine pregnancies, would look at her wonderingly, as if her coolness was an abnormality. Well, there was always Mrs. Woodbine. Raised on a farm, she must have taken her late husband's advances in the same spirit as she took the spectacle of a stallion and its mare.

"The lobster is as good as what we get at home," Helen Eiger was saying. No one replied. Joyce wasn't listening. She was still turning her husband's vanity over in her mind. After he was done examining himself in the closet-door mirror, he would say something about joining the YMCA, where there were weights and a pool that reeked of chlorine. The idea never came to fruition. His efforts at self-improvement were strenuous but short-lived. On the beach, he performed calisthenics and challenged the boys to foot races; swam a few strokes and came back winded, flung himself down in the sand so that his body looked as if it was coated in breadcrumbs. Oh, it was too pitiful in a man of fifty! Was he trying to keep up with boys of eighteen? Boys like Gary Dover, whom she'd loved in her last year of high school? The Dovers lived in a house with an ordinary back yard, nothing like the acres she went home to after school. She had liked the fact that Gary's origins were, if not humble, at least ordinary. She had flirted with him; he had overlooked her. Why? Was she not pretty enough? Were her parents too high and mighty? What had become of him? He must be married now, with a couple of normal, nice-looking children.

Arthur was saying to Marcus: "I was the same shape when I was your age—a little extra in front—and I outgrew it." He waved in the direction of the desserts. "I've never seen so much sweet stuff in one place. It's probably all Cat Fat. It's a pity when they don't use real butter and cream."

Joyce felt herself blush again. The Eigers must be baffled by her husband's fastidious tastes. His disdain for cheap substitutes was a carry-over from his pampered childhood. Certainly, *Katzenfett* had never appeared on Hermann Lasch's dinner table.

"Of course," Joyce said to cover her shame, "we'll all start to put on weight once we get to Vienna. Arthur's stepmother is a wonderful cook." She forced a laugh. "But I refuse to eat her salad. It's made with boiled peas."

"The boys will have to watch out they don't burst from her delicacies," Arthur said."

"I know when to stop," Marcus said in an indignant voice.

"They have rice pudding, when you're ready," Joyce said quickly. "Your favorite!"

She knew she was trying too hard to protect him. He was getting to be a big boy. She must rein in her mothering instincts. More than just mothering. Marcus was like a second husband. She could spend hours listening to him talk. And yet she had been disappointed—crushed almost—when she'd given birth to a third boy. She had hoped for a girl before it was too late. She and Arthur had agreed to stop after three children. But she had quickly gotten over it and then she had begun to worship Marcus. He had seemed to worship her in return.

"Can I have cake *and* rice pudding?"

"It won't do you any harm this once." Joyce felt an impulse to take him in her arms. There he sat, eating his food with precise movements of knife, fork and napkin, like a little adult! He had worn glasses ever since having surgery to straighten out his eyes, and that only added to his quaintness. And he said such dry, funny things, without even trying. If only she could have him to herself, forever. She knew it was wrong. As wrong as when she still sometimes—not very often—wished he was the little girl she would never have. But she could count on Marcus to pull away. She liked it when he taught her a lesson. She had once, in a dreamy mood, offered to paint his nails and he'd refused indignantly. Another time she'd dressed him up "just for fun" in a worn-out, beady-eyed fur stole. But Marcus had stopped the game, torn the costume off and cut the fur with scissors. Afterwards, he kept the amputated tail in a drawer.

Of course she loved her other two boys. There had been a time when Adrian was the center of her existence. Val could be endearing when he felt like it—how easily people fell for his looks!—but was growing more and more untrustworthy. Not a week went by when she didn't catch him in a lie. She felt sorry for the "flaxen prince". It was Arthur, in a satirical mood, who'd come up with the nickname, and it had unfortunately stuck. Val's untruthfulness, she felt, must flow from some mysterious grudge. But when he put his arms around her and begged her forgiveness, how could she resist? His hair brushed against her like the coat of some sensitive animal.

'Can I get dessert now?" Val was asking.

"Be patient," his mother answered. "The rest of us are just getting started. If you've finished, you can go over and look out the window."

What did it matter if he ate dessert before anyone else? Somehow it *did* matter! But why had she told him to look out the window? There were curtains covering the glass and, any-way, there was nothing to look at: grey clouds and a greenish-grey ocean. In another hour it would be dark. Joyce noticed that Julie had a sly look on her face, as if the suggestion of looking out the window struck her as foolish. Apparently, the girl took after her acerbic father. Suddenly Joyce resented Val. She prized Marcus, and then Adrian, and then Val, in that order. Where exactly Arthur fit in was not easy to say. He joked that he occupied the bottom of a totem pole, atop which Marcus and Horace perched in triumph. Well, she couldn't help but laugh. There was a grain of truth in it!

A full glass of wine stood in front of her. When had Arthur ordered it? It seemed to her that she had just sat down a mom-ent ago. Was she becoming one of those women who were never quite connected? Once her children were grown up, she might drift permanently. Adrian would leave home in another year. No doubt girls would occupy him more than his studies. Soon enough, he would fall seriously in love, if he hadn't fallen already and the replacement of her in his heart would become final.

Lately she had caught herself staring at her eldest son when he came out of the shower with a towel wrapped around him. She had to look away quickly in case he noticed. A girl would be lucky to have him pay attention to her! He simply needed to build up his confidence. There had been a time when the boys in the neighborhood had followed his lead. The clubhouse he'd built in the back yard had been their lair; the model train layout in the basement a source of wonderment. But now that he was well into his teens—seventeen the month before last—his talents mattered less. Girls didn't care about model trains! Joyce glanced at Julie Eiger. The girl was eyeing Adrian. She was too young for him. Fourteen, probably. But Adrian must be enjoying the attention. Sooner or later some nice girl, maybe a little older than he was, would come along. Adrian would be devastated if a girl led him on and then, after getting what she wanted, cast him aside. Well, whatever happened, Adrian had one ever-faithful admirer. Marcus hung on his every word.

Val was getting up from the table. He dropped his napkin on his chair and walked off by himself, without a word. Had he decided to stare at the Atlantic? Now there were two empty places at the table. Why hadn't Mrs. Woodbine joined them yet? Joyce felt a tightness at the back of her neck, which on top of her dizziness spoiled what little appetite she had. She arranged her knife and fork on the tablecloth and pushed her chair back.

"I'm going to go and check on Mrs. Woodbine." She turned to the Eigers. "Mrs. Woodbine is traveling with us. She's almost a member of the family." She tittered nervously. Idiotic! What business was it of theirs?

"How fortunate!" Helen Eiger said.

"Don't be gone too long, Joyce," Arthur said. It was clear he didn't want to carry the full weight of the conversation.

"If I'm not back in fifteen minutes, send out a search party." Joyce forced another laugh. But now Marcus looked alarmed.

"Don't let her go, Daddy. It's getting dark out there and the ship's rolling like crazy."

"She won't have to go outside."

"She could still get lost. I almost couldn't find my way back from ping pong. I had to ask about ten people for directions."

Arthur pulled his mouth down and made a serious face. "Yes, I suppose she could get lost. We may never find her."

"Listen to you two men worrying about me!"

"Maybe Mrs. Woodbine fell overboard," Adrian said.

Hank Eiger spoke up. "The railings out there are pretty high."

A quarter of an hour later, Joyce was still trying to locate Mrs. Woodbine's room. Marcus hadn't been wrong about the ease with which one could get lost on an ocean liner. The corridors were confusing. She had to retrace her steps after she'd mistaken a turn and gone up and down a wrong flight of steps. She had asked for help twice, once from a steward and once from a fellow passenger.

At last she knocked on Mrs. Woodbine's cabin door. No answer. She tried the handle. Unlocked. She went inside, cautiously. The lights were turned off. The room felt stuffy. She heard a groan.

"Mrs. Woodbine?"

"Over here, Mizz Lash. I'm on the bed."

Joyce switched on the overhead light. Mrs. Woodbine lay flat on her back, fully clothed except for her shoes. Her stockinged feet hung over the foot of the bed. Another, unoccupied bed stood against the opposite wall. All the remaining space was taken up with suitcases. It was a small room for two people.

"I'm not used to all this rollin' and swayin'," Mrs. Woodbine said.

"Poor Mrs. Woodbine! Should I order something light? They can bring it to your room."

"I don't believe I'd get anything down. I felt pretty good until it started rarin', and then it hit me. You all go ahead and finish your dinner without me."

"Do you need a seasickness pill?"

"I'll get used to it by and by." Joyce observed that Mrs. Woodbine's complexion was approximately the color of the sky outside the porthole.

"Are you sure you'll be alright? There's a ship's doctor."

"I'm all right. It's just I thought it would be a bigger room for what I paid. Never mind! It's a real nice lady I'm sharing with. Name of Lucille Shiflett. I told her we used to know a bunch of Shifletts. My cousin Earl married one."

But Joyce was listening with only half an ear. She suddenly wondered how Horace was faring, penned up in choppy weather. Tomorrow she would have to find out about visiting him in his kennel.

FROM WHERE HE was standing on the far side of the dining room, half hidden by a trellis of artificial ivy, Val was able to keep an eye on his family without being observed. His mother was getting up from the table and saying something apologetic. Probably she was going to check on Mrs. Woodbine. Stupid! Why had they let her come in the first place? Marcus was too old for a babysitter, and Mrs. Woodbine would soon realize she wasn't needed.

On Val's left, a mural of Christopher Columbus discovering the New World covered most of a wall. On his right, a padded door led to the kitchen. When the door swung open, a bustling noise swelled for a moment and then subsided as the door swung shut. It seemed to Val that most of the staff were speaking Italian. The boat was flying the American flag but the employees had apparently been gathered from elsewhere. It reminded him of the crew in the abridged edition of *Moby Dick* that he'd had to read the year before. Mr. Wind had explained that Captain Ahab secretly loved the enormous, blubbery thing he wished to kill. Mr. Wind had lost the lower part of his right arm to a Japanese grenade; when the teacher wore short sleeves and waved his stump in the air, you couldn't help but think of Ahab's missing leg.

Bang! The door swung open violently. A busboy came out carrying a tray on one shoulder. Val pictured the boy's home back in Italy: a crumbling farmhouse, sleeping quarters shared with animals. Probably there were a lot of children with dirty faces; Italian women had too many babies. Val recalled the moment his mother carried a new baby into the house. Marcus's head was too big for his body. A monster! Later on, it occurred to him that the baby might develop into an acceptable playmate; he would enjoy taking the part of the older, stronger brother. But after the first year, it was clear that Adrian was Marcus's favorite, and Val decided that the superfluous child, in its innocent, unconscious way, was changing everything for the worse.

For a while he'd wondered if his jealousy was making him physically ill. A child psychologist diagnosed the mysterious pains in his legs as a fictitious bid for sympathy that must be ignored. But he wasn't pretending! Finally, a new doctor recognized the symptoms of juvenile arthritis. Aspirin brought down the illness. His parents felt guilty for not believing him. What sort of present would he like to make up for their blunder? He had to think about it. How about a puppy? He'd picked out a terrier with black and white markings and named it Horace because it sounded Roman, like his own and his brothers' names. But Horace soon transferred his affections to Joyce. She couldn't help it: she bathed, brushed, fed and walked him. Dogs had always been her best friends. As a little girl, she told him, she had wanted to *be* a dog; around the age of four or five she'd walked around the house wearing a collar.

It was about that time that Val started wondering if he might be someone else's child. Was Joyce his real mother? Her baby might have been accidentally switched with someone else's at the hospital. But this was unlikely considering how closely he resembled his grandmother; their kinship was obvious in the silver-framed photograph of Gran, dressed for her coming-out party not long after the turn of the century. It was Arthur, then, who wasn't his real father. His mother had had an affair. Such things happened all the time in books and movies. The thought of it alarmed and excited him. At any rate, his parents, real or impostors, didn't understand him. How could they? He spent much of his time in private worlds, some of which he associated with geography class. In the Torrid Zone, for instance, boys walked around in loin cloths and shot arrows at wild animals, and at night there was a campfire with meat roasting on a spit, and songs and dancing and stories. The Tropic of Capricorn, on the other hand, was a place of towers and turrets where a good percentage of the grown-ups were wizards.

A clatter of plates interrupted his daydream. The busboy was stacking his tray. What if he noticed he was being observed and returned the attention with a dirty look or a cutting remark? That kind of thing happened in school, where certain classmates said that he looked like a girl and probably still didn't have hair where it most counted. If only he could be more like Adrian, who brushed off all sorts of trouble! Adrian was fearless. There was the time he'd taken the Dodge around the block three times. He must have been about thirteen. Arthur and Joyce came home from Gran's house in time to catch Adrian pulling into the driveway with his brothers beside him in the front seat. Val confessed to having been the one who found the car keys and dared Adrian to use them. The two of them were getting too old to spank, so they were sent to their rooms for the rest of the day. Marcus, by contrast, lived by the rules as if they were constructed for his personal benefit, and had never in his life gotten so much as a telling off.

If Arthur wasn't his real father, Val thought, then Adrian must be only his half-brother. Why not? Arthur and Joyce always remarked how different the two of them were. Adrian was handy with tools and Val wasn't. Adrian outshone Val in sports, except for swimming. And Adrian was girl crazy, like a character in a T.V. comedy. Val worried that he didn't share his brother's yearning. Instead, he studied his own face in the mirror, and couldn't help looking at certain boys in school. Not Curtis Blow, who was cynical and hollow-eyed, but boys who looked as if they'd never been sick or unhappy a day in their lives.

He told himself that he was "going through a phase"—one of his mother's favorite expressions. But what if he never outgrew it? A few weeks earlier, Father Dormond had mentioned in his sermon movies imported from Europe. Adultery! Degeneracy! *Sodomy!* The congregation had snapped to attention. Afterwards, Val thought of Professor Ludovic Kalb, his father's friend, whose nature prevented him from marrying and having children. Professor Kalb was a connoisseur of food and wine. His manners were courtly. He kissed Joyce on the cheek when he came for dinner, and his eyes twinkled pleasantly when he and Val shook hands. But for all that, there was something wrong with him.

Any day now, Val told himself, his mind and body would catch up with Adrian's. When the time came, he would pick someone out from the female pool and without further ado satisfy his curiosity, probably in a secluded nook somewhere. Val didn't see himself submitting to procedures that for Adrian were a necessity—like being driven to pick up a date, then being taken to a movie theater, and then retrieved at a designated hour. After they got back to America, Adrian would have his license and demand the use of the car, Arthur would lecture him on drinking and driving, and Joyce would worry about *going too far.* Suppose Adrian did go too far, and the girl acted as if something terrible had happened? Val pictured a girl sitting in the back seat, pressed up against Adrian with her blouse undone. She wore eye shadow and smelled of perfume. Her wiry bra had slipped halfway off. Nothing in the picture excited him. When he did think about the female body, which was seldom, he imagined nymphs like those in his illustrated book of Greek mythology: sleek woodland creatures, pursued by centaurs.

The trouble was that the things that used to give him pleasure no longer did. He remembered when he and Adrian had been happy to catch fireflies in jars in the front yard of the Lashes' summer cottage. The nights were warm enough for bathing suits. At the beach, he and Adrian rode the waves on a rubber raft until their lips turned blue and they were ordered to come out of the water while Marcus, floating in the shallows on his inflated ring, stayed out of their way. Their father left them alone, except for occasional attempts to organize a race or long jump. He had his books to read, or else he lay on the sand and dozed.

Lately, though, the thought of another summer at the shore felt like a prison sentence: the same old beach, nothing to do on rainy days, and no friends of his own. The sandwiches Joyce made from tomatoes and mayonnaise when she ran short of ham and salami were awful, and when no one wanted them she fed the soggy crusts to the seagulls. How had he ever thought it was fun? He remembered being especially happy the summer he was eight, when Gran had been well enough to travel from Buffalo. She'd sat in the back yard under an umbrella, annoyed by the smoke from a steam locomotive that passed behind trees that marked the edge of the property; Arthur and Joyce had discovered the tracks too late, after they'd already signed papers. That summer Adrian was away in camp, and one of Arthur's more promising students had been invited to spend an extended weekend. In the morning, Val spotted Lloyd Hedges in the bathroom, wearing only his pajama bottoms, his black hair in a tangle, regarding his skinny body in the mirror with a moody expression. Lloyd's features were angular, and the skin on his sunburnt back and chest was peeling off; he refused Joyce's offer of Coppertone. Lloyd was obviously depressed. But he had a dry sense of humor. Everyone, even Gran, laughed when he imitated the president's mangled locution. On Saturday, Lloyd accompanied them to the nearest town, Seaford, where there was an old-fashioned hotel, and shops that sold comic books, beach chairs and towels patterned with starfish and dolphins. On the sidewalks, ladies in white shoes and straw hats paraded slowly by. It all seemed like a dream now.

"*Prego!*" The busboy was motioning with his head. Val held the kitchen door open, so the boy could get through while supporting his heavy tray with both arms. "*Venga!*" The boy was evidently inviting him into his kingdom. Val stepped through the portal. The busboy carried his tray to a steel counter and came back and pointed Val to a stool. He stood back and regarded the young passenger.

"*Guard'il principino!*" The rolled r's were pleasant to the ear. "You like rock and roll?"

"*Si,*" Val, said. "*Molto bene!*"

"*Bravo! Parl' Italiano, tu?*"

Val felt his confidence swell. He had picked up a few Italian phrases from Mr. d'Ambrosio at the Kleencut; the old man was in the habit of talking to himself. He would try out what he'd learned on his new friend and let him laugh at his mistakes. Then he would revert to English. Foreigners were drawn to all things American.

"*Come ti chiami?*"

"Val."

"*Valentino!*" The busboy, who said his name was Massimo, chattered in a mix of Italian and English. A wave of dark hair fell across his forehead. Val recalled a word from his mythology book: *Faun.* He imagined pointed ears hidden behind the hair, and shaggy goat's feet underneath the white trousers.

"You want job, *Valentino*?"

Val shrugged and smiled. "*Si. Molto.*"

Val thought that he wouldn't mind at all spending the rest of the voyage working along side of Massimo and the rest of the kitchen staff, several of whom assumed that the *Americano* was familiar with soccer teams, a misunderstanding that gave rise to much laughter. Later, a cook in a striped apron made a game of asking him for assistance; handed him an enormous knife and let him cut a cake into sections. But the staff had work to do, and not wanting to overstay his welcome, Val wished Massimo *buona notte* and went back to the dining room, where most of the guests had already gotten up, leaving behind tablecloths littered with crumbs.

From the dining room, a hallway led into the bar and lounge. A trio—violin, piano, and xylophone—occupied a stage decorated with oversized scalloped shells. The violinist swayed from side to side as he led his colleagues through *Arrivederci Roma*. Val felt his happy mood dissipate. He spotted the Eigers ordering something at the bar. Hadn't they had enough to drink at dinner? What about his parents? There they were, in plushy armchairs. His mother looked tense; no doubt she was wondering where he'd gone. She was saying something to Arthur. Probably she was pestering him to go look for their lost sheep, and Arthur was telling her not to worry. Adrian and Marcus were nowhere in sight. They might have gone to the game room, or maybe they were taking a walk on deck.

Joyce caught sight of him lingering in the passageway. She sprang from her chair and hurried in his direction.

"Where have you been? You can't just wander off!"

"What's the big deal? I'm fourteen."

"You could spend time with your family instead of running away. Where were you?"

"The game room."

"Don't lie to me, Val. I checked the game room fifteen minutes ago."

"You must have just missed me." Val shrugged and headed into the lounge. His mother followed after him. He sank into her vacated seat. A dark-skinned woman with full lips and a sharp nose—Val guessed she might be Brazilian—was staring and nudging her husband. Typical! He reached inside his jacket pocket for his sunglass case.

"Val! You're not going to wear those indoors?"

"This lighting gives me a headache. I should have my eyes checked when we get home. Can I have coffee?"

"First," Arthur said, "get up and fetch another chair. Don't make your mother stand."

"What story has he made up this time, Joycie?" Arthur asked, while Val was dragging over a heavy chair.

"I'm too tired to talk about it."

Val sat down and stretched his legs out in front of him. He adjusted his sunglasses. Joyce gave him an angry look and twisted her wedding ring.

"Don't sit with your legs spread out like that," Arthur said. "And next time let us know where you're off to." But then his tone softened. "I suppose you and Adrian can take care of yourselves at your age."

"That's fine. Let them run off by themselves." Joyce's face suddenly looked old. "Why not? I'm only their mother."

"Dad! Tell her to lay off. She's always picking on me."

"He's safe and sound, Joyce. Let's enjoy the evening."

"Where are Adrian and Marcus, anyway? Did they kidnap that Julie Tiger or whatever her name is?"

Joyce sighed heavily. "The three of them said they were going to walk around the Promenade Deck. I wish you hadn't let them, Art. It's getting so dark."

"The railings are pretty high. Isn't that what Hank Eiger said? Besides, the ship isn't rolling nearly as much. The weather's clearing." Arthur gestured towards a tier of windows and a sky where one or two stars had made their appearance.

"Well, if you won't, I'm going to see if I can find them. I don't trust those railings. Anyway, I want to check on Mrs. Woodbine again." But no sooner were the words out than Joyce felt ridiculous. Adrian was practically a grown man. Mrs. Woodbine was as strong as an ox.

Arthur shrugged. "Give my condolences to Mrs. W. In the meantime, Val and I will drink coffee. Cream and two lumps of sugar, right Val? I might persuade the Eigers to join us, if they aren't too far gone. If not, we'll start a game of chess." He smiled at his son. "I intend to win for once!"

"Don't get your hopes up. You won't win unless I let you." Val softened. Maybe Arthur was his real father after all.

Joyce left them and headed for the Promenade Deck. Near the exit, it occurred to her that she was wearing only a light cardigan sweater over her dress. She buttoned it and opened a pair of doors. The Promenade Deck was partly enclosed by glass so that passengers, if they wished, could take their walks protected from the elements. She knew Adrian would want to be all the way outside. She pushed open another set of doors and was hit by a blast of air. Joyce hugged herself for warmth. Which way? She headed towards the bow. The ocean, faintly illuminated by lights from the ship, frightened her. She passed a pair of lifeboats hanging from divots, and then a couple sensibly dressed in trench coats, and a group of teenagers in shirt sleeves, apparently impervious to chilly weather. She felt self-conscious. Why hadn't she made Arthur come with her? The deck chairs were unoccupied, except for an elderly lady sitting straight up under a wool blanket. Joyce guessed from her chiseled, weather-beaten features that she hailed from Maine or maybe Nova Scotia. Joyce recalled the winters of her childhood: drifts piled high, and a horse-drawn sleigh carrying revelers down a broad avenue. She had been allowed to play in the snow all day until her fingers and toes were numb. Parents had worried less about their children's safety in those days, and there had been no such thing as polio vaccines or antibiotics.

A man with a white moustache approached with a German Shepherd on a leash. Joyce felt a rush of indignation. Was he allowed to keep the dog in his cabin? The man wasn't blind! It wasn't fair. She must insist, first thing tomorrow, on her right to walk Horace in the open air.

She judged that she was a hundred yards from the bow. She pictured Marcus leaning off the very tip, like a figurehead on a clipper ship. No, it was impossible; she was letting her fears get the better of her. She bowed her head against the breeze, wishing for a scarf to wrap around her head and tie under her neck, like the Queen of England. Her hair, beaten back, must look awful! She was conscious of the groaning of the ship's engines—a horrid noise, as if the boat were in pain.

Then she stopped short and gave an involuntary cry. There was Marcus, sitting on the deck with his hands folded around his knees, supporting his back against a sort of funnel. He was all by himself. Coming closer, she saw that his face was tear stained.

"Marcus! Where's your brother?"

Marcus got to his feet and wiped his face with his sleeve. "He told me to wait here for a few minutes. He said he wanted to tell Julie something in private. He said a few minutes, but it's been more like twenty." He checked his wristwatch to see if he was right.

"You're coming right back inside with me." Joyce felt his head. "You're all damp and shivering."

"I'm not cold. We should wait for Adrian and Julie. They'll come back and wonder where I went."

"Serve them right for leaving you!" But she recognized the logic in his words. "Let's go look for them. They can't have gone very far."

The nerve of them to have abandoned Marcus! Adrian should have known it would hurt his brother's feelings. And the girl! Wasn't she worried that Marcus might be swept overboard? What were they doing, anyway? Joyce thought she knew the answer and worried that Julie might report it to her parents. Whether it was the absolute truth wouldn't matter once Helen Eiger got wind of it. Then Joyce might have to defend Adrian. *My son knows better.* But was that the truth? Didn't she want Adrian to be a courageous young man? A bold lover would have swept her off her feet at Julie's age.

"Come on, Marcus. Let's find the runaways. First Val, and now this!" She took his hand, but he pulled it away.

"Don't tell them I was … you know."

"Tell them what? You were sitting and watching the stars."

Marcus gave her a grateful smile and took her hand back in his.

It didn't take long before they sighted two figures leaning against a sidewall surmounted by a railing. A ring hung from hooks. For a long moment Joyce imagined the girl drifting out to sea, clinging to the life preserver.

Neither Adrian nor Julie noticed their approach. She was about to call out to them, but then she saw the girl lean closer to Adrian and kiss him on the cheek. In her own day, Joyce thought, she'd have waited for the first kiss, and it would have been the boy who made the first move. Either way, it wasn't the sort of thing she wanted Marcus to see. A little boy, and so sensitive. But then Joyce doubted herself. Why should she want to shield him? A jealous mother!

"Mom, can we go now? Just let them know I'm okay."

Joyce pressed Marcus's hand and prepared to shout Adrian's name into the wind.

MRS. WOODBINE DREAMED that she was under the ocean, surrounded by huge fish. If only she could stay clear of their squishy bodies! But there were so many of them, and any second now they would rub up against her.

She woke up with a quickened heartbeat, thinking she was in her own bed at home. Was it time to get up and fix breakfast? Then she realized that she was aboard a great ocean liner. The room was dark. She checked the alarm clock next to her bed. Luminous hands pointed to a few minutes past midnight. Mrs. Woodbine gave a low groan. Another seven hours before she'd get any breakfast. She'd been afraid to order food in her room, even after she stopped feeling seasick; she thought they'd probably charge extra for room service. She'd gotten ready for bed, put a sweater on over her nightgown (there didn't seem any way to raise the room temperature), wrapped her hair around curlers, and lain down under a thin blanket. Her feet had felt icy, so she'd got up again and put on socks. A little later someone had knocked softly on the door, and Mrs. Woodbine, suspecting it was Joyce Lash coming to check on her again, had lain quite still. She'd not wanted to be seen in her bedclothes! Whoever it was had gone away. She'd dozed for a while until she heard Lucille Shiflett unlock the door and come in on tip toe. Mrs. Woodbine pretended to be asleep; she was keenly aware of Lucille's footsteps, the hiss of the bathroom faucets, and the flushing of the toilet. My Land, the woman took forever!

She checked the clock again. Still only fifteen minutes past midnight! She was acutely aware of sleeping in the same room as a stranger, in the middle of a vast, treacherous sea. Suppose she felt a powerful urge to step onto dry land? It would be like jumping out of a roller coaster in the middle of a ride. Mrs. Woodbine felt a twinge of panic. Had she made an awful mistake? No doubt her children thought so. She'd sent each of them a telegram. They must think she'd taken leave of her senses.

Her neck ached. It was a lumpy pillow they'd given her! Her stomach rumbled. She wondered if they served any sort of hot cereal for breakfast. If not, she'd settle for corn flakes. Afterwards, she meant to explore the ship. She would ask Marcus to come along. She might coax Adrian into joining them, but not Val. She suspected Val of saying mean things behind her back. Well, she mustn't expect the boys to depend on her the way they used to. She wondered if she didn't love them more than she loved her own two children. The Lord had placed both sets of children in her care. What wouldn't she do for them? Suppose she had to throw herself in front of a bus that was about to run down Marcus? Her soul would fly straight up to Heaven. *Purgatory* was Roman Catholic foolishness. Like taking your sins to the dry cleaner! Besides, she wasn't much of a sinner. Jesus would take her just as she was.

Mrs. Woodbine lay very quietly in her bed, listening for any cracks that might open up in the hull. She thought she would hear something if the ship hit an iceberg. Tomorrow she would go out on deck and see if she could spot any icebergs or whale spouts. She might sit in a deck chair, but not too long; it was no fun staying put when you could be moving around. If she sat by herself, a stranger might choose an empty deck chair next to hers. She wondered if there were any black people on the boat. Suppose Nat King Cole happened to be on board and sat down next to her? She enjoyed his recordings. His voice was like a white man's. He seemed very polite on television. She wouldn't have to move her chair if it was Nat King Cole.

It would be safer to sit with the Lashes, though. The Lashes appreciated her. They prized her honesty and dependability; laughed at her country ways. Not that anyone could call the home state of George Washington and Robert E. Lee backward! She had nothing to feel ashamed of. None of her family had ever owned a slave, as far as she knew.

Mrs. Woodbine felt a pang of self-pity. Nobody except Marcus was truly interested in her stories anymore. Lately, even Marcus lost patience. The days when she was his second mother were long gone. Why then had she intruded on their vacation? The expense alone should have held her back. She'd turned the question over in her mind while standing in line for a passport, and then later, while going through her bureau drawers and sorting out clothes, just in case the Lashes insisted she join them. She had rehearsed what she would say if they offered her a ticket plus her weekly salary. "Why, I'd be tickled to come along, Dr. Lash!" But no such offer had been made and, at the terminal, seeing them off, she'd made up her mind that it was all a big mistake. Until Horace's bag! She smiled at the thought of it. *A sign!*

When all was said and done, she had her reasons. One of the boys would get sick and need caring for. Worse things might happen. Once they got over there, the grandfather might drop dead from working long hours; she'd have to mind the children while the Lashes grieved and made funeral arrangements. Having no clear idea of what the boys' grandfather looked like, she pictured a very old man with a long white beard. Yes, the grandfather was probably hanging on by a thread! Another, more fascinating possibility occurred to her. What if the boys' father suffered a fatal attack? Mrs. Woodbine thought she detected a jaundiced pallor in Dr. Lash's cheeks. Her own husband, James Woodbine, had died at roughly the same age. Cancer had carried him off in no time at all. If something like that should occur, Joyce Lash would bury her head in Mrs. Woodbine's bosom and pour out her grief. They would kneel and pray together and Joyce Lash would bless the Lord for having provided a consoling friend. She would finally call her "Ruby".

There were other, more selfish considerations. The idea of traveling to a foreign country pleased Mrs. Woodbine immensely. She had never in her life taken an excursion remotely comparable. Nobody would have called her late husband an adventurous man. James Woodbine had been a good provider, though. His work in the lumber mill had been sufficient to raise a family in comfort. During the Depression he'd gone on relief until the mill reopened and the family were back on their feet— a necessity that some men hated but that James Woodbine faced rationally. What was the government for, he said, but to help honest families down on their luck? Even in the best of times, she and James were satisfied to stay within the boundaries of Virginia. But right before the cancer set in, they'd gotten as far as Arkansas, where James had relations. They'd visited a famous cave and dined at a restaurant with a view of the capitol in Little Rock. That was the same year the Blacks decided they wanted to attend the white schools. James Woodbine had refused to blame them. It was Communists, he said, who were stirring up trouble.

Mrs. Woodbine kept herself too busy to dwell on her bereavement. She was proud that James had been a hard-working, fair-minded man. And brave! You couldn't call a man who'd served in the First World War at nineteen years of age anything but brave. James had been shot at, and he'd shot back, though that was something he wouldn't ever speak of in any detail. She had pressed him on it a couple of times. The most she'd ever gotten out of him was that he was so scared he hadn't been able to aim his rifle straight. Nothing like shooting at a possum! She imagined James's bullet piercing the heart of some German soldier who was fixing on doing him in. It frightened and thrilled her to think of it. Like cutting the head off of a chicken!

And now here she was, about to see for herself what it was like in countries where they wouldn't stop having wars, and American boys had to go over and straighten out the mess. There must still be a lot of people around who had wanted to kill James, and even more who had killed about a million Americans in the last war. Turned on each other too! She'd seen the photographs of corpses stacked up, skin and bones. She'd heard of the showers that, when you turned them on, let out poison gas instead of hot water. Private John-Wesley Woodbine was over in Germany right now, making sure something like that didn't happen again.

Austria, Mrs. Woodbine speculated, might not be any better. When she thought about Austria, she couldn't help it that a kangaroo popped into her mind. But Italy sent a thrill down her chest and into the pit of her stomach. The Pope of Rome, carried around in a litter with a golden canopy! Suppose she happened to see him? He might wave at her and smile. It would be something between a blessing and a magic trick. And then the hundreds of falling-down palaces and fountains and churches.

She smiled. Dr. Lash would cough and turn up his collar in the grottoes they had over there. Mrs. Woodbine had only a vague idea of what grottoes were; she suspected they were wet and cold, and spooked by the departed. It wouldn't alarm her to visit one of them, though. Although she believed in ghosts, she wasn't afraid of them, and she never suffered unduly from unhealthy climates. As a little girl she'd withstood all kinds of illnesses. There hadn't been money for fancy doctoring. Take a spoonful of molasses-and-turpentine! Measles, mumps, scarlet fever, hookworm … . She might even have had a touch of the polio. Her brother Gabel had died and been resurrected during a bout with diphtheria. Mrs. Woodbine felt she was hardened by old sicknesses and wouldn't catch any new ones.

On the other side of the cabin, Lucille Shiflett's body rose and fell rhythmically. Lucille Shiflett was a divorced woman, forced to make her own way in the world. Mrs. Woodbine admired and pitied her. Traveling alone like that! It was a comfort knowing the Lashes were asleep in their cabins not too far away. Dr. Lash was a good man, never mind that he was a foreigner and belonged to the wrong church. The fact that he was dimly connected with the Hebrews brought to mind stories from the Old Testament; he might, with the addition of a flowing beard and robe, have stood in for Noah. Joyce Lash, too, was a good woman, and she'd be an even better one if she didn't look down from her high horse. Mrs. Woodbine remembered how she had once boldly called her "Joyce" to her face and had in return been emphatically addressed as "Mrs. Woodbine". Well, it was on account of how she was raised. Joyce Lash's mother, in Mrs. Woodbine's opinion, was a cold, unfeeling woman with money she didn't know how to spend. She couldn't bring herself to like her, or even feel very sorry for her now that she seldom spoke and spent her days in a wheelchair. But it wasn't for her to judge! How many times had her Daddy told her, "Ruby, put yourself in the other fella's shoes, and you'll understand him a sight better"? And when she had asked, "Is it because his shoes are too tight that he's ornery?" her Daddy had laughed.

The memory of her Daddy had a relaxing effect. It generally

did. Her mother, on the other hand, had a sharp, angry voice that had made her nervous as a child. She was ashamed to admit it even to herself, but she did not really love her mother. She didn't blame her, however. It hadn't been easy running a farm with six children and bills to pay and blighted crops and animals continually sickening and dying. Mama had always favored the younger children, Gabel and Moley, but Daddy had singled her out as his favorite. "Ruby," her Daddy liked to say, "has more sense than the other five put together." It had been his special concern that her good sense should not be spoiled by temptations; that was the reason he made her promise never to drink, dance or play cards. He had winked at her afterwards, as if to say that he wouldn't think the less of her if she now and then faltered. Mrs. Woodbine recalled something else her Daddy had told her: that if she ever had a chance to "see the world", she ought to take it. Strange that for years she'd not thought of those words, and now they were as clear as though he were lying next to her. *You're different, Ruby. Somebody gives you the chance, you take it!* Sitting astride his bony knees, kicking her bare feet, she had piped up, "And s'pose nobody offers me a chance?" He had laughed and said: "Why then, you'll have to make a chance all by yourself, Honeypie!"

The pet name revolved pleasantly in Mrs. Woodbine's mind. She felt her eyelids grow heavy. She would sleep until morning and wake up refreshed. It did not worry her that on rare occasions she walked in her sleep. It had never yet happened when she had gone to stay with the Lashes. On her very first visit, she had warned them, just in case they caught her wandering in the middle of the night. "I don't ever touch anything I oughtn't to." James Woodbine used to say it was because her mind wanted to get up and do something useful, but her body wanted to go on sleeping.

By half past twelve Mrs. Woodbine was snoring along with her cabin mate. Most other passengers were also in their cabins. A few insomniacs lingered over drinks; the bar and lounge stayed open until two. All the Lashes were asleep except for Joyce, who was sitting up in bed with a book. She was having a hard time ridding her mind of the scene she had witnessed a few hours earlier. She hadn't said a word about it to Adrian. She hadn't wanted to sound like a prudish mother, or a jealous one. She had simply chastised him for leaving Marcus alone. Adrian had looked sheepish and apologized to his brother. The four of them had walked back inside together, and then Julie had said something about having promised to meet her parents for cards. She hadn't acted the least bit ashamed. Just a kiss after all! Adrian had spent the rest of the evening watching Val beat his father at chess and casting glances over at the table where the Eigers were playing gin rummy.

Joyce checked her watch, sighed and plumped her pillow. The inside of it felt more like sand than feathers. She turned a page of her book: *Lady Chatterley's Lover*. She had bought it at the Book Worm; something to read on the boat. The Book Worm was Garnet's outpost of nonconformity. The shop's owner, Sheila Rath, was a bohemian. "Imagine having to wait for a bunch of old judges to give us permission!" Sheila Rath had said, ringing up the purchase. A cloth imported from the South Seas hung on the wall behind her cash register. Sheila was unmarried; she wore wooden earrings, ate at cheap restaurants in the "Village", and went to see movies forbidden by the Catholic Church. Joyce assumed that Sheila must have slept with a lot of different men.

So far, she had finished two chapters of *Lady Chatterley*. She was disappointed. It might have been any other English novel of the period. The "explicit" parts must come later on. She was sure she wouldn't be shocked. Already she was picturing Sir Clifford's gamekeeper as a cross between the author and Gary Dover. The same fair skin, dark hair and swimmer's body as Gary's, but with a soft beard and moustache and more somber eyes. Surely whatever happened between the gamekeeper and Constance Chatterley wouldn't be brutal or repulsive. She resolved not to give in to the temptation to skip ahead. It wouldn't be fair.

She glanced at Arthur, breathing peacefully next to her. After the boys had retired to their own cabin, and she and Arthur were both in bed, she'd told him all about Adrian and Julie. As expected, he'd been amused; Adrian's adventure gave him a vicarious thrill. She knew perfectly well how vivid, even extravagant, her husband's fantasies were—which didn't prevent him from being faithful. Imagination was better than the actual thing, he often told her, since there was no possibility of disappointment. What was the harm? Down with Puritanism! Americans, Arthur said, only pretended to be pure; they committed the most incredible transgressions. But then, not wishing to be ungrateful, he conceded that his adopted country had its virtues compared with his native land. Not so many years ago, he might have been taken away, starved, gassed and burned up to a pile of ashes. Americans hadn't treated their slaves and Indians with such cruel efficiency!

Arthur had promised her to take Adrian aside and have a talk. First he would say that it was hard at Adrian's age to rein in a very natural desire. Then he would say that Julie was learning to swim, as it were; not old enough to plunge into the deep end of the pool. And he would remind him that unless he took measures that were illegal, there was always the danger of a calamitous outcome.

Afterwards, excited by the topic of teenage lust, Arthur had pressed close to her under the sheet. She'd said she was tired out from the long and exhausting day. Of course that had disappointed him, almost angered him. "*Ach!* You say that all the time!" But it was the truth; she was tired, and seasick on top of it. "I just need a good night's sleep." Which hadn't stopped her, after Arthur had turned his back on her and fallen asleep, from picking up her book. But now she found that she was going over and over the same line of type. She couldn't read any further. She might as well get dressed and walk over to the lounge. A waiter would bring her tea or a cup of cocoa. The hot milk would make her sleepy. If she slept soundly, she would be in the mood to please her husband in the morning.

Five minutes later she was walking towards the lounge. The ship was more to her liking, now that there were few people up and about. She saw only one passenger in the corridors: a little old man in pajamas and robe. Where was he going? She passed him and walked on.

The tourist class lounge was occupied by a dozen souls. Half of them were sitting at the bar, the women heavily made up, the men running to fat. Were they old friends or simply kindred spirits? A few of the stuffed lounge chairs were occupied by quieter passengers. The trio were packing up their instruments. They must have played for hours. Joyce pitied them. Probably they'd once hoped to play in concert halls. Well, it was better than a dingy night club, but not as good as playing in the first-class lounge.

Joyce settled herself in a chair. On the table before her was a little menu with a tasseled cord running down the middle. Evidently it wasn't too late to order snacks. The thought of hot cocoa now made her feel slightly nauseous. She would order mineral water, and sit and watch her fellow passengers until the lounge closed for the night.

An apparition at the entryway caught her attention. It couldn't be! Was Mrs. Woodbine going to keep showing up at the oddest moments? And what on earth was she wearing?

For an instant, Joyce thought that Mrs. Woodbine had gone mad. She had on a pink sweater buttoned over her nightgown. Her hair was wrapped around curlers. She wore slippers and white socks. The strain of traveling abroad had been too much for her! She looked like some huge, migratory bird—like the albatross in the *Ancient Mariner*. But then Joyce remembered that Mrs. Woodbine wandered in her sleep. She had almost forgotten about the disorder, since Mrs. Woodbine had never, not even once, walked by night while under the Lashes' roof.

Judging from her bizarre outfit and the glazed look on her face, it was clear that Mrs. Woodbine was having a relapse. People were staring. The men and women at the bar seemed to think it was a great joke. Joyce tried to remember if it was advisable to interfere with somnambulists. If you broke the trance, did they go into shock? At the very least, Mrs. Woodbine would be mortified.

Mrs. Woodbine sat down on a tall stool at the bar.

"Does the *Signora* wish to order?" The barman's voice was deferential, but he was obviously suppressing laughter.

Joyce got up and hurried across the room. Mrs. Woodbine turned and gave her a determined look. "I already told you,

Mama," she said in a clear voice. "I'm done washing my hair." Then she swung her head toward the barman. "It takes an awful long time to dry."

One of the ladies at the bar let out a cackle. The drunk sitting next to her made a choking sound.

Joyce felt a flash of indignation. "She's not well. Can't you see? She's walking in her sleep."

The barman gave a sigh of relief. "*Ho pensat' uno spirito.*" The people at the bar gave each other looks. *A ghost!* Just like an Italian!

Joyce took Mrs. Woodbine's hand, gently led her from the bar and guided her towards the exit, as if she was accustomed to deranged people. A woman leaned forward in her chair and said the people at the bar ought to be ashamed. A man offered his assistance. Another suggested summoning the ship's doctor, but Joyce shook her head and said she would see that her friend was safely back in bed.

But Mrs. Woodbine was still in a talkative frame of mind.

"I ought to be in bed," she said in a confiding voice. And then, as they left the lounge: "That fella I was talking to doesn't even speak English."

No Extra Charge

THE NEXT FEW days on board the *Columbus* passed uneventfully. Joyce and Marcus spent their last afternoon on deck chairs. Joyce read some more of *Lady Chatterley*. Marcus read a book about a young soldier fighting alongside General Washington. Passersby regarded him with bemused looks; Joyce guessed that they were wondering why he wasn't playing with children his age. She would like to have explained that Marcus preferred the company of older boys and girls. Or grown-ups. It was because his mind was a couple of years ahead of his body. A school psychologist had told her so in so many words.

Marcus inserted a swizzle-stick between the pages of his book and closed the covers.

"You don't have to keep me company," Joyce said. "You can go look for Adrian and Julie if you want to."

"In a few minutes. By the way, I forgot to tell you that Adrian wanted to stick his head out of the porthole and look up at the passengers. You know, people leaning over the railing. It would have been funny if they saw Adrian staring up at them."

Joyce laughed and said that it was a good thing the portholes were bolted shut; someone would have to pry his brother loose if he got stuck. It saddened her to think that Marcus wouldn't have Adrian around much longer.

"We're going to have to keep an eye on Adrian, aren't we, Marcus? If he gets into trouble over there."

"The Bastille!" Marcus pictured his brother chained to a wall; rats nibbling a crust of bread. "He'll get pretty hungry. And he'll miss all the sights."

"We're only staying one night in Paris, remember dar—?" Joyce checked herself.

"Can't we stay longer? The Eigers will be in Paris for a whole week."

"Lucky Eigers."

"Will we at least have time for the Eiffel Tower? We should walk up." Marcus went on to explain the number of steps and the height and date of construction—information he'd gotten from the *World Book Encyclopedia*. The blue volumes filled two bookshelves in his bedroom.

"Our train gets in at three o'clock. We'll go in the evening, when it's all lit up. Julie can come with us. You'd like that, wouldn't you?"

"Adrian won't enjoy it otherwise." Marcus thought for a moment and then added: "I wouldn't mind if she was my sister."

"We'll invite her. But it means putting up with the mother."

Marcus looked puzzled. "You don't want Helen to come? I like her."

"Oh, she's all right."

Joyce reached over and squeezed his hand. She could count on Marcus to act as her conscience. She would have felt lonesome sitting by herself. Arthur had gone to the gym. Afterwards, he intended to stop at the ship's travel agency and ask about the relative merits of trains and rental cars. Mrs. Woodbine was taking a stroll with Lucille Shiflett, probably talking the poor woman's ear off. She had even struck up a friendship with Helen Eiger. "You're lucky to have her," Helen had whispered to Joyce over lunch, loud enough for Mrs. Woodbine to overhear. "A treasure!" As for her other two boys, Joyce had no definite idea where they were. She assumed Val had attached himself to one or another of the crew. She had gotten it out of him that he'd made himself welcome in the kitchen, and he boasted that a friendly officer had taken him up to the bridge. She pictured a gentleman with a white beard, like the captain in *A Night to Remember.* Yes, the captain might, as Val claimed, have allowed him to put his hands on the wheel.

She needn't wonder what was keeping Adrian busy. He and Julie were already an acknowledged couple. At meals they ate quickly, in a hurry to get away from the adults. Arthur made a wry face and joked that it was a good thing Marcus was keeping an eye on them. Julie and Adrian made a point of including Marcus in their fun. Last night, during the celebration of *Quatorze Juillet,* Julie had urged Marcus to perform. The trio, transformed for the occasion into a lively band—the violinist had switched to electric guitar and the xylophonist to a set of drums—were prepared to accompany passengers who wished to show off their talent. Marcus had gone up on stage right after a little girl who had sung something from a Broadway musical. His treble voice had sailed out into the room, loud and clear. *Chantilly lace and a pretty face, and a pony-tail hangin' down ... .* Adults and children pressed close to the stage, enthralled by the approximation of rock and roll. *Makes me feel real loose, like a long-necked goose ... .* Arthur had practically wept, he was so touched by his son's fearlessness. So what if the lyrics were borderline indecent?

In the morning, Joyce overheard Julie teasing Marcus about forgetting to take off his party hat the whole time he was up on stage. Elvis Presley would have remembered! Marcus had beamed with pleasure. Joyce had to admit that Julie was a generous girl. But she was reserved around Val. Joyce wondered if he minded the snub. It was so hard to tell with Val. As for Mrs. Woodbine, she was pleased as punch with Julie. "Adrian's sweet on that girl, Mizz Lash," she said during a walk on deck. She gave Joyce a nudge. "Not one of those stuck-up ones. But not *fast,* either."

Joyce reached for the cup resting on the arm of her chair. She sipped her tea, tepid from having stood too long. Mrs. Woodbine, she decided, *was* a treasure. For instance, she'd come along for moral support to confront the officer in charge of "live cargo". Might they not take Horace for a walk for half an hour? The man made a face and mentioned "unsanitary conditions"; if he made an exception for Horace, he'd have to do the same for everybody's pet. As if the ship were as full of animals as Noah's Ark! Joyce told the man that she understood perfectly well that the crew prided themselves on cleanliness, but then why had she spotted a load of trash trailing the hull? And what about the old gentleman walking his German Shepherd? The officer turned pink and said something about making an allowance for persons with disabilities.

Afterwards, Mrs. Woodbine clucked and shook her head. "Imagine that fella acting so ugly, and everybody else so nice and polite!" Earlier, in the lounge, a waiter had brought a Coca-Cola over to where she was looking at the pictures in *Life* magazine, without her even asking for it. On the house! He'd spoken to her as if he thought he owed her an apology. Several passengers had asked her how she was feeling. My Land, but she hoped she wasn't the sort of person people felt sorry for!

The fact was, Mrs. Woodbine was none the wiser. She had appeared at the breakfast table the morning after her nocturnal ramble in high spirits; consumed her cereal, eggs, sausage, toast and coffee with relish, exhibiting none of the seasickness that had marred the previous evening. Joyce decided to say nothing. Imagine Mrs. Woodbine's shame if she knew! Nor had she said anything to the boys. Marcus might let something slip out. Val was capable of saying something from pure malice. Arthur had agreed. Why let the cat out of the bag? No doubt witnesses had spread the story far and wide, but so long as no one said anything to her face ... .

"Joyce! Marcus!"

Joyce looked up at the sound of her husband's voice. Dressed in athletic attire—polo shirt, white cotton pants, tennis shoes—Arthur was hurrying along the Promenade Deck. He stopped and kissed his wife on the top of her head. Then he reached into his pocket and drew out an envelope.

"Train reservations. Private compartments all the way from Paris."

"Did you even ask about renting a car?" Joyce interrupted.

"And be at the mercy of crazy drivers?"

"I won't make Horace go back in a crate."

"Europeans are understanding about pets. The agent assured me Horace can ride with us in comfort."

"I would have done the driving. We could have stopped whenever we felt like it."

"Believe me, Joyce, it's not what you're used to. Over there they don't follow rules of the road the way we do."

Joyce sighed. As if there weren't terrible drivers back home! But Arthur was opposed on principle to the automobile. Engines were a complete mystery to him. They would have had to rely on Adrian to change a flat.

"Compartiment privé. Reduced fare for *le plus jeune."* Arthur was mimicking the travel agent; for some reason the man had

wanted to show off his French. "You should have heard him, Joyce: No extra charge *pour le chien.*"

"Will there be a dining car?" Marcus asked. "Like in *The Lady Vanishes?*"

"*Bien sûr!*" Arthur turned to Joyce. "You see? Our son has the right idea." He described the scenery they would take in: landscapes with haystacks, like paintings by Monet, and lakes and rivers that were a far cry from the streamlet that ran through Running Brook Park. Once they were in Austria, they would see charming woods, delightful parks; Marcus would love the giant Ferris wheel that loomed over the Prater fairgrounds. And then, after a few weeks in Vienna, they would take another train to Italy.

"Rome, Lake Como, Venice and departure from Genoa. What do you say, Joyce? We'll introduce our children to the world's most beautiful city. A room on the Grand Canal! I only hope the crowds won't spoil it. How about a gondola ride, Marcus?"

Joyce frowned. "I thought Venice was supposed to be for just the two of us."

"You don't really mind, do you? I wouldn't want the boys to miss the opportunity. *Piazza San Marco* … ."

"Of course not." Joyce's voice sounded hard in her own ears, but she couldn't help it. "Too bad the Eigers aren't coming with us; Hank could tell us all about the pigeons." She let out a short laugh.

Arthur put the tickets back in his pocket. He started to speak but then he checked himself. Joyce felt a ripple of satisfaction. Good! She had reduced her husband to silence.

"I don't suppose," Joyce said, "those are refundable?"

"Aren't you being unreasonable?"

"You mean I'm being selfish."

"I want to see the pigeons," Marcus said. "But it's okay if I see them some other time." He hated it when his parents argued. He picked up his book and began reading where he'd left off. Joyce picked up her own book. Out of the corner of her eye, she watched Arthur walk over to the railing and stare out to sea with his back to her. Oh, it was useless to fight. It would only place her further in the wrong. Marriage! In her book, the heroine was in the process of discarding her incapable husband. A woman's prerogative. Joyce suspected it was really the author who yearned for his fictional gamekeeper. She was only pretending to read. She recollected a family holiday, before the war, when she was fifteen: posters proclaiming *Il Duce Ha Sempre Ragione*; mustachioed *bersagliere* promenading in black-plumed hats; tourists in white linen suits; a delicate wafer poised upright in *gelato*; the silvery dish shaped like a little pedestal. From the balcony of her hotel room, she'd watched sleek, olive-skinned boys splashing in a canal, not minding the trash. Wherever she showed her face, locals whistled and shouted compliments. She had brought a camera encased in brown leather. She took snapshots of her parents; fed the pigeons in St. Mark's Square from a paper cone filled with corn. Marcus wanted to see the descendants of those same pigeons. Why ruin his fun? Besides which, a romantic Venetian holiday unencumbered by children would stir up passions in her husband that she would feel unable to match. Arthur would expect miracles; he would be disappointed when they failed to occur.

"I'm sorry" she said, getting up and taking Arthur's hand at the railings. Marcus, overhearing, put his book down and looked at her wonderingly. "I'm spoiling everything," she went on. There was a quaver in her voice. "Don't let me, Art. I don't want to be that sort of person."

ON DECK, IN the lounge, at the mock steeplechase, passengers made sly comments at Adrian and Julie's expense. During the lifeboat drill on the first morning of the voyage, an officer asked Adrian if he and Julie were prepared to go down with the ship together. At meal times, Helen Eiger alluded to the "shipboard romance". On these occasions, Adrian slid his leg closer to Julie's under the table cloth, Hank Eiger grunted, Joyce assumed a forced smile and Arthur laughed merrily. Privately, the Lashes agreed that Helen wasn't as pleased as she pretended to be. Joyce said that she understood a mother's fears. But Arthur was enjoying the affair. At dinner on the last night of the voyage, he compared the lovers to Hero and Leander. The unfamiliar tale was cause for confusion and hilarity. Why hadn't Leander simply sailed in a boat across the Hellespont, Marcus asked, instead of trying to swim the whole way? Drowned lovers! It was a fine story, Joyce said, to tell in the middle of the Atlantic. Still, she couldn't help laughing.

After dinner, Joyce gave Helen Eiger her address in Vienna; Helen was anxious to send postcards. Then the two women exchanged their home addresses and phone numbers and promised to keep in touch when they got back home, a promise that neither of the women expected the other to keep. At eleven o'clock, the two families retired to their cabins, but it was too soon for a farewell; the Eigers and the Lashes would be taking the same train from Le Havre to the Gare Saint-Lazare. Adrian and Julie, Helen Eiger said, glancing coyly at her daughter, would have a few more hours together.

Disembarkation at Le Havre the following morning went smoothly, as if the ship was eager to get rid of its passengers. While people waited for the unloading and inspection of baggage, they removed their coats and fanned themselves with folded magazines. Normandy was suffering from a heatwave. Outside on the pier, the temperature was already in the nineties. Not everyone minded, though. Horace strained at his leash, sniffed at everything and yelped at the seagulls. *"C'est la libération!*" a porter joked. Even Mrs. Woodbine, who generally treated Horace with reserve, as if he were a farm animal, let him jump up on her and lick her hand. "My Land!" she exclaimed. "I must be a sight for sore eyes!" Meanwhile, little boys ran around the dock in sandals and bathing trunks, offering packets that unfolded into postcards with views of Saint-Malo, Rouen, and Mont Saint-Michel. They, at least, were sensibly dressed. Everyone else looked ready to expire. An old woman, swaying under her heavy garments, circulated with a cart filled with sandwiches. Porters, sweating from their exertions, distributed luggage and then, after a glance at the amount, pocketed their tips.

"They're pretending not to care," Joyce said, after the Lashes had collected their belongings. "I'm sure they complain if they don't get enough."

"French workmen don't like to appear subservient," Arthur said. "It's a holdover from the Revolution. On the other hand, they feel entitled to their just reward."

"You over-tipped."

"*Noblesse oblige.*"

"Let me tip next time," Marcus said. "I don't want them to think Americans are stingy."

"It seems one of our children is a born aristocrat." Arthur laughed and wiped his brow with a crumpled handkerchief.

After a customs official inspected their luggage, the Lashes found a taxi and drove to the station with time to spare. Arthur cashed traveler's checks at Thomas Cook and helped Mrs. Woodbine convert a five-dollar bill into francs. While she counted her change, he speculated that she'd probably brought insufficient funds. A nuisance! He'd already paid for her train tickets and booked her a hotel room, despite her protestations. It would be simpler, he thought, to cover her expenses until they got to Vienna. Once there, she might make herself useful. He calculated a small salary, neither insulting nor too generous. He was about to tell Joyce the figure he'd settled on when he spotted the Eigers at the other end of the station. Hank Eiger was reading a newspaper. Julie and her mother had their backs turned. Arthur exchanged quick glances with Joyce. It would be rude to ignore them.

"I suppose we ought to make an effort," Joyce said. Adrian had already darted ahead to be with his girlfriend. The others followed dutifully.

"Here we all are again!" Arthur said after the two families had rejoined forces.

"Our train doesn't leave until one forty-five," Helen said. "I don't know how much longer I can stand this heat."

"It's certainly unusual." Arthur felt responsible for the weather. Europe was his continent, after all. He thought for a moment. "The beach is a few kilometers from here. Why not leave our baggage at the station? We can have an early lunch on the *quai.*"

"I sure could eat a sandwich," Mrs. Woodbine said. "A breeze would feel real good too."

Joyce suppressed a groan. If Arthur had suggested a ride in a hot air balloon, Mrs. Woodbine would have gladly complied.

"I don't know," Helen said. "Won't we miss our train?"

"*Ach!* We have hours." Arthur put his hand to his mouth and coughed into it. "These railroad stations are full of germs. You don't want a summer cold to spoil your vacation."

"We so rarely get sick," Helen said.

"I don't know that I want to get into another cab," Hank said. "There ought to be some place to eat around her. That place we passed on the way in looked all right."

Arthur made a face. "Bad food and worse wine! I dined there many years ago and I doubt it's improved."

Helen Eiger dabbed her face with a handkerchief. "Some decent food and fresh air might do us all some good."

Since there were too many to squeeze into one taxi, it was arranged that the Eigers would follow the Lashes in their own cab.

"Is it all right," Adrian asked, "if I ride with Julie?"

Helen Eiger whispered to Joyce, loud enough for her daughter to hear: "They grow up so fast, don't they?"

"I guess that must be why I'm still treated like a child," Julie said.

Helen made a tragic face and touched Joyce's arm. "Children!"

Ten minutes later, the families were seated at two tables pushed together on an outdoor terrace. The waiters at *La Petite Normande* were delighted to accommodate a big group at an hour when the restaurant was more than half empty.

"Feel the breeze?" Arthur directed the question to no one in particular. He pointed out the new cathedral, visible in the distance.

"The old one was bombed to pieces. This new one might as well be a bank somewhere in the Midwest." Arthur laughed and turned to Hank Eiger. "I suppose one can't expect another Chartres."

"Looks all right to me." Hank Eiger apparently didn't see much wrong with Midwestern banks. "The temperature's going up," he said. "We ought to have taken a table inside."

"The French don't believe in air-conditioning."

"Ought to be a fan at least."

Helen Eiger studied the menu. "I see they have mussels." She leaned over and whispered to Joyce, "I think it's wonderful that Julie and Adrian … ." Her words trailed off. She paused a second, then brightened and showed her teeth. "I was worried she'd be lonely on the boat for four whole days. And your son is such a gentleman."

Joyce forced herself to smile back. She decided that she rather disliked the Eigers. Hank was rude; Helen was an actress. Did she really imagine Adrian was a gentleman? For that matter, Julie wasn't so very innocent. The girl, it turned out, was older than she looked: sixteen, not fourteen.

It took a while for everyone to order. Joyce, Arthur and the Eigers decided on omelets. Marcus and Adrian wanted *steak frites*. Joyce said it was too early in the day for a big meal; Arthur overruled her. Nothing wrong with a hearty appetite! Now that he was almost on home ground, he wasn't worried about overeating.

Val chose onion soup, and Mrs. Woodbine, who would have liked a tuna fish sandwich, settled for *potage aux legumes*.

"That's awful good soup, Dr. Lash," she said, after she'd taken a sip.

Horace sat under the table, panting. Joyce gave him bits of

omelet and French bread. Arthur asked Hank about birds, and Helen made remarks about hotels. No one ordered anything alcoholic. By the time they had finished it was well past noon. Arthur suggested that, while the adults drank their espressos, the young people might as well take Horace for a jaunt on the beach. Mrs. Woodbine got up to accompany them but Arthur made her sit back down. No reason why she shouldn't relax and enjoy herself! Privately, he was thinking that Adrian would like to spend a little time with Julie away from the adults.

Val took hold of Horace's leash. It was a Saturday; people were spread out on towels and long chairs, shielded from the glare by broad hats and umbrellas. Children splashed in the waves or dug their shovels in the sand. The adults were content to lie still or cool off in the ocean. Everyone talked non-stop. Adrian took it all in with satisfaction. The French, he decided, were more relaxed than Americans, who went around as if they were guilty of something. Some of the littlest children were playing without anything on at all. At home, they'd get arrested. For that matter, French mothers and fathers let their children smoke cigarettes and drink wine, and no one thought there was anything wrong with it.

Adrian took off his shoes and socks. The others, following his lead, deposited their footwear in a pile. Adrian drew his polo shirt over his head and tied it around his waist. He took Julie's hand.

French people, he was thinking, wouldn't think that what happened last night was anything to get all upset about. He wanted to ask Julie if she'd enjoyed it, but the question was embarrassing and she might not tell him the truth anyway. What if she was disappointed? She might act as if nothing had ever happened. On the other hand, she might decide she'd done something to be ashamed of. Suppose she confided in her mother? Helen Eiger would tell Hank, and Hank would tell Arthur. Adrian's imagination raced ahead: His parents would be so furious they'd refuse to pay for his college education. In that case, he'd join the Navy and get assigned to a nuclear submarine. Better than going to some second-rate college. Or any college! His grades generally fell short, and his teachers' recommendations were bound to be lukewarm. Arthur said that if he didn't study harder, he'd end up in his father's classroom.

From the way she was looking up at him, Adrian was pretty sure that Julie Eiger hadn't been disappointed. After they got home, maybe she'd want to be his steady girlfriend. If things went on long enough, she might want to get married. Trapped! But for now, shouldn't he be glad? He'd wanted a girlfriend ever since seventh grade.

"I hate the beach at home," Julie was saying. "It takes forever to get there, and there's hardly any sand, and the water's cold. *Ugh!* The boys are … ." She hesitated, considering what it was she disliked about them.

"They're what?"

"They aren't anything like you, anyway."

"What am I like?"

"Better than them, anyway." She thought for a moment and then giggled. "Mom said I was too old to share their cabin."

Adrian felt himself blushing. If his parents ever found out, they'd never forgive him. But his father would be impressed, even if he never said so. And wasn't his mother always trying to build up his confidence? She ought to be happy. There was nothing for either of them to be scared of. Julie had promised that she was safe. She'd timed it. He hadn't needed the item he'd bought on a school trip to the city. *I have a bad headache, Mrs. Croon. Can I go get aspirin at the drugstore?* It had been Robert Boardman's idea. Robert wanted a packet for himself, just in case an opportunity ever came up, and there was no place in Garnet that would sell to a teenager. Robert suffered from acne and bad posture, and he still wore braces. Girls ignored him. He wouldn't be needing protection any time soon. But he was Adrian's best friend.

"What are you so quiet for?" Julie looked up at him.

"No reason. Just taking in the sights."

Suppose Julie had miscalculated? He ought to have used what was in his wallet. But then the complication of putting it on, even though he'd practiced at home, would have spoiled everything. He suddenly recollected that he'd kept his white socks on the whole time. He was in too much of a hurry; he'd been nervous that Helen or Hank might barge in at any moment. It was his first time, not counting Joanne Platt. He and Joanne would have gone all the way on the couch in her parents' garage, but he'd lost control while they were both still dressed. She'd promised she wouldn't report it to her girlfriends.

"I wish the sun would shine properly," Julie was saying. "Or it would rain or something."

The overcast sky dulled what would otherwise have been a cheerful scene. Horace at least was undaunted; he pulled ahead with all his strength. Val broke into a trot to keep up. The others followed behind.

"We should go for a swim," Adrian said. He untied his shirt from his waist and swung it around his head.

"We didn't bring our suits," Marcus objected.

"Marcus is a typical American. Worried about appearances." Adrian smacked Marcus on the back.

"At Lake Frogmore, we went skinny dipping," Marcus said. "Remember, Adrian?" He explained to Julie that the previous summer he'd gone to Camp Waban in Vermont for two weeks. Adrian had been a junior counselor.

Julie giggled. "I wouldn't mind. We should find a little cove."

"There might be some coves around here," Adrian said.

Julie grabbed Adrian from behind and gave him a kiss on the back of his neck. Adrian turned around and kissed her on the mouth. Marcus stood spellbound. Val turned around and scowled. Horace, excited by a flock of shore birds, broke loose from his grip.

"Val, go get him!" Marcus shouted. "What are you waiting for?"

Val had his hands on his hips, and was smiling, as if he didn't mind at all that the dog was bolting down the beach, trailing his leash.

"He's getting away!" Julie screamed. "*Il s'en va!*" Now was as good a time as any to practice her French; someone would hear her and grab hold of Horace. "*Le chien! Au secours!*"

Horace was already far ahead. A hundred yards away, a Frenchman bent sideways and extended his arms, but his quarry deftly evaded capture. Now Horace was heading into the surf, barking at a poodle who was swimming with a rubber ball in its jaws.

They all ran. A moment later they were standing at the edge of the water. Horace was in up to his neck, clearly enjoying himself. But suppose he got tangled up in his leash and the tide pulled him out to sea?

"Why won't he come out?" Marcus shouted Horace's name and waved his hands frantically. "Maybe he can't hear us!"

"He doesn't want to come out, stupid. You should stop yelling at him."

"I'm not the one who's stupid. You let go, remember?"

"Shut up. I got distracted." Val shot Adrian and Julie a look. "Certain people have to show off." Then he punched Marcus in the arm. "Don't tell Joyce and Arthur." Lately he had taken to calling his parents by their given names, as if they were random acquaintances. "Just say Horace needed to cool off, and I let him wade a little."

Julie jumped up and down, using the back of Adrian's shoulders as leverage.

"You've got to go get him, Adrian." By now Horace was dog paddling in the surf.

Adrian gave Julie a searching look. She looked back with mingled fear and excitement. She would remember it forever if he rescued Horace. He hesitated; Horace was sure to come out on his own once he got tired. But then he seemed to hear his mother's voice. *Poor Horace! You let him drown.*

Without making any conscious decision to do so, Adrian found that he was taking off his trousers. People were giving him satirical looks. A boy laughed and shouted something. It didn't matter. This was France, after all. He started running into the surf.

Adrian's a good swimmer, isn't he, Marcus?"

"Not as good as Val."

"Don't expect me to act like an idiot," Val said.

Adrian waded through a breaker. The water was up to his armpits. Horace was still yards away. A middle-aged woman, watching the drama, murmured disapproval. An old man with a fat belly shouted encouragement. A little girl was beside herself.

Maman, il va s'noyer! Did she mean the dog or Adrian was going to go under? A crowd gathered. Americans! So simple, so childlike; they did the craziest things. Didn't the boy own a bathing suit? What was it all about? *Ah, c'est ça!* They were afraid for their dog. *Bêtise!* Didn't they know that a dog never takes to the water unless it's sure it can get back to dry land?

Adrian grabbed Horace under his chest. He let a breaker carry the two of them, and then, finding his footing, carried the waterlogged dog to safety and deposited him on the sand. Horace shook himself vigorously. People clapped, an elderly gentleman came up and congratulated Adrian, and some boys and girls petted Horace. Adrian tried to think of something to say in French but his mind was a blank. The crowd was already dispersing. Julie knelt down and hugged Horace. "Poor wet doggie!" She jumped up and put her arms around Adrian. Then she took Marcus's hands and made him dance circles around Adrian and Horace.

"Wasn't your brother a hero? Val should thank him. If it hadn't been for … ."

"Show offs!" Val broke in. He turned on Julie. "You shouldn't have made him do it. You're not the one who's going to get in trouble."

"Forget it, Val." Adrian threw Horace's leash in the sand and began drying himself with his shirt.

Val picked up the soaking wet leash. "Your hair's wet. You think nobody will notice?"

Adrian gave Val a push. "He's supposed to be your dog, remember?" He turned to Julie and laughed. "*The flaxen prince!*"

Val let go of the leash and pushed back against Adrian's chest with both hands. Marcus grabbed hold of Horace's collar. A fight! What if one of them got hurt? Still, it was exciting.

Adrian pulled Val into the water; he was taller and stronger, and Val hadn't much of a chance. The two boys splashed and shouted at each other, and then Val punched his brother in the stomach. Adrian forced Val's head underwater. People gaped and got to their feet. Evidently the fun had turned into something worse. Americans were prone to savagery. Most of them had a drop of *peau rouge* in them.

"Adrian, stop!" Marcus was so excited he hardly knew that waves were breaking over his legs and splashing his shorts. "We're going to miss our train! Julie, make them stop!"

But Julie grabbed Horace's leash from Marcus and raced the dog along the water's edge. She didn't seem to mind that she was getting wet and sandy. Marcus heard someone calling from a great distance. He could make out his father, striding up the beach, a hundred yards away. Marcus checked his watch. The train to Paris was due to depart in half an hour. Barely enough time! He must warn the others. He inhaled deeply. He would need air in his lungs.

But his voice seemed to stick in his throat, the way that something stops you getting out the words in a dream, and in another second Adrian and Val were running toward him, lifting him up, and dropping him like a log into the waves.

THE LASHES AND Eigers sat in separate coaches on the train to Paris, and after their arrival they checked into different hotels; the Eigers had booked a suite at the Hotel de Crillon, much more luxurious than the Lashes' accommodations at the Saint James and Albany, where Hermann Lasch had stayed on business trips half a century ago. The two families stayed clear of each other. Joyce said it was understandable from the Eigers' point of view. She herself would have been embarrassed to spend more time with them, especially Helen, who'd acted as if the Lash children were a pack of wild animals. Arthur said the Eigers were making a mountain out of a molehill: why make such a fuss over a little fun and some wet clothing?

After their one night in Paris, the Lashes rose early and proceeded to the Gare de l'Est, from which a train would take them to Vienna before nightfall. Joyce led Horace to a patch of gravel at the end of the platform, while Arthur bought sandwiches, mineral water, orange soda, biscuits and chocolate in the terminal. Mrs. Woodbine and Marcus picked out postcards and Val spent four new francs on a cigarette lighter. The reformed French currency, Arthur said, made transactions much less cumbersome.

Once settled in their compartment, they had only a few minutes to spare before departure. Arthur said that something felt different. What was it? Oh yes, there was no plume of smoke and no hiss of steam; the locomotive ran on diesel. He glanced out of the window and noticed a derelict whose shoes were falling apart; the man gave a *gendarme* a dirty look and spat on the platform. Arthur turned away and shook his head. Not everything continental was charming. Earlier Marcus had been astonished that the railway station's urinals consisted of holes in a filthy tile floor. He had tried to explain that a certain amount of decay was the price one paid for thousands of years of history.

The train lurched forward. Arthur bent down and stroked Horace, stationed on a blanket between his legs. He glanced at Joyce.

"I told you he'd be all right."

"He's bound to get restless," Joyce said.

They stopped at Strasbourg and again at the border. A German official, youngish and pink-cheeked, stamped their passports. He was about the right age, Arthur thought, to have fought in the *Wehrmacht*. One of the lucky ones who'd survived the Eastern Front? Or perhaps a corporal in the SS? Arthur felt his neck tighten. He had promised himself not to bear a grudge. The younger generation, at any rate, weren't to blame.

The customs officer saluted and handed back the passports. *Danke schön!* The train gathered momentum and the officials jumped nimbly down onto the platform. As the train pulled away, Arthur caught sight of the pink-cheeked officer laughing and slapping his mate on the shoulder. German soldiers might have behaved like that after closing the doors on box cars jammed with bodies. What was the use of dwelling on it? The gruesome play was over; the actors lived on. Arthur glanced over at his children. What was that mocking jingle they used to sing? *Whistle while you work! Hitler is a jerk! Mussolini lost his beanie ... .*

Joyce caught her husband's morose expression.

"What's the matter, Art? Want to turn around and go home?"

"Not at all. It's just something of a shock." She would know what he meant.

Arthur distributed food and drink. Mrs. Woodbine lifted up the top of her sandwich and eyed the slice of pressed meat with suspicion. "Looks sort of slick." She laid the sandwich down on a cushion and reached for her pocketbook. "I almost forgot to give you money for my sandwich, Dr. Lash." She still had plenty of francs; her costliest purchase so far had been a souvenir model of the Eiffel Tower. From now on, she meant to pay her share.

Joyce watched her three boys unwrap their food. Yesterday's meal at *La Petite Normande* came back to her in a rush. When Arthur had brought the boys and Julie Eiger back, she could tell he was suppressing laughter. He'd scolded them but his heart wasn't it. Besides, he said, they ought to thank Adrian for rescuing poor Horace. A Frenchman had told him that *"ce jeune homme est formidable."*

But Joyce had been mortified by the waiters' grins and by people twisting around in their chairs to stare at the uncouth Americans. Americans weren't *that* uncouth. And then Mrs. Woodbine's "I told you so" face, which expressed as plainly as words that if only she'd been allowed to chaperone, none of it would have happened. Worst of all was Helen Eiger gaping at the half-naked culprits and pawing at Julie's soiled dress with a cloth napkin. Hank Eiger had turned his mouth down. "That other place by the station would have saved us a lot of trouble," Hank said, and Joyce had felt like throttling him. Marcus had made matters worse by describing the oily film on the water, and the bits of floating garbage. Arthur said that salt water and sunshine took care of the pollutants; what you could see and smell, he explained, wasn't nearly as risky as airborne germs. No one was convinced. After reckoning up their share of the bill, the Eigers hurried their daughter into a taxi. "I'm sure we'll all laugh about this some day," Helen said, but she looked ready to weep.

They would have missed their train if it hadn't been running late. The station's W.C. served as a changing room. Joyce made Arthur follow the boys inside—didn't perverts frequent railway toilets?—and afterwards she made sure they wrapped their wet things in newspaper. By the time they had boarded, everybody except Mrs. Woodbine was exhausted, and once they'd pulled into Paris, Joyce was too drained for sight-seeing. She slept through most of the afternoon, while the others visited a couple of rooms at the Louvre. Dinner in the hotel dining room wasn't nearly as good as the simple meal they'd had in Le Havre. Afterwards, in the taxi to the Eiffel Tower, Arthur tried to cheer everyone up. You couldn't travel, he said, and not expect a few mishaps … .

The train's whistle brought her back to her surroundings. They were well into Germany now. A sign flashed by: *Leibniz-Keks. Das Original!*

"That sandwich they gave me was real good," Mrs. Woodbine was saying. "Not what I'm used to, but that's all right." She took out a ball of yarn and resumed knitting something for her grandchild. Was it a hat or a tiny jacket? Too soon to tell and Joyce didn't feel like asking; it would encourage another long-winded story. She closed her eyes. It would be good to sleep for a while.

On the opposite side of the compartment, Adrian was looking out at homes and yards that were similar to and yet different from the outskirts of an American city. A pit filled with rainwater looked like a casualty of war. Everything was poor and ugly compared with Paris.

"What's happening in your book?" Adrian asked his brother.

"Johnny's getting a medal from General Washington. For saving the troops from an ambush."

Adrian smiled. Marcus liked to read the books he was assigned in school. Adrian's summer reading, *Lesbian Love Stories*, was packed away in the folds of one of his dress shirts. He'd picked it out from a rack at the Book Worm; Sheila Rath had congratulated him on his choice. Sheila seemed to like him. But what if she was only pretending? Maybe she didn't really care one way or another. The school psychologist at Garnet High said that it was natural for adolescents to mistrust adults. Everyone in the eleventh grade had to see Dr. Epsom at least once. The psychologist's bitten fingernails indicated that he had problems of his own. Towards the end of his thirty minutes, Adrian noticed that Dr. Epsom was yawning and glancing at his watch. Probably the doctor was wishing he were in a lab, experimenting on helpless monkeys.

Adrian glanced over at Val, who was leafing through an old issue of *Mad* magazine. Val had all sorts of secrets, all kinds of grudges. What was wrong with him? At Val's age, Adrian recalled, he'd wanted Nina Kusterman to be his girlfriend. He'd been fascinated with her white socks and slender ankles, the mole on the arch of her neck, the dark hair framing brown eyes that looked a little vacant but promising, and the two mounds poking against her blouse. He liked to imagine her changing into her field-hockey uniform in the girls' locker room. Nina had acted interested for a week before she dropped him. After that he found fault with her. When she chewed gum it made a snapping sound.

The warm compartment, the smell of tobacco and stale upholstery, were making him drowsy. Adrian felt his eyelids closing. Images paraded before his mind's eye: a fat man shouting something in French, and Julie running back and forth with Horace. Then suddenly he was in a classroom. He turned around in his chair. The English teacher, Mrs. Croon, was looking over his shoulder. *Lesbian Love Stories* was open on his lap, underneath the desk. *I'm disappointed in you, Adrian.* Now Mrs. Croon was writing something on the board about venereal diseases. But hadn't they already been through all that in Health Education? All at once, he was standing on top of a submarine. The water was grey and icy cold. He ought to get inside before they closed the hatch and submerged. Too late, the thing was locked! He was going to drown. He pounded on the hatch but no one could hear him.

Adrian opened his eyes. His heart was beating fast. Everyone else had fallen asleep. Mrs. Woodbine still held her ball of yarn; her head rolled to one side and her mouth was slightly ajar. Adrian had never before noticed how large, almost wolfish, her front teeth were. He turned away and looked out the window. They were in the real country now, with farmhouses, cows and tractors.

His mother yawned and rubbed her eyes.

"I was dreaming of that train we took to Buffalo," she said. "I don't know if you remember. You were only five."

"I remember. I had the lower berth. I kept thinking of the wooden train set on the overhead rack. You said I had to wait until we got to Gran's house before opening it."

"Did I?"

"You warned me that where we were going was a lot colder than home."

"There were snow banks up to your shoulders. I made you bundle up so you could hardly move. You wore a fur hat *and* earmuffs. You'd just recovered from the mumps, and I wasn't taking any chances."

"Where was Val?"

"I left Val with Mrs. Woodbine. He was only two, and I thought ... ." Joyce's voice trailed off.

"Why didn't Dad come with us?"

"Your father had a job."

"Couldn't he have taken time off?"

Joyce looked pensive. Adrian was sorry he'd asked. There was something she didn't want to tell him. He hadn't given his father's absence any thought at the time. He'd liked having his mother to himself. Gran had taken up much of her time, but there were delicious meals prepared by Gran's cook—shepherd's pie was his favorite—and mornings when a groom put him on a horse and led him around in the snow. The groom's name, funnily enough, was Mr. Grooms, and he doubled as Gran's gardener and driver. Adrian saw comparatively little of his grandmother. Frieda was struggling with the aftermath of a stroke. She took long rests in her room and barely acknowledged her grandson's presence. Her mind wandered. "Who's that little boy?" she asked, when they met in a hallway.

"I'm glad you got a chance to see where I was born," Joyce said. "Gran put it up for sale a year later."

"It must have sold for a lot of money," Adrian said. "All those acres."

"Less than you think. Land wasn't so expensive in those days. If you're wondering what became of the proceeds, they're going towards Gran's care."

"Then there won't be anything left?"

"What a question!" Joyce hesitated. "I suppose you're old enough to know. You and your brothers will each get a present."

"Really? How much?"

"Ten thousand dollars plus interest. You won't be able to spend it until you turn twenty-one. It's called a 'trust.'"

Adrian felt like jumping out of his seat. "Ten thousand? That much?"

"It sounds like a lot, but if you're not careful, it will slip through your fingers. You'll want to invest it."

"I guess you'll get something. More than ten thousand."

"All this talk about Gran's money! I want her to live as long as we can make her comfortable." She hesitated, feeling a lump form in her throat. "She still smiles when you and your brothers pay her a visit."

"It's sort of a half smile. Crooked. Kind of sad."

"It sounds cruel, but I think she's too far gone to mind much."

"I don't think it's cruel. I'd feel the exact same way if something like that happened to you or Dad. I wouldn't want you to know you were falling apart."

"Let's hope your father and I live to a ripe age, in full possession—." She stopped, on the verge of tears. At least her father had made enough to provide for his widow's comfort. *Provide! Provide!* She knew the poem by heart:

No memory of having starred
Atones for later disregard
Or keeps the end from being hard ... .

She glanced at Adrian, who was eyeing her sympathetically.

"I wish you'd known Gran when she was young. She was very beautiful."

Adrian smirked. "Like Val?"

"Sort of."

"I guess Val will be able to get any girl he wants. *If* he wants."

"Oh, I'm sure he'll take an interest pretty soon."

"I'm going to call Julie when we get home. Maybe I'll write to her in the meantime."

"She's a nice girl." Joyce giggled. "I suppose that's the last thing you want to hear from your mother; it's bound to make you lose interest in her."

"I don't know. I was thinking maybe Julie and I could meet at Grand Central. Go to a play or something."

"It sounds romantic. You'll have to see. I don't know if the Eigers will ever forgive us for what happened yesterday."

Adrian instinctively lowered his eyes. If his mother only knew! Yesterday was nothing compared with the night before. But was it really such a crime? It happened to lots of other boys, younger than he was. Ronnie di Angelo, for instance, who was in the tenth grade. He'd never heard of anything tragic happening as a result. Girls kept pretty good track of their "cycle", didn't they? And even if Julie got things wrong, what were the odds, after only one time?

"You do know that you have to be careful with girls Julie's age," his mother was saying. "No matter how impatient you might feel."

"Dad already went over all that. What are you worried about, Mom? I'm seventeen. It's not as if I'm thinking of leaving home and getting married or anything."

"Oh, I didn't mean that!" For an instant, Joyce pictured Adrian and Julie as newlyweds, like the miniature couple on top of a cake. "You've got years ahead of you before you need to think about marriage. Your father was thirty-one. I was much younger; only twenty-three."

Adrian yawned. "I know Mom, you've told me a million times. If it's all the same to you, I'm going to take a nap."

"We stayed up pretty late last night, didn't we? All those steps! It's catching up with you."

"Marcus had fun, didn't he?'

"He never would have forgiven you if you and Val *hadn't* thrown him in the ocean. He hates being left out."

Adrian smiled. His eyelids were heavy again. "I meant at the Eiffel Tower. Nobody appreciates things the way Marcus does." He closed his eyes and let his head fall back. In another moment he was breathing deeply.

Joyce studied her three children. *They who watch o'er what they love while sleeping … .* In college, she'd written her senior thesis on *Don Juan*. Of course she'd tried composing her own verses. She could still recite certain lines by heart: *I dreamed of a tower / In Buffalo's frozen dawn … .* Almost all her poetic models were dead or soon would be. How many people read Byron nowadays? As for the moderns, Yeats and Auden weren't a complete waste of time but who in all honesty understood Ezra Pound, much less Wallace Stevens?

She was picturing a classroom at Colfax College for Women. She'd felt older than her classmates; she'd delayed college a full year on account of a long recovery from pneumonia. In the fall of senior year, Professor Burgrass, an elderly gent in a tweed jacket, held forth on the Lake Poets, all the more poignant considering what the Nazis were doing to Britain. War with Germany, the professor said, was imminent. A girl sitting beside her murmured that Burgrass was wrong; America would never again stick its nose into Europe's business. Joyce thought the professor knew what he was talking about. After graduation, she would apply to be an English teacher at a private academy; they didn't normally hire women but the draft would siphon off the younger male faculty and they'd be forced to make adjustments.

And then in her final semester, Arthur Lash, a victim of "war-torn Europe", arrived on campus. You had to feel sorry for someone who had been kicked out of his country. Colfax was a step up; evidently his previous job had been at an all-black college in Tennessee. Some of the girls spread a rumor that he lived in sin with a fellow exile. But the fellow exile, on closer investigation, turned out to be the professor's father.

Her first day in Dr. Lash's Ancient Philosophy class, Joyce was pleasantly taken aback. Not exactly handsome, Dr. Lash was youthful and full of life, and his accented English conveyed a gentle melancholy and amusement. She paid very little attention to Plato's Theory of Justice; more entertaining were the professor's digressions on his adopted country. *Time* magazine, Dr. Lash opined, was on the level of an intelligent nine year-old. The Jack Benny radio program, on the other hand, was priceless. Jack Benny, the professor said, had honed to perfection the persona of a fussy homosexual pretending to be happily married; his love-hate relationship with his black butler, Rochester, was the giveaway. Some of the young women in the classroom tittered nervously. The rest looked puzzled, even frightened. A forbidden topic! Joyce thought she ought to warn Professor Lash to be more careful; word might get back to the dean.

On occasion, Dr. Lash sounded grateful. Only in America, he said, could you walk around freely, without worrying that someone was watching you; even the British, for all their national greatness, were too deferential to authority. Of course the Blacks were terribly mistreated, but then no place was perfect. The political arrangements in America, he said, combined the virtues of the Roman republic with those of a

Swiss canton. In his native country, Dr. Lash said, a man in a wheelchair was an object of pity or ridicule, whereas over here, the president was respected all the more … .

A loud yawn interrupted Joyce's reverie. Val opened his eyes and stretched.

"I think I'll go for a walk."

"Not too far, Val."

"I can't walk off a moving train, can I?"

"Just be careful crossing between cars."

"Should I make Mrs. Woodbine come with me?"

Joyce sighed. Just a moment ago, Val had looked like an angel. *There lies the thing we love with all its errors … .*

"Don't be too long."

She closed her eyes. Once again she was back at Colfax College. By March of senior year, she had fallen in love with Arthur Lash. She devised reasons to meet him in his office. There was a "paper" she wanted to go over; an exam on which she'd gotten a mediocre grade; poems she'd written, on which she wanted his unbiased opinion. The professor said he was no expert, but he thought they were not without merit; they put him in mind of Heine. Then he smiled, looked her in the eyes, and told her that if only she wasn't still his student, he'd show her what he really thought of her.

The summer after graduation, Arthur Lash was traveling on weekends from Colfax College to Buffalo, where he took his former student to dinners and movies. They strolled through the Botanical Gardens, watched the animals at the zoo and swam at the country club, where Joyce was entitled to bring a guest. In July, she made Frieda invite him to dinner. A Landseer painting hung on the wall across from the dining room table and Arthur joked that he couldn't help but feel the two horses were keeping an eye on him. Then in August, Arthur brought his father with him to Buffalo. At a restaurant where the atmosphere was hushed, Hermann Lasch kissed her hand and said that he hoped his son wouldn't let a jewel slip through his fingers. Then he insisted on paying for the tip.

Things had progressed rapidly after that. By September she and Arthur were planning a weekend visit to New York City.

Joyce showed her mother the hotel reservations for two separate rooms. In fact, as Joyce hoped and predicted, nature took its course. It seemed to her natural that the man to whom she'd lost her virginity should become her husband. Arthur had, on his part, declared his love and his urgent desire to wed. He hoped she knew he wasn't marrying for money! Of course he couldn't help being impressed by thirty acres, a stable and staff. But he was no social climber; his own family had once been well off. It wasn't his fault that their assets had been stolen by gangsters dressed up in uniforms.

They had had long talks about their childhoods and adolescences. Arthur told her about his previous affairs. To these confessions she listened with breathless excitement. You couldn't expect a thirty-one year-old Continental to be a pure lamb, and it amazed and delighted her that a man could freely admit to his past conquests without sounding either coarse or conceited. Arthur even alluded to certain experiences in the Austrian Boy Scouts; the "Grey Wolves" had apparently shared their blankets on their overnight hikes. Then he had shaken his head and laughed the whole thing off. Joyce decided that what she loved about Arthur Lash, in addition to his foreignness, his wit, his easygoing nature and the warmth with which he held her in his arms, was that they could tell each other anything and everything without embarrassment.

They were married in Buffalo two months before Pearl Harbor. Arthur had found a genial, not-too-demanding priest to guide her conversion. Her instruction had lasted only a few weeks; the expectation of war speeded things up. But certain doctrines were hard to believe. Bread and wine turning into flesh and blood? A trick! But later, it pleased her to cling to something holy. Arthur felt obliged to volunteer. He thought he ought to do his part. Joyce steeled herself to pray for his safety. She would light candles. But Arthur was turned down on account of his tachycardia—an irregularity that, as it turned out, was no great cause for concern.

For the next four years she had been happy with her husband and her first child. The town of Vanburgh, on the banks of Lake Erie, was a pretty place, especially in the fall, and

Colfax College gave it distinction. And then shortly after the birth of their second child, Arthur was offered a higher-paying job at Seven Sacraments, with the added attraction of living in Garnet, within reach of New York City. Arthur said it was only a matter of time before he attracted the notice of Columbia. It was simply a matter of cultivating the right connections; publishing a few articles, eventually a book. He had an idea about Aristotle's *Ethics* that was sure to attract notice.

Joyce had long ago gotten used to her husband's failure to advance. It was because he'd published so little. Still no book! There might have been other barriers. Protestants in high places, Arthur said, were suspicious of Catholics, and on the other hand certain Jewish luminaries resented his conversion. Just as likely, Joyce thought, people were put off by his conceit; the impression he gave of considering himself brighter and more sophisticated than his colleagues. Gradually he'd settled into fatalism. What did it matter, anyway? His family was adequately provided for, and his students and colleagues, though hardly top-notch, were pleasant, unassuming people. One could do worse than encourage a curious undergraduate, or debate morals with a clever Jesuit.

All well and good. The trouble was that after they'd been settled in Garnet for a couple of years, Joyce found herself unhappy. Did it mean she no longer loved her husband? Or was it the institution of marriage she was sick of? She didn't know. She had read a number of feminist tracts but they didn't seem to apply to her. She had no desire for a career. Nor did she pine for independence. What then? Was it the unremarkable fact of being tethered to a man who, in spite of his virtues, irritated her? She woke up in bed in the early hours of the morning and felt she was sleeping next to a stranger. She began to resent the hold her children had on her. Clawed at by hungry animals! Oh, it was shameful. She was an unfeeling, ungrateful, unnatural woman. The wives of lesser men would gladly switch with her. It wasn't as if she was in love with anyone else. And yet she had been glad to leave Arthur behind when she'd taken Adrian with her to Buffalo. "You'd only be bored," she'd told him, "hanging around while I take care of Frieda."

After three weeks away from home, she didn't want to go back to Garnet. The house on Blackwood Road had begun to feel like an airless room overcrowded with knick-knacks. She couldn't breathe! Suppose she stayed on in Buffalo? She would send for Val and settle in with her mother; there was plenty of room in the big house. She would reconnect with the Davidsons and other old friends; take a job in a school or a library. Arthur would visit from time to time. At some point, she and Arthur would agree to divorce amicably, in spite of the Church. She'd never really believed that divorce was a sin. Arthur would be terribly lonely at first. But he was still virile enough to attract a healthy woman. An attractive female scholar—Jewish, probably —would help him wake up the philosophy department at Columbia.

Naturally she had gone home at the appointed time. Arthur had rushed into her arms: "For God's sake, Joyce, I haven't been able to sleep at night!"

"Me too, Art." And although this was untrue—she'd slept soundly in her old bed, snug under a feather comforter—she knew that she could never abandon her husband and children.

Memories of her abortive plan faded. She opened her eyes and glanced outside. The train was hurtling through a village station without stopping; its whistle rose to a shriek and fell away. Joyce felt Arthur stirring next to her. He gave her a sleepy smile.

"It's been a wonderful trip so far, eh, Joyce?"

Kommerziellrat

HERMANN LASCH SENT his car to pick up his family at the station. The driver, a fellow with dark curly hair and prominent cheek bones, was waiting at the platform. Joyce and Mrs. Woodbine and the boys got into the back; Val and Marcus sat on folding seats, facing the rear. Arthur sat up front next to the driver with Horace wedged between himself and the chauffeur. Outside, a light rainfall spattered the pavement. It was already dusk. Lights twinkled. Arthur thought of asking the driver to close the window but then he decided the nostalgic smells of coffee grounds and wet masonry were worth the risk. They crossed streetcar tracks. The dark contours of the cathedral appeared and disappeared. Wide boulevards gave way to narrower streets, neat houses and small shops. Everything looked well cared for. The city had apparently recovered from war and occupation.

The chauffeur pulled up to an address in a quiet neighborhood: Schaffgasse 17. Hermann's new house was surrounded by a high fence. Arthur understood that the locked entry gate served as a kind of drawbridge, not that it would have deterred Nazis from forcing their way in. "Men dressed like gangsters from an American movie came to arrest me," his father liked to reminisce. "I found myself with businessmen, professors, artists, shopkeepers, not to mention the poorest Jews of Leopoldstadt, all of us packed together in a converted schoolroom." Evidently the lower classes made everything worse, especially when one was forced to share a filthy mattress. A month's detention had dragged on like a life sentence, and then, miraculously, Hermann had gotten permission to leave the country in exchange for signing over what remained of his assets. The official in charge had signed the release with a grin on his face; probably, Hermann said, the man was entitled to a commission on confiscated bank accounts.

Arthur wasn't sure he would have held up as bravely. He'd been on a short holiday in Italy at the time, and when he'd gotten news of his father's arrest, he hadn't gone back. His brother hadn't gone back either; Philip had stayed in Cambridge, where he was finishing up his dissertation. Returning would have been senseless. Perhaps if their mother had still been alive, Arthur told himself, he might have acted differently.

The driver got out and ran around the side of the car. He opened the back door and offered Joyce a helping hand, but she waved him aside and climbed out under her own steam. Mrs. Woodbine and the boys followed. Arthur let himself out. He was pleasantly shocked. He hadn't expected such a modern, comfortable-looking house.

"What do you think, Joyce?"

"It's so dark, I can hardly tell." She sounded disappointed. An elegant apartment near the stores and museums would have suited her better. But then she added: "Imagine coming back and building a house from the ground up, at his age. After all he'd been through. It's like a fairy tale."

"It looks big for two people," Val said.

"Wait until you see the factory," Arthur said. "It's the same buildings as when I was a boy, but your grandfather has installed some modern equipment."

A light went on over the front steps, illuminating the clean, rectilinear façade. A buzzing from within unlocked the gate. Arthur led his family up the flag-stoned front walk. Hermann and Anna-Maria appeared on the doorstep. Hermann kissed Arthur lightly on the cheek but Anna-Maria was not so formal. She remembered him as a youth of eighteen, when she'd kept house for the Lasches; she hadn't been much older than that herself. Arthur submitted to her hugs but he couldn't help comparing the current Frau Lasch with his mother. The Braunfels were exporters of glass and patrons of the arts, successfully assimilated Jews, like the Lasches; to think that Johannes Brahms had more than once been a guest in the Braunfels home!—whereas Anna-Maria was a product of rural Austria. But he ought to be happy for his father. Hermann was Anna-Maria's hero. After his arrest, she'd bribed an official so she could bring him decent food. There was no doubt she loved him. But when his father tried to bully her, she brought him up short. Who did the cooking, managed the household, kept him from being lonely, soothed him when he woke from a nightmare? Yes, she let him know how things stood.

Arthur told Anna-Maria she looked just the same as always. It was almost true; she appeared to him much as she had when she'd served at the table thirty years before: a large-bosomed woman with unremarkable features, a ready smile, and crisp curls now turning grey. She'd had a rough go of it during the war, but of those dark days she rarely spoke. Arthur wondered whether his father still had what it took for a full-fledged marriage, now that he was fast approaching eighty. He couldn't rule it out. It was just as well that Anna-Maria was considerably past child-bearing; Arthur had no room in his heart for a new half-brother or half-sister.

"So, *mon cher fils,* how was the journey?"

Evidently Hermann intended to speak English with a sprinkling of French for the benefit of his American family. He'd learned English as a young man and had perfected it in exile. The French touches hearkened back much further, to a pretty governess imported from Paris.

"The trip went very well, Father." Arthur turned to his sons and winked. "We had a few adventures along the way, right boys?"

"You must tell me about it, after you've eaten something." Hermann kissed Joyce on both cheeks. "*Charmante, comme toujours!*" Then he shook hands solemnly with each grandchild. "I trust you are enjoying your holiday," he said, in a half-joking, half-accusing voice that Arthur knew all too well. It was their own fault, the tone implied, if they weren't pleased to death with everything. He turned to his favorite grandchild. "Of course the automobiles are not as big as in America, eh Marcus?"

Marcus opined that the food was sure to be much better, especially the desserts.

"We must see about fitting you boys with *Lederhosen.* Don't you think so, Joyce?"

Joyce murmured something polite. She wouldn't be surprised if leather shorts had fallen out of fashion. Probably blue jeans were the thing.

"I'm sure Marcus will want a pair," Arthur said.

Hermann nodded toward Mrs. Woodbine, standing awkwardly and a little apart from the others. "You've brought me another guest!"

Arthur felt blood rising to his cheeks. "I mentioned it in my telegram, Father. Don't you remember?" He'd tried to explain in his lengthy wire that Mrs. Woodbine was the sort of servant who sat at the table, like an equal. But his father's expression was blank. Arthur felt a little spasm of fear. Hermann's genial manner could quickly turn to deadly sarcasm. The words would be cutting, a source of excruciating embarrassment: *Did you imagine I was running a hotel?* Arthur looked anxiously at Joyce. Why wasn't she coming to the rescue?

"I hope you'll let Mrs. Woodbine help in the kitchen, Anna-Maria," Joyce said. "She's so good with everything ... ." Now it was her turn to falter. What *was* Mrs. Woodbine good with? Moral support, chiefly. If only she didn't offer to cook! Hermann wouldn't know what to make of her "white cake", which weighed as much as a baby.

"*Nein danke,*" Anna-Maria said. "I do all the work." Anna-Maria wasn't as fluent in English as her husband but she knew enough to follow a conversation and make herself understood. "To do nothing is ... is ...*langweilig.*"

Hermann made a dismissive sound with his tongue. "*Langweilig!* Only a fool finds life boring. Life's pleasures are there for the asking. *Nicht wahr, Artur?*" For a second his expression darkened. "There's nothing like peace and quiet, after all that I've had to put up with."

"I'd be tickled if you all tried some of my recipes," Mrs. Woodbine said, on the assumption that her creations qualified as "life's pleasures." She smiled fondly at Marcus. "You always take a second slice of my white cake, don't you Sugarfoot?"

Arthur felt a fresh wave of anxiety. But Hermann wasn't at all angry. He was smiling and extending a welcoming hand to Mrs. Woodbine. It appeared he was quite willing to house a *dame de compagnie.*

"Delighted to make your acquaintance. I'm afraid I didn't catch the name."

"Ruby Woodbine. I'm sure pleased to meet you, Mister Lasch."

Mrs. Woodbine had imagined a different sort of old man. Hermann had lost most of his hair years ago, he was round and short, but his shoulders were straight, his mouth resolute and his blue eyes as keen as ever, behind his bifocal lenses. A sharp dresser, too! Mrs. Woodbine greatly approved of the light grey suit and vest, the crimson, white-dotted bow tie, and the gold pocket watch on a chain.

"Fortunately we have plenty of room."

"I sure hope I won't be in the way."

"Don't think of it, Mrs. Woodfein."

"I'd be real proud to stay with you all."

Arthur suppressed a giggle. *Woodfein!* Hermann was deploying his best continental manner. But Anna-Maria's smile was weak. Arthur foresaw having to move Mrs. Woodbine into a *pension*.

"We have plenty of room," Hermann repeated. "My wife will be delighted ... ." He was interrupted by Horace, who was pawing at his trouser leg. Hermann chuckled and reached into his pocket for a treat he had prepared in advance. Two years earlier, he and Anna-Maria had visited Garnet. Horace evidently hadn't forgotten the little rewards that had nothing to do with good behavior.

"Perhaps we shall put Mrs. Woodfein in charge of Horace, eh, Anna-Maria?"

Anna-Maria rolled her eyes. She was no great admirer of dogs. Like Mrs. Woodbine, she had grown up in the country, where animals were prized for their usefulness more than their personalities.

The guests were given a tour of the house: living room, adjoining study, dining room, kitchen, and master bedroom suite; then upstairs to more bedrooms, a bathroom fitted with a gleaming porcelain *bidet*, and a toilet in a closet-sized room all by itself. Marcus wanted to share a bedroom with Adrian, which meant Val would have a smaller one to himself. The room assigned to Mrs. Woodbine was smaller still; it had been designed for a live-in maid. Before descending, Hermann opened a cupboard in the upstairs hallway. Row upon row of toilet paper rolls stood on the shelves. He explained that an insolvent wholesaler had turned over his inventory as compensation for an unpaid debt. Hermann thought this was a great joke.

Marcus felt the paper. "It's scratchy."

"Not as good as what you have at home?" Hermann cast Arthur a significant look. "There was a time not so long ago," he told Marcus grimly, "when your Granddaddy had to make do with a scrap of newspaper."

After the house tour, the three grandsons played with Horace in the back garden. Hermann had planted two cherry trees, and there was a well-watered lawn, flower beds, a pedestaled bust of a female opera singer, a limestone representation of Leda and the Swan, and colored lamps at the bases of trees and bushes. Val had brought a Frisbee in his suitcase and Horace was having a fine time chasing it in the dusk. Arthur, Joyce and Hermann sat together in the living room while Anna-Maria got a snack ready in the kitchen. Mrs. Woodbine, eager to make herself useful, followed her. Her status wasn't quite clear to Anna-Maria, who kept glancing out of the corner of her eye at her new assistant. The American woman rattled off a barbaric dialect that was difficult to understand. Hermann, she was sure, would soon tire of the intruder.

Hermann's guests retired early and slept soundly, exhausted by the journey. In the morning Hermann left early for *Lasch & Söhne*, after giving Anna-Maria instructions that his family must not be wakened on his account. The whole family would tour the factory at eleven, after which there was to be a festive midday meal at a fine restaurant; Hermann said he'd forego returning to work and would spend the rest of the day at home.

After entering his private office and changing from his suit jacket into a long white coat, Hermann seated himself at his polished desk. He felt keyed up. He asked himself whether he ought to broach his great plan at dinner tonight or wait until Philip arrived. He hadn't yet told anyone beside Anna-Maria that his younger son was coming in from Chicago for his eightieth birthday celebration. A grand surprise! But Hermann's happiness was tinctured with regret. How shabby Arthur was looking in his rumpled clothes, and carrying a worn-out suitcase! Philip, on the other hand, was a star at his university; his suits were expensive, well tailored. Hermann reminded himself that it wasn't entirely Arthur's fault that he didn't shine as brightly. Exile had held him back. Another thing the Nazi swine had spoiled! Well, at least he had provided heirs, one of whom would run the factory some day, whereas Philip's chances for marriage and children were almost used up.

. The telephone on his desk rang shrilly. Hermann lifted the receiver; it was only Anna-Maria on the other end, wanting to know whether she should make reservations at the Hotel Sacher or the Café Central. She knew he'd told her at breakfast, but now she wasn't sure. Hermann told her the Central would be more amusing for Joyce and the children. Then he chuckled and said not to forget to reserve a place for *Frau Woodfein.*

He replaced the receiver and sat in his swivel chair, musing. In a few moments Herr Luftig, head of sales, would knock timidly, and they would go through the weekly reports. Luftig was getting on in years but Hermann was loathe to force him to retire. The man had actually broken down in tears when the Nazi thugs had come to seize the factory, and he had refused to work under the new owner, a Herr Mittwald. Hermann would have liked to have been present when Mittwald signed papers restoring the factory's rightful name and ownership. A long time to wait, but all the sweeter for that! The ceremony had been handled by Dr. Hagenfeld, Hermann's attorney, who'd thought it best to keep the two enemies at a safe distance from one another. To think that that idiot Mittwald had renamed the factory after his beloved Führer! *Adolf Hitler Papier und Kartonfabrik!*

Imagining the scene, Hermann smiled. How often had he looked forward to his return, during all those years! He could never recall without disgust a certain boarding house in Tennessee where he had lain awake at night, plotting how it could be achieved. Arthur had begged his father to be realistic. Even assuming an Allied victory, he said, *Lasch & Söhne* might no longer exist. Bombed to bits! And even if it remained intact, how did Hermann expect the conquering Russians to behave? A

Jewish capitalist wouldn't exactly be welcomed back with open arms. On the other hand, if the Americans got to Vienna first, they would say Hermann was lucky to have escaped with his life and send him away. Better to try and adjust to their new life in the New World, Arthur said, than be insulted all over again.

Bien! It had taken him almost two years to move his claim through the necessary channels, countless hours in stuffy waiting rooms and offices, countless excuses and delays. The factory was one thing. But when he'd brought up the stolen paintings, books and furnishings, the American officer on the other side of the desk had lost his temper, just as Arthur had predicted. What about the millions of dead, including all those American boys who had given their lives? Wasn't he fortunate to have lost only material goods? Hermann refrained from mentioning the cousins and intimate friends who had perished at Mauthausen and Dachau. He understood that Major Ryle was more lazy than malicious; the man simply wanted to avoid trouble. In the end, the confiscated paintings of ruminating cattle, the Louis XV inkstand, the leather-bound French volumes remained where they were, in the possession of unknown and untraceable persons who had bought them at fancy auction houses.

But the factory was the main thing. In the courtroom, Herr Mittwald—fiftyish, with a fat face and a bald head—had literally wrung his hands. As far as he had understood the matter, it was all perfectly legal! Hermann, sitting in the front row of the courtroom, observed the American military judge, whose physiognomy reminded him of a portrait bust of Voltaire. Judge Lefferts's German was very good and he had the driest of smiles at his disposal. That smile had filled Hermann with hope. A decision had been handed down: *Restitution of Stolen Assets.* Yes, Herr Otto Mittwald, hand over the factory and never show your fat face again!

Soon thereafter he had addressed his three-hundred-and-sixty-eight workers, gathered amid the rolling presses. The few who had accused him of "treasonous statements" had been dismissed. "I wish all of you to know that I bear no grudge," Hermann had told the throng. A fine sentiment! He had achieved what everybody said was impossible. And now? Exports up eighteen per cent. And an official title: *Kommerz-iellrat Hermann Lasch.* Of course "commercial councillor" wasn't on the level of a patent of nobility—if the Empire had held together, he might have ended up with a more impressive title—but a few friends from the old days came to congratulate him, all of them old enough to reminisce about the monarchy. There was even talk of resurrecting a bombed synagogue. A handful of returned Jews and a number of conscience-stricken gentiles would contribute. He himself had pledged a sum. Not that he was religious. As far as he was concerned, Judaism, setting aside the beautiful Old Testament stories, was superstitious nonsense. Not that Christians didn't have their own rigmarole. But please, spare him the Orthodox, wasting their lives dissecting the Talmud under a microscope! At any rate, they hadn't deserved to be wiped out.

Hermann inspected a framed photo that stood on a corner of his desk: Adele and their two young children, taken shortly after the First World War. Had he ever truly loved her? Not in the romantic sense. Adele was one of three daughters of a family very like his own; the two sets of parents had picked them out as a suitable match. Adele had made a good wife and mother, if somewhat inclined to crying fits. He himself had sobbed with grief during the last days of her illness. And now, any day, he might come down with something equally bad. His time was nearly up. Five more years? Ten at most. The changes he'd witnessed in his lifetime! His father, Julius Lasch, had kept a horse and carriage until his dying day. A terrible shame that Viktor, his younger brother, had died fighting Italians in the First World War. Had Viktor lived, married and had a business-minded boy, the lad might have taken up the reins when the time came.

The easiest thing would be to turn the factory over to the American firm that wanted to buy it. It would mean a nice sum of money to leave his widow and his descendants. But he had another idea. He would wait until the guests at his birthday party had gone home for their early bedtimes. Then he would unveil his plan.

Gor-litch-*ee*

After their heavy meal at the Café Central, the grown-ups were ready for a siesta. Arthur suggested the boys try to catch some butterflies: there were thousands of them in a nearby field, and he had an idea that Philip's old nets and receptacles were packed away in the garage somewhere; somehow they'd survived war and exile. Hermann's driver, Franz Gorlice, would show the boys where to find them. But where was Gorlice? He'd disappeared somewhere. Anna-Maria sighed and shook her head. The man always made himself scarce when he was needed!

All three boys took an interest in the chauffeur. The way they mispronounced his name—Gor-*litch*-ee—sounded, Arthur said, as if the poor man suffered from a rash; the correct way was *Gor*-litz-eh. But Arthur soon gave up correcting them and the chauffeur didn't care how his name was pronounced. Gorlice was about thirty years old and looked almost young enough to be in high school; Joyce said he was handsome in a rugged, outlaw sort of way. Arthur wondered what the man had been up to during the war. *Hitler Jugend?* It was just like Hermann not to have inquired about his past. There was a Frau Gorlice and a child, but these were seldom spoken of. Evidently the family had moved around a great deal. The surname implied roots in Poland.

When he wasn't behind the wheel, Gorlice was supposed to be at Anna-Maria's disposal. There were things to do around the house: unblocking a drain, digging a hole for a shrub, cleaning up Leda and the Swan. But on this particular afternoon, Gorlice had slipped off to a favorite spot bordering a lane that branched into the woods. He took off his jacket and sat down under a tree in his undershirt. A bottle of beer stood within easy reach. Gorlice considered that Anna-Maria, if she came after him, would be secretly pleased by the sight of his strong neck and shoulders. Suppose she scolded him for shirking? He needn't worry. There were lots of jobs to be had for the asking, now that the economy was booming again.

Besides, the old man was patient. Firing an employee would mean admitting he'd made a mistake in the first place, and then going to the trouble and expense of finding a replacement. Herr Lasch was averse to wasting time and money: a trait Gorlice admired because it was the opposite of his own free and easy temperament. The Jews, he thought, should be proud of their so-called vices.

Franz Gorlice had never thought very hard about the "Jewish Question". He'd been bored by the Nazis, even as a boy. He remembered a patriotic celebration, right after the war had started. He'd watched a pretty little girl present a cake to some minor official; the icing was decorated with a swastika. The old imperial eagle was more to his liking. His father, Karl Gorlice, counted himself lucky to have grown up in a part of Poland ruled by Kaiser Franz-Josef. Nowadays Poland was pushed around by a fat Russian with a bald head. Gorlice resented being governed by coarse people: Hitler, for instance: what was that shrieking, self-important little oaf thinking? He ought to have known about the Russian winters, and of course there was no chance of winning once the Americans got involved.

Gorlice remembered the war as if it had all happened yesterday. He'd spent the six years of it stealing, loafing and learning about automobiles. An SS officer had hired him to wash his car, had let him drive it around a little, just for fun. And then, right before the end, the SS man's wife seduced him, a boy of fifteen: a desperate move, right before the walls came crashing down. Another month or two of war and he would have been forced to put on a uniform and fight alongside even younger boys. By the time it was over, he found himself poorly educated and unemployed. But he had always gotten along somehow or other.

Sunlight filtered through the leaves and warmed Gorlice's shoulders. He felt very lazy and oddly satisfied with life. He glanced upward. What kind of tree was it? He hadn't the least idea. It occurred to him that it would be good to know the names of trees, birds, flowers, other things. People would look up to him as someone with knowledge. He ought to have paid more attention in school. But he was too lazy to excel at anything. The main thing was to avoid working too hard. People liked you better if you didn't go around gloomy, weighed down by regrets and responsibilities. The old man's American grandchildren, for example, seemed to admire him. They appreciated his relaxed approach. It would be funny to get them into a bit of trouble, especially the oldest, who looked cut out for it. Perhaps he would show them some fun. There was that pack of playing cards in his jacket pocket, with the amusing pictures on the backs.

Speak of the devils! The three Lash boys and their dog were rounding the corner. The middle one held the leash. The oldest and the youngest carried nets over their shoulders. Butterflies! A carefree pastime. People of their class had no idea of real hardship. It didn't matter a bit that they had Jewish blood. In America only the Blacks were despised. The Red Indians, as far as he could make out, were left alone on land that nobody else wanted.

"Gor-*litch*-ee!" the youngest was shouting. "You're supposed to be working!"

"He doesn't speak English!" the middle one interjected.

"*Nein, Herr Valentin*," Gorlice said. "I understand okay." In fact, he'd learned quite a lot during the occupation. Some of his stupider pals had clung stubbornly to their native tongue. But not he! He'd ingratiated himself with a Sergeant Jarwell by mimicking his slang. The good-natured sergeant had given him cigarettes and chocolate bars as a reward.

Gorlice picked Marcus up and set him on his shoulders.

"*Also, Herr Markus*. I should more work hard?"

"I don't want you to!"

"I have trouble, eh? With the grandmother?"

"Step-grandmother," Marcus corrected him.

Gorlice ran with Marcus on his shoulders toward a tree and stopped short just in time to avoid a collision. Then he repeated the performance twice over. Marcus wrapped his arms around Gorlice's neck and screamed each time they almost crashed.

"He's not a horse, Val said. "You're going to choke him."

Gorlice stamped his feet, tossed his curly head and neighed. Then he swung Marcus down to the ground. He pretended to be winded; clutched his knees and puffed out his cheeks. "*Ouf!* Too much kilos!"

"He eats like a pig. *Wie ein Schwein!*"

Gorlice laughed and complimented Val on his German. Then he asked the boys how they'd liked their tour of the factory.

"There was a lady folding boxes," Marcus said. "Really fast. Like a machine."

"And afterwards, you go to Café Central." A touch of resentment swelled in Gorlice's normally placid soul. The grandsons had ordered *Schnitzl*, no doubt.

"The soup was good," Marcus said. "And the cake."

"Where you go now?

Marcus thought for a moment. Why not try out his own German? But he didn't know the word for "butterflies."

"We're going for a walk," he said finally. "*Mit Hund*.".

"Good dog." Gorlice bent down and stroked Horace. Then he stretched his arms out and yawned. "I have better idea." He gestured toward a wall on the opposite side of the lane, made of stone and mortar, about four-feet high. On top was a long row of stacked clay pots of different sizes—most of them cracked, chipped and discolored by mold and moss. Gorlice had not the slightest idea what the pots were doing there. But they were an inviting target. He picked up a stone and took aim. *Crack!* A pot shattered and fell to pieces. He picked up another stone and handed it to Adrian. Val, noticing Marcus's anxious expression, made a face.

"What's the matter? Afraid of getting caught?"

Gorlice giggled. "*Polizei?*"

Crack! Adrian's stone hit its target.

Val picked up two stones and threw them, one after the other. *Crack! Crack!* Two more pots down. Forty or fifty to go.

Marcus's stone went through a gap. On his second try, he knocked down two at once. For the next quarter of an hour the boys fired away while Gorlice shouted encouragement. Horace, tied up to a sapling, barked and whined. When it was over, the ground below the wall was littered with shards.

"Do you think anyone will care?" Marcus asked.

"Nobody saw," Adrian said.

"If somebody did see, we'd get in trouble."

"We should get going," Val said.

"Wait one moment!" Gorlice fetched his bottle of beer, took a gadget from his pocket, pried open the top, and took a long drink. He offered it to Adrian, and then Val. After they'd each swallowed some, Gorlice took the bottle back and held it out for Marcus. Marcus hesitated. But Gorlice and Adrian were grinning in an encouraging way and Val was eyeing him scornfully. He wasn't a baby! The liquid was pleasantly fizzy, slightly bitter. He swallowed a second time, then a third, a fourth, and a fifth. He would have kept going but Adrian yanked the bottle away.

"I wasn't finished!"

But what was this? Anna-Maria was rounding the corner. She stopped short and put her hands on her hips.

"*Was macht ihr alle?*"

Anna-Maria grabbed Marcus by the chin, studied his glazed expression, and then glared at the chauffeur and slapped him across the face. Was this the Anna-Maria who was always so nice and kind? Was Gorlice going to hit her back? But no, he looked shocked for an instant, and then stood with his head down, shame-faced, his lanky arms hanging at his sides.

"It wasn't Gor-*litch*-ee's fault. I drank ... and I drank ... ." Marcus could see the imprint where Anna-Maria had struck Gorlice. "Don't tell Granddaddy.".

But Anna-Maria was staring daggers at Adrian now. She grabbed the beer bottle out of his hand.

"*Und du, Adrian!*"

"We're sorry, Anna-Maria. You won't say anything, will you?"

"Please don't," Val said in his sweetest, most persuasive voice. "We promise it won't happen again."

Anna-Maria gave an exasperated sigh. Then she shook her head and laughed. And as quickly as it had broken, the storm passed. She turned her back and marched homeward, having forgotten what she had wanted from Gorlice in the first place. She called out over her shoulder: "I don't tell Granddaddy. But next time ... !" She shook her fist.

The boys and the chauffeur parted ways. Gorlice shrugged

and said not to worry; he would take care of raking up the mess. Everybody had forgotten about hunting for butterflies.

The remainder of the afternoon the brothers stayed out of sight in the back yard. At teatime, nothing was said about beer or broken pottery; evidently Anna-Maria had said nothing to Hermann. But Joyce said Marcus looked as if he might be coming down with something. She felt his forehead and made him lie down on the sofa. From time to time, Mrs. Woodbine gave the boys knowing looks, as if she were privy to their misdeeds.

There were a few hours to kill between teatime and dinner. Marcus fell asleep on the sofa and the other two boys stayed upstairs. Val got out his *Mad* magazines and Adrian took a bath. Soaking in the tub, he finished reading a long story in his paperback about two women living on a farm. At the end, one of them was killed by a falling tree. Adrian was disappointed. Why wasn't there any sex in the story?

By seven o'clock everyone had changed into clean clothes. At the supper table, Hermann poured red wine to go with the boiled beef. Anna-Maria gave Marcus only a drop. She looked at him significantly; he'd had more than enough for one day. Marcus couldn't get it out of his mind how she'd slapped Gorlice. A big, strong man letting a woman hit him in the face! No one would ever dream of striking their maid at home. His mother and father were always extra nice to Ellen. Black people, Joyce said, had it hard enough.

Over dessert and coffee, Hermann told a humorous story about his son. It seemed that when Arthur was a lad of four, he'd crawled under the dining room table when no one was looking and grabbed his mother's ankle. Poor Adele had let out a shriek! Of course Arthur had been punished—one couldn't have children frightening their parents like that—but in retrospect it was amusing, wasn't it?

"His mother tried to protect him," Hermann said. "Always sticking up for the two boys!" He laughed and turned to Arthur. "I imagine you've forgotten the sad affair?"

"Actually … ." Arthur was about to say he recalled it all too well but Mrs. Woodbine cut him off.

"My Land! It reminds me of the time I made believe I was a

snake and bit my Mama on the foot. Daddy just laughed and said Mama ought to thank the Lord it wasn't an honest-to-goodness rattlesnake."

Mrs. Woodbine leaned back in her chair and spread her hands on the tablecloth. The Lashes knew the look on her face. There would be no stopping her now.

"I didn't get a licking that time, but Mama licked us all pretty good, except for Gabel, whose foot was twisted sideways. Mama felt too sorry for him to punish him ever, even after he cut off all his hair."

"It sounds—" Arthur began, but Mrs. Woodbine ignored him.

"Gabel finally did get his foot operated on, though. The doctor charged fifty dollars, which was more than we could afford. Daddy said he'd rather die poor than leave Gabel with a limp. After that Gabel carried on like anybody else and the little black boys and girls didn't make fun of him the way they used to."

"*Diese Neger!*" Hermann turned to his son. "That college in Tennessee! I can never forget it!"

Arthur felt his neck tensing up. His father was surely about to say something offensive. But Mrs. Woodbine nodded wisely; she understood perfectly well what was meant by *Neger.*

"I reckon Tennessee's got just as many of them," Mrs. Woodbine went on. "Daddy wouldn't let us go near their shacks; said there was liable to be witchcraft and what-all. I do believe Daddy said it just to scare us children, so we'd stay out of trouble." She gave Marcus a conspiratorial glance. "Sometimes, though, we'd sneak out, creep right up and look. Once Gabel swore he saw a cat come clear out of a chimney and fly away."

"I'm sure it must have been—"

Hermann, greatly amused, interrupted his son. Mrs. Woodbine was as good as a Grimms' fairy tale! He turned to her with a smile. "You must tell us more about your childhood, Mrs. Woodfein. Uncle Tom and his Cabin! I suppose your people owned slaves at one time?"

"Oh no!" Mrs. Woodbine exclaimed. "Daddy said slavery was a sin."

"What was his opinion of the Indians? How I loved Winnetou as a boy!"

"I don't believe I know that name."

"Winnetou was a made-up character," Arthur explained. "Karl May was a German writer of boys' fiction in the last century. I believe his books still sell in the millions."

"Like Tarzan?" Marcus asked.

"Something like that. Winnetou was the hero. Old Shatterhand was his white blood-brother. The funny thing is that Karl May never set foot in America and never met an Indian. I admit I found it all very exciting as a boy."

"Perhaps Mrs. Woodfein will tell us more stories," Hermann said. "I believe she must have hundreds."

Mrs. Woodbine turned pink with pleasure. In America, she decided, Hermann Lasch would have presided over a courthouse or run for Congress. Still, he had a lot to learn about the South and its ways.

She would be pleased to set the old man straight.

Schwimmbad

MARCUS WANTED TO see the dancing horses and spend a day at the amusement park, but Arthur kept putting him off. The *Lippizanner* horses at the Spanish Riding School were a tedious affair, he said, and the Prater was hardly better than Coney Island; he seemed to have forgotten how, on board the *Columbus*, he'd praised the giant wheel. Of course museums and palaces were worth visiting but the chief attraction was the countryside. And so, on a cloudless morning, the Lashes rode a streetcar that let them off near a meadow buzzing with insects and fragrant with summer blossoms. Adrian brought a remote-controlled model airplane that he'd bought in a hobby shop. He got the propeller moving, the plane soared up into the blue and after a short flight crashed into the field. While the boys made further attempts to keep the toy aloft, Arthur and Joyce picked wildflowers and let Horace sniff for rabbits. Afterwards, they walked all the way home along a road where hundreds of snails sat sunning themselves on the grassy margins. Along the way, they stopped at a snack bar at a crossroads that sold fruit cake and little bottles of cold raspberry juice.

The real, old Austria! Sipping the delicious red juice—the tiny berries were illustrated on the bottle's label—Arthur said the vacation wouldn't be complete unless he took the boys mountain-climbing. Joyce hoped he'd forget about the idea. His boyhood friend, Max, she reminded him, had died after falling from a precipice. Another boy had been holding one end of a rope and had somehow lost his grip. Since then, Arthur had never again attempted a climb difficult enough to require rope. Even so, Joyce imagined Marcus sliding off a cliff.

They got back to Hermann's house in time for lunch. Anna-Maria and Mrs. Woodbine, both of whom had stayed behind, set out cold cuts and rolls. Anna-Maria had gotten used to having Mrs. Woodbine lend a hand. Much of what the American said was unintelligible, but at any rate Anna-Maria had nothing to fear in the way of culinary competition. The cake Mrs. Woodbine made was a failure. Hermann had put his fork down and pushed the plate to one side. He smiled politely and said something to Arthur in German about the cake's being inedible. Mrs. Woodbine imagined the old man must be apologizing. She explained to herself that it wasn't what he was used to. She gave Hermann a smile back. She pitied his inexperience.

The days went by quickly. On a cloudy morning, after letting Joyce and the children off at the zoo, Arthur had Gorlice drive him to the university and climbed the majestic staircase where he'd once jostled students in flannel trousers and silk ties. There weren't many people around during the summer. The Jews, of course, were gone for good. On these same steps, Arthur recollected, the philosopher Moritz Schlick had been murdered; the crime had been excused in certain newspapers on account of the professor's "Jewish sympathies". Did the present generation of young scholars give thought to the recent past or were they experts in forgetting it? As he rounded the corner of a landing, Arthur thought he recognized an elderly janitor. The old man looked at him suspiciously. Arthur wondered whether any of his professors from before the war might still be teaching. He could find out and try to meet them. No, it would be a mistake; he had no desire to assuage their consciences.

He felt better outside. He walked to an antiquarian shop that was nearby and bought an engraved map of old Vienna. At another shop he bought each of his sons a pair of *Lederhosen*. He'd have to explain to them that the leather softened and blackened with age: the marks of a true *Wandervogel*. He'd have to explain that the "Wandering Birds" were a sort of continuation of the Boy Scouts, but with a rebellious streak. He might skip their penchant for nude sunbathing; it wasn't something American boys would understand.

In the afternoon it started to rain, which didn't prevent Hermann from joining the family for a shopping expedition. This was a grand occasion for bestowing gifts. Hermann bought Swiss Army knives for the boys, Italian-made shoes for Adrian, a camera for Val, Roman coins for Marcus and a wristwatch for Arthur. Then it was Joyce's turn. Hermann insisted she pick out something at a jewelry store. If only he hadn't stood right over her all the time she was looking! The high prices embarrassed her. She finally settled on a gold and silver charm bracelet, just to get it over with.

The next morning, a Friday, the weather was much improved. Hermann decided to take the day off. Gorlice dropped his boss, Arthur and Joyce at the Belvedere Gardens. Then he drove the boys to a swimming pool that Arthur remembered from the old days. It would be an opportunity, Arthur said, for them to mingle with the local youth. Afterwards they would all meet for lunch at the Hotel Sacher. Val objected that oceans and lakes were one thing but he didn't like swimming pools. He was overruled.

In the *Schwimmbad's* changing room, boys and grown men —even those with pot bellies and wizened shanks—wore tight bathing suits that exposed all but a few square inches of flesh. Coming outside, the boys were dazzled by the bright sunlight. They laid out their towels on the pool's perimeter near some teenagers. Val, arranging his towel, noticed a boy observing him out of the corners of his eyes. He suddenly felt ashamed of his baggy American swimming trunks. He put on his sunglasses and rolled over on his stomach, wishing he were somewhere else.

Adrian surveyed the girls sitting adjacent to him. One of them had a thick waist and sturdy calves. Another had a nicer shape. Her fair hair hung down in a thick braid. If he started talking to his brothers loudly enough, she might perk up her ears at his English; foreigners were always interested in Americans.

But Marcus was impatient to go swimming.

"Aren't we going to try out the pool?"

"You go first," Adrian said. "I want to watch you dive." He watched his brother shrug and put on his pink nose clip. Poor Marcus's nostrils were extraordinarily sensitive; it was on account of his allergies. But that was only the half of it. A vast number of trees, grasses and flowers made him sneeze and cough; his eyes would water and he'd make a funny croaking sound at the back of his itchy throat. But he rarely complained. Now he was climbing down a ladder and easing into the pool.

Probably, Adrian thought, he was nervous about diving in. The pool was so crowded, you couldn't swim more than a few strokes without bumping into someone. Gor-*litch*-ee would have put Marcus up on his shoulders and started a game with the other children. But no one had suggested that the chauffeur bring a bathing suit. Why? It wasn't nice to make him wait in the hot sun.

In fact, Gorlice was feeling very sorry for himself. Of course it hadn't occurred to anyone that he might want a swim himself! Typical! A servant's place was on the outside of things. From the parking lot, where he stood smoking with his back against a chain-link fence, he could hear splashes, shouts and laughter. He envied people who could take the day off. He would have liked to dive from the highest platform. People would admire his form, not to mention his broad shoulders and narrow waist. Well, he had the next day off. Playing with the kid all day! Not exactly something he looked forward to. And then dinner time would be a disappointment. Klara's cooking wasn't up to the standards of Frau Lasch.

Gorlice threw his cigarette butt on the ground and stamped it out with his shoe. He consoled himself with the thought that he had Saturday night to look forward to. He'd meet some pals at the *Gastshaus* opposite the petrol station, just around the corner. Beer, darts and dirty stories! He'd get home very late, past two in the morning, after promising to be back early. Klara would wake up and cry real tears. Why should she stay home by herself on a weekend evening while he went out and had fun? But someone had to watch the kid, and there were no friends or relatives either of them trusted. It wasn't his fault. Well, she'd get over it. He'd promise to pay for a babysitter next time, and then, if he wasn't too drunk, he'd make it up to her in bed.

Gorlice wiped the sweat from his brow. There wasn't a single tree anywhere in the parking lot; no shade at all. On top of that, he couldn't help thinking back to how he'd been slapped in the face by that woman. *Mistvieh!* That woman gave herself airs, when she'd been nothing more than a housekeeper before the old man made her his wife. He ought to have smashed her face in, right in front of the grandchildren, who looked on as if she had just kicked their dog. Nice kids, though, all in all. Especially the youngest. Of course if he'd talked back, she would have gotten her husband to fire him. If he'd given her a good punch in the stomach, he'd have been charged with assault. He wasn't a timid man but he was cautious. It wouldn't be fun being dragged off to the police station. They would have looked up his record. Theft. Driving while intoxicated. Surprising that the old man had never checked.

Gorlice lit another Memphis; he couldn't afford the American brands he'd developed a taste for during the war. There must, he told himself, be some way he could get even. He'd thought and thought about it for days, but so far nothing had occurred to him. Well, give it time. An opportunity would come along, sure enough.

He heard someone calling out to him. The Lash boys were coming back with wet hair, holding their swimsuits wrapped in damp towels. So soon? The pool must have been a disappointment. Gorlice eyed the middle boy. Nice-looking kid! How old was he? Fourteen? Fifteen?

"Gor-*litch*-ee, you should have seen me," Marcus said. "I dove in at the deep end."

"*Gut gemacht!*"

"He doesn't care!" Val looked at Gorlice for confirmation. The chauffeur gave him back his warmest smile. His was proud of his very white, very even teeth.

"And you, *Herr Valentin*? You dive? Or just watch the girls?"

Val blushed. It wasn't the girls who'd interested him but rather the boy sitting a few feet away on a striped towel. "Joachim," his friends called him. Or "Achim". He had the smooth muscles of a practiced swimmer, waving brown hair and a snub-nosed face. He'd looked over at Val and smiled, just once; a moment later he'd jumped into the pool and swum expertly over to the deep end. Then he'd hoisted himself out and gone off somewhere with his companions. There hadn't been time to start a conversation. Too bad! If they'd gotten to know each other well enough, he'd have asked Joachim to come for dinner and stay overnight. They could have talked and played cards, after all the others were asleep.

Gorlice put his arm around Val's shoulders.

"*Was ist los, Val?* You not like our girls?" Then he laughed as if it was all a joke. But no one joined in. Adrian suddenly looked serious.

"Let's go, Gor-*litch*-ee. We're supposed to meet them at one."

On the way to the Hotel Sacher, traffic was heavy. When they stopped behind stalled vehicles, Gorlice kept glancing in the rear-view mirror at the grandchildren. *Herr Val* had a resentful look in his eyes; the kid was obviously choking back some grudge. Something was bothering him. Maybe he liked the boys more than he liked the girls? So what of it? He himself had had a few experiences at that age. He'd rather enjoyed them. Afterwards, it had been all girls. If the grandson made it a habit, it would be his own fault.

The truck in front of him wasn't moving: one of the Julius Meinl grocery trucks you saw everywhere. Gorlice recalled the shopworn riddle: *Why is Julius Meinl like a puppy? Because he does a little business on every corner.* Stupid! His head ached and his eyes felt hot. He checked the instrument panel: the Mercedes was overheating; there'd been trouble with the radiator all summer. His boss would blame him if they were delayed and he was in no mood for a reprimand, not after that woman had already humiliated him. He let out a blast from his horn. The Meinl truck picked up speed. More like it! Gorlice stepped hard on the gas pedal. A second later, the truck braked as suddenly as it had accelerated. Gorlice reacted quickly, but not quickly enough. *Crack!* He braced himself against the wheel and avoided hitting his head against the windshield. He turned around. Two of the boys were unscathed but Marcus had banged his forehead against the glass partition that separated the front from the rear seats. The boy was lying back with his eyes shut. A bump had already surfaced above his left eye. *Herr Adrian* was shaking him. *Herr Val* looked dazed. Outside, the truck driver was getting out and running toward them.

Gorlice felt as if the ground had dropped away from under him. Suppose the boy didn't wake up? He'd never taken remorse very seriously: once a deed was done, there was no point in wishing it undone. But now he felt like saying a prayer.

He found that he was lifting Marcus out of the car, without any thought of what he ought to do next. The two other boys got out of the car and stood around, useless. The truck driver was cursing, shouting something. A gash defaced the Mercedes's grill. A woman on the curb had her hands crossed over her bosom. Gorlice could tell she was enjoying the disaster. He felt like knocking her to the pavement. He knew his Austrians! Never let a good misfortune go to waste.

Hermann Lasch, seated across a white tablecloth from his son and daughter-in-law, looked at his pocket watch. "Over forty-five minutes late! If he'd allowed enough time … ."

"They're probably stuck in traffic," Arthur said. "These things happen. Don't upset yourself." What was supposed to be a treat was turning into an ordeal. They were all, Arthur thought, growing a little tired of Hermann's hospitality. His father had a knack for turning generosity into a burden.

"We should order something while we're waiting. What do you think, Father?"

Hermann grunted. Joyce didn't raise her head. She was pretending to read the Hotel Sacher's menu, trying to control her worry. Almost an hour late! Gorlice's fault. She didn't like the chauffeur. He was careless; rarely kept both hands on the wheel. And then the pool. All the boys were good swimmers but you could never tell what might happen. Maybe some local boys had ganged up on the foreigners and started a fight. Her sons had been hauled off by the police. Oh, she was being an idiot!

"*Herr Hermann Lasch?*" A hotel clerk materialized next to their table. The man's voice was soft, deferential. He explained that there was a telephone call. If the *Herr Kommerziellrat* cared to follow him?

Hermann rose quickly and adjusted his suit jacket. His first thought was that Anna-Maria, who'd decided to stay home with Mrs. Woodbine, needed to speak to him about something. But what? Was she ill? He asked the clerk if he knew who had placed the call. No. All he knew was that the party on the other end was a man. Joyce and Arthur exchanged quick glances. Hermann followed the clerk out of the room. Watching him, Arthur was struck by his the straight carriage and brisk pace. Really, there was nothing elderly about his father. He might have been sixty, not eighty.

"It's probably nothing," he told Joyce. "Someone from the factory. Or maybe it's Gorlice. The car might have gotten a flat."

"I told you not to let them go by themselves. What if something awful happened at the pool?"

"Philip and I used to swim there unsupervised."

"I'm sure it's something bad. I don't trust that Gorlice."

"You're letting your imagination get the better of you. Remember when you had a premonition that your mother was dead?"

"She might have died, if the doctor hadn't come in time. Go see what it is, Art."

Arthur sighed and pushed back his chair. "Order a drink in the meantime."

He was directed to the front desk and from there to the manager's office. Then a boy in a uniform led him down a corridor. Arthur shook his head as he was shunted from place to place. Typically Austrian! He found his father in a private room reserved for telephone calls. Hermann looked up at his son, spoke a few words into the phone, and hung up.

"There's been a slight accident. Marcus struck his forehead in the car. Gorlice has taken him to a doctor's office. It's not far from here. A Dr. Schöndorf."

Hermann felt his heart pound. "Is he all right? "

"That was Schöndorf on the telephone. He says Marcus suffered a … ." Hermann was for once at a loss for the English word. "*Eine Gehirnerschütterung.*"

"Concussion!"

"It's all right, he's wide awake now. The doctor says we must simply keep him quiet."

"Shouldn't he have an X-ray?"

Herman shook his head and took his son by the arm. "Come. Let's find Joyce and take a taxi to the doctor's office. As for that rascal, Gorlice, we shall see!"

When she saw Arthur and Hermann, Joyce knew from their faces that something was very wrong. Arthur explained the accident in a few words. Dr. Schöndorf, he said, was sure the skull wasn't fractured. Not even any bruising to speak of.

"That Gorlice! I could kill him!" Joyce got up from her chair so suddenly that she overturned her water glass. A waiter sprang forward to mop up the mess.

"Marcus is awake now," Arthur said. "They have him lying down with a cold compress."

"He could have a hemorrhage. There was that man who worked for my father. Something hit him on the forehead. An iron chain, I think. He seemed all right, and then died in his sleep that same night."

"You mustn't worry, Joyce," Hermann said, once they were all seated in a taxi. "After the horrors I've seen, a bump on the head doesn't look so very serious." Cheerfulness, he believed, was the best antidote to fear.

Joyce suppressed an urge to turn on her father-in-law. What did his sufferings have to do with her child? Hermann was brave but he was also an egotist. *His* horrors!

"I'm sure I must have told you," Arthur was saying, "how I blacked out at Marcus's age. We had boxing matches after school and my opponent was much better at it than I." The scene came back to him. Just before the match, he'd overheard the other boy calling him a *schmutziger Jude*. How vividly he recalled the boy's greasy, pimply face, the smell of sweat and boxing gloves!

"I remember it well," Hermann said with a laugh. "Arthur came home with a bump and a black eye. Of course his mother was terribly worried. Adele was inclined to pamper him, I'm afraid." He turned to his son. "I confess I've never understood what good all this maternal fussing does. A boy ought to be … ."

"It's no use making light of what's happened," Joyce cut him off. "Any mother would feel the same. The two of you can stop treating me like a hysteric."

Hermann, offended, turned pink. She ought not to use that tone with him. Not after he'd paid for their trip! He concealed his irritation by facing toward the taxicab's window. They were passing the cathedral. The *Stefansdom*'s lofty black façade was badly in need of cleaning. It gave an impression, Hermann thought, of rottenness. It seemed to him that the whole city was like that, never mind all the money people were making now. The Viennese, despite their reputation for light-heartedness, harbored a guilty conscience—all sorts of shameful secrets. Hadn't the founder of psychoanalysis made his reputation treating their sick souls? Hermann's thoughts wandered back to the pre-war years. He used to see the famous man taking his evening walk, accompanied by a large dog with a pink tongue. The Freuds and the Lasches were acquainted. They had once stayed at the same resort hotel with their respective families. The two mothers had compared their children's quirks and illnesses, and the fathers had chatted about literature. He had of course refrained from discussing anything of a professional nature; he'd long since decided that the sensational theories amounted to what everyone believed but preferred not to talk about. And a good deal of it was probably nonsense.

"Why aren't we there yet?" Joyce craned forward and gripped the back of the driver's seat. When she felt like making the effort, her German was adequate. "*Kannst du nicht schneller fahren?*"

The driver shrugged and grumbled something unintelligible.

"He can't go any faster," Arthur said quickly. "It's not his fault if there's traffic," Of course Joyce was upset. Naturally. But she shouldn't have spoken harshly to his father. Hermann's hurt feelings were liable to freeze into a permanent offense. If only they were at the doctor's already! Joyce would calm down once she saw that Marcus had suffered no serious harm. But the snarl of autos and trucks was unbelievable. No wonder there'd been an accident; Gorlice was an impatient driver.

"Not his fault! Oh, of course not!" Joyce's sarcasm was like an icy hand on his bare skin. "Nothing is ever anyone's fault!"

"I wouldn't go that far." Arthur felt a profound weariness settle on him. He glanced sideways at his wife, seated between himself and his father. It certainly wasn't *his* fault that Gorlice had rear-ended a truck. A common enough sort of accident! And why make such a fuss over a swimming pool? The good old *Döblinger Bad* was nicer—and no less safe—than the Garnet YMCA.

Still, it was true enough that the accident might have caused a worse injury. Joyce had every right to be angry. It was obvious she was under a strain. His father had a way of making even the calmest temperaments uneasy. Perhaps, too, Joyce's irritable mood had something to do with the city's ugly past. The majority of Viennese, after all, had welcomed Hitler. Joyce was less willing to forgive than he was. Strange! If the Germans had never marched in, he would have had a different life altogether. Different wife, different children, different job ... even different food! Everything familiar and comfortable. All through those early years of falling in love, courtship, marriage and fatherhood, he'd counted his exile a kind of backhanded stroke of luck. But all the same, suppose he'd never had to leave? Weren't there other women who could have made him happy?

Arthur's thoughts drifted back to the affairs he'd had before his marriage. How many? A dozen? More? He could make a list, with a column for grades. Well, it was nothing to boast about. Nothing unusual. Only one or two had meant anything more than a passing thrill. Strange to say, the most attractive of the lot had proven the least satisfactory: a Norwegian girl a few years younger than he was. They'd been on holiday in Italy, on the island of Ischia, because it was cheaper than Capri. Her body, as she lay on the stony beach down the road from his *pensione*, had affected him so strongly, he'd felt light-headed and short of breath. Her smile, when she'd raised her head and caught him staring! Yes, he'd felt something painful between his shoulder blades! Cupid's arrow! He'd hardly dared imagine success. In fact it had all gone off rather easily. Easily and disappointingly. She'd proven passive, rather cool. It had been the beginning of a lesson that had taken him years to learn once and for all. Touch was the thing. Not that looks and personality were unimportant. If you ran across some good-looking woman with whom you could stand to spend more than fifteen minutes, and then you discovered she appreciated your virtues, laughed at your jokes, tolerated your vices, forgave your errors ... . Yes, those were things to consider. But without the mysterious sense of touch, all else was bound to disappoint.

He recollected the time Joyce had taken Adrian with her to Buffalo and he'd known that she was half-wishing for an escape. Well, she'd returned to him all right, revitalized for a time and then gradually indifferent. Nowadays, her compliance was most often a sort of sacrifice. Maybe it wasn't her fault that her feelings had altered with age. Female hormones! He told himself that she loved him still, but in a different way from in those early years. Half the time he convinced himself it was true. He wondered whether his wife would some day experience a rebirth. Why shouldn't such a thing happen? In spite of it all, he'd never urgently wanted anyone else. His daydreams were harmless enough. That girl in his seminar on Schopenhauer ... .

His father's voice jolted him. "*Gut!* We're almost there. In a moment you'll see it's nothing." Arthur could tell that this father had decided to bury his hurt feelings and treat Joyce like Adele: fragile and in need of guidance.

The car drew up to the curb. On the side of a building a brass nameplate read: *WALTHER SCHÖNDORF Dr. Med.* Arthur got out of the car, with Joyce at his heels, while Hermann counted out money for the driver. They were directed into a room where Marcus lay on a couch with a pillow under his neck and an ice pack on his forehead. He sat up and smiled at his parents.

"See?" He removed the ice pack. "Just a bump. It doesn't hurt too much any more. I'm lucky it happened right outside a doctor's office. I might give an oral report on it when I get back home."

Oral report! Joyce wiped away tears and laughed. Thank heavens the other two boys hadn't suffered so much as a scratch! They were seated on straight chairs near their injured brother, watching everything with curious eyes. Val, of course, had a skeptical, mocking look on his face. But where was the doctor? Val said he was busy treating another patient. Marcus, he added, had only been unconscious for ten minutes at most. Or maybe he was faking the whole thing!

"Don't be spiteful, Val!" Joyce sat next to Marcus and hugged him. Then she told him to lie back down and replace the ice pack on his forehead. Arthur gave him a handshake and congratulated him on his bump.

"The size of a walnut! Mine wasn't half as big, that time I got knocked out."

"He shouldn't have been leaning forward in his seat," Val said wisely.

"I'm sure he'll remember that," Arthur said.

"I was looking for my Swiss Army knife. I thought it might have fallen on the floor. But it wasn't there."

"As long as you're safe." Joyce kissed Marcus. "We'll get you another knife. An even nicer one! Won't we, Art?"

The door to the office opened. Hermann had waylaid the doctor outside his examining room. The two men looked as if they had reached an understanding: Parents nowadays were absurdly anxious!

Dr. Schöndorf was about sixty, with a full head of white hair and a dark moustache. Joyce thought he looked a bit like the man she'd glimpsed walking his dog on board the *Columbus*, but of course it couldn't be the same person. Dr. Schöndorf said he didn't mind a bit taking care of a child who wasn't his patient, especially when the child was as brave as Marcus—a *Mensch!*—and then he explained all over again why an X-ray was unnecessary. The boy was lucky. So many of these automobile accidents ended tragically. But then children weathered all sorts of scrapes, didn't they? If there were any changes in his condition, they must let him know at once.

By the time they were ready to leave, Hermann was saying he would recommend Dr. Schöndorf to his business associates. He insisted on paying in cash. On their way out of the office, Arthur supported his son's arm, just in case he had another fainting spell.

"Where in God's name is that fellow?" Hermann asked after they'd exited onto the sidewalk. "What's he done with the car?"

"He wanted a cigarette," Adrian said. "He seemed pretty shaken up."

"Shaken up!" Hermann shouted. "I'll shake him up all right!" His face was flushed, almost youthful in its righteous anger. "He deserves to be kicked out into the street!" A suspicion seized him. "If he went for a drink while you boys were swimming … ."

"It wasn't Gor-*litch*-ee's fault," Marcus said. "He wasn't drinking. I would have smelled something." He was remembering the day when he'd drunk from Gorlice's bottle. As soon as he'd gotten home, he'd brushed his teeth. "That truck," he went on, "stopped so suddenly."

"He must have gotten too close," Arthur said.

"The truck driver was really excited," Adrian said. "I guess he was in too big a hurry to hang around."

"He'll be in trouble if they find him. Did the police show up?"

"I don't think so," Adrian said. "We've been waiting inside almost the whole time. The car should be parked somewhere around here."

Arthur shrugged. "He may have driven it to a repair shop. Perhaps he's ashamed to face us after what happened

"Maybe he ran away," Val said. "Left the city. We might never see him again."

"He'll crawl on his hands and knees," Hermann shouted. "He'll apologize to Marcus and the rest of us! The damages to the car will come out of his salary."

"He ought to be fired," Joyce said. But Marcus was all right; that was the main thing. The only thing really. She was too relieved to care very much about Franz Gorlice.

THE NEXT DAY, Arthur got up early and sat down to breakfast on his own. Joyce and the boys were not yet awake but he could hear that Anna-Maria and Mrs. Woodbine were already busy in the kitchen. He unrolled his napkin and set it beside his plate—the same gravy-stained cloth he'd used the night before. Arthur smiled and shook his head. Another custom that came as a shock to his American family!

Anna-Maria came in with a soft-boiled egg, toast and rolls, butter, honey and jam on a tray.

"*Guten Morgen, Artur. Tee oder Kaffee?*"

"*Tee, danke.*"

Anna-Maria leaned over the table, arranged his breakfast and retreated into the kitchen. Still treating him like the rather pampered youth she'd once served at his parents' table! Arthur cut the top off the eggshell and dipped a corner of toast into the yolk. A curl of steam rose from the innards. Before taking a first bite, he remembered to say a silent prayer of thanks. Nothing worse than a bump! Even so, Joyce had insisted on putting Marcus to bed as soon as they were back from the doctor. Mrs. Woodbine had brought him a bowl of soup and told him a story about her brother Moley Woodbine, who'd been knocked senseless after jumping off a roof. A little later, Gorlice came back from dropping the car at the shop; he'd had to take a streetcar and walk part of the way. The family gathered around as witnesses to a dreadful spectacle: Gorlice, on Hermann's orders, stammered an apology, while Marcus hung his head in embarrassment. Afterwards, Hermann dropped his threat of making Gorlice pay for damages; after all, the car was fully insured. But Joyce said that she would never trust the chauffeur again. From now on, she and the children would take taxis and streetcars. If Hermann and Arthur wanted to his risk their lives and Anna-Maria's, that was their business.

A few hours later everyone but Marcus, who was still resting in bed, sat down to dinner. Hermann tried to lighten the mood by reciting *The Grasshopper and the Ant* in French. He was disappointed by Val and Adrian's incomprehension. What sort of education were they getting? Surely the fables of La Fontaine weren't so difficult! Arthur and Joyce were relieved when the time came to say goodnight. Upstairs in the bedroom, Arthur circled Joyce in his arms. Shouldn't they celebrate Marcus's recovery? Their son had dipped his toe into the River Styx and pulled it out again. But Joyce was tired out, drained, wishing for home. She hadn't imagined the protracted visit would be such a strain. The charm bracelet she'd picked out under Hermann's scrutiny lay on the nightstand. She wanted to tear it to pieces. Or give it to Mrs. Woodbine. No, she simply wanted to close her eyes and sleep. After she'd fallen asleep, Arthur lay awake, ruminating. Hopeless! Even if she'd given in to him, she would have tensed up, worried that Hermann and Anna-Maria might hear their lovemaking all the way downstairs. As if either one would care! His father, at any rate, would be pleased that the marriage was a passionate one.

He was finishing his breakfast when Mrs. Woodbine came in with letters and deposited them on the table.

"Mail sure comes bright and early around here, even on a Saturday." She lifted the lid from the emptied teapot. "Did you want more tea, Dr. Lash?"

"Don't tempt me! I might burst." Arthur felt carefree. Mrs. Woodbine was a kindly soul. Soon Marcus would come down to breakfast. Perhaps the bump had already vanished. He thought of Joyce, still in bed upstairs. Well, there was bound to be a next time. His marriage wasn't ideal, but what of it? No marriage was a bed of roses. The world wasn't such a bad place. Tomorrow, he would take the boys to the Prater. They would ride the wheel.

"There's one for you, Dr. Lash. I put it on top." Mrs. Woodbine watched him closely.

"That's funny. It's from Hank Eiger. Or rather *H. Eiger.* He's written from Paris. I wonder how he knew where to send it?"

"I believe Helen wanted to send postcards. I recollect she asked for the address."

"That explains it. But why a letter?" Arthur felt a cramp in his stomach. Like Marcus, he was prone to nervous aches. What could Hank Eiger possibly wish to communicate? He slit the envelope with a table knife, blew into it, and extracted two leaves of paper. He spread them out. Somehow Hank had gotten hold of a typewriter. It took Arthur two minutes to read the letter. Mrs. Woodbine observed his expression change from confusion to anger. She recollected that James Woodbine had looked almost the same way the day he'd lost his job at the lumber mill.

"Would you mind asking my wife to get dressed and come down? Tell her there's something we need to discuss right away. But don't frighten her!"

"I'll tell her to get a move on, Dr. Lash." Arthur listened to Mrs. Woodbine practically gallop up the staircase. He should have run upstairs himself. But he felt rooted to his chair. He was terribly upset and at the same time felt like laughing out loud. But it was no laughing matter. If he sat quite still, he ought to be able to think everything through calmly. He stared at a half-eaten piece of toast. Of course he must talk it over thoroughly with Joyce. He ought to let Hermann read the letter. His father wouldn't give way to panic.

Joyce came down in her nightgown, robe and slippers. She'd delayed just long enough to splash her face and pull a comb through her hair. Mrs. Woodbine trailed behind her, caught sight of Professor Lash's pained expression and, despite her curiosity, decided it would be a good idea to see if she was needed elsewhere.

"What is it, Art? You look like your best friend died."

"Sit down. You need to read this." Arthur slid the letter to the opposite end of the table.

"Hank Eiger? I wasn't expecting to hear from either of them." Joyce pushed a stray lock of hair behind one ear, seated herself and began reading.

Wednesday, July 20

Dear Prof. Arthur Lash,

I am not a man to beat around the bush, so I will get right to the point. Your son Adrian is not the gentleman that Helen thought he was. Frankly, I always had my doubts about him. Be that as it may, facts are facts. Yesterday, Helen dragged it out of Julie that Adrian took advantage of her, right under our noses, our last night on board the *Columbus*. I trust you're not such a fool as to feel proud of the boy's success. I don't like to mention mention my daughter's intimate functions, but Julie has informed her mother that she is late for her time of the month, and it seems your son failed to take precautions.

I guess you understand what I am getting at. We are all sick to death over it, as you may imagine. Julie refuses to leave her hotel room, eats very little, and takes no interest in the sights they have over here.

We are leaving Paris today. A change of scenery may do all of us some good, though I can't be sure. If there's no change in Julie's condition, we will of course have to have her tested. In the meantime, Helen feels that we all ought to meet as soon as possible. She expects your son to tell Julie in person that the whole thing was a mistake for which he is prepared to take the full blame, and that she should forget all about him. She feels this will give Julie some peace of mind.

We stop overnight in Munich and arrive in Salzburg the day after for the Mozart Festival. We should make Vienna by Sunday night. I don't think you will object to giving up an hour of your time on Monday. We may be reached at the Hotel Zauberflöte.

Yours truly,

Henry Eiger, Jr.

P.S. Helen says she isn't surprised after what happened on that beach, which was bad enough. She says that if worst comes to worst, she's willing to raise the infant and pass it off as our own, at least until the parents are old enough to get married. I hope you will agree with me that this sounds like foolishness.

P.P.S. I have nothing personal against you or your family. I guess it hasn't been easy for you, a foreigner, raising three boys in a free country. Your people haven't had it easy. The other two boys are all right, for all I know, though the middle one strikes me as secretive and the youngest abnormally precocious. As for the oldest, there's something unhealthy about him. My advice is, enlist him in the military.

P.P.P.S. Don't think we won't take legal action.

Joyce placed the letter down on the table. She smoothed the sheets. Arthur waited for tearing of hair and rending of garments. But Joyce only cleared her throat and began speaking in a level voice.

"I knew your little talk with Adrian would be useless. I'm sure he could tell how excited you were. You may as well have egged him on."

"You're exaggerating," Arthur said. But he couldn't pretend that he hadn't enjoyed watching the romance. "Adrian ought to have known better," he went on. "It was careless of him."

"You mean he ought to have had something handy in his wallet? Where would he have gotten it?"

"Nowadays they probably sell them in the school cafeteria."

"Is that supposed to be funny?" Joyce sighed and scanned the letter again. "The girl must have told Adrian not to worry."

"The girl has a name, doesn't she?"

Joyce rose from her chair and began pacing the room. She held her arms tight across her chest.

"I know something about teenage girls. She invited him into her cabin, didn't she? She knew exactly what she wanted to happen. There's something shameless about her. That day on the beach, when Helen was trying to get her into the taxi, she looked like a wild animal ready to bite."

"If anyone was a wild animal, it was Adrian." Arthur thought for a moment. "I can't quite make out what Hank Eiger wants from us."

"Maybe Hank wants us to bring up the baby. He obviously doesn't like the idea of Helen playing make-believe mother. It doesn't matter. The blood will flow once Julie stops imagining that she's carrying Adrian's child. She's obviously head over heels in love, and it's affecting her hormonal balance."

"You think so? Let's hope you're right." Arthur felt taken aback. How much did his wife really know about hormones? He glanced at her. A protective mother! It was clear she would willingly turn Julie Eiger to stone. Either that or a babbling stream.

"Even if she *is* pregnant," Joyce went on, "there's no proof it's Adrian's." She sat down in her chair. "For all we know, she gave herself to one of the crew."

"Joyce, please! She's a nice girl. You said so yourself. She was kind to Marcus. Even Mrs. Woodbine approves."

"Nice girls do things. I would have slept with you when I was still your student at Colfax, if you'd given me half a chance, Suppose I'd gotten pregnant?"

"I would have married you the minute I found out you were carrying our child."

"You would've been fired regardless." She gave him a curious look. "You're not seriously imagining Adrian and Julie as a married couple?"

"Who knows? It might not be such a bad idea, once they're of age."

"Wonderful! Why wait? The legal age in Kentucky is thirteen."

"Now you're the one making light of the situation," Arthur hesitated. "Do you really think it's a false alarm? How do we know it's not the real thing?"

"Female intuition. Mr. X will arrive sooner than later."

"Who?"

"Mr. X. It's what a child in our neighborhood called it. Marcus got all excited. I had to explain it to him." To Arthur's surprise, she giggled. "He really ought to have come to his father for answers." She picked up one of the sheets of paper from the table. "*There's something unhealthy about him.*" She crumpled the paper in a ball. "I don't know if I'll be able to restrain myself. You'd better handle the meeting."

"It might be a good idea if the fathers and mothers talked it over in separate rooms."

"Are you planning to tell Hermann?"

"It may be too late to keep it a secret. It's awfully quiet in the kitchen. I suspect that Anna-Maria has her ear to the door."

Joyce laughed bitterly. "And Mrs. Woodbine? It seems unfair to deprive her of a family scandal."

Arthur sighed. "Perhaps Hank is right. We ought to get Adrian into uniform before he ruins more girls."

"Because soldiers and sailors are known for their chastity? Hank Eiger's a fool."

"It's good of him to inform me that he has nothing against my "people". He means the Jews. I wonder how he found out?"

"Mrs. Woodbine must have said something to Helen."

"The threat of legal action is a nice touch. I wouldn't be surprised if it all comes down to money."

"Oh, I'm sure that's the case, aren't you?" Joyce handed her husband the sheet she had crumpled. "I feel dirty just handling this." She hesitated. "Do you think Marcus is *abnormally precocious*? He does gravitate towards grown-ups."

"He takes after his father. At his age, I liked standing in the doorway and listening to the adults talk. I wasn't much interested in football."

"He's begun reading *Uncle Tom's Cabin*. I warned him it was boring."

"Is it? There's that part where the hounds chase Eliza across an icy river. I remember seeing it on the stage. I must have been Marcus's age." Arthur folded the letter and put it in his pocket. "I'd better find Adrian and fill him in. I ought to be boiling with righteous indignation. Why aren't I, Joyce?"

"Because you see yourself in him."

"Is that it?" He felt a tightness in his throat. "You know, don't you, how much I love you and the boys?" He kissed her and walked towards the staircase. He would tell Adrian to throw on some clothes and then take him for a walk in the woods. He wasn't looking forward to being a scold. After pretending to be angrier than he felt, he would reassure his son that the chances of Julie's being pregnant were slight. Of course Adrian would worry anyway.

Arthur climbed the stairs—it felt as if lead weights were attached to his legs—and walked down the hallway toward Adrian and Marcus's bedroom. Why hadn't his son had more sense? Still, it was understandable. A picture of entangled bodies took possession of him, and of himself as a crab clinging to the hull of the S.S. *Columbus,* watching the two lovers through the porthole. Shameful, but what could he do? It was human to envy the young.

Swiss Army Knife

USUALLY MARCUS DELIGHTED Hermann at the dinner table but not tonight. When he held up his glass and asked for more wine, his grandfather gave him a stern look. "Wait until someone offers it!" Marcus blushed and stayed quiet for the rest of the meal. Yesterday, everyone had made a fuss over him; tonight they seemed to have forgotten his brush with death. Conversation lagged. Even Mrs. Woodbine was subdued. As for Adrian, he might as well have been a ghost. He ate his food in silence, with his head down and his shoulders hunched.

It was a relief when Anna-Maria and Mrs. Woodbine removed the remaining bits of pancake left over from the *Palascinta.* Adrian pushed back his chair and said he wanted to take Horace for a walk before it got dark. When Marcus offered to join him, he said he wanted some time to himself.

"Why don't you play badminton? Val said he wanted to."

Joyce and Arthur retired to the study with Hermann; there were evidently things they wanted to talk over in private. Marcus fetched the rackets and birdies from the garage. He and Val left their shoes and socks at the edge of the lawn. The grass was fresh and cool under their feet.

"You're getting better at this," Val said, after dropping a volley. He swung his racket sideways; the mesh made a swishing sound as it cut the air. He was in a rare good humor. Marcus remembered that Granddaddy had taken Val into his study at teatime: just the two of them. And then, at the dinner table, he'd asked Val about school and what sort of books and music he liked. He'd shaken his head in mock bewilderment, pretending to be unfamiliar with the latest tunes, when Val tried to explain rock and roll. When he overheard American music blaring from open car windows, his reaction was always the same: "*Dees-gusting!*"

When it grew too dark to play, Marcus threw his racket down and pulled his brother by the arm to a corner of the garden where a bench abutted Leda and the Swan.

"There's something I have to ask you."

118

Val raised his shirt tail and wiped the sweat from his forehead. "There's too many mosquitos out here."

"Just sit down for a minute."

"Okay. I'm sitting."

"I don't get it. Adrian's sort of pale and doesn't want to talk. They're all acting funny. Granddaddy's been ignoring everyone except you." It occurred to Marcus that Val might take that as an insult. "I don't mean he shouldn't pay attention to you. It's just strange, don't you think? Nobody's told me anything."

Val gave a short laugh. "Since when do they tell me things? But as a matter of fact, I do know. I got Adrian to tell me a while ago. He wasn't supposed to, but he did. I don't know if I should tell you, though."

"I'm old enough."

"They wouldn't like it."

"I promise I won't say anything."

Val thought for a moment. "First you have to think of something to trade."

"You can have one of my Roman coins."

"You didn't really lose your Swiss army knife in the car, did you?"

"It was in my drawer in the bedroom the whole time."

Val laughed. "You almost got killed looking for it. Let me have the knife and I'll tell you what's going on. But don't say you gave it to me. Let them think you lost it for real this time. Maybe they'll buy you another one."

"You have your own knife, exactly like mine."

"I want an extra one." Val saw himself giving it to Joachim. Of course he'd have to see him again at the pool first.

"All right. You can have it when we go upstairs. Now tell me."

Val lay down on the bench with his knees bent and his toes curled over the edge. His arms hung down on either side. As he spoke, he stared up at the sky, plucked blades of grass and crushed them between his fingers. Marcus stood facing him.

"It's like this," Val said. "Adrian did you-know-what with that girl, Julie."

"What's *you-know-what*?" Marcus felt his heart racing. It was like Mr. X all over again, but more alarming.

"Do I have to explain? They fooled around in her cabin. You know. S-E-X."

"I don't believe you. You're making it up."

Val shrugged. "You don't have to believe me if you don't want to. But you still owe me the knife." He yawned and then continued in a world-weary voice. "There was a letter from Hank Eiger this morning. He wants a meeting, so Adrian can tell Julie to forget about being his girlfriend or something. I guess the Eigers will be in Vienna in a day or two." Val giggled. He had left the best part for last. "Oh, and another thing. She might be pregnant."

Marcus felt his stomach turn over. Intercourse! Adrian a father! Things like that happened in movies, not in real life.

"You wouldn't lie about something like that, would you Val?"

Val stood up and stretched. He stroked the Swan's limestone feathers.

"Maybe I would," Val said finally. "Everyone thinks I lie all the time, so why not?" He sounded bored, as if the topic was of no further interest. "But it happens to be the truth."

Marcus left Val and walked back into the house. He no longer wanted to be around his brother. He was sorry he'd pried the secret out of him. Upstairs, he lay on his bed, picturing Julie's stomach growing big and round. A tiny infant splashing out in a pool of blood and looking like Adrian. No, it was impossible! After a while, he got up and went downstairs to the kitchen, pulled up a chair and watched Mrs. Woodbine and Anna-Maria dry off some silverware. Mrs. Woodbine studied his morose expression for a moment.

"What ails you, Sugarfoot?" She pulled on his ear lobe. "I believe you've been hearing things. Did someone let the cat out of the bag?"

"I guess Val did."

Mrs. Woodbine sighed deeply and Anna-Maria shook her head and muttered something about Marcus being *zu jung*. Mrs. Woodbine didn't seem concerned, though. In her opinion, Marcus, far from being too young, was wiser than most adults.

"I declare, I didn't expect it from Adrian," Mrs. Woodbine

said. "I reckon boys that age get up to all kinds of mischief. There was my cousin, C.J. Woodbine … ." She launched into a story about an overturned convertible and a young woman thrown from the front seat onto a patch of dirt.

Anna-Maria brought a plate of biscuits to the table. She had more than enough to do, without all this new trouble: the worst time for such a thing to happen! Hermann's birthday celebration was the day after tomorrow, with invited guests, and Philip due to arrive. Really, it was all too much! She sat down, took a biscuit for herself, and addressed Marcus.

"In two days, your Granddaddy is eighty."

"I declare," Mrs. Woodbine put in, "he's like a young fellow still!"

Anna-Maria smiled uneasily. It always gave her a little jolt when Mrs. Woodbine made personal remarks.

While the two women kept Marcus company in the kitchen, Hermann, closeted in his study with Arthur and Joyce, was working himself up into a fine state. How dare those people threaten his family! As his hatred for the Eigers waxed, his anger toward his grandson waned. Adrian's behavior was only natural in a young fellow. He recalled a parallel situation. At the age of twenty, on a trip to Paris, he'd had a brief affair with a married woman. Somehow or other the husband, an excitable man with waxed moustaches, had found out. He had offered to soothe the man's injured pride with a check. To his credit, the fellow had refused. But those Eigers! They were scheming something. The giveaway was the threat of legal action. The rest was a smoke-screen.

"Do they think I can't summon lawyers of my own?" Hermann banged his fist down on his desk, rattling a paperweight whose concentric rings produced the profile of Napoleon Bonaparte when held up to the light. "If it comes to it, let them try to prove that Adrian is the father. Afterwards, we sue for defamation."

"Please, Father! Let's not get ahead of ourselves. I have no idea of the jurisdiction in a case like this. Don't forget it happened in the middle of the Atlantic Ocean." Arthur made a hopeless gesture. "I'm not sure—"

"All this talk of money and lawyers," Joyce interrupted. "She's not pregnant, I tell you."

"Maybe not. But she's refusing to eat. I've heard of these eating disorders. Girls waste away and die."

"Don't be silly, Art. Nobody's going to die. I told Adrian it wasn't all his fault," Joyce went on. "The girl is responsible too. I don't know what they expect us to do. Even if there *is* a baby on the way, which I seriously doubt … ."

"I thought we were all in agreement that, if worst came to worst, putting it up for adoption would be the lesser evil," Arthur said.

"I didn't agree to any such thing," Hermann interjected. "These things can be remedied, and the sooner the better." He made a contemptuous gesture. "You're welcome to your moral scruples." He subsided into an aggrieved silence.

"There's no point in bringing it up," Arthur said. "Hank Eiger is a vestryman. That means he's involved in running his local parish. He and Helen wouldn't go along with something they considered sinful."

"Wouldn't they? It's money they're after, I tell you."

"Julie would refuse," Joyce put in. "Don't forget she's in love with Adrian. She probably yearns to be the mother of his child."

"*Verrückt!*" Hermann shouted. "A crazy girl of sixteen?"

Joyce rose from her seat and crossed to the window. She stared out at the lawn, so that the other two wouldn't see her if she began to cry. Outside, Val was idly swishing his badminton racket to and fro. Did he know? Probably. Adrian was no good at keeping secrets. She felt her eyes grow hot and moist. Surely her life wasn't meant to go like this! But Hermann was right, even though it was against the law, and a transgression in the eyes of the Church. But wouldn't ruining the lives of two young people be a greater evil? Joyce walked back to her chair and sat down heavily.

"Helen and Hank," Arthur was saying, "might decide to keep the child for good … ."

Hermann cut him off. "Nonsense, Arthur!"

"Please, Father, let me talk. We needn't decide anything at present. I'll call up the Eigers first thing Monday morning.

They're expecting it. I don't see how we can refuse a meeting; it would look as if we were evading responsibility." Arthur looked at his watch. "We ought to call it quits for the night."

Hermann grunted. "Make sure the diplomacy takes place in their hotel and not in this house. I don't want them to think I'm worth a lawsuit."

Arthur smiled. "It might help if you were present. You'd intimidate them."

"Intimidate? What do you mean, Arthur? I treat people fairly. My employees will vouch for it."

"I only meant—"

"*Assez!* It's true I've had to stand up to all kinds of trouble. Long before that *canaille* marched in and stole everything. Trade unionists, socialists, Communists! They had more in common with Herr Hitler than they imagined. Some day you should ask Anna-Maria what she had to suffer at the hands of the Reds. She's too ashamed to go into the details, even with me.

"You've told her what happened between Adrian and Julie?"

"Naturally." Hermann gave a dismissive shrug. "I imagine your Mrs. Woodfein knows everything too. That woman seems strangely clairvoyant."

"She knows," Joyce said. "Eavesdropping, most likely. She's going around with a look on her face. We can trust her, though; she's extremely loyal."

"Then we should all try to get a good night's sleep." Hermann opened the door for Arthur and Joyce. But as they were about to pass through, he stopped them. "There is something else I meant to say. Philip arrives the day after tomorrow, in time for my birthday."

"Philip?"

"It was supposed to be a surprise," Hermann went on, "but you might not be able to stand another shock, either of you." He chuckled. "Birthday celebrations! Under the circumstances, it will be difficult to sustain a mood of gaiety. No matter. Soon enough, I won't need to worry about such things. *Je vais où tant de braves hommes sont déjà venus ... .*"

"Father! You'll live to be a hundred!" Of course it was only natural that Hermann had begun to contemplate mortality. Still, it came as a jolt that he was preparing to follow in the footsteps of "so many great men". He'd always behaved, even in the darkest times, as if he had his whole life ahead of him.

"Do I surprise you, Arthur? It's time I set my house in order. After the guests have departed, I shall make a proposal."

Joyce and Arthur exchanged looks.

"Don't be alarmed! It will take your minds off Adrian. We've all heard a bit too much of that *jeune monsieur*. As a matter of fact, my plan doesn't include him. It particularly concerns Valentine."

"You'd better tell us now," Joyce said. "Otherwise we won't sleep a wink."

"No, we must wait for Philip. I'd like him to be present. I've already said too much."

Hermann's eyes were bright with anticipation.

ARTHUR HUNG UP the phone in Hermann's study and turned to his wife. "We can forget about the Eigers."

"You should have left a message, Art. Maybe they haven't checked in yet. It's still pretty early."

"The letter said they were due to arrive last night. Anyhow, the clerk says there's no reservation for a Henry Eiger."

"I wonder if they decided on a different hotel. The Zauberflöte isn't what I expected of Helen. I looked it up in our guide book; the *Magic Flute* has lost its magic. Not high-class enough. Don't forget they stayed at the Crillon in Paris."

"They would have let us know."

"How? The phone number here is unlisted." Joyce sat down on a chair opposite Hermann's desk. *Life* magazine lay on a small table next to her; on the cover, a French actor with a face like a horse planted a kiss on Marilyn Monroe. "Do you think," she continued, "they've changed their minds about coming to Vienna?"

"Hank sounded pretty determined in his letter." Arthur shrugged. "I don't see what else we can do. I'm not going to call up every hotel in the city."

"My guess is they've calmed down. If it's turned out there's no baby on the way, there's no reason for them to annoy us."

"I wish we could be sure about the baby. If Julie is pregnant, I wouldn't put it past Hank to start a lawsuit once he's back in the States. We'd better be prepared to fight back."

"You sound like your father."

"Do I? I should ring him up and keep him abreast."

"It's just like him to go to work on his birthday, and in the middle of a crisis."

"My father is a firm believer in the stiff upper lip. He doesn't understand that we're not all cut from the same cloth. Certainly my mother wasn't. Nor Philip. Nor I for that matter."

"What now, Art?"

"I should find Adrian and tell him the meeting's cancelled. He'll be relieved."

"Really? He was looking forward to seeing Julie."

"I wonder if our other two sons will turn out to be as amorous? We'll have our work cut out for us."

"Don't think you're fooling anyone. You're impressed with Adrian. Hermann's impressed too. Even Mrs. Woodbine has a gleam in her eye."

Arthur chuckled. "She's not easily shocked, is she? I suppose it's because she grew up around farm animals." He stretched his shoulders and rubbed the back of his neck. "My father has more important things on his mind. I have a pretty good idea what proposal he's been hinting at. He knows that I have no talent or inclination for the business, that Adrian is unreliable and that Marcus has his head in the clouds. Which leaves Val. I imagine Hermann would like us all to move to Vienna."

"I see. We hang around until Val's old enough to take over the reins?"

"My father will put us on a stipend and find us a place to live. He'll think of something for me to do at the factory while Val's learning the ropes."

"You make it sound like a *fait accompli*."

Arthur sat down in the chair behind his father's desk. He fingered the edge of Hermann's blotting paper. "On the contrary. I'm comfortable in my burrow. We'll have to disappoint him." He sighed. "He had better make up his mind to sell out. He's had a generous offer from that American firm, you know."

"Shouldn't he give Philip one last chance?"

"Philip has too much to lose. He's risen much farther in his field than I ever will."

"Envious?"

"I've had to travel at my own gait." The words sounded unconvincing in his own ears. "It's never been my nature to make a big noise in the world."

"I wonder what my nature is?" Joyce asked. "I'm not sure I know myself, and you've never explained to me."

"You ought to start thinking of something to do with your free time. Something that truly interests you. In another few years the house will be empty of children."

"Won't you like having me snug at home, all to yourself?"

Arthur hesitated. In truth, he'd prefer things to stay more or less as they were. "I'd never stop you from branching out." He hesitated again. "So long as you don't stop loving me. I haven't forgotten that time you took Adrian to Buffalo."

"That was a long time ago, Art."

"History has a way of repeating itself."

"You needn't worry. I'm not going anywhere. I suppose I'll have to pull myself together and find something to do."

"You might go back to writing. Your poems were no joke."

"Nobody except you wanted to read my verses. Snowfalls and withered leaves! Robert Frost has that sort of thing pretty well covered."

"You could try something completely different. Something enterprising."

"Like Julius Meinl? A little business on every corner?"

"Seriously, you'll have money when your mother goes. Enough to start something."

"Let's not rush her into the ground. First Adrian, now you!"

"I just meant, you might build something of your own."

"Such as?"

Arthur pondered for a moment. What truly interested his wife?

"Why not breed dogs and sell them to the public?" he asked finally. It was all that came to mind.

Joyce laughed. "I'll be an independent businesswoman, like Sheila Rath."

"Sheila strikes me as tragic. Spinsters often are."

"*Spinster* doesn't fit, does it? I'm sure she's had lots of thrilling affairs. She's no worse off than most married people. In the end, she'll turn into a spry old lady." Joyce caught the look on her husband's face. "Don't worry, Art. I'll need a husband waiting for me when I come home at night." She reached out and squeezed his hand. "I'm warning you though. I'll smell of dogs and flea powder"

"Then there's no problem, is there? I'm going to look for Adrian. Want to come?"

"No, I'll let you break the news."

Arthur left Joyce leafing through her magazine and went out

into the hallway. The house was quiet. No sound of children or dog. Where to look? His step-mother might know. He turned into the kitchen. Anna-Maria, busying herself with preparations for the festive dinner, pressed him to sit down and take a cup of tea. They began discussing the celebration. Anna-Maria went down the list of Hermann's guests: the Hagenfelds, the Silbers, Dr. Otter, and Sophie Fluss. There would be fifteen at the table, counting the family. She'd asked Hermann to hire an assistant for the occasion: Fräulein Greta, who worked in the factory's canteen.

At the mention of Sophie Fluss's name, Arthur glanced at his stepmother. Sophie Fluss was the opera singer whose bust occupied a place of honor in Hermann's garden, and Hermann didn't conceal the fact that the two had had an "understanding" before the war, while poor Adele was still alive. "My first marriage wasn't a love match," his father admitted, "but in time I grew very fond of Adele." No, it certainly hadn't been a *Liebesheirat!* Sophie and Hermann still enjoyed a cozy friendship. Anna-Maria must be jealous. Probably she had nothing to fear, though; her rival was close to seventy. Anyway, it was really none of his business.

Arthur asked where Mrs. Woodbine was. Shouldn't she be helping to get everything ready? Anna-Maria made a face. She'd sent *die Woodbine* into the garden to cut flowers. Mrs. Woodbine was kind and good, Anna-Maria said, but got on her nerves. On and on her stories went, always about her relatives, their illnesses, their misfortunes, their dealings with *die Neger.* Anna-Maria had enough on her mind at the moment; they all did. Arthur told her she needn't worry about Adrian; the people who were causing trouble had apparently changed their minds. Of course Adrian ought to have known better. But as he said this, Arthur knew that deep down he was rather proud of Adrian. Well, "proud" was too strong a word. But he couldn't help feeling pleased. Adrian was sure to provide him with grandchildren in the years to come, at the rate he was going, and the "shipboard romance" would become a family legend.

Anna-Maria began arranging cherries in a cooking pan;

apparently there was to be *Kompott* along with the birthday cake. Tonight, she told Arthur, everyone must put their worries aside. There would be *gutes Essen,* champagne and her husband's jokes. As for Adrian's troubles, Hermann would know how to make them go away. Best of all, the factory would stay in the family after all. It would all turn out well in the end.

"Alles wird gut, Artur."

Arthur wasn't so sure everything was going to turn out for the best. The Eigers, he thought, might yet prove a nuisance. Naturally, they were angry. Julie was very young. But then so was Adrian. It was an old, old story. *Daphnis and Chlöe.* Why all this fuss about an irresistible urge that was perfectly natural in the young? Joyce was probably right: Julie Eiger's "pregnancy" was wishful thinking. Were her parents really as outraged as they pretended to be? All this hypocrisy over sex was a disease! The churches only made the illness worse. It was driving the young away from religion.

Before thanking Anna-Maria for his tea and leaving the kitchen, Arthur asked if she'd seen Adrian. No, she hadn't seen the children since breakfast. She thought they must have taken the dog for a walk. Maybe they intended to fly the toy airplane again that made such a dreadful noise. Arthur decided he'd wait until the boys got back home; in the meantime, he would take a nap on the terrace.

Around the time Arthur put his feet up, Adrian and Marcus were lounging in a vacant lot, sharing a shady spot with Gorlice. Val, in one of his sour, solitary moods, had gone off somewhere by himself. Horace lay next to the two boys. His sides expanded and contracted; intermittent moans indicated he was dreaming.

"What do dogs dream about?" Marcus wondered.

"Die nächste Mahlzeit." Gorlice laughed. The next meal! He was in a good humor. He leaned over and examined the bump on Marcus's forehead; screwed up one eye and made ruminant sounds, as if summoning his medical expertise.

"Sehr nett! I have hundred percent success!"

"You didn't do anything! It got better by itself."

"They wanted to put on disgusting stuff. I told them just ice. I learned from army."

"You were in the army?" Marcus pictured Gorlice in a Nazi uniform.

"*Nein.* But I see many soldiers."

The talk circled around to Gorlice's little daughter, who was suffering from *Bindenhautentzündung*; it took some time for the boys to understand that the complicated word meant "pink eye". The conversation shifted to the American election. Gorlice said that it would be better if *der Ike* stayed in office a few more years; he had a bad feeling about Vice-President Nixon, and Kennedy was too young and inexperienced: the Russians would run rings around him! Adrian contributed little to the talk; he lay on his back and stared up at the sky, where wispy clouds hung in the blue.

"*Was ist los, Herr Adrian?* You not so good today?"

Marcus waited in suspense for what, if anything, his brother would reveal. He had a feeling Adrian wouldn't mind confiding in Gorlice. After a moment, Adrian turned his head so that he was facing away from the chauffeur. He cleared his throat.

"It's just this girl I met on the boat," he said finally, still avoiding Gorlice's eyes. "Her parents found out. They told my parents."

"What means *found out*?"

"You know. We *did* it ... ."

Gorlice's eyes sparkled. He laughed and made a sly gesture with his forefinger.

Marcus felt his ears and cheeks turning pink.

"The first time, *eh?*" Gorlice recalled the SS officer's young wife. "I am more young than you even. She forgets me right away."

"You don't understand!" Adrian's face was tight with anxiety. "She could be pregnant. She's *late.*"

Gorlice made a skeptical face. "Maybe she makes a story. Happens so."

"But what if she really is? I'm supposed to meet her parents. They're coming to Vienna; probably already here. They want us to break up so she can get back to normal. But if she's going to have a ... ." He couldn't say the word, for fear that doing so could make it come true.

Gorlice said something under his breath that might have

been a German obscenity. Then he put an arm around Adrian's shoulder.

"Your Papa make it right. And the Granddaddy." Gorlice recalled the old man's behavior following the accident. After he'd calmed down, Lasch had been fair. "Not so bad a man, your Granddaddy. He help you all right." He made a face. "*Die Anna-Maria,* I don't like."

"Probably," Marcus put in, "Julie's not even … you know. Mom doesn't believe it."

"Your Mama has good sense." Gorlice reached into a pocket of the jacket that lay folded up on the ground. He drew out a pack of playing cards.

"Look here."

Adrian examined the card Gorlice held up for him. On the back was a picture of a half-naked woman with a large bosom. Adrian snickered. Marcus slid closer and craned his neck to get a better look. There were four different women in all, corresponding to the four suits in the deck.

"Nice," Adrian said simply.

The pictures didn't excite him in the least but Marcus thought he should show some appreciation. "*Very* nice," he said in a whisper, and both Adrian and Gorlice laughed.

Now Gorlice was reaching into his pants pocket. He took out his wallet and withdrew a laminated card that displayed a different image depending on the angle at which it was held. He showed it to Adrian and giggled. "We maybe don't let your brother see."

But Marcus squeezed himself between Adrian and the chauffeur. Held one way, the card showed a woman in a nightie. Held another way, the nightie flew up, revealing what was between her legs. The sight came as a shock to Marcus. There was nothing like it in paintings or sculptures of naked women.

Adrian snickered again. "Better put it away. It's giving Marcus ideas."

Gorlice replaced the card in his wallet. "You feel okay now?"

"A little better."

Some fifty yards down the road, a stout young woman and a small child were approaching them. The chauffeur got to his feet and muttered something. The woman stopped in front of him; the child rubbed her eyes and grinned. Gorlice bent down and embraced the little girl. She gave him a kiss. Horace, awakened from his nap, sniffed at her legs. The child patted the dog's head while the adults conversed in German. The woman glanced several times at the two boys. Gorlice clarified the situation for the benefit of Adrian and Marcus.

"The big one is Klara, my wife. The little one is our Monika." He turned to the child and instructed her to say "*Guten tag.*" The little girl looked up at the boys, too awe-struck to utter a word. Gorlice shrugged and explained that Frau Klara and the child had gotten on a streetcar—no, two different streetcars—and traveled for an hour because little Monika wouldn't stop fussing on account of her pink eye. "Moni" had been driving Mama crazy! So here they were, since Frau Klara couldn't think of anywhere else to go.

Marcus was astonished at Frau Gorlice's appearance. She was about the chauffeur's age but fat. She reminded him a little of the "marzipan pigs" that Anna-Maria arranged on a platter, to go with his tea. Shouldn't the chauffeur have picked someone more like himself: trim, athletic, good-looking? It was puzzling. As for little Moni, she kept rubbing her eyes. Marcus felt sorry for her; she was on the plump side, like her mother, and her face was dirty. There was a large stain—fruit juice, it looked like —on her white smock.

The dialogue between husband and wife resumed. The boys understood enough to tell that Gorlice was irritated with Frau Klara for having dragged the kid right out to the outskirts of the city. Did she expect him to take time off work, just like that, and drive her and the child around in the Mercedes? Or maybe she wanted him to introduce her to his boss? The child wasn't present-able with that dirty frock and face! And why hadn't Frau Klara given the child ointment? She kept rubbing her eyes! Hadn't he given her the money for the clinic before leaving the house?

Frau Gorlice began to shout. She *had* been to the clinic, and she'd put ointment in both eyes, but the *Gott verdammt* medicine wasn't working, at least not yet, and who knew whether the nurse at the clinic had given her the right stuff?

"I think we'd better go," Adrian said. "Horace needs his exercise." Then he remembered his manners. "Nice to meet you, Frau Gor-*litch*-ee. And nice to meet you too, Monika." He bent down and gave the little girl a formal handshake.

Klara Gorlice watched the brothers disappear down the road. Nice kids! But her husband was considering how he might use Adrian's story to his advantage. There was that trashy newspaper, the *Wiener Blatt*. He had a contact there, a junior editor by the name of Klaffer who spent his Saturday nights at the *Gasthaus*. Klaffer would lap up a scandal. Gorlice chuckled under his breath. He would have to exaggerate a little; say that the girl's pregnancy was as good as certain. It would amount to no more than gossip, but he knew his Viennese. They liked the Jews no better than they did in the old days—especially the better-off ones. The *Blatt* even managed to insinuate that the Chosen Ones were not altogether blameless for the mess they'd gotten into.

Gorlice chuckled some more. How that witch Anna-Maria would tear her hair out!

But suppose Herr Lasch found out who had spread the rumor? What if he flew into a rage and fired him on the spot? Well, it would be worth it. He hadn't forgotten about that vicious slap in the face. He wasn't going to spend the rest of his life as a slave! A happy thought occurred to him. Klara had an uncle. She could ask him for a loan. He, Franz, had always dreamed of opening a garage, or maybe a little snack bar, somewhere in the country.

He gave his wife a kiss. She was fat, not too bright and none too capable, but she was a faithful creature and knew exactly what he liked in bed. He hoisted Monika onto his shoulders. The child shrieked with delight. Gorlice began singing a folk song: something about a lusty fellow who finds himself stuck in a bedroom window. Klara and Moni pranced around to the melody. At the end of the chorus came a stretch of yodeling. Franz Gorlice was an accomplished yodeler. Suddenly all three were in the best of moods. Gorlice told his family to wait for him. He could afford to waste an hour. He would fetch the car and drive them to the nearest ice-cream vendor.

Hotel Prinz Eugen

HELEN EIGER CROSSED the length of her sitting room at the Hotel Prinz Eugen. Stopping before a pair of tall windows, she considered the view. In the distance, the dome of the Hofburg shone coppery green in the afternoon sunlight. She couldn't give it the attention it deserved. The whole voyage was spoiled! Still, she was glad they'd decided on the Prinz Eugen. A friend back in Connecticut had recommended the Zauberflöte but after reading in two different guide books that the place had gone down in recent years, she'd cancelled the reservation and booked a suite instead at what was said to be one of the best hotels in Vienna.

She turned to face her husband.

"Don't you think we should have heard by now?"

Hank Eiger put his cup down on a glass-topped table. It was his third coffee of the day. He avoided meeting his wife's anxious eyes.

"I wouldn't be surprised if you can't trust the mail over here. Maybe they never got the letter. Or maybe they tore it up. I don't know what you expect me to do about it. There are no Lashes in the book. The number may be unlisted."

"We could send a wire."

"And have them ignore it?"

"You're sure you gave them the name of our hotel?"

"I'm not an idiot."

"You might have said the Zauberflöte. They might have tried to reach us there."

Hank made an impatient gesture.

"Well, if you're sure." But Helen had her doubts. Hank hadn't wanted to write the letter. She'd had to stiffen his spine. He'd huffed and puffed before acceding to her wishes.

"I suppose there's only one thing we can do," Helen continued. "Just march right over there and have it out with them. I'm worried to death about Julie's nerves."

"Suppose seeing that boy again rekindles the flame?"

"I thought we agreed it was a good idea. I expect Adrian will be glad to break it off. I doubt he wants to be saddled." Helen blushed. She was making Julie sound like a burden, when in fact, any boy would be lucky to have her. "What I mean," she went on, "is that they're both much too young."

Hank made a sour face. "You had the two of them as a married couple—" he allowed himself a dry chuckle "—after you and I were finished pretending it was our child."

Helen blushed. "I suppose it was a foolish idea." She picked up a cloth napkin from the table and dabbed her eyes.

"Let's not start the waterworks again. Worst case, we put the child up for adoption and sue the other side for damages."

"I won't drag our daughter into court."

"We've been over that. Almost the same thing happened to that Briarly girl. Nobody had to appear before a judge."

"Hank! Deborah Briarly was a—." She was about to say "tramp" but stopped herself.

Hank grunted and picked up a copy of *National Geographic* that he'd located at a newsstand. There was a story he wanted to finish about Antarctic birds. Helen sighed and said she might as well go down to the lobby, since certain people didn't seem to appreciate the gravity of the situation.

Lying face up on her bed in an adjoining bedroom, Julie Eiger heard her parents' voices, muffled by the closed double doors. She couldn't make out all the words but she could tell they were discussing her for the thousandth time. She knew she ought to get up and tell her mother that her period had arrived just a short while ago, while she was sitting on the toilet. Yes, she should tell them right away. It wouldn't be fair not to. Everyone would be tremendously relieved.

Instead, she felt strangely disappointed. Of course it would have been absolutely awful to hide for nine months, even if missing school was no hardship. Probably there was some place she could have gone, like a convent, but without strict rules. Afterwards, she and Adrian would have gotten married and moved to New York City. They would have lived like beatniks. The grandparents would have helped out. She would have missed her horses but Connecticut wasn't so far off. Anyway, it wouldn't have mattered. She hadn't felt really happy at home for years. It would be all right to visit just once in a while.

Julie went over to the bureau and examined herself in the mirror. She pushed the skin away from her cheekbones. She wasn't sorry to have lost some flesh, after hardly eating anything for a week. It made her look older and more interesting. Maybe she'd give up meat altogether and stick to vegetables in the future. Why not? Jennifer Westermark, her best friend's older sister, was a vegetarian. Jennifer felt sorry for the animals. She had a point. Julie recalled how once, on a field trip in third grade, she'd watched rows of cows attached to milking machines. The sight of those swollen udders attached to rubber tubes had made her feel sick. Maybe she would give up dairy products as well. If only she wasn't always hungry! She was only pretending not to want to touch her food. It was just that an appetite seemed out of place, considering her situation.

Yes, she really ought to tell her parents the news. Everyone would be overjoyed. Adrian had a right to know too. The families were supposed to meet. Her parents wanted her to break up. But she was dying to see Adrian. She couldn't stop thinking about him. It was strange how she felt even more attached to him now than when they'd actually been together. The sex part wasn't so important. Everything had happened so fast, and she'd been worried about a key turning in the lock: her mother kept an extra one.

Of course, in a way, it was her fault: once she'd given him permission, Adrian hadn't thought of refusing. Boys never did, from what she'd heard. But suppose Adrian told her to forget about what had happened? He might be tired of her; she had to prepare herself for that. At times it seemed a certainty. Then the remainder of the European vacation would be a torment. She'd turn sickly, and they would have to go home early. She'd spend the rest of the summer brooding, plotting to get Adrian back. Her predicament fascinated her. What else did she have to look forward to? Another year of being stared at by pimply, gawky boys, none of them as nice as Adrian. Not the straight-A boys, and certainly not the ones who thought *Playboy* magazine was the height of sophistication. Adrian probably stared at the centerfolds too, but in his case she forgave him. His face reminded her of that actor in the Hitchcock movie about two people on a train. It didn't matter that his nose was too big and he looked gloomy half the time. No, she had no intention of giving him up.

A startling thought entered Julie's head. She no longer cared much about Buck, her favorite of her three horses.

She opened the top bureau drawer and took out a photograph Adrian had given her. It was a color photo of the Lash family, lined up on the New Jersey seashore. The photo was creased from having been carried around in Adrian's wallet. In the picture, Adrian, sunburnt, wore a straw hat. Val stood next to him, wearing sunglasses. Marcus, in a floppy bathing suit and a baseball cap turned backwards, held his mother's hand. Mrs. Lash wore a two-piece suit whose bottom ended in little pleats. The father, dead center, grinned happily at the camera. He looked proud of his hairy chest.

Carefully, Julie tore the paper so that Adrian was separated from the others. She disposed of the rest of the Lash family in a wastepaper basket and trimmed the remaining fragment with a pair of nail scissors. Then she lay back on the bed and held the photo in front of her face. She kissed it tenderly and placed it on the night stand. She closed her eyes. Where was Adrian at this very moment? What was he doing? Maybe he was just as unhappy as she was.

Adrian, it so happened, was at that moment riding a streetcar. It was his father's idea to get him out of the house. It wouldn't hurt, Arthur had said, to spend a couple of hours by himself to think things over. He might stop at the *Stefansdom* and offer a prayer of thanks for his narrow escape! Joyce gave him her grudging approval, but she made him promise to be back in good time for the birthday party.

Seated next to a bony, nervous-looking woman wearing a Tyrolean hat and laced up boots, Adrian brooded. His father expected him to be relieved. The Eigers had apparently given up the idea of a conference; it meant that Julie wasn't pregnant and her parents had decided to forget what happened. But instead of relieved, he was depressed. He'd been looking forward to the meeting. He would have refused to make any promises. Let Helen and Hank carry on as much as they liked!

A baby at the other end of the streetcar fussed loudly. Its mother gave it a pacifier to suck on. She was young but not as young as Julie. It would have been terrible if Julie had to give up nine months of her life; even more terrible if they'd had to hand a baby over to Helen and Hank, or to complete strangers. But none of that would have happened. Everyone would have seen there was only one thing to do. There must be places you could go. Granddaddy would have known whom to call. After that, he and Julie would have shared a dark secret. It would have brought them closer. She was in love with him. He was starting to think he loved her too.

Adrian got off in the central district. He wasn't sure where he was, but it wouldn't be hard to retrace his steps and board a car going in the opposite direction. He looked around him. So many of the women, young and old, were dressed in shapeless clothing. A few wore peasant *dirndls* that exposed their fleshy arms. The young men carried thick briefcases, wore up-to-date tab collars, and had hair combed up like Elvis's. Their sturdy thighs and calves bulged through their narrow trousers.

He stopped at the window of a book shop. Granddaddy had forbidden birthday presents. What did he need them for, at his age? All the same, Adrian suspected he would be pleased with an unexpected gift. Something in French? Everyone would be thrilled by his thoughtfulness.

Inside the shop, everything was in German and nothing looked particularly valuable. Just as well. Anything Granddaddy would appreciate was bound to cost hundreds of dollars. Adrian pretended to examine a few books before leaving, relieved that his good intention had come to nothing. Another store displayed women's handbags. He ought to buy something for Julie. Why shouldn't he give her a present? If the meeting was off, he'd mail it to her once they were back home. Better yet, figure out a way to meet her in person. But ladies' handbags were a mystery, and too expensive. What then? Across the street was a toy shop. Julie was too old for toys. Or was she? Girls liked frivolous things, reminders of their childhood.

Adrian crossed the middle of the block and opened a door with KINDERWELT written across the glass. The inside was poorly lit; it took his eyes a moment to adjust. What would Julie like? Obviously not a wooden railroad, or dolls or dolls' houses. But what was this? A monkey wearing traditional Austrian garb sat amid a collection of stuffed animals. Adrian studied the monkey for a moment and then carried it over to the cashier. A young man with thick eyeglasses rang it up.

"*Hundert zwanzig, bitte.*"

A hundred and twenty schillings! Adrian summoned up his German. "*So viel?*"A woman who'd been arranging games and puzzles in the back of the store—evidently the manager—overheard. She hurried to the front and gave Adrian a wide grin.

"For you, one hundred schilling!"

The woman's eagerness to make a sale was embarrassing. Maybe he ought to forget the whole thing. But then Adrian pictured the monkey in a place of honor on Julie's bureau. She might go to sleep holding it in her arms. He got out his wallet.

By the time he was back at the streetcar stop, it had started to rain. Adrian checked his watch. Four forty-five. Later than he thought. He would arrive home with barely enough time to bathe and get dressed. The prospect of a boring evening, with elderly guests and long-winded toasts, weighed on his spirits. At least Uncle Philip was coming in from Chicago. Maybe Philip would liven things up.

A clanging bell alerted him to the approach of a streetcar. Was it the right line? He'd forgotten to take note of the route number. Well, it looked just like the car he'd taken an hour ago and it was headed in the opposite direction. He boarded, dropped coins in the box and found a seat next to a small girl who looked curiously at his parcel. The fancy pink box might have rolled off the presses of *Lasch & Söhne*. Adrian smiled at the little girl. He ought to explain. What was "girlfriend" in German?

"*Für meine Freundin.*"

The child looked quickly away, as if she'd dared too much.

At the same time as Adrian was leaving the central district, Franz Gorlice was standing in a crowded streetcar traveling in the opposite direction, heading toward the apartment building where he rented three small rooms. Usually he dozed off during his homeward ride, even when he had to stand and hold on to a strap, but on this occasion he was deep in thought. An interesting day! He was picturing a pile of money. American dollars, preferably. Mustn't be greedy. A thousand? Enough to put a down payment on a nice little bar somewhere in the country, with living quarters upstairs and a yard where Moni could play in the fresh air.

At the next stop, several passengers got off. Gorlice found an empty seat, clasped his hands behind his head and stretched his long legs out into the aisle. An elderly lady with a cane gave him a dirty look. Look as much as you like, old *Mistvieh!* Yes, life was decidedly looking more interesting, now that he'd heard Klara's crazy story about Frau Lasch. Except it wasn't crazy!

He and Klara had glimpsed Anna-Maria on their way to fetch ice-cream for little Monika. Frau Lasch was watering the front lawn. She'd looked up and given him a suspicious look. No doubt she was wondering about the woman and child sitting beside him in the Mercedes. He'd driven right past her with his eyes straight ahead, but Klara craned her neck and stared back at his employer. Then she asked him if he knew who it was.

"*Natürlich. Frau Lasch.*"

Klara had sucked in her breath and then let it out, slowly. She'd recognized the woman's face. After so many years! Oh yes, she knew quite a lot about her! He was so taken aback—what could she possibly know of Frau Lasch?—that he'd swung the car over to the curb and hit the brakes hard. Monika's head fell forward but this time the sudden stop caused no harm.

"*Wass meinst du, Klara?*"

She would explain herself, she told him, after Moni was busy with her cone.

They found a table and chairs under an umbrella. While Monika licked her ice cream, Klara recounted the time when Russian troops had broken through the city's defenses. She had been fifteen years old—no, not even, her birthday didn't come until June—and working all hours in her parents' grocery store. No one was bothering about school just then; they were worried about surviving the Russian Army. The Reds had arrived in April. The rear echelons were the worst; animals who'd take turns on the same helpless female; nobody too young or too old. Klara let out a short, ugly laugh. She was handled no worse than thousands of others. She was lucky to have been picked out by just one soldier: a smooth-faced boy with wide cheekbones and narrow eyes—the face of a simpleton.

Klara's story shocked Gorlice. He always thought she'd gotten away in time. Didn't her uncle have a place in the country? And what did all of it have to do with Lasch's wife? She was getting to that, Klara said. It was a strange coincidence, wasn't it? Anna-Maria Wensch, as she was then called, worked for the butcher across the street from Klara's grocery, ringing up sales. She told Klara that she'd been in the service of a wealthy man. Klara guessed it was a Jew, since he'd apparently disappeared, and it was hard for people who'd been employed by Jews to find decent work. Klara said that she and Anna-Maria got to be friends; the older felt sorry for the younger; gave her scraps from the butcher shop. Eventually Anna-Maria showed her a trapdoor cut into the floorboards in a back room, padlocked and covered up with a thick rug. Underneath was the basement.

Gorlice interrupted her: A hideout? Suddenly he felt excited. This was as good as the cinema!

She was getting to that, Klara said. She must tell the story in her own way, bit by bit.

She and her parents, she said, were living in one tiny room above the grocery. A month earlier, coming up from the air-raid shelter, they'd found nothing much left of their apartment. Her mother bought used mattresses, laid them down on the floor of the room over the shop, and got hold of a few sticks of furniture. Then came the day when a Russian squad dragged what little remained of their stock—flour, canned goods—into the street. They'd already searched Anna-Maria's shop but the butcher had shrewdly emptied out all the movables before fleeing to the countryside.

Tears were running down Klara's face. The man behind the counter looked away, embarrassed. Little Moni looked up at her mother and began to cry. Her cone fell from her grip; chocolate ice cream formed a puddle on the table top. Gorlice had to take her on his lap and explain that it was nothing; *Mutti* simply wasn't feeling so good. Klara dried her own eyes with a napkin; then she continued with her story. Who would have believed it? Anna-Maria had a bed, food, water, clothing down in the butcher shop's cellar. There was even a makeshift water closet. It was her burrow. She'd been afraid to leave the city with no money and no family within hundreds of kilometers. She hadn't any other home. Maybe she couldn't afford rent. Who knows? *Ach!* Her frightened, angry face, when Klara had begged Anna-Maria to share her hideaway! *Nein!* She mustn't! There was only enough room and supplies for one. Klara and her mother and father must fend for themselves.

Klara remembered the following day exactly: a Tuesday, with cool weather and showers. The Russian soldier had barged into the room over the grocery shop and had laid his rifle carefully on the mattress. Her parents, helpless, had covered their faces and stopped their ears. He hadn't touched her mother, *Gott sei dank*; her sickly appearance saved her.

Gorlice murmured something sympathetic; he hardly knew what he was saying. He asked her what had happened to Anna-Maria. Klara supposed she'd stayed holed up for days or even weeks, until things calmed down; she couldn't say for sure. That same evening, Klara and her parents started walking on foot to her uncle's place, some sixty kilometers to the west. For four days they trudged through the rain and dirt. If only they'd had the sense to leave sooner! But a voice on the radio kept promising the city would never fall. Only traitors and cowards, the voice said, were leaving.

When Klara was finished, her husband hugged her, kissed her and then got up from the table with a sigh. Just what he might have expected! Pretending to be Klara's friend and then leaving her to wolves! He took Klara by the hand and carried Monika, nestled in his arm, back to the Mercedes; then he drove to the streetcar stop where his wife and child would start their ride home. Before parting, he asked Klara why she'd never confided in him until now. Klara said that talking about it only made her feel worse. Just imagine, though—he was working for that woman! No, it was too much!

The rest of the day, Gorlice occupied himself with odd jobs. That loose floorboard in the hallway was absorbing work. He took pains to do it right; you didn't want anyone tripping on an exposed nail. When Anna-Maria came into sight, checking to make sure he wasn't idle, he imagined how she might have looked fifteen years earlier. Perhaps much the same. To think she'd slammed the cellar door against a girl of fourteen! Had she panicked? Or was she simply selfish? He wondered if the woman the Lashes had brought with them from America would have done likewise. A peasant woman, obviously, just like Anna-Maria. *Die Woodbine* talked too much and had a habit of looking at him suspiciously when their paths crossed. All peasants were the same: took good care of themselves, their land and their livestock, and everyone else could go to hell. His own family was a cut above. A grandfather had been quartermaster in the Imperial Army. Another had been skilled with his hands: a gunsmith, back in Poland. And then there was a cousin who'd played the violin in a provincial orchestra. But that was neither here nor there. The shame of it! Leaving a young girl to face the whirlwind! It was something he could use against Anna-Maria, surely. There was money in it! A good deal of money, if only he handled it right. The only question was how.

The lurch of the streetcar as it stopped near his home brought Gorlice back to the present. As he disembarked, he noticed a car on parallel tracks that was just leaving in the opposite direction. He glanced idly at the passengers sitting and standing behind the windows. Wait! Wasn't that the Lash kid? Was he imagining it? No, there was no mistaking the features— more like the father's than the mother's. But where did he think he was going? The streetcar line led to warehouses, cheap housing. Nowhere near Hermann Lasch's address.

Gorlice chuckled softly. Clearly the boy was lost.

Telegrams Are Always Bad News

HERMANN'S GUESTS ARRIVED promptly at six. Dr. Ulrich Otter, professor of classics, handed over his umbrella, cape and hat to Fräulein Greta. On his heels came Dr. Wolfram Hagenfeld, retired attorney, arm in arm with aristocratic Hannelore Hagenfeld, née von Trautheim, looking frail but bright-eyed. Last came Sophie Fluss, upright, full-chested, wearing a gown that reached the tops of her shoes and a necklace of crystals or diamonds—impossible for the untrained eye to tell which.

Hermann, greeting each in turn, felt ill at ease. At the last minute, the Silbers, his aged cousins, had begged off because Florian Silber had come down with a cold. And to think they'd made a special trip from Zurich! Their absence meant thirteen at the table. Thirteen! Anna-Maria had panicked. Their guests would be nervous the whole evening! He'd lost his temper; shouted at her that it was all the same to him if she set a fourteenth place for the dog. Still, thirteen was an unlucky number, there was no doubt about it.

Worse, Philip hadn't shown up yet. His flight from London had landed on time; he ought to have arrived hours ago. And where was Adrian? Damned if the boy hadn't gotten into more trouble! Dr. Otter, perceptive as a cat, sensed something was amiss. He took Hermann by the arm and delivered a remark about Cato the Elder, suitable for the occasion. Just imagine! Cato had begun learning Greek at the age of eighty! But Hermann, caught in his friend's grip, felt the chill of mortality. Ulrich Otter must be well into his seventies. How little time they both had left on this earth!

Sophie Fluss, noticing Hermann's discomfiture, wasn't about to be thrown off her game. She kissed her old admirer on both cheeks and told him how well he was looking; it must be because he had his family with him! She'd neglected to have young ones of her own, and her two husbands—the first divorced, the second disappeared—were ancient history. Her career, she admitted with a rueful smile, had always come first. Her "children" were young people with whom she shared the concert stage. Nowadays it was all recitals. Just last season, she'd taken a young female accompanist under her wing, a Belgian girl not yet twenty.

Hermann interrupted her. She was still young enough for the opera stage, he told his old friend. She had a good ten years ahead of her! Nobody else had ever played the Countess Almaviva so well.

Sophie Fluss bowed before Hermann's compliment. Then she turned toward Val, tilted her head, tittered, and gave him a kiss on the cheek. *Wirklich ein Engel!* An angel! He ought to be on the stage! Val scowled, Joyce averted her eyes, and Arthur suppressed an urge to laugh. Flirting with a fourteen year-old! It might as well be a scene in *Der Rosenkavalier.* He wondered if Marcus, staring up at the great lady in awe, would be next. But no, Sophie Fluss had already resumed her conversation with Hermann, who was relaxing a little under her influence. It was too bad, Sophie Fluss said, that poor Adele wasn't alive for the occasion. Hermann nodded, but Arthur could barely contain his impatience. Really, the woman was shameless! He glanced at his step-mother, who appeared to be doing her best to ignore the diva; she was exchanging polite words with the Hagenfelds. It wasn't long before Anna-Maria excused herself; Fräulein Greta couldn't be expected to do everything by herself. Mrs. Woodbine bustled after her. Hermann tried to explain to his guests where Mrs. Woodbine stood in the family hierarchy. He'd never encountered anyone quite like her! *Ein echter Charakter!* Arthur chuckled along with his father, pleased that Hermann found his uninvited house guest diverting. But the best Joyce could summon up was a wan smile; she was worried about Adrian. If only Arthur hadn't let him go off by himself! After a decent interval, she said she too must see how things were going in the kitchen.

Hermann's guests settled themselves on the sofa and soft chairs in the living room. Hermann poured glasses of dry sherry. Dr. Hagenfeld, who had played an important role in recovering the factory, inquired how the business was going. Frau Hagenfeld turned to Arthur and mentioned a former mutual acquaintance, a certain Professor Linzmann. The poor fellow, she whispered, had come down with cancer of the larynx and was refusing to be treated. Just imagine! Arthur uttered polite sympathies. Sophie Fluss posed questions to Val and Marcus in rapid-fire German. Were they enjoying their journey so far? Such a shame the opera season was over! The two boys, barely comprehending, answered with *ja* and *nein*. Dr. Otter, at a loss, got up and studied the bindings in Hermann's glass-fronted bookcase.

The evening ran according to a schedule: Hermann wanted everyone gone at an early hour, to leave ample time for family business. At six-thirty, he conducted his guests to the dinner table. Dr. Otter, observing two vacant chairs and place settings, made a polite inquiry. Hermann replied that Philip must be held up in traffic; as for his grandson, young fellows his age were apt to lose track of the time. Arthur, watching his father out of the corners of his eyes, knew he was only pretending to be indulgent. In the old days, if he or Philip had shown up late for a dinner party, it would have taken weeks to be forgiven.

Family and guests sat down and unrolled their napkins— white as snow. Hermann poured wine. Fräulein Greta, sweating and red-faced from nervousness—never before had she waited on so formal an occasion—brought in the soup. Dr. Otter, seated next to Arthur, asked how Philip's academic career was going. Arthur suppressed irritation. The old man hadn't thought to inquire about his own career! Well, Philip was the star. He told Dr. Otter about a paper of Philip's that had won a prize. Of course he himself, who'd had to struggle with Euclid, hadn't been able to make heads or tails of it. He wondered in the back of his mind if Philip wholly deserved his reputation. So much that struck a spark faded into obscurity! Someone might point out an inconsistency, a faulty equation. Immediately he felt ashamed of himself. It was spiteful of him to doubt Philip's eminence. What was the matter with him? It was because he'd been jealous of his mother's preference for her younger child. It wasn't Philip's fault, of course. Philip's finely drawn features, his affectionate nature, the dry sense of humor ... . Irresistible! Yes, he had always been envious of his brother. Not that this had prevented him from loving Philip and pitying him when he was gripped by hopeless despondency. But Philip was spoiling things by his absence. Something must have happened. Anna-Maria would say that the bad luck was a result of the dreaded number thirteen.

The doorbell rang.

"Don't you all get up. I'll see who it is." The guests stared at Mrs. Woodbine. Sophie Fluss stared hardest of all; if she had worn a lorgnette, she would certainly have used it. But Hermann's face brightened and Arthur joked that it must be the two prodigal sons arriving home at once.

There was a ripple of laughter. Wolfram Hagenfeld, who had tucked his napkin into his collar, turned around in his chair, so as to be able to get a clear impression of whoever was about to join the company. Mrs. Woodbine's footsteps could be heard, then the buzzer to unlock the catch, then muffled voices and the front door shutting. Mrs. Woodbine came back into the dining room and handed an envelope to Hermann. She had gotten it from a boy in a uniform, she said. A nice young fella!

The guests' faces turned from expectant to anxious. Telegrams were always bad news! Hermann opened the envelope and scanned the contents. Then he folded the message up and placed it in his vest pocket. For a second or two, he played with the napkin ring beside his bowl. He removed his spectacles, rubbed his eyes, then rose to his feet, cleared his throat, and asked Arthur to come into the study. His guests, he said, must excuse them for five minutes.

"Is anything wrong, Father?"

"*Was ist denn geshehen, Hermann?*" Anna-Maria's voice quivered with fright. "What is it? Tell us!"

Hermann changed his mind about withdrawing to the study, withdrew the telegram, handed it to Arthur and instructed him to read it aloud. What was the use of hiding its contents? Everyone would find out soon enough.

Arthur took the telegram and read it silently Then he stood up and read it aloud:

REGRET TO INFORM YOU PROFESSOR PHILIP LASH
ADMITTED SAINT AGNES HOSPITAL.

BULLET WOUND TO LEFT SHOULDER AND LUNG.
NO EVIDENCE FOUL PLAY. DEEPEST APOLOGIES.
TIMOTHY R. ZELLNER
DEPARTMENT OF MATHEMATICS
UNIVERSITY OF CHICAGO.

Arthur tried to take in the shocked faces ranged around the table. He was having trouble focusing. His legs felt weak. Sophie Fluss and Anna-Maria give little cries of horror. Dr. Otter stared at his bowl. Frau Hagenfeld, whose English was poor, turned to her husband. What did it all mean?

Val felt excited: it sounded to him as if Uncle Phil had been involved in a duel. But Marcus felt as if he might start to cry. He had just one uncle, but even if he'd had a dozen, Philip would have been his favorite. Some of his earliest memories were of Philip's holding up objects: an orange, a funnel, a paperweight. *Is it a cone, a cube or a sphere?* With a little practice, he almost always got the right answer.

"Mom, what happened? Is he going to die?

Joyce gave him a look. "How dreadful!" she said in a whisper. Did she mean Philip's plight or his question? Apparently he'd spoken out of turn. Marcus felt ashamed and afraid. The atmosphere had turned unbearably solemn, as if they were already at Philip's funeral.

"It doesn't seem possible." Arthur was still holding the telegram. "But why does it say *deepest apologies?* What does the fellow have to apologize for?" He tried and failed to control an unseemly urge to laugh.

"Just like Philip, isn't it Father? Ruining your birthday party! I suppose he was fooling around with a pistol."

Hermann struck the table with the palm of his hand. There was a silence. From upstairs, Horace could be heard scratching at the door to the bedroom where he had been confined for the evening.

But Mrs. Woodbine absorbed the news with philosophic calm.

"I declare! James Woodbine used to say the trouble with guns is they're liable to go off. Accident, I reckon."

"It *must* have been an accident," Arthur said. But he

doubted his own words. Philip had always been prone to excitability followed by despair. Once possessed of a new interest—butterflies, chess, mathematical puzzles—he was apt to go without sleep for nights on end. Finally, he'd lose interest and develop an illness. At fifteen, he'd suffered a breakdown and been shipped off to a *Kurhaus* in the Vorarlberg. The mountain air, lake and wholesome diet had effected a temporary recovery.

Hermann raised his hand. He begged everyone to go home now. Under the circumstances, he could hardly be expected to entertain his friends. He was terribly sorry. A great shame!

A flurry of dismayed and consoling sounds rose from the guests as they gathered themselves for departure. Fräulein Greta, frightened out of her wits, helped them with their coats and umbrellas. Hermann took his pocket watch from his vest and made a mental calculation.

"It will soon be morning in Chicago," Hermann told his son. "We must place a telephone call. The overseas connection will take some time."

Mrs. Woodbine told Joyce she would make sure the children were fed. Should she bring a tray into the study? Joyce hardly heard her. She was thinking of her brother-in-law. Philip was such a sensitive creature! *No evidence of foul play.* What did it imply? A suicide attempt. Philip had fired the gun wide of its target. But why aim at the heart? Didn't suicides choose the temple? Or take the barrel in the mouth? The grotesque image made her nauseous. Another possibility. Someone had shot Philip. A jealous rival for a woman's affections. Someone on the faculty! The university was covering it up. No, it was absurd. Philip was the last man on earth to get seriously entangled.

Suppose Philip died. A punctured lung was no joke. Philip might be in terrible pain. Of course the trip to Italy was off. They would have to return to the States at once. Arthur would want to rush to his brother's bedside.

And on top of everything, Adrian not yet home!

"I sure hope Dr. Lash's brother is all right," Mrs. Woodbine was saying. She checked her wristwatch, shook her head and made a worrying sound in the back of her throat. "I expect Adrian's gotten into another fix."

Joyce felt a flash of indignation. Just like Mrs. Woodbine to read her thoughts and add to her anxiety! She imagined her son sprawled on a sidewalk, blood trickling into a gutter. No, she was being hysterical; probably Adrian had gotten on the wrong streetcar. She ought to follow Arthur into the study. Hermann must already have placed a call to the hospital. Transatlantic connections took ages to set up; it might be a long while before they had more information.

Joyce got up and hugged Marcus and Val, still sitting stiffly in their chairs, and told them that Philip would make a good recovery—lungs healed pretty easily—and wasn't it strange that he had accidentally hurt himself that way? But strange things did happen, all the time, and they mustn't think Philip had harmed himself on purpose. Mrs. Woodbine was going to bring in food for them, she said, and after that they could go outside until it was time for bed.

She stopped herself. Marcus was gazing up at her with trustful eyes, but Val's lips were curled in an ironic smile, a sign that he didn't believe a word she was saying. She wondered why she had lied. What was she protecting them from? She must find the strength to explain things honestly.

But now someone was ringing the bell again. She almost ran to the front door. Without looking through the front window to see who it was—surely it must be Adrian—she pressed the buzzer. Then she opened the door, ready to forgive Adrian regardless of whatever excuse he might make. But it wasn't Adrian. Hank and Helen Eiger were making their way toward her. Beyond the gate, parked at the curb, she could make out Julie Eiger in the back of a taxi.

"I do hope you'll excuse the intrusion." Helen said nervously. "Hank was against it, after we didn't hear from you at our hotel, but I said we ought to come in person right away and tell you the news. I'm sure you'll be relieved to know that Julie's out of danger. We can all breathe easier now."

"We're not out of the woods yet." Hank Eiger's voice was defiant. He didn't like the look of the house. Except for the shingled roof, it reminded him of the newest houses in Rushton. He felt he would be at a disadvantage once he and Helen were inside, outnumbered by so many Lashes. "I'm going to get our daughter now," Hank went on, in as commanding a voice as he could summon. But then his voice cracked. "The poor kid's embarrassed to come in. We expect your boy to apologize. If he's any kind of man, he'll tell her how sorry he is to have put her—to have put *us*—through all of this." He glanced at his wife, knowing she disapproved of his tone. "We want him to promise the whole thing is over and done with, once and for all. Julie can't have anything more to do with him." He wanted to leave it at that, but then his resentment got the better of him. "One more thing. We expect a fair settlement, considering all we've had to put up with."

He noticed—and Helen noticed—the look on Joyce's face. Joyce held her hands behind her back so that the Eigers wouldn't see them shaking.

"I see. You've chosen this moment, with my brother-in-law in the hospital with a gunshot wound, and my son missing, to show up on our doorstep." She turned to Hank Eiger. "I'm perfectly delighted that Julie's in the clear. As for a settlement, I'm sure I have no idea what you mean."

Marcus and Val, who had come into the front hall to find out what was going on, heard their mother break into a peculiar laugh. The laugh sputtered out, and then she said something that sounded like an invitation. Helen went back to summon Julie. The girl seemed almost to crawl out of the taxi. Marcus was shocked at how thin she looked. When she reached the front door, all three Eigers trooped solemnly inside.

Home

SOME THREE MONTHS after her father-in-law's calamitous birthday party, Joyce Lash sat at her kitchen table with a letter lying unopened in front of her. Arthur wrote to her at least twice a week; Val less frequently. For a moment she delayed opening the envelope, knowing that the contents would make their separation all the harder to bear. She had not seen Arthur or Val since August, and now it was already the last day of October. She wondered if Val, thousands of miles away, was thinking about Halloween. Probably the holiday was unimportant. Probably *she* was unimportant! Did Val ever think about Marcus and Adrian? Maybe it had been a terrible mistake to let him return to Vienna with his father.

She was dimly conscious of voices coming from the back yard. From the sound of it, she guessed that Marcus was trying to persuade Adrian to go trick-or-treating with him one last time. Adrian was past the age for it: eighteen next spring. In less than a year he would be finished with high school. What then? On the coffee table in the living room, a stack of college catalogs lay untouched. Lately Adrian had been talking about working on a ranch. His friend Boardman had an uncle who said he could get them jobs in California, right after graduation. Doing what though? Weren't the workers out there Mexicans? Did they even speak English?

Joyce opened the pale blue envelope and took out four thin, typewritten sheets. Arthur must have used his father's Olivetti. She sighed heavily. It would be another two months before the family reunited. Well, she had made her bed, and she must sleep in it. Perhaps, after all, the letter would cheer her up.

Wednesday, October 26

Darling Joyce,

    Sorry for not having written sooner, but I hardly have a moment to myself, between spending most of my day at the factory with Val and then in the evenings giving him German lessons. Hermann and Anna-Maria are amazed by how quickly he's picking

152

up the language. Where there's a will, there's a way! In my "free time," I sit up with my father half the night talking over everything from the factory (profits up, but you can never tell from one year to the next) to Val's business aptitude (high marks) to the sorry state of the world (another war likely, this time with the Russians). I can hardly refuse, since it helps take his mind off Philip. Not that he doesn't finally get around to asking the same questions: How could Philip be so weak, so selfish? Isn't he proud of his achievements? Hasn't he had numerous opportunities to marry and have children? And so on.

Hermann has gotten it into his head that Phil's current unhappiness might be a case of acute homesickness. He wants him to fly to Vienna. I remind him that Dr. Vache thinks Phil is making progress in the sanitarium, and that interrupting his treatment would be a mistake. I myself don't think Phil's visiting Hermann would be helpful. My father loves his son, but we all know that Philip timed the disaster to coincide with Hermann's birthday party. Not exactly a good start for a reconciliation!

Evidently Dr. Vache's regular chats with Philip have given him a pretty good idea of the lie of the land. The doctor has informed me that it's a case of "manic-depressive tendency exacerbated by childhood trauma". That sounds pretty definitive! Of course it's quite true that Philip had a rough go of it as a child, torn in two by a demanding father and an indulgent mother. Still, I can't help thinking that he ought to have worked through his resentments by now. Remember I told you how annoyed I was when I saw Philip in the hospital? Uninterested in anything except the fellow in the next bed—a youngster recovering from some sort of groin injury. The two of them were obviously anxious to get back to their chess game. Really, I felt I might as well have not rushed to my brother's bedside. He certainly didn't want my sympathy. The most I could get out of him was that he'd had a particularly bad week, couldn't bear the thought of a family reunion, and couldn't bring himself to make up an excuse. I almost want to believe the whole thing was one of his pranks! Someone who seriously wants to die takes more careful aim.

I'm sure there must be more to it than I can make out and I only hope Dr. Vache can find a way through the labyrinth. The treatment seems to boil down to rest, counseling and pills. We can be thankful Vache hasn't resorted to more drastic measures. The Mayo Clinic, so I've read, is currently treating no less a personage than Ernest Hemingway with high-voltage therapy.

I should mention that the doctor was excited when I informed him that my brother spent an hour on the Great Man's couch, when he was still a teenager. My father only agreed to it because Adele insisted. I'll never forget the day Philip came home and announced that he wasn't going to any more sessions because Dr. Freud's theories were "not sufficiently proven"!

It occurs to me that Philip might benefit from a visit to Garnet, once he's discharged from the sanitarium. You know how fond he is of you and the boys. It makes me uneasy to think of him returning straight to his lonely apartment, after having been coddled for so long. I've written to Vache, and if he agrees (and if you agree) I'll suggest it to Philip.

Enough about my troubled and troublesome brother! The chief thing is that Val and I are both giving the "trial run" our full cooperation, and it looks as though Hermann's plan has every chance of succeeding. I can picture you frowning. Remember, though, that you were the one who came up with the brilliant idea that I take a leave of absence and you were the one who kept pointing out that we hadn't seen Val so happy and excited in years. Please don't think the part I have to play is easy for me, though. Val and I have become more like distant relatives than father and son. Outside of his German lessons, we don't talk much. He prefers following Hermann around at the factory and chatting with the workmen. As for boys his own age, he's befriended an aristocratic young fellow he recognized from the swimming pool. The boy turned up at the church where we go for Sunday mass and one thing led to another. Joachim von Neuwander is a constant visitor at the house; he and Val seem to have endless amounts to talk about, and the boy has quite won over Hermann with stories about his illustrious family and their castle in the Tyrol.

Well, for another two months I must try to take an interest in the affairs of Lasch & Söhne. My father fervently hopes that we'll all move to Vienna next summer and stay at least until Val is old enough to take over. Is it really such a crazy idea? Curiously, I find I don't miss the college. If I withdraw from academia, will it matter to a single soul? It's Philip who's contributing to the world's store of knowledge, not I.

I've been thinking, in the event that we do end up as expatriates, that Adrian might go to the university here. Perhaps he ought to begin studying German. You wrote in your last letter that he seems to have gotten over Julie Eiger. It's a great relief we haven't heard anything more from the parents. I lie awake at night reliving that evening when Hank and Helen showed up at the worst possible moment. Really, those people have achieved a sort of mythical status in my imagination! At the same time there's something pathetic about them, with all that bluster about a settlement. But it was a memorable scene, wasn't it, when Adrian finally turned up and Julie rushed into his arms? We have my father to thank for keeping his head and getting everyone to calm down.

I haven't forgotten for an instant that there's you and Marcus to consider. I suspect Marcus would be quite happy to trade Garnet for Vienna. I couldn't help laughing when I read in your letter about his *lederhosen* making a hit, and the other children in the neighborhood wishing they had a pair—especially since I wasn't able to get Adrian or Val to put theirs on even once!

Could you be happy living abroad, Joyce? I miss you every day and even more so at night. Have you given it any more thought? Are you dead set against giving it a try? Perhaps a fresh start would do all of us good. I must tell you that Val is absolutely determined to stay on with Hermann and Anna-Maria, even if means separating from the rest of us. The idea of inheriting the factory has completely taken possession of him. I suppose young Joachim figures in the calculus as well. I'm not sure I have it in me to forbid him. Yesterday he said, in all seriousness, that you and I shouldn't worry about leaving him with my father and Anna-Maria, since he'd be able to visit us in Garnet "at least once a year"! I didn't quite know whether to applaud his independence or cry over his indifference.

Well, we needn't decide now. I promised you I wouldn't act against your wishes and I meant it. Val and I will be home before Christmas and then we'll have plenty of time to discuss the future.

I almost forgot to tell you the latest about Franz Gorlice. The fellow was pulled over by the police for running a red light. The officer smelled alcohol on Gorlice's breath. (Don't worry! Val and I have been taking the streetcar to and from the factory.) Hermann had to post a bond to get him released from custody. Afterwards, there was a painful scene at the house. Herr Franz, apparently still inebriated, or at any rate lacking his usual submissiveness, came out with the most incredible accusations. Instead of thanking Hermann for bailing him out, he announced that he knew all about Adrian's having "ruined an innocent girl", and that he would see to it that the whole city found out; it would make an amusing story! Then before we knew what to make of his threat, he switched to a garbled

tale about a locked cellar; apparently it was somehow Anna-Maria's
fault that Frau Klara Gorlice had been violated by a soldier in the
Red Army. All of Vienna would find out about that too, Herr Franz
declared, unless Anna-Maria apologized on her knees to Frau
Klara. She must apologize to him as well, for having struck him in
the face in front of our boys—it seems she caught them drinking
beer and I don't know what else. Finally he drew himself up to his
full height—the fellow is an imposing figure when he's not cringing
—and told Hermann that the price for his silence was a thousand
American dollars, evidently enough to get the Gorlices started on
the path to prosperity.

Of course none of us knew quite what to say at first. Then
floods of tears on Anna-Maria's part! Really the story about the
Russian Army was so confused, I hardly understood what she was
denying. As for the slap, she insisted the chauffeur deserved it for
getting Marcus drunk, and she had a good mind to repeat the
punishment. Anna-Maria's counter-attack weakened Gorlice's
backbone and Hermann demolished what was left of it. Did he
really think, my father shouted, that someone who had had survived
the Nazis would give in to a pitiful attempt at blackmail? Not a
living soul, Hermann said, gave a damn about Adrian's tomfoolery,
and as for Anna-Maria, did the chauffeur imagine he had a right to
accuse a woman who'd risked her neck to bring her employer
decent food?

In sum, the chauffeur was humiliated and then dismissed,
though I wouldn't be surprised to find Gorlice back on the job in a
week or two. It would be just like Hermann to enjoy watching him
beg for "one last chance", and then to extend a merciful hand.

Time for bed! I will miss holding you in my arms and covering
you with my kisses. Love to Adrian and Marcus and Horace, and
regards to Mrs. W.

Your faithful husband

Arthur

P.S. I hope your mother is doing a little better than when you
last wrote. Or at any rate no worse. Please give her my best wishes.
Even if she seems not to understand, one can never tell.

Joyce laid the sheets on the table. She was conscious of Mrs.
Woodbine humming one of her hymns as she folded freshly
laundered clothing in a room behind the kitchen, and of Horace

snoring as he lay asleep next to the refrigerator. She wondered why the dog was always dozing off these days; the vet said there wasn't anything wrong with him. Well, she had other things to worry about. She'd have to think about starting dinner soon; the boys were always hungry by six o'clock. There were the makings of a quick supper in the cupboard: chow mein in a can, rice, crispy noodles and, for dessert, fortune cookies. By seven the dishwasher would be stacked, the garbage taken outside. She would leave the distribution of Halloween candy to Mrs. Woodbine. By eight o'clock Blackwood Road would be deserted except for middle-school boys armed with shaving cream and toilet paper.

She would have the rest of the evening to herself. Another night in front of the television. Or else she would read *To Kill a Mockingbird* or sit with Horace at her feet and pretend to listen to Mrs. Woodbine talk. Arthur had no conception of what her evenings were like. He'd persuaded himself that because she had the two boys and Mrs. Woodbine for company, she must be bearing up. Well, it was her own fault for encouraging the "trial run." She should have vetoed the plan from the outset. Looking back, it seemed to her that everything had moved too fast. She hadn't had time to consider things sensibly. As she sat listening to Hermann's grand proposal, she'd watched Val and Arthur out of the corner of her eye: Val excited to have been singled out as heir, and Arthur weakening. She could tell where things were heading and refused to have any part in it. If the earth was about to move under her feet, she would run for safe ground.

That same night, in the bedroom, she'd come up with her "brilliant idea". Once they were home, Arthur ought to apply for a semester's leave of absence and then, after visiting his brother in the hospital, fly back to Vienna with Val, leaving her and the other two boys behind. Val would miss the first months of high school but she was sure he didn't care. Let him live abroad for awhile—say until Christmas—and get a feeling for what was involved in running *Lasch & Söhne*. They would give it a year before making a final decision.

She had felt so noble, so unselfish! And Arthur had taken her advice. He had Val's welfare at heart and he was worried about his father. He was sure Hermann secretly blamed himself for Philip's suicide attempt, never mind that he put it all down to his son's weak character. The bond between father and son had long ago foundered on misunderstandings and recriminations. In his old age, Hermann needed moral support.

She picked up Arthur's letter and read it over again. Val was taking to his new life far better than she'd expected. It was his chance to blossom. But to leave him for good, with Hermann and Anna-Maria as surrogate parents? Never! She might yet call off the whole scheme; Hermann would simply have to sell out to the Americans—there were worse things in life than clearing a couple of million dollars. But wouldn't Val resent her for the rest of his life? It was wrong of her. He would be fifteen in February. Not really a child any longer. She mustn't give him cause to hate her. And then there was the new friend he'd made, Joachim. Friends were vital at his age. She'd never liked Curtis Blow; aristocratic Joachim von Neuwander was doubtless an improvement. Arthur said they spent hours together in private. What did that mean? Boys had crushes on boys at that age. Arthur would scoff and say it was nothing to worry about. Hadn't he had a crush or two of his own? Common enough, and something most boys outgrew. *Most boys!* Val had never shown the slightest interest in the opposite sex. It was a phase. But what if it wasn't? The "five percent", Sheila Rath called them, with a tolerant smile. Lonely outcasts!

No, it was wrong to leave her son to his own devices at such an impressionable age. He needed a mother and father. She and Arthur and the other two boys would all have to move next year for Val's sake—lock, stock, and barrel. Arthur had mentioned the International School for Val and Marcus. Maybe Adrian would agree to try the university. But there wasn't enough room in Hermann's house; she'd breathe easier if Arthur found a place in the central district. What about Frieda? Her mother's current live-in nurse, a German girl, was a model of kindness and efficiency. She would have to bring Frieda and "Leni" to Vienna too; their new home would have to be spacious enough to accommodate an extended family. It would all cost a great deal of money. But Hermann would be glad to subsidize their new life.

Vienna! Museums, concerts and chocolate cake. On the other hand, they'd be surrounded by ex-Nazis. Or Nazi sympathizers, at least. Their beady eyes and tight lips would give them away. Women in ridiculous clothing who only a few years ago were singing Hitler's praises. And the men! Some of them former SS officers at the camps. It wasn't as if they'd all been brought to justice. Not even the higher-ups. Perhaps some felt remorse. Most simply went on with their lives. Why did Arthur talk as if it didn't trouble him? Even Hermann seemed to have wiped the slate clean.

Gorlice's tale about Anna-Maria's locked cellar puzzled her. Hermann had more than once spoken of how hard it had been for her during the war. Anna-Maria preferred to draw a curtain over the details. Now it turned out she'd survived in some kind of hideout. Joyce pictured her huddled in a basement, listening to the thud of boots overhead. What had she done wrong? Joyce felt no inclination to judge her. She felt that she would have acted no better and maybe worse.

But what about that slap? In America you didn't treat a servant like that. Joyce thought of Ellen, who took the train from Harlem twice a week. She didn't actually need Ellen, so long as Mrs. Woodbine was on hand. But she hadn't the heart to deprive the maid of her twenty-five dollars a week. Ellen wasn't especially hard-working but even speaking sharply to her was unthinkable.

Gorlice must have done something to provoke Anna-Maria. Alcohol! She tried to remember if she'd noticed any of the boys acting tipsy. Come to think of it, Marcus had seemed not quite himself. She hated drunks. If one of her sons turned out like her own father, she'd never stop blaming herself.

She heard footsteps. Marcus and Adrian must have come inside and gone up to their rooms when she was reading her letter. Now they were coming into the kitchen in their Halloween outfits. Marcus's mask bore an uncanny resemblance to Senator Kennedy. Adrian had dug out a rubber wolf's head from the attic. It fit like a hood, with holes for seeing and breathing.

"I'm too old for this," Adrian said. "Marcus should call up one of his friends." He adjusted the hood and let out a growl. It occurred to Joyce that, despite his protest, he was looking forward to scaring the younger children.

"It's your last chance," Joyce said. She thought of reminding him that Marcus's only real friend, a little boy named Danny Nightingale, had transferred to a private school and that no new friends had materialised in the fifth grade. But saying so would only embarrass Marcus. "You'll never go trick-or-treating again," she told Adrian instead. "Not until you have children of your own."

"That's what I told him," Marcus said. "Besides, I only want to go out for a half hour. I hate it when kids start spraying shaving cream." He adjusted his tie, so that it fit snugly against his collar. Over his white shirt he wore his grey flannel suit jacket.

"You're not going to eat dinner dressed like that, are you?" Adrian asked. "Senator Kennedy's family are very informal."

Mrs. Woodbine, overhearing the conversation, came in to inspect the costumes.

"Why Adrian, you scare me to death!"

"That's the general idea."

"Now let me guess, Marcus." Mrs. Woodbine laid a stack of towels on a chair and put her hands on her hips. "Calvin Coolidge?"

"Kennedy!" Marcus shouted.

Mrs. Woodbine laughed. She liked getting the better of him occasionally. "I was only funning, Sugarfoot! My, doesn't he look handsome in that suit!"

"You mean Marcus? Or Senator Kennedy?"

Mrs. Woodbine gave another laugh. "I declare, Adrian, I don't know whether I'm coming or going!"

Joyce waved Arthur's letter like a flag. "I've had a communication from your father. He and Val are doing wonderfully well over there." She made an effort to drop the sarcastic tone. "Granddaddy is still beside himself over Philip's accident. But Daddy and Val sound like they're doing okay. And Gorlice has managed to get into more trouble."

Adrian snickered through his mask. "We're still pretending that what happened to Uncle Phil was an accident?"

"What do you mean?" Marcus sounded offended. "Daddy said he was just fooling around and it went off. That's what I think happened. Daddy wouldn't lie."

"That's right, Marcus,' Joyce said soothingly. "You miss your father, don't you?" She hesitated before adding: "Do you wish Val were at home with us?"

Marcus pushed his mask up over his forehead.

"I miss Daddy. And Val a little bit. But they'll be home in a couple of months." In the back of his mind he was thinking that if it were the other way around—if Adrian and his mother were on the other side of the world—he wouldn't be able to bear it. "I guess me and Adrian can hold out."

Adrian sat down at the table "What kind of trouble is Gor-*litch*-ee in?"

"Traffic violation." Joyce didn't want to share the whole story. Let them think the chauffeur was a charming character a while longer. "Granddaddy fixed it."

Adrian snapped the elastic band behind Marcus's mask. "He misses Gor-*litch*-ee and he'd be happy if Val stayed over there forever."

"You boys ought to know that we might all move to Vienna, at least until Val's older."

"Mrs. Woodbine too?"

"Marcus! Mrs. Woodbine has a family of her own."

"I don't expect I can just pick up and leave for good," Mrs. Woodbine said. But she sounded doubtful. In fact she felt cheated. Cutting the trip short had deprived her of Italy. She wasn't ready to forgive Dr. Lash's brother, although on the whole she was fond of him. He reminded her of a boy cousin to whom she'd once felt attached. But imagine a grown man shooting himself because he was feeling down in the dumps!

"Come on, Marcus," Mrs. Woodbine said. "Let's me and you go count up how much candy there is. I've got an idea your Mama wants to talk to Adrian."

Marcus was about to protest but then he shrugged and let Mrs. Woodbine lead him away to the front hallway.

"Mrs. Woodbine always knows what I'm thinking without my telling her," Joyce said. "It's very strange."

"She learned it from the Blacks. Most of them practice voodoo."

"Adrian! It would terrify her! Anyhow, her church wouldn't approve."

"So what is it you want to talk about?"

"Take off that mask. I feel funny discussing it with a wolf."

Adrian pulled off the hood. His face was sweaty from being trapped inside the rubber.

"I was just starting to get used to it."

"Be serious, Adrian. There are things we need to talk about. Julie Eiger, for instance. I wouldn't pry, but it concerns me and your father too. We don't want any more trouble from Hank and Helen."

Adrian took a cupcake from a cellophane package that lay on the table and carefully removed the icing. The chocolate slab was so pliable it could be pulled off without breaking into pieces.

"You'll spoil your appetite." Joyce realized too late it was something mothers said to small children. "I hope," she went on, "you don't blame yourself for the Eigers' showing up when they did. Their timing was off, to put it mildly."

"Granddaddy was pretty cool." Adrian ate the icing and started on the cake. "It was like he forgot all about Uncle Philip."

"He didn't forget. And then when the call from Chicago came through sooner than anyone expected and the doctor said Philip was in no immediate danger, the Eigers suddenly seemed less important." Joyce giggled. "I'll never forget Hank's face when your grandfather asked him if he'd like to examine some rare book plates. Tropical birds, I think."

"I remember. By the time they left, Hank and Helen were shaking my hand."

"I suspect they would have liked to stay for dinner. Anyhow, the way you handled Julie was very impressive."

"All I did was take her out in the yard and walk her back and forth. I hate it when girls cry. I gave her a present but it was all damp from the rain. She said she'd put it on a radiator to dry out."

"She's very fond of you, isn't she?"

"Like when you hug a puppy?"

Joyce laughed. "You're right. I'll never say use the word *fond* again."

"I guess the Eigers aren't suing us or anything."

"Why would they? They've come round to liking you a little. Or else Hank's lawyer told him there was no case. Nowadays—." She was about to say that nowadays sex between an underage boy and girl wasn't an actionable offense, but she held back. It wouldn't do for Adrian to brush off the affair too lightly.

"Julie wrote that they might let her see me again during Christmas vacation, if she keeps her grades up."

"Is that what you'd like?"

"I don't know. I still think about her a lot." Adrian shot his mother a defensive glance. "It's not just because of what happened on the boat. There's lots of girls in school who'd do the same thing."

"You're pretty sure of yourself." Joyce was taken aback. But she was flattered by her son's willingness to confide in her.

"There's this new pill. If a girl is on it, nobody has to worry."

"I know all about the new pill. I wasn't born yesterday. I would have thought the girls you know are too young for that sort of thing." She paused. "You know, even if you take precautions, there are consequences. Suppose the girl feels she made a mistake. She might feel ... *used*." She was conscious that her words sounded like an article in the *Reader's Digest*. Adrian must think she was a prude. "I can't help thinking that you ought to have waited. Julie is—." She wanted to say "unstable" but she stopped herself. "Sensitive", she said finally.

"Is that a bad thing?"

"Not necessarily. A true Romantic feels things deeply."

"Oh, Mom."

It was hopeless. Joyce decided to switch to a topic she had mapped out in advance.

"Your father wrote that he thinks you can get into the University of Vienna. You know it's his alma mater. Philip's too. He thinks you can learn enough German in advance, if you put your mind to it."

"I already told you, Boardman's uncle can get us jobs on a ranch. It's called the San Joaquin Valley. Picking almonds, I think."

"Aren't all the workers out there migrants?"

"They need a few people around who can speak English. I'll probably learn Spanish on the side."

"What about after the ranch? You could come with us to Vienna and enroll in the university next fall."

"It's Val's future. Why do the rest of us have to go along?"

"I can't imagine leaving Val all alone. He's much too young."

"He wouldn't be alone. He'll have Granddaddy and Anna-Maria. He wrote to me that he met some rich kid who has a place in the country. He'll be happy."

"Families ought to stick together, don't you think?"

"All I know is, I'm not college material."

"The draft, Adrian … ."

He cut her off. "Maybe I'll enlist in the Navy."

The image of her son in a naval uniform didn't displease her. Her own father had been lieutenant on a troop carrier, towards the end of the First World War. If there was to be a new slaughter, the Navy was safer than the Army.

"In that case, you ought to be an officer. Annapolis."

"I wouldn't get in. You have to be at the top of your class or else know a congressman or an admiral or something. You can rise through the ranks though, and get to be an officer without going to college first. I checked."

Joyce sighed. "I just want you to think carefully. If you make the Navy your career … ."

"Who said anything about a career? It'll be character-building. Isn't that what Hank Eiger said in his letter?"

Joyce laughed. "We're taking advice from Hank, are we?"

"You worry too much, Mom. Anyway, I'm starving. What are we having?"

"Chinese."

"My favorite." He got up. "If I know Marcus, he's arranging the candy in neat rows."

"It's nice of you to go trick-or-treating with him," Joyce said. "Remember when the two of you painted Halloween designs on the shop windows? Yours won first prize. *The Ghost in the Grey-Flannel Suit.* Marcus was proud of you."

"I'm going to feel like an idiot ringing doorbells at my age."

Joyce giggled. "Little Red Riding Hood might answer the door." She suddenly felt unburdened. Adrian was right. She worried too much.

Walpurgisnacht

GENERALLY JOYCE VISITED her mother in the mornings, when Frieda's attention was less apt to drift, but tonight was special; a few trick-or-treaters might come to her house. Joyce decided to take Adrian and Marcus with her after supper, before they went door to door. She called ahead, so that Leni, the live-in nurse, wouldn't be taken by surprise.

Gran's house—more a cottage really—was only a block-and-a-half away. On the walkway stood a candle-lit pumpkin that Leni had carved in her spare time. Joyce had her own key to the front door. Before going inside, she reminded Adrian to leave off his wolf mask. She made a joke of it, alluded to the fate of the grandmother in the story. Marcus, she added, had better leave off his own mask too, in case Gran thought Senator Kennedy was paying a visit.

They found Frieda sitting in her wheelchair. A television dominated the living room, solid as an idol. The set was tuned to an evening news program. Frieda raised her head, startled. She looked, Joyce thought, ten years older than her seventy-two years. Not much was left of the fine features that fifty years earlier had reminded connoisseurs of a painting by Burne-Jones.

"Mrs. Michelson, you have visitors." Leni Kramer spoke excellent English, with hardly any accent. She got up from her chair and snapped off the T.V. One of the things Joyce liked about the nurse was that she addressed her mother matter-of-factly. There was no talking down or false enthusiasm.

Joyce embraced her mother. Adrian and Marcus took turns bending down to kiss Gran. A crooked smile passed across Frieda's face, Her hand fluttered in her lap. Did she mean to take hold of her grandsons? The moment passed.

"Has it been a busy evening, Leni?"

"Not a single child has rung the bell, Mrs. Lash. And I worked hard on the pumpkin!" Leni sighed. "Really, I was looking forward to it. There's nothing like it where I come from."

"The children might be afraid to disturb an old lady. Their mothers probably warned them."

"It would cheer up Mrs. Michelson. Your mother had not so much appetite tonight, I'm afraid. I was just going to clear away and bring dessert."

The remains of roasted chicken, baked potato and peas sat on a tray clamped to the wheelchair's handlebars. Joyce was grateful that her mother could still use a fork and drink from a glass. But the tray irritated her. Was it too much trouble to bring the chair up to the dining room table? She would mention it to Leni, but not tonight.

"I made *Apfel strudel*," Leni added. "There's enough for everyone."

Joyce smiled. "I'm afraid the boys have already had their ice cream and those horrible cupcakes from the Shopwell." No doubt, she was thinking, Leni was just as contemptuous of Cat Fat as Arthur.

"I can't eat another bite," Adrian said.

"What about it, Marcus?" Leni didn't talk down to children any more than to invalids.

"Maybe half a *Strudel*." Marcus patted his stomach. "I don't want to go overboard."

Joyce knew that lately her son had gotten into the habit of walking over after school, not for his grandmother's sake, but because of his friendship with the nurse. Evidently they entertained one another. Marcus never tired of Leni the way he grew bored with children his own age, and quite a few adults too, for that matter. Tonight, at the dinner table, he'd complained about his fifth grade teacher, Mrs. Roubini, who treated the class like babies and didn't know anything except what she got out of the school books; she'd even asked him, after he'd given an oral report on his summer vacation, if he spoke "Austrian" with his grandfather. Then there was the gym teacher, Mr. Strohman, who yelled so hard the veins on his neck stood out. Gym class, Marcus said, was the worst period of the day. He especially hated "bombardment"—children hurling rubber balls at each other—and Joyce knew he was ashamed of his awkwardness at somersaults and rope-climbing.

"A spoonful of vanilla ice cream on the side?"

Joyce watched Marcus nod and give the nurse an adoring smile. Leni was slight of build, with straight brown hair cut fairly short, a very pretty nose, blue eyes and a serious expression that broke into a merry smile when she thought Marcus was being funny. Joyce estimated she was about twenty-five or twenty-six.

"I'm sorry, Mrs. Lash. I forgot to offer you a piece. Shall I get you one?"

"I'd better not. I had my fill of rich food in Vienna. I must have gained five pounds and I haven't been able to lose an ounce since I've been home."

Leni's face turned wistful. "*Ja!* The food over there is not easy to resist."

While Leni was in the kitchen cutting *Strudel* for Marcus and Frieda, the visitors found places to sit. The room was furnished with pieces saved from the house in Buffalo. Marcus and Adrian sat on a sofa with wooden armrests. Joyce sat opposite her mother in a chair upholstered in velvet. On a cherry table next to Frieda's wheelchair stood a framed portrait photograph of Joyce's father, wearing a double-breasted suit jacket and a tie pin in the shape of a horse's head. The photograph, Joyce recalled, had been taken toward the end of his life. She would have been sixteen at the time. Henry Michelson had been older than most of the other girls' parents. He hadn't married until his thirties, and fatherhood had been delayed by war until the age of thirty-nine. And then, just one year after their Italian holiday ... .

Leni, coming back into the room and handing out dessert, brought Joyce back to the present.

"Your mother had a good day, Mrs. Lash. It was warm enough to sit in the front yard. That woman stopped and rolled down her car window."

"Oh? Which woman?"

"Mrs. Cloy. The Christian Scientist. I think she means well but she gets on my nerves. She shouts at Mrs. Michelson as if she's deaf. She says your mother lacks faith. We should pray together! And then she says her diet works miracles. No milk, butter or cheese."

Joyce sighed and shook her head.

"So few people even bother to say 'Good morning.' They walk right past."

"Amy Cloy is in my class," Marcus said. "She always brings a special lunch. They won't let her eat anything with dairy products either. Not even ice cream."

"I bet you give her some of yours when no one is looking," Leni said. "Eh, Marcus?"

Marcus blushed. "She sits with the other girls."

"When I was a girl, we always sat with boys we liked."

"That couldn't have been so long ago," Joyce said. Then she remembered that Leni had been born into the Third Reich. There must have been a picture of the Führer over the teacher's desk. Leni wasn't shy about expressing her disgust with Hitler, although the East German Communists came in for even more abuse.

"So, Marcus," Leni was saying. "No girlfriend yet? Better hurry and catch up with your big brother."

"Oh, I think he's a little too young still—" Joyce began, but Adrian interrupted her.

"He's got a girlfriend. Her name's 'Leni.'"

"Shut up, Adrian!" Marcus's face burned.

But Leni let out a peal of laughter. "Who knows? If I was younger, and Marcus a bit older?"

It seemed everyone had forgotten about Frieda. But then the old lady made a warbling sound in the back of her throat. Was she making one of her rare efforts to speak? Joyce got up and walked over to the wheelchair. She bent forward over her mother.

"What is it, Mother? Is there something you want?"

Leni interrupted without waiting for Frieda to answer. "*Ach!* I should have known. Excuse me, Mrs. Lash." She hurried Frieda away to the bathroom.

"You boys can go," Joyce said, "after you say goodnight to Gran. I'll stay a while longer. Mrs. Woodbine can take care of the trick-or-treaters at home."

"Marcus wants to hang around with his girlfriend some more," Adrian said.

Marcus gave Adrian a punch in the arm, not hard enough to hurt.

"Don't tease him, Adrian."

"I'm proud of Marcus," Adrian said. "He's getting an early start."

Leni, wheeling Frieda back into the room, giggled. "Never too early, isn't that so?" She'd apparently overheard the two boys even with the bathroom door closed.

"The two of you are impossible!"

Joyce worried that Leni was leading Marcus on. Was it usual for a young woman to harbor romantic feelings for a ten-year-old boy? No doubt in Europe such things were tolerated with a smile. Joyce wondered if she ought to put a stop to it. Apart from her brisk efficiency, there was something untamed about Leni. She came from a town deep in an enchanted forest; the locals observed a yearly *Walpurgisnacht* as protection against evil spirits. The woman had cast a spell on Marcus! Tonight of all nights she mustn't leave her child alone with a witch.

"It wouldn't be the same without Marcus's visits," Leni was saying. "My day would be dull otherwise."

"I'm glad he cheers things up. Just let me know if he gets to be a nuisance."

"Mom!"

It was rare for Marcus to get angry. But now his face was compressed with resentment. He ate the entire piece of *Strudel* with a vengeance. Her son, Joyce suddenly understood, was in love. Just yesterday he'd brought the nurse a bag of home-made cookies. In exchange Leni had given him a wax envelope containing a sprig of dried flowers, a keepsake she'd brought with her from her faraway mountains. Marcus had fondled the fragile blossoms. A gift from one lover to another! Even Mrs. Woodbine was taking notice. "Sometimes a foreigner has to be told how we do things over here," she observed sagely. Honestly, it was all beginning to be a bit much. But perhaps it would be best not to interfere.

The boys went up to Gran and wished her goodnight. Before he left the room, Marcus put on his mask.

"I almost forgot to ask Senator Kennedy!" Leni called after him. "Can we count on you to win?"

Marcus cleared his throat. "It's going to be a *hahd* fight right up to the *lahst* minute!"

Everyone except Frieda laughed. But another crooked smile flitted across her weary face. Joyce wondered if her mother had any idea whom her grandson was imitating. It didn't matter. It was a small blessing that she found him amusing.

On the sidewalk outside Gran's cottage, Adrian said it would have been better if the stroke had finished her off. What was the point of living a half-life?

"Mom says she looks forward to our visits, though."

"She says that to make herself feel better. She'll be relieved when Gran goes. Sad but relieved." Adrian adjusted his rubber hood. "I can't see a thing through these holes."

Marcus glanced at his brother's loafers. "You should have borrowed Val's boots. They look sort of like hoofs."

There were a lot of children on the sidewalks, now that it was past dinner time. A robot and a Frankenstein were heading up Gran's front walk.

"I hope Leni has enough candy," Adrian said. "Germans don't know much about Halloween. She might think it's okay to hand out *Strudel.*"

"Leni knows all about American things."

"Of course," Adrian said. "I shouldn't have doubted your girlfriend."

"Stop! I just like her, is all."

"Maybe I do too. Maybe I'm jealous."

"I don't believe you. Besides, what about Julie Eiger? Isn't one girlfriend enough?"

"Maybe not." Adrian hoisted Marcus onto his shoulders. "Let's ring the Pearls' bell," he said. "It's on Rocklin Road. Joanne Pearl is in my homeroom."

But it wasn't Joanne Pearl who answered the door. Mrs. Pearl informed them that her daughter was at a Halloween party in another part of town.

"You're the Lash boys, aren't you? It ought to be a donkey mask, Adrian, considering who's sitting on your shoulders." Mrs. Pearl tittered. "I must tell you that my husband and I will be voting for Nixon." She dropped some Tootsie Rolls into Marcus's shopping bag.

Heading up Rocklin Road, they were stopped on the

sidewalk by Robert Boardman. His fake upper teeth somehow drew attention to his bad complexion. He was holding a little girl dressed as a fairy princess by the hand.

"Nice monster fangs," Adrian said. "Where's the rest of your costume?'

"Look who's talking." Boardman bared his teeth. "I'm only wearing these because Laurie wanted me to." He glanced down at his sister. "The dentist was giving them out to kids. It was either monster teeth or a rabbit's foot on a chain."

"He gave me both," Laurie Boardman said.

"All I ever get is a toothbrush," Marcus said.

"Senator, there's something I need to talk to your brother about. Privately. Can you take Laurie for a few minutes?"

"I don't know if I should. She might get scared."

Boardman placed a hand on Marcus's shoulder. "You owe me. My parents are planning to vote for you. Even though we're Republicans."

Laurie Boardman stamped her foot, shod in a white tennis shoe. "You said you'd take me to all the houses, Robbie!"

"I will, Laurie. All except the ones Marcus takes you to. You know all the best houses for candy, right Marcus?"

"Well, I—"

But Laurie Boardman interrupted: "I don't even know who he is!"

"It's Adrian's little brother. You like Adrian, don't you? Marcus is even nicer. He gets straight A's."

Laurie Boardman waved her spangled wand. "Oh, all right then."

Marcus shrugged and took Laurie's hand. "Come on Laurie. We'll start with the Krafts. They always give out bags of M&Ms."

When they were alone, Robert Boardman guided Adrian to the front porch of a house with dark, curtained windows.

"They're out of town. Death in the family or something. We can talk here." He seated himself on the front steps and pulled Adrian down next to him.

Adrian took off his rubber mask. "What's the big secret?"

"You've got to promise not to tell anyone."

"Not even Mrs. Woodbine?"

"Funny. Just listen, okay? You remember I joined up with the Good Samaritan Club? My Dad made me do it, so I'd have something to put on my college applications. They assigned me to this retirement home, Crestview Manor. You have to spend time with one of the old people. Mine is Mrs. Huntress. She's pretty old but her mind is still sharp. She remembers the Spanish-American War. A soldier asked her to dance or something."

"So? Have you talked her into putting you in her will yet?"

Robert Boardman snickered. "Not quite. But she says she wants to help me get a start in life."

Adrian laughed. "What makes her think you need help? You're not a poor orphan, are you?"

"Not exactly. I just said my parents don't understand my ambitions. I said there was a great opportunity waiting for me in California after I graduate, but it would be tough keeping my head above water until the money started coming in. I said I have an uncle out there who knows a Hollywood agent, and the agent's sure he can get me into the movies."

"She believed that? Is she blind?"

"Not all movie stars are gorgeous. Anyway, it came up when we were in the activities room playing dominoes. The conversation got around to my future plans. I didn't mean to lie to her, but somehow it just came out. I was afraid she was going to laugh in my face or report me. But she didn't. She seemed pretty interested, in fact."

"How do you know she has money?"

"I can just sort of tell. She told me she's a widow, and her only daughter died a couple of years ago, and she doesn't have any grandchildren. She said it makes her sad sometimes that she has no one who needs her help."

Adrian patted his friend on the back. "Very nice. Until you get arrested."

"Arrested for what? I never asked her. It's all her idea. It makes her feel good. Anyway, she has this friend who's even older. They want to discuss my future over lunch at some restaurant they've picked out. I guess the friend is supposed to size me up, so Mrs. Huntress doesn't do anything dumb. I asked if I could bring another guest." He grabbed Adrian's arm. "I need you to be there, otherwise I'll get too nervous. Besides, you'll make the right impression." Boardman hesitated and then added, "I told Mrs. Huntress I'm bringing my twin brother."

"Are you crazy? We don't look anything alike."

"Fraternal twins. Just don't let on that we're not related."

"Let's say she hands you an envelope. How much, do you think?"

"I don't know. I get the feeling she's generous. Anyway, you're not the one she wants to help, so don't worry about it."

Adrian thought for a moment. "I don't get it. What do you need her money for? I thought we were going out to California. We'll get paid, won't we?"

Boardman shrugged. "It won't hurt to bring some extra. What if we don't like the ranch? We can quit and spend the rest of the summer in San Francisco. There's all these beatnik girls."

He stopped abruptly. He'd spotted Marcus and Laurie. In another minute the two trick-or-treaters were sitting next to their older brothers.

"It's been ten minutes," Marcus said. "More like fifteen, actually."

"I think we're about done here," Adrian said.

Laurie gave her brother a look. "Done with what?" Then she reached into her shopping bag and took out a packet of M&Ms. "Look, Robbie. My favorite!"

Cryptography

EARLY ON THE first Saturday of November, Joyce dreamed she was back in college. Except she was much older than the other students. Someone was walking toward the lectern. Philip Lash! Philip arranged his notes and surveyed the class, singled out Joyce and gave her a sardonic smile. Strange! She'd never studied math beyond high school. Now they were in her bedroom. Philip held her in his arms. His embrace was pleasurable but at the same time upsetting. They kissed … .

She woke up; it took her a second to realize she'd been dreaming. Well, she shouldn't be too surprised. Philip was due to arrive from Chicago in a few hours. Dr. Vache—the name made Joyce think of a cow wearing a white coat and a stethoscope—had given him his blessing. When Philip had called up to ask her if it was alright, he'd laughed and said the pills they were giving him must be working; he felt almost human!

Joyce lay in bed, remembering that Philip had spoken as if he was discussing some patient other than himself. It was unsettling to say the least. Of course, she couldn't refuse him but she would keep a sharp lookout. She could count on Mrs. Woodbine to provide a cheerful atmosphere. Their visits had sometimes overlapped before. Philip always called Mrs. Woodbine "Ruby" and insisted she call him by his first name too. His gentle teasing and good looks pleased her. Lately she appeared to have forgiven him for trying to take his own life and she was looking forward to his arrival, especially given her fascination with any sort of physical or mental disorder.

Joyce glanced at the bedside clock and snuggled back under the covers. Six forty-five. Another fifteen minutes before the alarm. She smiled. To think she'd been dreaming of Philip's hugs and kisses! It seemed she was as susceptible as Mrs. Woodbine. What was there about Phil? He was still boyish. The last time he'd visited, he'd looked much younger than his forty-five years. His dark hair (it had once been blond) waved around his ears and away from his forehead, like Ashley's in *Gone With the Wind*. His eyes were thoughtful like Wilkes's, at times bright with mirth. And then there was something appealing about his finely drawn lips, more like the mouth of a sensitive boy than of a full-grown man.

She smiled again. Asleep, she had enacted the impossible; awake, Phil made her uneasy. Moody as an adolescent! The attempted suicide frightened her, even allowing for its having been a sort of stage performance. She couldn't help being anxious. What was that line from the poem? *Once they are bowed so low for long, they never right themselves ...* . Well, the pills were apparently helping Philip right himself. She herself needed righting! She'd ask him for a few capsules, just to see; one or two couldn't hurt. If they did wonders, she might ask Dr. Hexter for a prescription.

She threw aside the covers, got up and prepared herself for the day. While she brushed her teeth, she remembered that since it was Saturday, Marcus would be able to spend the whole day with his uncle. They might take a long walk together in the woods that surrounded Running Brook Park, or even farther afield. They would have to leave the dog behind, though; Horace was laid up with a lame ankle from jumping off the bed. Really, the dog was becoming old and frail before his time! Adrian had somewhere important to go with Robert Boardman so Marcus would have Philip to himself. He'd like that. In the meantime, she would plan a special dinner for the guest. Mrs. Woodbine would insist on baking a cake. Philip would pretend to find it delicious.

At a little past ten, Philip arrived in a taxicab, set his suitcase down in the front hall, hung up his stylish sport jacket on a hook and greeted the family. Marcus questioned him about the overnight train. Adrian hung back a little and eyed Philip closely, curious whether his ordeal had changed him. Joyce noticed that her brother-in-law wasn't wearing socks. Catching her curious glance, Phil explained that no, he wasn't trying to imitate Albert Einstein, it was just that his laundry had piled up at the sanitarium and that, at the last minute, he'd discovered he didn't have a clean pair for the journey. Mrs. Woodbine threw up her hands, vastly amused by the confession. It wouldn't take but a minute, she said, to throw a few things in the washing machine.

When Philip planted a soft, warm kiss on her cheek, Joyce was reminded of her dream. Was it really so out of the realm of possibility? Arthur had been eager for his brother to pay a visit. Too eager! Did he expect her to heal his unhappy brother? In *Lady Chatterley*, crippled Sir Clifford had wanted Connie to be unfaithful so she could have a child. But Arthur was no cripple and they already had three boys. Still, Phil might be tempted. Weren't they going to be together quite a lot? Immediately she felt ashamed. Was she so vain that she must have her brother-in-law bewitched by her charms?

She covered her self-consciousness by going into the kitchen to help Mrs. Woodbine, who was busy making a late breakfast for the house guest. Philip followed her in and sat at the kitchen table. While Joyce and the boys watched him eat his eggs and bacon, no one said a word about the sanitarium. It was as if the awful event and its aftermath were forgotten or had never happened. While Joyce wondered if the scar was very ugly, Philip complimented "Ruby" on her robust health and asked about her family. Amazing that he remembered the names of each sibling, child and grandchild! Then he quizzed Marcus about the fifth grade and teased Adrian about certain things he had heard from Arthur: "Better have your adventures when you're young. You'll be less likely to mope around when you're an old man like me." Then he went back to asking Marcus what he knew about circles and ellipses, squares and trapezoids, and Marcus was forced to admit, shamefacedly, that his class was still on long division and fractions.

After breakfast Philip was anxious to stretch his legs. The boys followed him outside. Joyce stood at the kitchen window and watched her brother-in-law reach up for the Frisbee that Adrian sent sailing toward him. He missed, stumbled and fell back on the grass, laughing. His tie was off, his shirt tail loose. She had expected to find him aged or depressed. On the contrary!

The game continued until Adrian came inside to take a shower and put on clean clothes. He'd earlier hinted at a formal occasion—something about a "luncheon" arranged by Robert Boardman. He'd resisted providing any details, and she hadn't wanted to pry; he had a right to his secrets, after all. But since when did unpopular Boardman have a social life?

Philip and Marcus came inside too. Philip said he would take a bath after Adrian was finished getting ready, and Mrs. Woodbine said that there would be clean socks waiting for him in the bedroom. In the meantime, Marcus put on a record he knew his uncle liked: songs about banana boats and brown-skinned girls. The two of them sat on the living room sofa and sang along with the tunes they both knew by heart. Then they discussed the election that was only three days away, and finally Philip yawned and suggested they get started on their walk in the woods. Afterwards, of course, they would both be starving. Philip said he didn't want anybody to go to any trouble about lunch. Marcus said he knew several places in town where they could eat in private.

Adrian came downstairs dressed in a white shirt, tie and blue suit. He stood in the middle of the living room, facing Philip and Marcus.

"Do I look all right?"

"You look very handsome," Philip said. "It must be an important occasion."

Adrian blushed. "My friend Boardman has this friend who's bringing another friend."

Marcus giggled. "I guess you won't let Julie know about it."

"Tell me," Philip asked Marcus in a confidential whisper, "is this Julie the young woman with whom your brother enjoyed himself?"

"I'm not supposed to know anything about it. But I know most of it."

"I'm positive even Mrs. Woodbine knows all about it." Philip laughed and ruffled Marcus's hair. Adrian grinned sheepishly.

Joyce and Mrs. Woodbine came in from the kitchen, drawn by the sounds of Philip's laughter.

"Great Day in the Morning, Adrian!" Mrs. Woodbine crowed. "You look fit for a wedding!"

"He and Boardman have a date with two *femmes fatales*," Marcus said. It was a phrase he'd come across in the *Saturday Evening Post*. He only slightly mispronounced the French vowels.

"He doesn't even know what that means," Adrian said.

"I wouldn't be so sure," Philip said. "Marcus knows many things. Just this morning he was able to tell me the difference between an atom and a molecule. Not that he learned it in school, I'm afraid."

"Danny Nightingale explained it to me last year. His father's a scientist."

"We're all sorry that boy isn't in Marcus's school anymore," Joyce said. "I keep telling Marcus he should call him up for a sleep-over."

"*Mom!* I told you I don't want to!"

Joyce sighed and turned her attention to her eldest son. "Aren't you going to be too warm, Adrian?" She fingered his suit collar. "You ought to wear your Madras jacket. Or your old seersucker if it still fits." It was on the tip of her tongue to ask where he was going that required formal attire.

"You gave my seersucker away, remember? You said the Davidsons could have it."

"All five Davidson boys will take turns wearing it." Joyce gave Adrian an appraising look. "I must say you look very nice. I hope whoever it is appreciates the effort."

"I told you. Just some girls Boardman knows. Friends of the family I guess. I never actually met either of them. Boardman said to wear something formal. They're used to fine dining or something. I don't even know what restaurant he's picked out."

"How interesting!" Joyce pictured an elegant dining room. The Country Club maybe? One or both of the girls might belong to one of Garnet's old families. There were no Van Riper girls of Adrian's age, but maybe a Stellenburgh or a Warren. She felt a flash of curiosity. Really, would it be asking too much to know the girls' names? But on the point of insisting, she was distracted by the sound of a car pulling up outside the house.

"That's him. I've got to go, Mom, or we'll be late."

Joyce drew aside a curtain and looked out. A Fairlane idled at the curb. No doubt Boardman would have preferred his father's Thunderbird convertible. She could make out a dark suit and a bow tie slipping to one side. Weren't ties like that, held in place with a clip, for children? There was a large bouquet of red roses on the back seat. The lengths the two of them were going to! On the whole she was pleased. It would be just as well if Adrian branched out from Julie Eiger and started over.

After Philip's bath and change into clean clothes, Joyce gave him the car keys. Marcus and his uncle had decided to hike in the Old Forest, just outside the town limits. There were more interesting trees in the Old Forest, Marcus said, and chipmunks, wild mushrooms and berries whose names Philip would know. When Joyce handed over the keys, Philip joked that the doctor had put a special stamp on his driver's license: FULLY RECOVERED. Joyce forced a smile. She told herself it was no more than a ten-minute drive and the speed limit was 25.

Philip parked the car in a clearing next to a trailhead where a wooden model of Smokey the Bear raised a warning paw. Philip said it was strange that a bear needed to wear trousers and Marcus agreed. They walked side by side along a marked path. Sunshine broke through the trees and they tied their jackets around their waists. Garnet was experiencing an Indian summer, which would be the last warm spell of the year. From now on, even on sunny days, cold winds would whip up the fallen leaves.

"I hate when it starts to get dark as soon as you get home from school."

"Be happy you don't live in Chicago," Philip said. "The winters aren't fit for civilized people." He sighed. "In Vienna, one always felt cozy inside the houses and shops. In Chicago one never feels really warm. And the streetcars! Freezing! Your father wouldn't last a year there."

Marcus laughed. He was a little ashamed that he was enjoying Philip's company more than his father's. It wasn't the first time. What would it be like if Philip *was* his father?

Philip, as if guessing his nephew's thoughts, added: "You're lucky to have Arthur for your father. Kind and generous fellow that he is." He smiled. "So long as he doesn't push the Catholic business too hard. Rosary beads and holy water! Heaven and Hell! It's all a bit much for a young fellow like you."

"You sound like Mrs. Woodbine. But she believes in the Heaven and Hell part."

"Heaven and Hell are what we make of our home on Earth." Philip hesitated, as if remembering he was conversing with a child. "You understand what I mean, don't you?"

"I think so. But what about Hitler? Doesn't he deserve to be in Hell?"

"The Führer was sufficiently punished the moment he realized he had lost the war. As for the victims, yes, it would be nice to think God is making it up to them."

They walked along in silence for a few minutes. One of the things Marcus liked about his uncle was that it didn't matter if neither of them felt like talking. They would always find something to say sooner or later.

"Daddy doesn't actually force us to believe anything," Marcus said finally. "He says it's up to us to decide once we're grown up." He broke a dried branch from a tree trunk and switched in the air, so that it made a hissing sound. "Actually, I don't think Mom cares, and Adrian and Val say they don't believe most of it anymore."

"What about you?"

"I'm not sure. I mean, there must be a God. But a lot of other things ... ." He was imagining the giant crucifix that hung over the altar at St. Thomas's. He'd always found it hard to look at. Why had God allowed such a thing to happen? Wasn't there some better way?

"Last year, there was this father-and-son dinner at school. It was a Friday and the main course was spaghetti and meatballs. I was afraid Daddy ... my father ... would tell me I couldn't it eat it."

"Meatless Friday!"

"But he said it was okay. He didn't want me to feel embarrassed in front of the other kids."

"You see what I mean? Kind and understanding! My father, on the other hand, would have made me go hungry. Hermann simply didn't care what other people thought."

"He must have been pretty strict."

"The trouble was, Hermann has no conception of other people's feelings. Not my mother's. Not Arthur's. Not mine. How many times he told me I was a good-for-nothing who was never going to grow up to be a man like himself! And now that I'm a famous name in my field, he says that it's because he pushed me to make something of myself. Your father weathered the slings and arrows better than I did. Still, I imagine he carries around a few scars." Philip put his arm around his nephew's shoulder, then quickly took it down again. "I expect Hermann finds it much easier to be pleasant with his grandchildren. It's obvious you're his favorite."

Philip suddenly sounded so downcast that Marcus felt an impulse to take his hand. But offering a sympathetic hand was what adults did to children, not the other way around.

"I used to think, if I had a family of my own ... ." Philip left the thought unfinished. Then: "I'd have liked a little boy just like you, Marcus. Not that you're so little any more. You've grown up since the last time I visited."

"Why didn't you? Get married and have children, I mean."

Philip shrugged. "That would take a lot of explaining. I'm not sure I know." He gave a dry laugh. "Dr. Vache thinks I've gotten too comfortable being unhappy." He glanced sideways at Marcus. "Don't worry, I'm not going to try anything foolish in the future. It must seem like a terrible thing to you, what I tried to do." His voice grew softer, as if he were talking to himself. "I thought I must either throw the gun into Lake Michigan or get it over with quickly; either action appeared perfectly undetermined—the ideal opportunity to prove to myself that I had freedom of action." Philip let out a harsh laugh. "I couldn't stop my hand from shaking! I was pretty certain I was going to miss."

"But why did you want to do it in the first place?"

"Well, for one thing, I'd broken it off with a young lady. For six months we were 'in love', or so it seemed, and then it got so that I simply couldn't bear her company for more than five minutes at a time. It was her unceasing jargon that got to me. Everything became a symptom of 'neurosis' or 'maladjustment'! I suppose it was because she was studying to be a psychologist. On the other hand, it seemed to me that I'd never find anyone better. And the thought made me restless. I couldn't sit still. Couldn't concentrate on my work, couldn't sit in a cinema or read a book. Couldn't sleep! And then, I couldn't bear the thought of having to pretend to enjoy Hermann's birthday party." Philip patted his hip pocket. "I've disposed of the weapon since then. Just carry my pills. If you notice I'm becoming overly excited, Marcus, tell me and I'll take one of the purple ones on the spot. Doctor's orders!" He plucked a feathery blossom from the trailside. "Dr. Vache advises me to develop a healthy interest in something besides numbers and my own sorry state. What do you think, Marcus? Shall I set sail for the South Seas? Take up butterflies where I left off?"

Marcus felt unsure whether his uncle was joking or serious.

"I guess everyone needs a hobby," he said finally. "Adrian used to spend a lot of time in the basement with his model trains. He hardly ever goes down there any more. The wires and tracks and things are covered with dust. He might have to pack everything up and store it somewhere, if we move to Vienna."

"Yes, Hermann's written me all about that. I suppose it's a great relief to him that Val's determined to go into the business. Unusual in a boy his age. It must be a sign he's cut out for it."

"Maybe you could come with us."

Philip laughed. "I'm grateful for the invitation. Perhaps the university would take me on. I graduated from there, you know, like your father. But really, the city can't accommodate Hermann and me. We'd make one another miserable, even if we lived at opposite ends of town. Not to mention my step-mother! Just between you and me, that woman is not my cup of tea."

Marcus considered telling Philip about the slap Anna-Maria had given Gorlice. But that would only make things worse. Instead, he added: "We're supposed to decide by next summer."

"A real Austrian boy. Is that what you'd like to be?"

"I'm not sure. I like Vienna. But I might feel homesick." He pointed to berries growing by the side of the path. "What are those?"

Philip gathered a few into his palm and examined them. "They look like blackberries but they're not. They're a species I'm not familiar with. I wouldn't recommend eating them. Your mother would never forgive me if you had to have your stomach pumped."

"I thought you knew all the plants in Austria. And the butterflies."

"Did I ever tell you that I'm practically an expert on the *Lepidoptera* of the south of England? That's the scientific name for butterflies. When I was stationed there during the war, I collected them by the hundreds. I asked the locals and studied butterfly books and wrote down lots of notes. It helped take my mind off things that weren't so pleasant."

"It doesn't sound like a war. You never had to shoot at anyone, right? That's what Daddy said."

"The United States Army saw fit to put me in a tank. During training exercises, I drove while the other fellow fired at targets. It was so hot inside, you felt every breath would be your last. I doubt even Mrs. Woodbine's late husband, of whom we've all heard so much, suffered as much in the trenches. I must have sweated away ten pounds. But I was lucky. Before I was sent into action, somebody high up in the chain of command realized there must be a better way to put my brain to work. They shipped me off to England and sat me down at a desk, decoding messages. 'Cryptography,' it's called. They gave me a pistol, just in case German spies disguised as tradesmen invaded the office. No one seemed to care that I kept it afterwards."

"I'm glad you never had to kill anybody." But in the back of his mind, Marcus thought he would have been proud of his uncle if he'd shot a few Nazis.

Philip smiled. "I'm rather glad myself. But I'm beginning to feel hungry. What if we turn back and find a really decent restaurant?

Marcus thought for a moment. You had to be a member to dine at the Country Club. The next best place was Lapine's, where parts of the menu were in French. Marcus would have just as soon eaten a hamburger at the Family Diner but he didn't want to disappoint his uncle, who seemed to be in the mood for something fancy.

"Well, there's Lapine's. The onion soup is pretty good."

"Excellent. Don't tell your mother, but I'm going to order a drink."

Fine Dining

THE MOST POPULAR items at Lapine's were the lobster bisque and the steak *bordelaise*. The offerings hadn't changed much since Prohibition. Guests rarely went into raptures over the cuisine; on the other hand they rarely sent anything back to the kitchen. If the food disappointed, there were always the drinks and the wine list and, for guests privileged to sit near the windows, a view of the weeping willows and two disheveled-looking peacocks.

When Adrian Lash and Robert Boardman entered the lobby a few minutes past noon, itchy and uncomfortable in their suits, they found their two dates already seated behind a velvet rope, as though cordoned off for their protection. Adrian guessed the younger-looking of the two was Mrs. Huntress; he thought she looked about eighty. Her companion, who had very little hair on her head, might have been a hundred and looked as though her flesh might flake off at the slightest touch. Both women had dressed for the occasion. Mrs. Huntress wore high heels, earrings and lipstick, and her friend had on a pearl necklace. While Boardman introduced him as "my twin brother, Chad," Adrian stood at attention with a strained smile. What was he doing here? Boardman would have called him a coward if he refused. He might still make up an excuse: *I can only stay a few minutes; I promised to have lunch with my uncle who's visiting from Chicago.* But wouldn't it be cruel to put a damper on the "luncheon"? If Mrs. Huntress decided to give Boardman some cash, that was her business. She looked smart enough to take care of herself.

Mrs. Huntress seemed pleased with the roses Boardman handed her. It took some time for the ladies to gather their pocketbooks and proceed from the lobby to the table reserved for four. Mrs. Huntress managed well on her own but her friend, whose name was Miss Small (or perhaps Stall—Adrian couldn't quite make it out), leaned heavily on a cane. Boardman helped her into her seat while Adrian drew out a chair for Mrs. Huntress. A waiter carried the cane away so that it wouldn't be in the way.

"Isn't this a nice place? I haven't dined here since my late husband passed." Mrs. Huntress gave the boys a radiant smile. "And that was, let me see, nine years ago … . "

"First time I ever set foot in it," Miss Small put in. "Too high-priced for a schoolteacher's salary."

Mrs. Huntress tittered. "Let's not spare any expense! Remember, Robert, lunch is on me."

"Gosh, Mrs. Huntress, that's really nice of you. Chad and I would have paid our own way."

"Nonsense, Robbie!"

Mrs. Huntress explained that she'd asked Johnny, the Crestview Manor's colored caretaker, to drive them over; she'd made Johnny promise to wait in the car until they were finished. Of course she'd had to give him a sizable tip to make it worth his while and to make sure he didn't spill the beans. She hadn't told anyone at the Manor that she and Miss Small were meeting two young men.

"I didn't want a lot of nosy questions!"

"Sounds like you planned it just right," Boardman said.

They were drawing curious glances from people at the adjacent tables. Adrian tried to persuade himself that it didn't matter; for all anybody knew it was Robert's grandmother they were dining with. But what if somebody he knew came in? The Van Ripers dined at Lapine's when they were tired of the Club. Adrian felt his heart beating. Well, it was too late to back out now. Besides, he was curious how it would all end up.

"Do you guys want appetizers," Boardman inquired, "or should we go right to the main course"?

Adrian suppressed a hysterical laugh. *You guys!* Obviously Boardman wanted things to move along quickly. The sooner he got what he wanted the better.

"I think we ought to enjoy ourselves, Robbie." Mrs. Huntress gave Boardman a searching look as if she feared he might already be finding the old people tedious. She picked up the wine list. "Dr. Woodworth would kill me if I ordered a drink. He's my cardiologist. Besides, you and Chad aren't old enough, and I think it's rude to drink when others at the table can't join in."

"In a couple of months that won't be a problem. Chad and I will turn eighteen."

"They look like a couple of children, if you ask me," Miss Small put in. "It used to be that eighteen meant you were ready to stand on your own two feet and get a job."

If anything was going to wreck Boardman's plans, Adrian decided, it was this sarcastic old woman.

Mrs. Huntress pointed a fingernail, varnished with red polish, at the menu.

"Did you see, Willa? They have *Vichyssoise*. They serve it cold, you know."

"All that cream! You oughtn't to, Mary-Louise. Not with your ticker."

"Well, there's *soupe à l'oignon*."

"Onion soup, you mean. I suppose the English language isn't good enough. I guess I wasted my time teaching it in the high school."

The discussion of appetizers went on for several more minutes, and then it was on to the entrées.

"Prime rib *au jus?*" I wouldn't if I were you, Mary-Louise. That means it's going to be undercooked."

By the time the waiter had taken their orders—shrimp cocktails for four, broiled chicken for the ladies, and steak *bordelaise* for the boys—it was nearly one o'clock. A stainless-steel cart materialized, divided up into compartments. While a busboy in a white tunic distributed cottage cheese, black and green olives, radishes, celery, sliced cold beets, rolls, butter and breadsticks, Boardman began talking about the "big Hollywood agent" who was certain he had "potential." Not to sound immodest, but his high-school drama teacher had telephoned the agency and said he'd never seen such natural ability.

Listening to Boardman's fable, Adrian felt his face grow tight. He said nothing; no one expected him to contribute to the conversation. His presence was merely decorative. Boardman might as well have left him out of it.

"*Romeo and Juliet* had to be extended for five extra performances," Boardman said with an innocent smile on his face. "I hate to brag, but I played the lead role." Adrian searched

Mrs. Huntress's face for any sign of skepticism. Boardman as Romeo! Surely she'd see it was all a lie. But Mrs. Huntress only nodded and said she wished she could have been in the audience; it was her favorite Shakespeare play.

"Hollywood must be full of talented youngsters. Of course it helps to know the right people. What did you say the name of the agency was, Robbie?"

"It's one of the new ones. They already have big clients though. And a lot of up-and-coming ones." For an instant he hesitated. "It's called the Thomas Prescott Agency."

Adrian looked down at his plate to hide a smirk. Thomas Prescott was the name of the coach at Garnet High. Mr. Prescott had been fired last year for taking overly long showers with the boys' basketball team. It had been in the local paper.

"Thomas Prescott," Miss Small piped up. "Seems to me I've seen that name some place."

"There was a Tom Prescott who ran the town council back in the thirties, remember Willa?"

"That was someone else, Mary-Louise."

"If you say so, Willa."

Miss Small shot a hard glance at Adrian. "You're a very quiet young man. Aren't you interested in your brother's plans?"

"I'm sure Chad is excited about his brother's opportunity," Mrs. Huntress chimed in. "I believe he's shy. Such a good-looking boy, too! I'm sure he'll have no difficulty getting ahead with whatever he decides to do."

"Don't worry about Chad," Boardman said. "He's going into the armed forces."

"Oh, that's wonderful!" Mrs. Huntress turned to Adrian. "Which branch?"

"My brother Frank," Miss Small broke in, "fought in the infantry. Battle of Gettysburg. Frank was killed when he was seventeen-years-old and I hadn't been born yet."

Appetizers were brought and consumed and the plates taken away. When the entrées came, Miss Small sent her chicken back to be "cooked all the way through". Mrs. Huntress complained about the buttered Lima beans and mashed potatoes. Too much salt! All the same, both ladies cleaned their plates. Adrian was sure the smile on the waiter's face wasn't entirely innocent. He was mocking them! Maybe he'd figured out that the ladies were somehow being taken advantage of. What if he whispered something to management? Any moment now, a couple of plain-clothes detectives would walk up to the table.

But no lawmen appeared. By the time four different desserts were brought out—brownie *à la mode*, apple tart, *crème caramel*, coffee ice-cream *parfait*—the dining room had thinned out. Adrian checked his watch. Two-fifteen! He'd been sitting for over two hours. He glanced at Robert's face, which had turned pale and oily from the strain.

"Robbie, I've been talking over your situation with my friend," Mrs. Huntress said. "She wanted to see what sort of a fellow I was intending to assist. We were anxious to meet Chad too, of course! It's hard to believe that the two of you are both twins, you're so unlike."

"Everyone says that," Robert said. "Chad's the quiet one." He laughed nervously. "I guess I've bored you ladies, haven't I? I shouldn't talk about myself so much."

"Don't be silly. It's why I invited you." Mrs. Huntress put down her fork and wiped a crumb from her face with a napkin. "Robbie, I want to help you with your career. But I feel I ought to discuss it with your father and mother first. I couldn't possibly act behind their backs. Willa—Miss Small—agrees with me. Isn't that so, Willa?"

"You bet."

Boardman gripped the edge of the table. His voice trembled.

"You don't understand! They think I should forget about acting and go to college—or else enlist."

Miss Huntress looked taken aback. "There's plenty of time for all of us to sit down and discuss things. I can be very persuasive, you know. I'm sure a nice talk with your mother and father ... ."

"I'm telling you it won't work!"

"There's no need to raise your voice, Robbie. I'm not hard of hearing."

"I'm sorry, Mrs. Huntress, I didn't mean to shout."

Boardman looked desperately at Adrian. "I almost forgot to tell you, the agency wants me to fly out during Christmas vacation for a screen test. I want Chad to come with me." The improvised words tumbled out of his mouth. "My parents won't give us the money for plane fare. They don't believe in me."

"But surely—"

"It's like this," Boardman interrupted. "They can't afford it. And they're too proud to accept help. Especially from a stranger. It's their Scottish blood. The truth is, my sister's operation cost a lot more than we expected."

"Operation!"

"Her eyes needed straightening. She's fine now."

Mrs. Huntress pressed her hands to her bosom. "Thank goodness!"

"They'd only think I was taking advantage of you. They'd talk you out of it."

"Oh dear! I certainly don't want them to think I'm interfering!"

Robert looked up at Mrs. Huntress with beseeching eyes. "I thought it was going to be our secret."

"Well, I don't know … ."

But Adrian caught a gleam in Mrs. Huntress's eyes. She might not be wholly averse to subterfuge. For a moment no one spoke.

"I'm not sure I like secrets," Mrs. Huntress said finally. "I don't think I can be party to a deception. Besides," she went on, "wouldn't your mother and father wonder where you got the money?"

"I'll say I saved it up. From Christmas presents and … and part-time jobs in the summer. It would only be a white lie."

Mrs. Huntress tittered. "I don't think they'd believe you, Robbie. Plane fare is so expensive, isn't it? And you'd need some place to stay. If I were your mother, I wouldn't be able to sleep thinking of you in some flea-bitten motel."

"Even the nice motels don't cost that much. Eight, nine dollars a night." Boardman's plea ended in a kind of squeak.

"I'm afraid you and Chad would need a lot more money than you think. I'm sorry, Robert. You know I would have been so pleased to help." Mrs. Huntress sighed deeply. "It would have been no hardship for me. I would have been happy to start you off on the right foot. I have no one else, you see."

"She's got all those stocks and bonds just sitting in the bank, is what she means," Miss Small broke in. "Her daughter stopped speaking to her even before she passed. Nobody else to spend her money on, unless it's the Humane Society. Maybe you ought to ask me instead of her! Maybe I'm not the type who minds going behind people's backs."

"Why, Willa!"

Miss Small jabbed a thumb in the direction of her friend. "I'm old enough to be her mother. Ninety-two last August. But what's the use? I can't help anybody. I've got nothing in the bank except three twenty-dollar savings bonds." Miss Small turned her mouth down. Her eyes were trained on Robert. "Maybe you'd better find someone else to fool, young man. You and your twin brother, if he *is* your brother."

"Willa! What dreadful things to say!" Mrs. Huntress touched Boardman's wrist. "I'm afraid," she whispered, "she's very old and doesn't always know what she's saying."

"She's ruining it! Can't you see?"

It occurred to Adrian that he ought to get away before things turned ugly. But before he could think of a way to make a graceful exit, someone was tapping him on the shoulder. He turned around and found himself face to face with Uncle Philip and Marcus.

"I see you've finished your desserts. We almost missed you!" Philip sounded perfectly calm, as if encountering his nephew in the company of two elderly ladies was nothing out of the ordinary. But Marcus looked as if he'd been struck dumb.

"I had to tip the *maître d'* to seat us," Philip continued. "The room generally closes at two. But where are your good manners? Aren't you going to introduce us to your friends?"

Adrian, stammering, introduced the two ladies. He turned bright red, trying to think of a way to identify Boardman without giving away the game. In the meantime, Miss Small stared at Philip Lash as if he reminded her of some unpleasant person from her past. But Mrs. Huntress was anxious to dispel the cloud that had settled over the occasion.

"You must be the boys' father! I saw the resemblance between you and Chad right away!" She gave Marcus a smile. "The boys didn't tell us they had a younger brother. But then Chad is so reticent."

Philip laughed. "Twins? There must be some mistake." He tapped Adrian's shoulder again. "This is my nephew, Adrian Lash." He laughed again. "He's never been called 'Chad', so far as I know." He clapped Marcus on the back. "And this young fellow is Adrian's brother, Marcus Lash." He glanced at Robert Boardman, who sat frozen in his chair. "As for the other one, I've not yet had the pleasure of making his acquaintance."

Mrs. Huntress gave a gasp. Miss Small cackled. Mrs. Huntress reached into her pocketbook and withdrew a twenty-dollar bill and a ten. She placed the money on the tablecloth and gave Robert Boardman a sorrowful look.

"These are for the lunch, Robert. Tell the waiter to keep the change. If you do go to Hollywood, it certainly won't be on my dime. And please don't come to visit me in the future." She gathered herself together. "Come, Willa, it's time we went home. The Manor will be wondering what's become of us."

"As if they care!"

The two ladies rose from their chairs; Philip helped Miss Small get to her feet. A waiter handed Mrs. Huntress her roses and brought over Miss Small's rubber-tipped cane. Mrs. Huntress held her friend by the arm. They left the room fast, considering Miss Small's frail condition.

"Shouldn't one of you call them a taxicab?" Philip asked.

"Johnny will take them home," Boardman said.

"Johnny? The ladies have another admirer?"

One of the dining room's French doors was open partway to let in an unseasonably warm breeze. Releasing himself from his chair, Adrian raced towards it, nearly colliding with a little girl who was on her way back to her table from the restroom. Outside, he sat on the grass under a willow tree, facing a peacock. The bird cocked its head. Adrian loosened his tie and put his head in his hands. What would his parents say? Maybe they'd disown him. Mrs. Woodbine would say it was a low, mean trick. Julie Eiger wouldn't want to have anything more to do with him.

In the dining room, Philip shrugged and turned to Boardman. "I must say, your companions seemed well past their first youth." He smiled at Marcus. "Your brother has obviously been up to some new mischief. Really, his animal spirits are an inspiration!"

The waiter, a haggard fellow well into his sixties, collected the cash that had been left on the table cloth. Boardman told him to keep the change. The *maître d'* watched the proceedings with suspicious eyes. Boardman sat slumped in his chair, turned to stone by the ladies' gorgon eyes.

"Leave him to his conscience," Philip said. "We'll soon find out what it was all about." He ran his fingers along the back of Adrian's vacated chair. "All things considered, Marcus, it would be best not to say anything to your mother." Then, taking his nephew's hand, he let the *maître d'* lead them to a table laid for two.

Heir Apparent

BY LATE AUTUMN, Val understood Austrian newspaper headlines easily and could manage a good deal of the fine print. On a Thursday morning towards the end of November, he lay stretched out on his bed with an assortment of daily and weekly journals. He left *Die Presse* for last. The front page carried a picture of the Kennedy family, grinning as they posed outside their home on Cape Cod. Inside, there was an article about the launching of a new submarine: the U.S.S. *George Washington*. The sub's nuclear missiles, the outgoing president declared, were equal in destructive power to all the bombs used in the Second World War. Val smiled sardonically. Was Adrian serious about joining the Navy? It was practically the last thing they'd talked about. Suppose he ended up on the *George Washington*? Something would go wrong: the hull would spring a leak; the sea would pour in and drown the crew. Even if nothing like that happened, the claustrophobia would be unbearable. But Adrian said it would be an adventure.

He checked his watch. Almost noon. He'd woken up feeling sluggish and out of sorts; couldn't lift his head from the breakfast table. Hermann said it was laziness but his father said he might as well stay home and work on his German lessons. Instead of which, Val had passed the morning reading newspapers and magazines and watching news on the television set Hermann had recently acquired. Austrian television carried just one channel: the programming consisted of news, *Fußball* and a variety show that featured men and women in Tyrolean outfits. Still, T.V. was better than poring over books.

He felt entitled to a break. His father was making him study European history and geography on top of his German lessons. And then there were the hours he spent at the factory, watching Granddaddy make phone calls, go over reports and try to explain to his chosen heir how everything worked. From time to time, Herr Rausch, the factory manager, led Val from room to room and did his best to go over the manufacturing process. It was very boring but worth it. Some day he would be in charge of the whole enterprise. Let Adrian submerge himself under the North Pole and Marcus squirrel himself away in college. In another five or ten years, Hermann would be dead or retired. Arthur would have to defer to his grown-up son. It was how Granddaddy had planned it.

Val got up and walked over to the mirror over the chest of drawers. He smoothed his hair where the pillow had pushed up some stray locks. His face was still lightly bronzed from the summer and early autumn. On weekends, he and his friend Joachim took streetcars and railroad trains to woods where they walked for hours and swam in lakes, while the weather held. Afterwards, there were places to buy sandwiches and beer, and Joachim offered Val a Memphis from the pack he carried in his shirt pocket. When Val wrote to Curtis Blow, he always made a point of mentioning Austrian beer and cigarettes. Not that Curtis Blow meant much to him any more. When he wrote to his brothers, he mentioned neither of his new habits. He would have liked Marcus and Adrian to know he was doing things forbidden in America but his letters might be read aloud to Joyce, and Arthur had hinted that it would be best if he wrote nothing that might worry his mother.

Val leaned forward and studied his reflection. In a couple of months he would turn fifteen. He supposed he still looked a little soft and childlike. Still no sign of facial hair. On the inside, of course, he was older. Mentally he felt equal to Joachim, who was almost sixteen and nearly two meters tall. Achim teased him; told him he was built like a girl. Once, when no one else was around, he'd kissed him on the cheek. Of course it was only in fun. Still, Val decided it would be best if it didn't happen again. He didn't want anything to spoil the friendship.

Next weekend, he would ask Achim if he wanted to see Alfred Hitchcock's latest. The shower scene, the critics said, was so frightening that people felt sick and left the theater; after the movie, they would sit in a café for awhile and trade sarcastic remarks. Achim found that most people were a little beneath him. On one of their excursions, he'd invited a few friends to come along. On that occasion, Gretchen Trimble had twisted her ankle and little Gerd Cronbeck had volunteered to carry her. The two of them had shrieked and giggled all the way to the lake. Achim had seemed positively annoyed with both of them. Then there were parties where the older girls wore make-up and tight skirts and teased their hair up like Brigitte Bardot. Achim was a good dancer and liked showing off the latest steps and Val always made a point of dancing with one of the prettier girls, but in truth he was bored. He was sure Achim felt the same way. He liked it that Achim was a hard critic. The young aristocrat allowed that Americans deserved credit for their skyscrapers and automobiles, and of course they'd beaten the Germans, twice, but what about the way they treated their Blacks? Besides, Americans were a relatively recent addition to the history books, whereas the von Neuwanders could trace their ancestry back to a certain knight who had followed Frederick II on his crusade to the Holy Land. Every year, there was a fantastic family reunion in the mountains, with banquets, solemn speeches and oaths.

Next fall, if all went as Val hoped, he and Achim would be in the same school. But first, he would have to persuade Arthur that the *Bundesgymnasium* was a better choice than the International School. It shouldn't be too difficult, seeing as both his father and his uncle had gone there; Arthur had told him it was where all the ambitious Jewish boys had matriculated in those days.

A scraping sound from the back garden distracted Val from his daydream. He gave his reflection in the mirror a final glance and went over to the bedroom window. Outside, Gor-*litch*-ee was raking wet leaves. Val smiled. Just a week ago, the disgraced employee had come, hat in hand, begging for any sort of work. It seemed jobs were not so easy to come by as he'd imagined. Hermann had taken pity on him. There were always menial jobs that needed doing, and the new chauffeur—a cautious man called Herr Pflüger—was unfit for heavy work. Anna-Maria protested but not very strenuously. She was in no position to stand on her grievances. It hadn't taken her long to admit that indeed she had shut the cellar door in young Klara's face and that it had been a cowardly act of which she felt heartily ashamed. Her tearful confession came out at the dinner table; it was unbearable, she said, to keep the truth from people who loved and trusted her. Hermann had taken her by the hand and kissed her cheek. Who was there in all of Vienna, in those terrible times, who hadn't done something of which they were ashamed? Besides, it was understandable that she'd looked out for herself; it wasn't as if Klara was a blood relative. Arthur had looked down at his plate, embarrassed; finally he'd said something about letting bygones be bygones. For Val, the painful scene was absurd. What difference did it make? Obviously Anna-Maria wasn't going to be punished or sent away!

He watched from his window as Gorlice put down his rake, wiped his face with a handkerchief, picked up an ax and tested it on a dead branch. *Chop!* The ax made a dent. *Chop! Chop!* In another minute the branch was off. Anna-Maria came out to inspect the work. She nodded her head and pointed out more dead limbs. These days Anna-Maria was polite to Gorlice; she even brought him out bottled drinks—but nothing alcoholic. It was understood that she had privately made peace with her enemy; had even asked him to convey an apology to his wife. At any rate she and Gorlice were no longer at war.

Val straightened his shirt, laced up his shoes and headed downstairs. His head ached. Better not complain or Anna-Maria would want to take his temperature. He would follow Hermann and Arthur back to the factory after lunch for more training. It was important to keep up an appearance of enthusiasm. The prospect of someday being in charge excited him; what did he care whether the machinery produced boxes or soccer balls? In the meantime, it wasn't as if he didn't have free time. Last Saturday he and Achim had visited the Prater. Many of the attractions were closed for off-season but there were still a lot of teenagers riding bumper cars: working-class boys in leather jackets and girls holding big stuffed toys that their dates had won at the shooting galleries.

Val wondered if Achim envied the boys who had girls hanging on their arms. His friend rarely discussed the opposite sex, just limited himself to smutty stories and verses he'd picked up in school. He'd once mentioned a certain place in a shabby suburb where *Ficken* could be bought by the half hour. Some of his acquaintances had already been more than once; Austrian boys evidently grew up faster than their American counterparts and had fewer moral scruples. The most experienced boys bragged that the girls for hire were *frisch* but Achim said they were more likely *krank*. Suppose Achim suggested that they pay the *Hurenhaus* a visit? The thought of it filled Val with disgust.

At the bottom of the staircase, Val checked his watch again. Hermann and Arthur would be home any minute. He wandered into Hermann's study. On the desk lay an air-mail envelope from home. You weren't supposed to read other people's mail but he was curious. In the letters he got from his mother, she wrote about inconsequential things: Horace's trip to the vet and Marcus's dissatisfaction with his new teacher. She wanted to know whether he was "having fun," and whether he wasn't feeling "dreadfully homesick". If only she'd leave him alone! Why didn't she realize that it didn't matter to him if the family reunited? He got along with Granddaddy and Anna-Maria and he could get along without parents and brothers. But his mother might thwart him. It would be like her.

He examined the envelope. It had been opened with a paper knife and the contents placed back inside. Arthur must have forgotten to put it away in a drawer. Val felt he had a right to know his mother's intentions. But first he closed the door to the study and locked it.

Joyce's neat handwriting covered the fronts and backs of two pale-blue pages.

Sunday, Nov 13

Dearest Darling Art,

Well, we have a new president, and it's a nice change to have voted for the winner! Did you remember to mail in an absentee ballot? I can't quite believe it. Kennedy seems too good to be true. He says he'll appoint Bobby to be attorney-general. Two handsome Irishmen running the country! My father used to say Joe Kennedy made his millions off bootleg whiskey, and wasn't he on the side of the Germans before the war? At least we've been spared Nixon!

I don't have to tell you that I'm counting the days. It won't be much longer until Christmas and we're a family again, and we'll have months to talk everything over and decide. I wish I could tell you that I've definitely made up my mind about what to do. When I sit by myself in the evenings, I start thinking for the thousandth time about leaving everything behind and all of us starting over in Vienna. Is there such a thing as homesickness before you even leave home? I think about silly things like milkshakes and drive-in movies! And then when I think of all of us just continuing on with our current life and not being especially happy—even Marcus isn't his old self; he has no real friends in the fifth grade and absolutely despises his teacher—I think maybe it would be for the best to pull up stakes.

You say you wouldn't mind giving up the academic life. But for what? Spending your days at the factory? I worry that you'd be utterly bored without your students and colleagues. Do you think they'd give you a job at the International School? Oh Art, if only I didn't feel so torn in two!

I'm sorry to say that Frieda seems to be slipping. Dr. Hexter says she probably won't live through another stroke, even a small one. Leni says that when the time comes, my mother will probably go gently, maybe in her sleep. I'm sure Leni thinks that a peaceful death is the best thing that can happen when someone's so far gone that she can't get any pleasure out of life. I dare say she's right. She's very matter-of-fact; it's only her politeness that stops her from going around whistling, even with a dying patient in the house. No doubt she's already looking around for a new job.

Well, I have to resign myself to the inevitable. It will leave me with nobody on my side of the family. Did I ever mention that Frieda once told me—I must have been six or seven—that it didn't matter that I was an only child? She didn't want any more children, she said, since I was her best friend, and she didn't need more than one. Then she gave me her little smile, which peeped out now and then when I did something that pleased her. I think I must have spent a good deal of my childhood waiting for that smile!

Philip is still with us. He says Marcus is better for his mental health than the pills. Of course I'm happy to have his company, and Marcus and Mrs. Woodbine practically worship him, but I'm convinced the real reason for the delay is that he and Leni have developed an attraction for one another. Who would have guessed? Marcus, for one, is certain that the two are destined for a lifetime of happiness. There's no denying that Leni laughs at all of Phil's jokes and is always asking me about him. Apparently she doesn't care about Philip's "accident" or that he was in a sanitarium. Maybe it's because she's a nurse that she doesn't mind; or maybe she feels Phil's assets outweigh his liabilities; she's continually remarking what a handsome brother-in-law I have and, like all Germans, she's tremendously impressed by an academic title. Wouldn't it be funny if Philip finally found a wife, literally just around the corner? Well, she's a good-natured, honest person and Philip seems steady in her company. He told me last night that Leni is the sort of good, understanding creature he should have set his sights on years ago.

I have to tell you, though, that Marcus is looking very downcast. He'd gotten used to being Leni's favorite. Our son is such an unselfish, forgiving boy that he's perfectly willing to sacrifice himself for the people he loves. Still, he's a bit young to be heartbroken. If he's anything like Adrian, we won't have long to wait for more love affairs. Speaking of your eldest son, he has once again gotten himself involved in a predicament, although for the life of me I haven't been able to get to the bottom of it. I suspect Philip knows much more about it than I can get out of him. It seems your brother and Marcus happened to stumble across him and his friend Boardman (how I dislike that boy!) at Lapine's, of all places, with two dates whose identities remain a mystery. Apparently something happened to ruin the occasion and Adrian came home sweaty, frightened looking and practically in tears. Philip assures me that it was all some kind of misunderstanding and no serious harm was done. He's obviously covering up for his nephew! I haven't gotten any angry phone calls from distraught parents, so perhaps it's all right. But whatever took place has brought about a remarkable change in Adrian. He no longer has any interest in working on the ranch, just goes around with a thoughtful look on his face and talks very seriously about joining the Navy after graduation. I do wish, if that's what he truly wants, there were some way we could get him into Annapolis. I'll speak to Bob Davidson about it; he has a cousin who's a state senator, I think.

Well, I've left the best for last: We've been invited to Thanksgiving dinner at the Eigers! Incredible but true! Evidently Julie informed her parents that our family is suffering from a temporary breakup and they've gotten it into their heads that Thanksgiving will be a sad affair for the Garnet branch of the Lash family and that we need cheering up. Apparently all is forgiven. Really, you have to admit that these old-school Protestants are impressive when they set their minds to doing good. Of course I'm nervous about going but I can't see how I can refuse without seeming ungracious. Adrian and Marcus are excited, and so is Mrs. Woodbine. Phil has been invited too. I shall have to leave Frieda with Leni; she's far too weak to travel. I feel guilty about abandoning her at Thanksgiving but, as Leni puts it, "Mrs. Michelson won't realize it's a holiday." Really, these practical German women!

My love to everyone,

Your long-suffering wife

Joyce

P.S. I can't bear to leave Val with Hermann and only see him once a year! I don't want him to hate me, which I suppose means that in the end we'll all become good Europeans. Won't the college be furious if you resign and they have to scramble for a replacement?

Val's face grew warm from excitement. His mother was on the very brink of giving in! It would be even better if he was left with Hermann and Anna-Maria and Joachim and didn't ever have to go back home. Apparently that wasn't going to happen. But the important thing was that his future was secure.

He heard his father and grandfather enter the front hall. Val folded the letter back up and replaced it in the envelope. Then he unlocked the door and walked into the living room. If Hermann asked, he'd tell him he'd gone in to get some letter-writing paper. But no one noticed him coming out of the study.

Ten minutes later, the family sat down to the midday meal. While drinking her soup, Anna-Maria complained that Gorlice had cut away too much wood, after her warning him to be careful. Really, the man was hopeless! Hermann grimaced and waved a dismissive hand; Val could tell he wasn't in the best of moods. But he recovered his humor when Val told him that he was feeling better and that he'd watched a morning news program, and wasn't that a good way to learn the language?

After lunch, Ann-Maria cleared things away and retreated into the kitchen. Hermann said he might be coming down with a cold and was not going back to work after his siesta. Val, relieved that he wouldn't have to spend the afternoon at the factory, said that he'd study for a while and then take a tram as far as the *Gymnasium,* where he'd meet Joachim. Would it be all right if he invited him to dinner? After all, today was … . His grandfather liked it when he practiced his German at the table but Val couldn't think of the word for "Thanksgiving."

"Danke Sagen!" Hermann said. He made a wry face and began recalling a long-ago Thanksgiving supper at a boarding house in Tennessee. Dry fowl, starchy pie and everything too sweet or too salty!

Arthur brightened. He'd forgotten to tell them, Joyce had been invited to Thanksgiving dinner at the Eigers. Hard to believe! Hermann laughed and said that anything was possible with those people. Joyce, he added, had better watch out that it wasn't some kind of trap. Before leaving the table, he told Anna-Maria that, considering what day it was, she ought to make a turkey dinner. Anna-Maria made a face. Where on earth would she find a *Truthahn?* What about a goose in its place? Or a pair of ducks? Hermann chuckled and said that it was too bad *Frau Woodfein* wasn't on hand; no doubt she knew some good stories for the occasion.

In the end it was arranged that Ann-Maria would do her best to approximate the American celebration. Duck, red currants and her *Käsekuchen* would stand in for turkey, cranberries and pumpkin pie. As he left the dinner table, Hermann suggested Val use the desk in the study to work on his lessons. He often put it at Val's disposal.

Val went upstairs to get his history book, dictionary and notebook. Before coming down, he paused on the top landing and eavesdropped on the conversation down below. Hermann was telling Arthur how pleased he was that Joachim was coming to dinner. But it was strange, he said, that the von Neuwanders had never invited Val to either of their two homes. Were the Lasches not good enough for them? These old families, he said, liked to pretend they'd been anti-Nazi, but most of them had pitched in. Arthur answered that, at any rate, it wasn't fair to blame the younger generation; it wouldn't matter if Val was a half-Jew or a half-gypsy, the boys were such good friends. Hermann switched to English, as if he suspected Val was listening and wanted him to understand every word. The newspapers and the politicians, he said, went around pretending that Austria had been a victim. They seemed to have forgotten how people had grinned and clapped their hands when Jews were forced to scrub anti-German graffiti off the storefronts and cobble streets; how they had applauded the deportations and profited from the sale of confiscated goods.

Val peeked over the bannister at the two men down below. Whenever Granddaddy got angry with the Austrians, he flushed red. But then he always corrected himself; it was a mistake to harp on the past; to do so would only put more power into the hands of the enemy.

Father and son retired to their rooms for their afternoon naps. After passing his father on the staircase, Val closed himself off in Hermann's study. He opened his textbook and stared at the page he'd marked off with a scrap of paper torn from his notebook. Arthur had chosen the book at a shop near the university. The volume was meant for younger pupils. There were a lot of maps and pictures, and the vocabulary wasn't overly difficult. *Der Kaiser errichtete seine Hof in Aachen.* "The Emperor set up his court in Aachen." Well, that was easy enough. Val skipped ahead from Charlemagne to Bismarck. There was nothing about more recent times. Did the students at the *Gymnasium* have to learn about the concentration camps? Val rather hoped they did not. If people found out about his Jewish ancestry and that he lived with a grandfather who'd been persecuted, they might feel embarrassed. On the other hand they might resent him. Not all Austrian boys were like Joachim, who called Hitler a trickster who'd had the misfortune of being taken seriously. Hadn't the Jews, Joachim said, been trusted by innumerable emperors and noblemen to handle their finances? And what about great men like the poet Heinrich Heine, and Albert Einstein? If the war had gone on any longer, Achim said, Germany would have been smashed to bits by atomic bombs engineered by Jewish scientists like Oppenheimer—and it would have served them right! Val decided that what Granddaddy had said about the von Neuwanders wasn't true. Joachim had promised they would spend a weekend soon at his country place. Somehow a definite invitation had not yet materialized but Val wasn't in any great hurry.

Val felt certain that, once he was enrolled in the *Gymnasium*, if any of the other boys sneered at him, Joachim would take his side. Achim had a temper when he was aroused. He was in trouble with two different teachers; reports had been sent home and punishments handed down. Joachim promised Val that he would get even with *gottverdammt Herr Matthias,* and *vertrottelt Herr Münster,* although how exactly he would take revenge remained to be seen. It wasn't just grown-ups who inflamed him. Val had seen Achim push another boy up against a wall outside the school and hit him across the mouth. It seemed that the boy had insinuated something about Achim's friendship with the *Amerikaner.* Achim wouldn't go into the particulars but Val thought he could guess what the taunt amounted to. Best not to think about it. He closed his book, made some room on Hermann's leather-trimmed blotter and laid his head down on his arms. For the next forty minutes he slept soundly.

He woke up at three, went to the hall closet and found his coat. He still felt a little tired and dizzy but he was determined to see his friend, and by three-thirty he was waiting outside the gates of the *Gymnasium.* A cold wind had come up, wet leaves stuck to the pavement, and boys were turning up their coat collars. Val's spirits lifted when he caught sight of Joachim. His friend's face struck him as slightly unfinished, as if modeled by a sculptor who'd abandoned his work before it was quite complete. That rough-hewn quality pleased Val; he liked it that Joachim's features weren't as polished as his own.

He watched Joachim say something to another boy. The two separated and then Joachim came over and threw an arm around his shoulder. How many American boys would have done that? Curtis Blow wouldn't have been caught dead! Joachim yanked at his tie, pulled it over his head and crumpled it in his jacket pocket. His eyes looked bleary, and his nose was red at the edges. Val decided that although he and Achim had probably caught the same cold, it wasn't serious enough to prevent an invitation to dinner. But afterwards, Joachim would be too tired to take the streetcar; he'd call home and tell his parents he was staying overnight. Anna-Maria would set up a cot in the bedroom. The last time Achim had slept over, Val remembered, the room had overheated, and his friend had kicked off his blanket and removed his undershirt during the night. In the morning, he'd woken up and seen Achim lying there, still asleep ... .

"*Wovon träumst du, Val?*" Achim's voice sounded hoarse. Yes, he was definitely coming down with something

"Not dreaming. Just thinking. Can you come over and stay for dinner tonight?" Val started to explain the significance of Thanksgiving but Achim cut him off. He knew all about the holiday: Indians and so on.

"Okay, I come to dinner. Practice English." Achim reached into his inside jacket pocket. "Oh, I almost forget." He took out a pistol, nearly small enough to be concealed in the palm of his hand.

"Is it real?"

"I find her in our castle. *Auf dem Dachboden.* How one says it?"

"In the attic?"

"*Ja!* Papa forget he put her there. I borrow her."

Val wanted to ask whether it wasn't asking for trouble to bring a pistol to school. But the question was cowardly. Better to approach the matter indirectly.

"It looks old. Maybe it doesn't work any more."

"I give her oil and clean her good. Then I shoot two times, in woods where nobody walk."

"It's not loaded now, is it?"

Joachim laughed. He reached into his pocket again and withdrew a small brass and copper object. "You see?"

Val forced himself to laugh in return. But suppose someone found out? Joachim would be expelled.

"Cool. But better put it away. If someone sees ... ."

"So much you worry!" But Joachim replaced the items in his pocket and took Val by the arm.

"Wait what I tell you. That *son-uffa-beetch* Herr Matthias—"

Val interrupted him. "Where'd you learn 'son-of-a-bitch'?"

"*Of Mice and Men.* We read in English class. 'Steinbeck' is German name, not so?" Joachim grinned. "Hitler always say 'Roosevelt' is Jewish. Same as 'Rosenfeld.'"

"Crazy! 'Roosevelt' isn't Jewish, it's Dutch."

The boys walked arm-in-arm toward the streetcar stop, shivering. It had grown colder and a few tiny flakes were drifting down from a grey sky. Even without *Truthahn*, Val was thinking, Thanksgiving was going to be a great occasion.

Frankie and Eric

At the hour that Val and Joachim were sent up to bed after Anna-Maria's improvised Thanksgiving dinner, both boys suffering from bad colds and too much wine, it was still late afternoon on the other side of the Atlantic. At five o'clock, Joyce Lash was headed toward the Eigers' home in western Connecticut. Adrian sat in the passenger seat; Marcus and Mrs. Woodbine were in the back. Uncle Phil had declined the Eigers' invitation. A long, drawn-out dinner with strangers, he said, would send him back to the sanitarium.

"We should have taken the train," Adrian said. He glanced out the window at the slow-moving traffic. "It's getting dark already."

"You don't need to keep reminding me." It was true they would have made better time on the train. But then Helen Eiger would have wanted to pick them up at the station and drop them off again for the last train back to Grand Central. And then another train home! Better to come and go under her own steam and in her own good time.

"It doesn't matter if we don't get there right on the dot."

But she knew she was at fault. Traffic was bound to be heavy on Thanksgiving. They ought to have left earlier. Why hadn't they? Sandra Van Riper, who went to the city three times a week to be psychoanalyzed, would say she was subconsciously trying to get back at the Eigers. If that was the case, she was being unjust. Helen and Hank were apparently anxious to bury the hatchet.

"It's so hot in here," Marcus said. He loosened his tie: he'd chosen a real one, not the clip-on kind. "We're never going to make it in time for dinner." He rolled his window all the way down—his father wasn't around to stop him—so that a blast of cold air ruffled his hair and disturbed the fake flowers on Mrs. Woodbine's hat.

"Better raise it up some," Mrs. Woodbine said.

Marcus rolled the window all the way back up. "Is that far enough?"

"Someone's acting kind of ugly." Mrs. Woodbine shifted her bulky frame; her clothing rustled under her winter coat. She was wearing a formal dress: dark blue with a white collar. On her head was a black straw hat decorated with artificial blossoms.

"I expect that turkey's nowhere near done yet," Mrs. Woodbine went on. She winked at Marcus and poked him in the rib. "I know someone who wants the wishbone!"

Marcus ignored her. He *did* want to pull the wishbone. But then everyone would watch and think it was cute.

"I hate the wishbone," he said finally.

Adrian yawned, leaned forward and checked his reflection in the rear view mirror. The pimple he'd discovered on his chin when he'd gotten out of the shower was still there. He turned around and faced the back seats. "There won't be any turkey. They're making a roast pig. You know, with an apple in its mouth."

"Oh, My Land, Adrian!"

"He's just teasing," Joyce said.

"Julie said there was going to be a special dessert," Adrian continued. "*Floating Island* or something." He wondered if Helen Eiger was a good cook. Maybe they had someone do it for them. He pictured a big Swedish woman in an apron; no, more likely a black servant. A black cook might be as good as the one at summer camp—Odell, who was famous for his Indian pudding, southern fried chicken and fresh corn. His mother, on the other hand, only went through the motions. Her heart wasn't in it; it was no wonder she always wanted to eat out. Well, the Lashes wouldn't be eating at Lapine's any time soon. Marcus had let slip, in his mother's hearing, that one of the women at the restaurant looked about a hundred years old and the other one wasn't much younger. Uncle Phil had dropped more hints. Adrian had confessed, finally, that Boardman had wanted to "borrow" some money from a lady he'd met at the old age home. Nothing, he told his mother, had come of the scheme. All the same, Joyce was furious. She'd never liked Boardman and now she knew why. Suppose they got an angry phone call? Philip had given away Adrian's last name and there was only one "Lash" in the phone book. Suppose the police got involved! Maybe she ought to warn Frank and Gail Boardman.

But the days passed and there was no phone call from either Crestview Manor or the police station. Joyce's fears subsided into relief. But Mrs. Woodbine wagged her head and said she'd never dreamt Adrian could sink so low.

Adrian checked his watch. Ten minutes to six. They had left the parkway and were driving past lighted-up billboards: a bear relaxing on a mattress, and then an exterminator in a top hat, preparing to pound a rodent with a sledge hammer. His mother wouldn't let him drive; it was her way of punishing him. Adrian tried to focus his thoughts on Julie Eiger. The strange thing was that he couldn't remember what she looked like exactly. Even the sex part wasn't all that clear in his mind. He imagined her in an apron, helping her mother get ready for the Thanksgiving dinner. Maybe he'd be attracted to her all over again. Or maybe not. They'd written each other a few times and talked on the phone. He'd had to strain to think of things to say. She always asked him if he'd made any new friends; obviously she was dying to know if he'd latched on to some other girl. He didn't want her to be unhappy. He told her that the girls in his high school, even the pretty ones, were boring. This wasn't strictly true; he'd gone on a few dates with a girl in the eleventh grade, Rebecca Harmer. They'd gotten as far as kissing in a movie theater. Then he'd put his hand on her thigh; felt her blouse. Rebecca Harmer had pulled away, offended. They hadn't spoken to one another since then. There was no reason why he shouldn't start over with Julie, if that's what they both wanted.

Thanksgiving dinner! Adrian foresaw that Helen Eiger would make polite conversation; maybe compliment him on his new herringbone jacket. Meanwhile she'd be wondering all the time if he and Julie had a future together. Hank Eiger would examine him from across the table, as if he were a specimen in a lab. Mrs. Woodbine would talk too much. And Marcus would get to pet the horses, and see the owl that Julie had said her father had recently acquired that lived in an outdoor cage. Apparently there were going to be other guests, including ten-year-old twins—real ones, this time. But Marcus was bored by children his own age. What his brother needed, Adrian decided, now that Leni was out of the picture, was a new girlfriend; someone old enough to appreciate him. Poor Marcus! He might at this very moment be imagining Uncle Phil and Leni on the couch in Gran's living room. Or would they wait until Gran was asleep and then sneak into Leni's bedroom and close the door? Mrs. Woodbine didn't think it was right. He'd overheard her talking it over with his mother: "I'd sure feel better, Mizz Lash, if Philip kept us company instead of staying behind with that gal." His mother said it wasn't her business what two grown-up people did in private but Adrian was sure she disapproved. If only Uncle Phil had come with them! He would have treated the whole occasion as a huge joke.

Adrian checked his watch again. They were supposed to have been there at five. Already an hour late. Traffic was building up again.

"You boys are acting like you're in the dumps," Mrs. Woodbine said. "Let's all have some fun. Who wants to play *I'm Hid?*"

"I want to play," Marcus said. "I want to be *it*." He sounded more like his usual self.

Mrs. Woodbine patted his knee. "That's right. We always start with the youngest and work our way up."

Mrs. Woodbine had played *I'm Hid* with her brothers and sisters half a century ago. The person who was *it* could be any size, anywhere in the world. The other players took turns narrowing things down with yes-or-no questions. A "yes" meant you could ask another question. A "no" meant it was the next person's turn.

Joyce asked the first question: "Are you in North America?" The questions dragged on until Adrian established that Marcus was hiding in the car radio, right behind the volume button. After that, the other three took turns being *it*. Last to go was Mrs. Woodbine. Marcus eventually located her inside a salt shaker in the shape of a lobster claw, behind the glass panels of her curio cabinet. He remembered Mrs. Woodbine's curio cabinet quite clearly, from the time they'd stayed overnight during a visit to "the nation's capital". It had been Arthur's idea to save on a hotel room. Mrs. Woodbine would gladly have let them stay for free but his father had insisted on giving her a few dollars.

Now they were driving on an unlit, two-lane highway bounded by a wooded landscape. There were few cars on the road. Rushton's single traffic light came and went. Mrs. Woodbine's eyes grew anxious and she craned forward.

"Shouldn't we be at our turn-off by now, Mizz Lash?"

Joyce slowed and pulled over to the side. She picked up a bill from the gas company, on the back of which she'd written directions.

"There's supposed to be a crossing next to a stand that says *Farm Fresh Produce*. I haven't see anything like that yet."

"I declare! Do you suppose we missed it in the dark?"

"I ought to be driving," Adrian said.

"Just be thankful you're not in the county jail." Joyce was about to remind her son that swindling the elderly was a crime, then thought better of it. They were supposed to be in a holiday mood. But Mrs. Woodbine shook her head. County jail! She'd barely been able to look Adrian in the eye, once she'd learned of his wickedness. Lord save us! Playing a prank like that on old folks! Worse than a prank, a sin! But she wouldn't write the sinner off as irredeemable. A few years in the service would straighten Adrian out. It had worked on her own John-Wesley, who'd been wild at Adrian's age.

"I think maybe we did pass it." Joyce made a U-turn and headed back in the direction from which they'd come. Mrs. Woodbine strained to see if there was anything outside that made the least bit of sense.

"There it is!" Adrian pointed to a broken-down stand that stood at one corner of a crossing. The weather-beaten structure looked as if it might collapse in a stiff wind. Joyce tried to imagine it in summer, stocked with eggs, vegetables and fruit.

"I don't see any sign. It should say *Farm Fresh Produce*.

"Maybe the paint wore off," Marcus suggested.

"Wouldn't the Eigers have known that?"

"Maybe they got mixed up. Like the time Hank gave us the wrong hotel."

"I suppose we have to try. Let me see." Joyce consulted her directions. "It says turn right at the crossroads, but we're pointing in the opposite direction, which means we turn left."

The narrow road they turned onto was deeply rutted. Marcus pointed out a pair of dark shapes: cows bedded down for the night.

Mrs. Woodbine's eyes grew rounder. "These old roads," she said, "just keep a'going."

"Look for a mailbox with the number 160. The Eigers live at 160 Wallford Road."

"I didn't see any sign for Wallford Road at the turn-off."

"I don't know, Marcus. Maybe it fell down." Joyce gave a short laugh. "Maybe they never put up a sign in the first place. Maybe you're just expected to know."

"I think we took the wrong road."

"Relax, Marcus," Adrian said. "We're not in Darkest Africa."

The car bumped and swerved on a rut. Mrs. Woodbine felt her heart beating. Suppose they broke down? There might be convicts on the loose, escaped from the state pen. But then she saw something that made her jump forward.

"There it is, on your left!" Mrs. Woodbine screamed. "A hundred-sixty! My Land, we just about passed her by!"

Joyce turned into a long driveway She had expected something white and colonial, with eaves, shutters and windows already hung with Christmas wreaths. But the house was all plate glass and rugged materials, and the only reference to winter holidays were tiny white lights strung around a sculpture of a female body that appeared to be missing parts of its anatomy. In the distance, Joyce could make out a tennis court and a stable—unless it was a guest house.

She parked beside a convertible sports car.

"An MG!" Adrian said. "The Eigers are cooler than we thought."

Joyce opened the car door and stepped into the night air. Wonderful, after having been cooped up for hours! But it was strange that there were no other cars in the driveway. Had all the other guests been sensible and taken the train?

A tall, striking woman with Nordic features answered the

doorbell. She wore a long wool skirt and a vest woven in rich earth tones. She stood bewildered for a moment. Then she let out a musical laugh.

"You must be the Kettelsons! Eric's been dying for us get to know each other." But her eyes looked uncertain.

"I'm afraid we're not the Kettelsons. I'm so sorry." Joyce pushed a strand of loose hair from her forehead, then caught herself. Why was she apologizing? Were these Kettelsons, whoever they were, more deserving than she and her children? "We're the Lashes," Joyce went on. "We met Helen and Hank on the boat. They were kind enough to invite us."

"Helen and Hank?" The woman extended a hand; the wrist was adorned with copper and silver bracelets. "There must be a mistake. I'm Frances Brainard. Won't you come in out of the cold?"

Joyce felt tears welling up behind her eyeballs. Marcus was right; they'd taken the wrong road. It was so bitterly cold on the doorstep and she must look like a fool! She wanted to run back to the car without another word. But instead she stepped across the threshold.

"Thank you," she managed to get out. "I'm so sorry to intrude. We were looking for 160 Wallford Road."

"I'm not sure where that is exactly. I'm almost a stranger here myself. My husband and I drive out on weekends and holidays. Our work keeps us in town." Frances touched Joyce's arm. "You've come to 160 Mill Pond Road. The right number at least! I imagine you'll want to use the telephone."

Frances took their coats and dropped them on a bench, then led the way to a big room with a beamed ceiling and a stone fireplace, where several people were gathered with drinks in their hands. Then she introduced her husband and explained the situation to him. Eric Brainard made a sympathetic face, uttered some reassuring words, and escorted Joyce to the telephone in his den. Frances made the boys and Mrs. Woodbine sit down opposite the fire. She was sure they must want something to "take the edge off."

"Oh, we're fine!" Mrs. Woodbine said. "We'll just wait until we figure out how to get to where we're going." She sounded uncharacteristically shy. She was doing her best to avoid looking at the very dark-skinned man and the young blond woman, evidently a couple, who were eyeing her and the boys.

"We sure hope we aren't holding up your turkey!" Mrs. Woodbine got out.

Frances Brainard laughed. "We won't sit down to eat until seven-thirty at the earliest. And there won't be any turkey! It's going to be partridges all the way. Eric shot the poor things this morning." She found a bottle and poured wine into the black man's glass. "But I'm rude! I've not made introductions. This is Lawrence Drury, the writer, and his very good friend, Vera Solotorovsky. And you are ... ?"

"Ruby Woodbine. Pleased to meet you all. And these two are Adrian and Marcus."

"You forgot to tell them that Vera's a writer too, Frankie," Lawrence Drury said.

Frances wagged a finger at her guest. "You're trying to pick a fight, Larry! I was getting around to that."

"He's just teasing you," Vera Solotorovsky said. Her voice was low, almost like a man's.

"I love the unexpected," Frances said. "Everything would be boring otherwise. And Larry here wouldn't have anything to write about."

The writer raised his glass. "I'm delighted to meet you two boys, and your grandmother."

Mrs. Woodbine's mouth tightened. Adrian was about to correct the mistake, but then he decided not to. Let people think whatever they wanted.

"Get them something to drink, Frankie!" Lawrence Drury boomed.

"Of course! What'll it be?"

Adrian felt he would like something alcoholic; he had a feeling Mrs. Brainard wouldn't object. But Marcus spoke up first.

"Would it be okay if I had a Coke?"

"I'd like a beer," Adrian said.

Mrs. Woodbine shot Adrian a grim look, but Mrs. Brainard acted as if both boys had chosen wisely. She walked over to a bookshelf and pressed a button. A moment later a foreign-looking woman appeared.

"Sophia, be an angel and bring two Coca-Colas with ice for Marcus here and his grandmother. And a cold beer for his brother." She winked at Adrian.

The servant nodded and went off to fetch the refreshments. She returned a moment later with a tray, just as Joyce re-entered the room, followed by Eric Brainard.

"The mystery is solved," Eric announced.

"Wallford Road is farther than we thought," Joyce said. She laughed nervously. "We shouldn't have turned around when we did." Her family, she noticed, had been given drinks. Adrian was holding a beer. Why did she feel so deeply embarrassed? These people were simply being hospitable.

She extended her hand to Frances. "I'm Joyce Lash. You and Mr. Brainard have been life savers."

"Our privilege," Eric broke in. "And please, call us Eric and Frankie." He went over to his wife and put a hairy paw on her shoulder. "I much prefer Frankie to Frances. I won't let our friends call her anything else!" His wide, stooped shoulders, beak nose and tangled eyebrows reminded Joyce of a bird of prey. The collar of his fisherman's sweater might as well have been a circlet of feathers. How old was he? Sixty? Seventy? Eighty? It was hard to tell. His craggy face and upswept grey hair gave no definite clue.

"What about the Eigers?" Adrian said. "Are they mad we're late?"

"Oh, I don't think so." Joyce forced a smile. "They have other guests to keep them company. Apparently the turkey's not out of the oven yet. I should have put you on the phone with Julie."

She was aware that Eric Brainard was watching her with a benevolent smile. His teeth, Joyce noticed, were long and ivory colored.

"I insist you have a drink, Joyce Lash, before you resume your pilgrimage. Something to fortify you against the cold. Besides, I have a feeling we've just begun to get acquainted."

"Oh no, I couldn't! We should be on our way. Our hosts

must be wondering ... ." But Joyce suddenly felt that this was one of those rare moments when a drink would do her a world of good. She glanced at the bottles lined up on a side board.

"It's okay, Mom," Adrian said. "I can drive the rest of the way. One beer won't make any difference."

"All right then. A glass of white wine, if it's not too much trouble."

Later, after she was home in Garnet, Joyce decided that she had never seen such good taste, such understated elegance. Nothing fussy or shabby, and on the other hand nothing that proclaimed its richness too loudly. Eric Brainard turned out to be an architect and Frankie was an interior decorator. They shared an office suite in the city. The two of them had planned and supervised the execution of every inch of their country house: tongue-and-groove woodwork, Danish tables and chairs, hand-woven tapestries and works of distinguished painters and sculptors. No, the hollowed-out woman on the front lawn wasn't a Henry Moore but when Frankie mentioned the name of the sculptress, Joyce remembered colored photos in an exhibition catalog in Sheila Rath's book shop. And then the guests! Lawrence Drury was the main attraction: Joyce had read his stories in *The New Yorker*. She remembered one of them in particular, about a colored child's first visit to a museum. While she sat sipping her wine, more people arrived: first a literary agent and his handsome, spoiled-looking young male companion; then a married violinist and horn player, both members of the Philharmonic; and finally two neighbors: a young couple who made hand-blown glass in their converted water mill.

But it was the Brainards' two children who captivated her. They came gliding in so gracefully! The girl was enrolled at the Rhode Island School of Design; the boy, a year younger, was in his first year at Yale. He, Jonathan Brainard, wore soft flannels and an olive-green turtle-neck; the girl, Olivia, had on a camel-hair sweater and a black wool skirt. Joyce saw that Adrian couldn't keep his eyes off her. She watched as the girl came over and sat next to him on the couch. How had she managed it so naturally, without seeming either bashful or forward? But then both children looked so self-confident and quietly amused by the unexpected company. Soon Olivia and Adrian were having a conversation, too low for her to make out what they were saying.

Jonathan Brainard wasn't as good-looking as his sister—he had a beak nose like his father—but his face, behind horn-rimmed eyeglasses, was sympathetic. Jonathan, she saw, was treating Marcus like someone his own age. He wanted to show him the moon up close; evidently there was an expensive telescope in his bedroom window. The two of them disappeared up the staircase.

Of course it was unconscionable to linger so long, knowing she was keeping the Eigers waiting. More than once she caught Mrs. Woodbine pointing to her wristwatch. The poor woman, Joyce thought, hardly knew what to do with herself; no doubt her instinct was to retreat to the kitchen and lend a hand. Lawrence Drury and his companion made her all the more uncomfortable. Joyce thought it was high time Mrs. Woodbine faced up to her prejudices.

Somehow she kept putting off her departure. It wasn't until well after seven o'clock that she gathered her dependents and made her exit. But first Eric Brainard insisted on an exchange of addresses and phone numbers. "We'll stay in touch, won't we?" He looked straight at her with his raptor's eyes. Joyce felt herself blush. The dominating type. Was he laying the groundwork for a seduction or did he merely like to collect strangers? What did his wife think? Apparently his manner didn't bother her in the least. Frankie Brainard was cordial: "We must meet your husband and your other son, once they return from abroad." Before Eric closed the front door all the way, Joyce overheard him say to his wife: "Imagine leaving a beautiful woman like that all by herself ... ." She caught the sound of Frankie's tinkling laughter.

Fifteen minutes later they were at the front door of a comfortable but quite ordinary house. Joyce summoned up her courage. She must think of an excuse.

Julie Eiger answered the door bell. Joyce was taken aback. The slender girl of the S.S. *Columbus* had filled out. She must,

Joyce calculated, have gained ten or fifteen pounds. While the girl was welcoming Marcus, Joyce glanced at Adrian long enough to gauge his reaction. He looked stunned for an instant but then he smiled and, blushing, let Julie kiss his cheek. Joyce felt proud of him. A gentleman after all! She could hear a hubbub from within the house and there was a smell of turkey and a wood fire. Helen Eiger was heading toward her. A couple of small boys raced down the hall and clung to Julie. Cousins perhaps, or children of old friends.

She would tell them, Joyce decided, that she'd taken a wrong turn and gotten stuck. "Those awful ruts!" Nobody would believe the story but what did it matter? The Eigers were insignificant compared with the Brainards.

Reckless Endangerment

AROUND MIDNIGHT ON the evening of Anna-Maria's *Danke Sagen,* the weather in Vienna turned much colder. The following morning, a little after eight o'clock, Franz Gorlice jumped down from a streetcar and headed toward the Lasch house. He turned up his collar and tried not to mind the early hour and the freezing temperature. It wasn't a real job, this business of doing odds and ends; any day now, something better was bound to come along. In the meantime, he couldn't very well sit around while poor Klara spent every night cleaning and polishing in one of the new office buildings. He recalled the look on Frau Lasch's face when he'd come begging for any kind of work. There was gladness in her eyes; no doubt she thought taking him back made up for the wrong she'd done to both of them. His first day back on the job she'd approached him in the back yard and offered a sniveling apology. He accepted her olive branch for the sake of the cash he was going to receive at the end of the week. But he'd drawn a line when she suggested he bring his wife to work one day, so that she might ask for Klara's forgiveness in person. As if poor Klara wanted everything dug up and dragged into the light of day! She was angry with him as it was, for having blabbed her secret.

He'd promised to show up extra early today. There were a thousand things, Frau Lasch said, that needed attending to. Yesterday she'd been in a flutter, planning a celebration in honor of some American holiday that involved a great deal of food, and she'd scarcely paid attention to his comings and goings. He'd been able to relax. But today she'd be on top of him. *Ach!* It was more than a man could bear! And then the grandson, Val, hanging around with a sarcastic smile on his face. The little hypocrite was being groomed to take over the family business. No doubt he'd be rich in not-too-many years. The other two ... *Herr Markus* and *Herr Adrian* ... were nice boys who would stick up for you in a crunch.

Gorlice halted opposite Schaffgasse 17, pressed the button on the front gate and waited for an answering buzz. Frau Lasch met him at the door. The boss, she informed him, had come down with a head cold and wasn't going in to work; Pflüger, the new chauffeur, had been given the day off. The grandson and his friend were both upstairs in the bedroom. Evidently both had woken up in the middle of the night with high temperatures.

Gorlice kept a polite look of concern on his face while Frau Lasch complained of the trouble that had fallen into her lap. The *Danke Sagen* feast had been a failure: the fowl overcooked, the boys drinking too much and becoming unruly and then suddenly turning pale and practically falling over from wretchedness. They were both much sicker than her husband. Frau Lasch sighed and twisted her hands. She must call the doctor, and then call the von Neuwander boy's parents. But first she rattled off a list of chores that she wanted taken care of: gutters to clean out, a ditch to drain, and the usual raking and sweeping. Oh, and he mustn't forget to patch the roof over the dining room; a spreading stain had appeared on the ceiling, which meant only one thing.

Gorlice swallowed his annoyance. The woman had given him enough work to last a week. Typical. And she wouldn't be so busy tending to the sick that she'd forget to keep an eagle eye on him. He nodded his head while she ticked off each item; then he went out to the garage to gather his tools. He would begin with the easiest tasks: raking and pruning. He might get around to the gutters before lunch, and then again he might not. Draining the ravine at the bottom of the garden would take the whole afternoon. The roof could be put off until another day. A fine thing if he broke his back!

At twelve o'clock, the doctor arrived, bag in hand; Gorlice, high up on a ladder where he was pulling leaves from a gutter, saw the car drive up to the curb. The doctor, young and self-important, stayed for half an hour. A little later, Gorlice sat in the kitchen while Anna-Maria made him a sandwich. She reported that Dr. Weber was not unduly alarmed. There was quite a lot of flu circulating. Nothing to be done except bed rest, fluids and aspirin. Young Joachim was suffering more than Val; the poor boy, despite the aspirin, was delirious from fever.

Gorlice, munching his *Leberwürst* sandwich, remembered to inquire about the *Herr Kommerzielrat*. Oh, there was nothing much to worry about, Frau Lasch said. Her husband was already feeling better and talking about going back to work on Monday. As if the factory couldn't get along without him! *Nicht zu stoppen!* Gorlice smiled courteously. Really, it was as if she was asking for his friendship. Perhaps she sincerely wanted to be forgiven, in which case she wasn't quite as rotten an egg as he'd thought. Well, you could never tell with people.

By teatime, Hermann, dressed in slippers, pajamas and robe, was seated in a big chair in the living room, reading the paper. The boys' fevers hadn't gone down very much but they were sitting up in bed and taking nourishment. It wouldn't be a good idea to send Joachim home just yet, the doctor said; the patient might catch another chill. Best if he stayed another night. Arthur had already called the von Neuwanders. Herr Otto von Neuwander had answered: he and Frau von Neuwander were grateful, they were certain Joachim was receiving the best of care but, no, they wouldn't be paying their boy a visit: it would only give Frau Lasch more work. As if a short visit meant a formal reception! Probably the parents feared catching the illness; these things were always more contagious in their early stages. Arthur didn't altogether blame them. Thankfully the windows were firmly shut and the furnace set to a comfortable temperature, but his own throat felt suspiciously scratchy. He remembered that it was around this same time of year that he'd come down with whooping cough. When was it? The year of Franz-Josef's demise.

While he sipped his tea, Arthur wondered if he should put in a transatlantic call to Joyce. She'd never forgive him if things took a turn for the worse and she hadn't been notified. On the other hand, it would only cause her distress and there was nothing she could do on the other side of the world. Everybody would be asleep. He stretched his shoulders and went over to a window with a view of the back garden. He could see Gorlice lugging a ladder and a pail of tar to the side of the house. He ought to tell him to go home but he didn't want to interfere. Hopefully the fellow would finish whatever he was doing quickly. Arthur turned his back on the window, yawned, went into the living room and took a seat opposite his father. They began discussing the deteriorating situation in Berlin.

By the time Gorlice climbed up on the roof, it was past five o'clock. He cursed himself for being a fool. He ought to have told the Lasch woman that it was too late and too dark. Besides, there wasn't going to be any rain tonight; a half moon was rising in the clear sky and a bright planet glittered. He had a good view of neighboring roofs, presumably all of them leak-proof, some with smoking chimneys and some with television antennae extending their arms up to Heaven. Well, he might as well finish what he'd begun. He'd brought an oversized flashlight with him; it shouldn't be too hard.

Gorlice judged that the problem must be located where the pitched roof over the dining room butted up against the second storey. Sure enough, two or three shingles looked rotten. His boss would have to see about having them replaced but for now it would suffice to patch the tar underneath. He put his tar bucket to one side, removed a claw hammer from his tool belt and proceeded to pry up a shingle. He grunted and swore softly. Damned if the thing wasn't stubborn as hell! It was going to take longer than he'd imagined. He ought to climb down and tackle it early the next day. *Ach!* What was the use? It would be just as much trouble tomorrow as tonight. He paused for a moment to catch his breath. When he exhaled, a puff of vapor swirled in the air. He pulled his knitted cap down over his ears. He had forgotten to bring a pair of gloves and his fingers were smarting.

There were lights on behind a dormer window that projected from the second storey. The grandson's bedroom. He and his pal were nice and warm! Gorlice felt an urge to see for himself, even though he knew it would only fuel his anger. Whenever he crossed paths with them, the grandson gave him a superior sort of glance, and the von Neuwander kid—conceited brat!—didn't even bother to look up.

Gorlice pulled himself up, planted his boots on the sloping eave and peered through the glass. He kept very quiet; the occupants mustn't catch him spying. The boys were sitting on the bigger of the two beds in their pajamas, playing cards. Not as sick as all that! The bedclothes were strewn with junk: orange peels, empty juice bottles, an open tin of biscuits, a comic book and what appeared to be a toy pistol. A good time they were having, even if their faces were flushed and damp with sweat!

But what was this? The older boy was throwing down his cards and was punching the other one in the arms and chest. The two flung pillows at each other and then the von Neuwander kid was flattening the grandson down on the bed, holding his wrists and keeping his body pinned between his knees. No, they certainly weren't as sick as all that! Now the boys were wrestling and laughing. Gorlice sensed something more than horseplay in the air. What next? It might prove worthwhile to stay where he was for a little longer, never mind his frozen fingers.

Hölle und Verdammnis! His feet were slipping! He grabbed the ledge harder; his boots scraped against the shingles. At the sound of it, the older boy sprang across the room, quick as a rat. Gorlice crouched low, not daring to move. The window was flung open and Gorlice had a clear view of Joachim von Neuwander glaring at him, as righteously indignant as one of his noble ancestors. It was almost comical! But what was that he was pointing?

Gorlice hoisted himself up and faced the two boys; the grandson had crept up beside his friend.

"*Was ist los, Val?* You don't know me?"

Val hesitated. Then: "It's only Gor-*litch*-ee."

Joachim scowled. "He want to steal from us. One time, a servant in our *Schloss*—"

Before he could explain the offense, the gun, which Achim was pointing out of the window, slipped from his hand. It clattered down the sloping roof and came to rest in a gutter.

"*Meine Pistole!*"

Gorlice laughed in spite of his discomfort. The kid's teeth were chattering so hard it looked as if they might fall out of his head. Really, he ought to go back to bed! Gorlice gave Val a conspiratorial glance. They were all in this together, weren't they? Then he let himself down and made his way to the edge.

He reached into the gutter and retrieved the little gun. He examined it. Not a toy after all! The pistol looked like a relic of the last century; these old families loved to save such things for posterity. He ought to keep it in his pocket for now; the Neuwander kid had behaved in such a peculiar, threatening way, there was no telling what he might try. But then, on the other hand, it might be best to give it back; things would go badly if he were accused of trying to steal the boy's prized possession.

Gorlice clambered back up to the window. He handed the gun back to its owner and made a little bow. Best to treat the whole thing as a joke and at the same time show he was in charge of the situation. He addressed Joachim: Did he always take a gun into bed with him? It wasn't loaded, was it? There was no crime worth mentioning in the neighborhood. Would it not be a good idea to put it away now and not tell anyone?

Val knew the pistol held a single bullet. Achim had been playing with it on the bed, unloading and reloading. *Possession of a lethal weapon!* Achim could get into a lot of trouble. Gorlice wasn't the type to snitch. But what business did he have peeping through bedroom windows?

"He'll say you pointed a loaded gun at him," Val said. He had an odd sensation that the words were coming from someone else. His voice dropped to a whisper. "He'll say he saw something through the window." Achim would know what he meant. "He's caused all kinds of trouble," Val went on. "He made us throw stones, and drink from his filthy bottle, and there was that car accident. He almost got my brother killed, and then he tried to ... ." He searched for the German equivalent of "blackmail". Achim wouldn't know the English word. Oh yes, he'd seen it in an article in *Die Welt.* "He wanted to *erpressen* ... ."

Gorlice let out a cry. "*Das ist alles vorbei!* All forgotten!"

"*Schwindler!*" Joachim's voice shook.

Gorlice felt a ripple of fear pass through him. A loaded pistol! He should climb down and tell the boss before somebody did something stupid. But he wasn't the sort to get a couple of boys in trouble. He'd done worse things at their age.

He let himself down the roof, moving slowly backwards, and picked up his claw hammer, then climbed back and held onto the window ledge with one hand while he held the tool aloft.

"*Siehst du, Val?* I come to fix roof. *Frau Lasch—*"

But Val wouldn't let Gorlice finish. "He could have used that to break the window. Maybe he didn't know we were inside."

"*Nein.* He know all right," Joachim said. "Kill us in our beds."

"*Mit seine Hammer,*" Val said. Somehow it was even more ridiculous in German. But he felt a rare pleasure in tormenting Gorlice.

He noticed that Achim's hand was shaking. If he fired, the bullet would probably end up in the trees behind the house. Gorlice would get a scare! It struck Val that the man had a habit of looking at him sideways, as if he divined a secret that amused him. From now on, after what he'd glimpsed through the window, that sideways look would be a thorn in his side. It would be good to watch Gorlice stagger and fall, if only from fright.

There was a bang, and Gorlice screamed and fell back. He rolled, arms flailing, and dropped over the edge of the house. The body lay face-up on the lawn. Arthur, hearing the gunshot and a noise like a barrel tumbling, came running. A moment later Hermann, wearing his hat and overcoat, followed. Lastly came Anna-Maria, who had at first taken the gunshot for a car backfiring. Gorlice was conscious but quite unable to speak. When Arthur unbuttoned the jacket, the shirt was bloody. The poor man, he said to Hermann, must have been attacked and fallen from the roof. Probably he'd seen someone trying to break into the house, and the man had fired and taken off in a panic. Hermann gave his son a skeptical look. Since when did housebreakers operate at five in the afternoon, when there were people up and about? No, there must be some other explanation.

Gorlice's mouth twitched and his eyes rolled up in his head. Anna-Maria wailed and held her head between her hands. It was her fault for making him work so late! Would she never stop bringing these Gorlices to grief? It was a curse on her head!

Hermann begged her to gain control of herself. It looked, he said, as if the man would survive. He led her into the house, sat her down in a chair, and went into his study to summon an ambulance. Arthur stayed outside, kneeling beside the victim. The man's face was white, vacant, sweaty. He was in shock. He shouldn't be moved. Arthur realized that the boys must have heard the commotion. He looked up and saw two anxious faces craning from a wide open window. Straight from an overheated room into the icy cold! He himself was shivering violently. They'd always made fun of him for feeling the cold, and now their curiosity was going to put them in the hospital!

"Is he dead?"

"Go back inside Val! And get back under the covers!"

The window slammed shut. But just before it did, Arthur caught sight of what looked like a toy pistol in Joachim von Neuwander's trembling hand.

THE SECOND WEEK of December, the weather forecast for Garnet called for clouds and snow. By Monday afternoon big flakes were falling, and drifts were already piling up. Children hurried home from school through the white, deposited their book bags and lunch boxes, and ran back outside to play.

Marcus Lash, stopping on the front porch of his house, watched some boys throwing snowballs on the opposite side of the street. He recognized one of them: freckled, red-haired Teddy Kroger, who was in a class for slow learners at Running Brook Elementary School. Today, Teddy was wearing a hat made of imitation leather, with a visor and two big flaps coming down over the ears. Marcus liked snowballs, but not Teddy Kroger. What he really felt like doing was taking some snapshots of the trees in the backyard; the bare branches looked especially fine under the fresh layer of snow. But then he remembered that there wasn't any film in his Brownie camera.

Marcus came inside the house, stamped snow off his shoes, deposited his coat and knapsack in the hall, and went into the kitchen where his mother was seated at the table with typewritten sheets spread out in front of her. She was staring straight ahead. Marcus often found her in a sad mood when he came home from school. He sat down next to her.

"What's wrong, Mom?"

Joyce managed a weak smile. "Oh, nothing special. Are you hungry? I forgot to buy cupcakes, and you and Adrian finished all the chocolate-chip cookies. I can heat up a bowl of tomato soup, if you like."

"I guess I'll wait for dinner. I kind of have a stomach ache, anyway."

"Want some ginger ale?"

"No thanks. I'm not really thirsty."

"I'm sorry meals haven't been very interesting lately. I'll try harder."

"Half the time, Adrian doesn't even eat with us. He's hardly ever home."

"What if we have dinner at that place out on Route 9? The King and Queen. The waitresses bring the food right out to your car. Adrian won't be able to resist."

"I don't know where he is. Maybe he went somewhere with Robert Boardman."

"Boardman!"

Marcus giggled. "You hate him."

"After what happened … ." Joyce's voice trailed off. She was losing track of her eldest son's complicated affairs. Last weekend, Olivia Brainard had invited Adrian up to Rushton. Joyce prayed that Adrian had learned his lesson. She hadn't the strength to weather another storm. She suspected that Eric and Frankie didn't keep a very close watch over their children's movements. The Brainards floated on a tide of money, talent and self-assurance. She envied them. She'd never before realized how ugly her own living room curtains were, with their crazy pattern of peaches and pears. It wouldn't cost that much to throw out the worst furnishings—starting with the awful curtains—and begin over. Why shouldn't she own something like the abstract wooden birds that stood on the Brainards' mantelpiece—the ones that reminded her of the famous carving by Brancusi?

She'd even had a dream in which she was an addition to the Brainard family: she and Frankie were waiting for a train; the two of them seemed to be best of friends. And now she had something tangible to look forward to. The Brainards were throwing a New Year's Eve party to which the Lashes were invited. Lawrence Drury was going to be there and Frankie hinted at a famous abstract-expressionist painter. Frankie wouldn't say the name on the phone; she wanted it to be a surprise. "I'll have to bring in a caterer," Frankie said.

Joyce could hardly wait. What a story to tell Sandra van Riper! Fortunately for all concerned, the boys' "grandmother" would have to miss the occasion; Mrs. Woodbine was going to be celebrating the holidays with her sprawling family. But poor, overweight, heartbroken Julie Eiger! And for that matter, poor Helen and Hank! All through that awkward Thanksgiving dinner, the Eigers had given every sign of viewing Adrian in a new, more favorable light. Future son-in-law? Better the devil you know! Of course they knew nothing of the debacle at Lapine's. But it looked as if Adrian was going to disappoint them once again. Olivia Brainard was his new favorite, and all because of a wrong turn into a wrong driveway. But Adrian might have lost interest anyhow, now that Julie had gained so much weight. With boys his age, looks were everything

Marcus's voice broke in on her thoughts. "Do you think that lady would have given Boardman money?"

"I don't know, Marcus. Maybe you and Uncle Philip saved him from getting into real trouble. You two showed up just in the nick of time."

"Like guardian angels."

"Something like that."

"Do you think Philip and Leni are going to get married?"

"I don't know. Maybe." Joyce sighed. Philip had "eloped" to Chicago with Leni soon after Thanksgiving weekend. She was more angry with the nurse than with Philip. Leaving her in the lurch, practically overnight! Leni had made a thousand apologies; had even taken it upon herself to find a replacement: a cheerful colored woman who seemed capable enough. Still, the whole thing was insane. What was the rush? If the affair didn't work out, who knew what crazy thing Philip might do? Next time, he might aim more accurately. Leni was so head over heels she'd taken leave of her senses. Or had she planned it all out? Maybe she'd learned some spells in that enchanted forest of hers. Arthur must have been astounded when he read her telegram breaking the news. And Hermann must be beside himself.

"You miss Leni, don't you? And Uncle Philip? It's been sort of lonely around here."

Joyce handed Arthur's letter to Marcus. "It's from your father. You can read it."

"Is there anything bad in it? Val's getting better, isn't he?" A terrible thought struck Marcus. "Is Gor-*litch*-ee's going to die?"

"No chance of that. Read it. You might as well know how things are going over there."

Marcus wiped his eyeglasses with a paper napkin, placed them back on his nose and ears, and began reading.

Dearest Joyce,

I hope this letter finds everyone well. I realize how painful it must be for you, thousands of miles away from Val and not being able to take care of him. How are you bearing up? My telephone call, after everything literally came crashing down, must have been a terrible shock. I wish I could have broken the news more gently, and in person.

The main thing is that Val should be out of the hospital as early as tomorrow. I'll wire as soon as I know for certain. The penicillin has worked wonders on his pneumonia, and the past few days he's been feeling much better. Thank goodness his recovery won't take anywhere near as long as yours did, in the bad old days before antibiotics! As for the other boy, Joachim has been up and about all week; his influenza never developed into anything more serious. Val was simply the unluckier of the two, since they were both shivering terribly from cold when I went up to their room. Haven't I always warned you and the boys about that sort of thing?

The not-so-good news is that I had a visit yesterday from two plain-clothes policemen, informing me that Val must remain in Vienna at least until a preliminary inquest into the shooting has been completed. I've been in touch with our consulate, and apparently there's nothing to be done except wait patiently for the wheels to turn. Hagenfeld says we have nothing to fear, as far as Val is concerned. As for the other boy, Joachim has signed a deposition stating that he never meant to fire the pistol; the gun went off because his hand was shaking violently from the cold. Whether he intended to cause harm may turn out to be moot, if the authorities judge that the act itself was involuntary. Well, apart from everything else, it's rather an interesting defense, isn't it?

I have no doubt that our son will stick to whatever story will get his friend off the hook. Val has been beside himself over the possibility that Joachim could be convicted of assault and wind up in a home for juvenile delinquents. I try to reassure him that his friend will probably get off with a slap on the wrist for possession of a loaded, unlicensed pistol. And I think that once Gorlice is fully recovered from his injuries, he'll be far more interested in a generous settlement than in ruining Joachim's life, much less ruining our son's. The fellow is not ill-natured and, when I went to visit him in the hospital yesterday, he didn't appear to hold a grudge against either of the boys. If anything, he blames Anna-Maria for making him climb up on the roof in the first place! Of course I can't guarantee how he'll behave once he's recovered. At the moment he's inclined to ramble, on account of the pain-killers they've been giving him. It appears that the broken ribs and sprained wrist, to say nothing of the wound in his shoulder, are healing nicely.

Anna-Maria and I are greatly concerned about my father. Philip's shooting himself was bad enough but the attack on Gorlice is more than Hermann can comprehend. He keeps asking how Joachim could have been so stupid as to point a loaded pistol at someone, and why Val didn't stop him in time. I confess I can't fully explain, and neither Val nor Gorlice has given me much to go on. At any rate, the final straw for Hermann was when two men in long overcoats showed up and handed us the document that forbids Val from leaving the city. An all-too-vivid reminder of 1938! Of course the police were well within their rights this time, but nevertheless it did feel decidedly sinister.

Besides all that, there's the unsettling coincidence that Gorlice will have a scar in almost the exact same spot as Philip's! It's a lot to digest, even for someone as level-headed as my father.

Anna-Maria goes around wringing her hands over the affair and bringing up Hermann's birthday dinner, and the number thirteen, and the curse she imagines she has brought down on the Gorlices, and says how sorry she feels for Val and the von Neuwander boy. Believe me, it's not been easy this past week! To top it off, Herr von Neuwander has informed me on the telephone, in his politely insinuating way, that our son is "partly responsible". No doubt he fears an exorbitant claim on Gorlice's part and expects my father to chip in over and above whatever the insurance covers. Hagenfeld says it's out of the question, since Val never so much as touched the weapon. All smoke and no fire!

Meanwhile, Joachim is forbidden for the time being from communicating with Val. Really, it's hard on both boys. Hagenfeld says that these legal procedures take time and that we can look forward to the process dragging on well into the new year. You must decide for yourself whether you want to join us here until it's all straightened out. Of course it would be a great thing for me, and for Val too, if you came as soon as you could, in which case you might consider leaving Marcus and Adrian at home, under Mrs. Woodbine's watchful eye.

I'm afraid there's no question of Val's now taking over the factory. He's quite heart-broken that Hermann has abandoned the plan. This latest catastrophe, I'm sorry to say, has left my father much the worse for wear; he suddenly looks like an eighty year-old man, or even older. One too many blows! He thinks that in view of the scandal (yes, it's been in the papers), he'll get considerably less from his American buyer than he would have gotten under normal circumstances. Who knows? He's mentioned retiring somewhere far away from the source of so many painful memories. I've suggested we find a nice place for him and Anna-Maria in Garnet, but he feels the south of France would be more to his liking.

I'm pleased to hear that Frieda is doing a little better and that the new nurse is satisfactory. I'm astonished by Leni even more than I am by Phil. The woman appears to charm men of all ages; first Marcus and then my brother! I've written to Philip cautioning him not to rush into a marriage, not that my warning will do any good. Hermann simply shakes his head and leaves it in the hands of Fate.

That's all I have for now. I need hardly add that I love all of you, and especially my long-suffering wife.

XXXOOOXXX Arthur

Joyce watched Marcus put the sheets back into their envelope. He looked up at his mother. His eyes were glassy.

"What is it, darling? Val will be all right, and we'll all be together again pretty soon."

"It's just that … ." The dam broke and tears began running down Marcus's cheeks. Joyce was shocked by his choking sobs. She remembered the last time she'd seen him cry, when she'd discovered him on the ocean liner's deck, abandoned by Adrian and Julie. But that time hadn't been nearly as bad. She put her arm around his shoulder and stroked his cheek. He leaned against her.

"It's just that—why does he say 'long-suffering wife'? Who's making you suffer, Mom? Is it Val? Or Daddy? Or Adrian or me?"

Joyce took him into her arms. "Don't be silly," she murmured in his ear. "It's just a figure of speech. A little joke. How could I suffer from three wonderful boys?"

"You love Daddy, don't you?"

It occurred to her, too late, that she'd neglected to mention her husband along with the "wonderful boys."

"Of course I do! All families have problems. Little fights. But we always make up, don't we?"

"Why did they have to shoot Gor-*litch*-ee?"

They! Even the littlest slips, the Freudians said, meant something important. Joyce released her son and gave him a moment to wipe his face. The tears made damp spots on his long-sleeved shirt.

"It was the other boy who pointed a pistol at Gorlice. Val had nothing to do with it. You know that, don't you? Joachim's fever was so high he didn't realize what he was doing. And it was so cold that night. You read what Daddy wrote. Joachim's hand was shaking and the gun went off by accident."

"That's what you said about Uncle Phil. But it wasn't an accident. He told me so."

"I know, Marcus. I wasn't truthful. I didn't want you to be frightened. I know how much you love your uncle. But this is different."

But Joyce doubted her own words. There must be more to the story than Arthur was able to say. Of course he wouldn't have pressed Val too hard while he was lying in a hospital bed with pneumonia. Would it make any difference, now that the crisis had passed? Val would never tell the whole truth. What about the victim? So far, Gorlice hadn't said much to the police; too muddled from the pills—or else he was holding back. It was only a matter of time before he lowered the blade.

" Gor-*litch*-ee didn't want to hurt anybody," Marcus said.

"Everyone understands that. I'm sure Val tried to stop his friend."

What more could she say? Secretive, untrustworthy Val! Her unhappy boy! She must see to it that what was broken grew back together. She ought to start looking for a really good psychologist who specialized in adolescents. Maybe Sandra Van Riper would know whom to call. But she couldn't wait to see Val. She would leave Marcus and Adrian with Mrs. Woodbine as soon as the holidays were over and fly to Vienna.

She glanced at Marcus's face. He looked so forlorn!

Nothing, of course, compared to the state Val must be in. She mustn't wait even another week! She must forget about the Brainards' utterly unimportant New Year's party and fly to Vienna at once. She would take the boys with her. The whole family would spend Christmas together. What difference did it make if Marcus and Adrian missed ten days of school? She'd send them home to be with Mrs. Woodbine after the holidays. Hermann would pay the air fares. First class this time.

"It must be hard for your brother over there. First pneumonia, and then all of his plans ruined, and not being able to see his friend. We ought to spend the Christmas vacation with Val and your father. It's the least we can do."

"Can we fly? I wish we'd never gotten on that ship in the first place."

"I can't say I disagree. It was fun coming home on a jet, wasn't it?"

"Horace was glad he didn't have to stay in another kennel."

"Where is Horace? He's so reclusive and his breath smells funny. I'm sure there's something wrong with him."

"He's depressed, if you ask me. I saw him asleep in the hallway. I was looking for a roll of film in the hall table. I guess I must have used it already."

"We can go into the village and buy some more."

"I don't know. I might go outside and build a snowman. It should stay light for another half hour."

Mrs. Woodbine came into the kitchen and observed the two despondent faces.

"Land o' Goshen! I expect that letter must have brought some more bad news!"

Joyce disengaged from her son and straightened his hair. "Nothing as bad as all that. The important thing is that Val is out of the hospital, and he and his father are coming home for good, as soon as the loose ends are tied up. It's just that it's going to take more time than we'd like." She decided to postpone discussing her immediate plans with Mrs. Woodbine. Doing so would only lead to endless talk.

"Gor-*litch*-ee," Marcus put in, "is going to be rich. He's going to get millions of dollars."

"I expect he'll spend it on all sorts of foolishness. I never believed anything that fella said to me. John-Wesley says—."

Mrs. Woodbine began a story about a disreputable Italian her son had somehow gotten to know over in Europe.

BY HALF PAST four o'clock, Marcus had put a knitted cap on the snowman's head and made a carrot-nose. A corn-cob pipe he'd bought two summers ago in a shop in Seaford completed the effect. Who was around to appreciate his work? Only his mother and Mrs. Woodbine. But then he remembered that old Mrs. Frohlich, whose back yard lay adjacent to the Lashes', might look out one of her rear-facing windows and see his creation.

Lonesomeness welled up in Marcus's chest. He would like to have shown off the snowman to Leni. The *Edelweiss* blossom she'd given him lay safe in a desk drawer. A vivid picture of Leni in her neat white nurse's uniform, laughing as she listened to one of his stories, passed before his mind's eye. On more than one occasion, she had taken him in her arms and given him a hug. It had felt very different from his mother's hugs. She had smelled of a pine forest. He'd felt a sort of warm thrill. But he wouldn't be seeing Leni anymore—maybe never again, unless she and Uncle Philip got married and they both came to visit. But even then, it wouldn't be the same as before.

Most of all, he wished for Adrian's company. Shouldn't he be home from school by now?

Marcus didn't know it but Adrian had stopped off at the public library. The library was practically empty and very quiet, a good place to concentrate on the letter he intended to write to Olivia Brainard. Of course there was the telephone but he thought a letter might be more romantic. Afterwards, he'd have to write a different letter to Eric and Frankie, thanking them for their hospitality. But first Olivia. So far he'd only gotten as far as telling her how much he'd "enjoyed everything". Not very original. He wanted to say more than that. On the other hand, he mustn't sound too eager. She'd drop him in a minute if she thought he was some desperate, awkward high-school kid. Late on Saturday night, when he'd been staying over in Connecticut, he'd thought about sneaking out of the Brainards' guest cottage and tip-toeing upstairs to Olivia's bedroom in the main house, but he'd decided against it. What if Jonathan had seen him in the hallway? Besides, Olivia might think he was acting like a little boy. She was the cool, reserved type. Which only made him want her all the more.

He felt a pang of guilt. It wasn't his fault that they'd driven up to the wrong house. Suppose Mrs. Woodbine hadn't spotted the number 160 on the Brainards' mailbox? He never would have met Olivia. Maybe he would have overlooked Julie's extra pounds. But Julie was a child compared with Olivia Brainard, who'd refused to let him even so much as kiss her, after she'd brought him upstairs to look at her modern-art books.

There wasn't an hour that he didn't think of "Livvy". She crowded out everything else, even the crazy stuff that had happened at Granddaddy's house. Val and that friend of his! He didn't quite know what to make of it. What were they doing with a loaded pistol in the bedroom? Weren't they supposed to be sick? What made them think Gorlice was breaking in? They might have killed him! His own misdeeds were tame in comparison. Not that breaking Julie's heart was a small thing. All through Thanksgiving dinner, she'd kept staring at him with a sort of hopeless expression on her face. She sensed things weren't the same. When he kissed her goodnight, he could tell she was holding back tears. He'd forced a foolish grin and promised to call her soon. But he kept putting it off. And then this past Saturday, when he'd been in Rushton Village, he'd had the strangest feeling that Julie was following him and Olivia and Jonathan. Wasn't that her peeking around the corner? When he looked a second time, it was some other girl. All his guilty imagination!

He ought to write to Julie and break it to her gently. He wondered how long it would take for her to get over him. She'd find someone else, especially if she got back down to her old weight. In *Lesbian Love Stories,* one of the characters got killed on account of jealousy. That was fiction, though.

Adrian stared out the library windows at an expanse of earth, already thickly covered with snow. He held his ball-point pen suspended over his letter. He must see Olivia again, soon, before she got distracted by some other boy. There must be some way they could meet in New York, or Providence. He didn't want to wait around until the New Year's Eve Party. He must think of a plan and present it to her.

While Marcus put the finishing touches to his snowman and Adrian pondered his strategy, it was already late at night in Vienna. In Hermann Lasch's house, the head of the family was already in bed; lately he was tired out by nine o'clock. Anna-Maria opened the bedroom door a crack to check on her husband. There he lay, tucked under a feathery comforter. She whispered his name but there was no answer. Asleep already! She'd always been able to convince herself that Hermann would never get truly old. But not anymore! These last few weeks had changed him. She was married to an old man who needed a good nine hours at night, on top of his siesta. She herself was to blame! She ought not to have pestered Gorlice about that leaky roof. She was consoled by the thought that her victim stood to get a lot of money. Enough to improve his lot in life. It might yet turn out for the best. These things were in the hands of God.

Anna-Maria closed the door gently and went downstairs to see if there was anything Arthur and Val wanted before bed. She found them seated in front of the television, with the volume turned down low. When she offered tea and hot chocolate, Arthur gave her a wan smile and refused.

"Nothing for me. *Danke schön, Anna-Maria.*"

"Then I go to bed. *Gut Schlafen, Artur.*"

Anna-Maria tried not to mind that Val hadn't bothered to answer—not even to wish her a good night. Well, the child was still terribly upset. His friend under house arrest and his plans spoiled! And then the poor boy must know that everyone was wondering why he hadn't acted to head off the calamity. She herself hardly knew how to explain it.

As soon as he heard Anna-Maria going up the stairs to bed, Arthur gathered up his resolve. Now was the time to have a real talk. He'd put it off too long. He glanced sideways at his son. Val, slumped in his chair, looked as if he were deep in his own thoughts. Not that there was anything worth watching; the final program of the evening featured yet another exhibition of *Schuplattler* dancers slapping their thighs and stamping their feet. With the sound turned almost all the way down, the effect was of marionettes executing a weird pantomime.

"Ready to turn in for the night, Val? I can't stand to watch it to the end. At least they could run some bad American shows."

No answer. His effort at levity, like all the others, had fallen flat. There was nothing for it but to take the plunge.

"You know Val, if you want to talk more about what happened, I'm always willing."

"I already told you everything."

"They'll probably ask you a lot of questions at the inquest. Gorlice may tell a different story from yours and Achim's."

"What do you expect me to say? I tried to get Achim to put the gun down. Maybe he didn't hear me. Anyway, he was shaking from the cold. We both were. He didn't pull the trigger on purpose."

"But why was he pointing the gun in the first place? You told him it was only Gorlice. Why didn't he believe you?"

"I don't know."

"Try to think, Val. It's not as if Achim had never seen Gorlice before. Could he have forgotten what he looked like?"

Val shrugged. "You think Achim's lying. You think we're both lying."

"I think you're worried about your friend. It's understandable if you feel you ought to protect him."

"What is it you want me to say?" Val's voice was trembling. "Do you think I wanted him to shoot Gorlice? Why should I?" Val stood up and snapped off the television. He turned and faced his father. "If you really want to know, I don't care about Gorlice. He shouldn't have been spying on us. It's all his fault Granddaddy's selling off the factory."

"Is it really Gorlice's fault, Val? Perhaps he was just curious when he saw the light was on."

"*Curious!* What was he doing up there in the first place? Couldn't the roof have waited until morning? Anna-Maria wouldn't have minded. Maybe he really did want to steal something. Maybe he wanted to wreck the whole house or set it on fire. He's been mad at our family for months."

Arthur sat in silence. His son's fury! He suddenly glimpsed

an explanation, as if someone had turned on a light in a dark room. The chauffeur had witnessed something he shouldn't have seen.

"You're right, Val. He shouldn't have been spying. But whatever Gorlice saw couldn't have been so terrible."

Val glared at his father. "What do you mean, Daddy? We were playing cards. It's not my fault if Gorlice ... if that creep ... if he ... if we—" Val stopped abruptly. There was a long silence. Arthur stood up and put his arm around his son.

"It's all right, Val. We'll talk about it some more in the morning. You ought to get some sleep now."

He led Val upstairs to bed. Tomorrow he would try to talk sensibly to his son. But now, the boy needed his rest. At the door to the bedroom, he kissed Val on the top of his head. The "flaxen prince"! It was wrong of him to mock his son's beauty.

"Don't worry, Val. It's just a matter of compensating Gorlice for his injuries. Granddaddy's insurance will cover some of it and the von Neuwanders will have to come up with the rest. No one wants to hurt you or Achim."

"I know all that. Anyway, like I said, we were playing cards."

Arthur went back downstairs, shaking his head. Val was sticking to his story like glue. The authorities might accept it. If not, Joachim would pay a heavy price and Val would have to live with his part in the drama. There must be some way he could help his son! He would discuss it with Joyce. Perhaps Philip would have some insights. His brother had his own complicated nature to cope with. All those years of battling a father whose blindness was somehow inextricably bound up with his virtues!

Arthur went into the study and picked out a book from the shelves, something to help him drop off to sleep. Henry James. *The Europeans.* On his way through the downstairs hallway, he noticed that there was no light at the bottom of the door to the master bedroom. Good. Both father and step-mother were asleep. Hermann had been complaining of waking up from his first half hour of sleep and then being unable to go back. Last night, he'd had his reading lamp on past midnight.

But Arthur was wrong to assume that a dark room meant slumber. Although Anna-Maria had already sunk into a sound repose, Hermann was lying wide awake in the bed next to hers. He was listening to her light snoring. It soothed him. A good woman he was married to! He couldn't quite grasp how she could have slammed the door on Frau Gorlice. Well, nobody, however good their character, could know how they would act under extreme conditions. The ugliness he'd seen in prison! Men squabbling over rations. Civilized people whining and groveling, wasting away from sheer despair! He'd witnessed stoicism and self-sacrifice as well but it was the bad behavior that was most fixed in his memory.

He tried silently reciting a passage that he'd memorized from Racine; a practice that usually sent him to sleep. *Je l'ai aimé trop* … . No good. What about La Fontaine? *La cigale ayant chanté* … . He gave up the effort. Tomorrow's appointment kept intruding. A Mr. Hawthorne from American Forest Products would arrive at his office at ten o'clock. The man had flown in from the firm's overseas office in Brussels. How much would he offer? A million at the most. A pitifully small sum, even allowing for the accompanying debt. But what could he do? Gorlice's plight had caused a scandal. It was in every newspaper, and even on the radio and television. Of course it wouldn't materially affect business but Hermann nonetheless suspected, probably unreasonably, that Hawthorne would try to use it to his advantage.

Damned if the von Neuwander boy hadn't ruined everything! Well, it was really the father who was to blame. Leaving a weapon and ammunition around the house! Austrian *Schlamperei!* And then his own grandson, his chosen heir, bore some of the guilt; Val should have stopped the wheels from turning, just as one threw a lever to stop machinery from spinning out of control. Well, it was too late now. His project was in tatters. He no longer had the heart for it. Let the Americans profit from his life's labor! To think how many months he'd spent wresting back his property, and all for nothing!

Hermann's thoughts grew fragmentary. Herr Mittwald … the Nazi swine could go to hell … Austrians had done all in their power to destroy him … Arthur had been right all along … Time to turn his back on his native land … Nice or Cannes, where the weather was mild all year around … Yearly visits to America … Garnet and then Chicago … Philip had taken up with that German girl just to spite him … The nurse, or whatever she pretended to be … It would end badly.

Hermann's eyes closed. He began to dream even before he was fully asleep. He was in a courtroom, facing a judge. The judge was explaining the conditions under which his property would be restored to him. There were innumerable cardboard boxes in the courtroom. He, Hermann Lasch, must go through all of them and vouch for his rightful ownership of each and every item. It would take years! Who could he turn to for assistance? His sons were far away. There was only Val, but Val was terribly sick. He would, as usual, have to handle everything on his own. It was how he'd always come through in the end.

At the hour when Hermann finally fell asleep, Franz Gorlice, lying on his back in his hospital bed, was contemplating his future. Now that they'd weaned him off the morphine, he could think things through more clearly. Klara's uncle had found him a lawyer, a Polish Jew who'd somehow survived Nazis and Communists and made a career in Vienna. Herr Epstein had already visited him in the hospital twice to go over everything. Criminal charges, the lawyer said, were certainly an option, if Gorlice wished to press them. Assault with a deadly weapon. Intent to do bodily harm! Well, he'd been young and stupid himself not so long ago, and he didn't feel like punishing the Neuwander kid, or the grandson either—at least no more than was necessary. The main thing was money, a lot of it; more than what Lasch's insurance would cover. He was perfectly willing to keep quiet but only if the other side showed a willingness to give him what he wanted. Otherwise he would say that Val had provoked the other boy to take aim and fire. Epstein had cautioned him that it would be his word against the boys'. What of it? Did the parents want him to tell his side of the story and have it repeated in the papers? He might stretch the truth a little. How should he put it? The boys had panicked because he'd caught them red-handed, so to speak. Indecent behavior! Why not? It wasn't too far from the facts.

The other side would cave in. He was sure of it. He would

get a large sum without any unpleasant complications. Just how large remained to be seen. Hermann Lasch might be persuaded to chip in; Epstein had heard that the old man was about to sell the business. *Herr Valentin* would have to find some other line of work! Gorlice laughed silently, so as not to awaken the man in the next bed. He glanced over at his roommate. The poor fellow coughed all day and night. The doctor said that the cough wasn't in the least contagious. Still, it was enough to drive anybody crazy! Thank God he'd be discharged soon; his lung was healing nicely and his ribs ached less than before. The future was looking better than he'd had any right to expect. A lucky misfortune, when all was said and done! Lucky for him, and lucky for Klara and little Moni. Maybe they'd decide to have another child—a boy, this time.

Gorlice let out a yawn and shifted his weight in the bed. *Herr Val!* A mixed up, cursed sort of kid. He wondered about the other two. Probably *Herr Adrian* was busy chasing girls back home. And *Herr Markus*? He had a soft spot for the youngest. So trusting! So honest! What was he up to over there? Skating? Sledding? Reading a comic book? American children had every-thing so easy.

If, at that moment, he could have seen Marcus putting the finishing touches to his snowman in the fading light, Gorlice might have felt sorry for him. Where were his friends? Didn't he have any? The snowman's carrot nose stuck out crookedly, and a top hat would have been an improvement over the knitted cap. Marcus stood back a few feet, surveying his handiwork. A verse from "Frosty the Snowman" came back to him:

> *Frosty the Snowman knew the sun was hot that day*
> *So he said let's run and we'll have some fun,*
> *Just before I melt away … .*

When he was a little boy, the words had made him cry. It was unbearable to think that Frosty had so short a time left! Even now, the thought of it made the back of his throat tighten up.

Mrs. Woodbine, watching Marcus from the kitchen window, thought she would miss him awfully, when it was time to go home and spend the holidays with her children and grandchildren. She suspected that, even before Christmas rolled around, Marcus would be over in Europe again with the rest of his family; Joyce Lash didn't look as if she could wait much longer.

Maybe, Mrs. Woodbine decided, she'd be too busy during the holidays to think about the Lashes very much. She'd have visits from Gabel's family, and Esther's, and she'd have to go to the old folks' home and see her mother, at eighty-nine in better shape than Frieda Michelson, who would probably not last another year.

But no, in spite of all her obligations, Marcus would be on her mind. She loved him as if he were her own!

Mrs. Woodbine wagged her big head. What a lot of foolishness and sinfulness she'd witnessed over the past few months! But it would all come out right, if not in this life, then on Judgment Day. She recalled something she'd learned in school, forty years ago. Sir Isaac Newton had proven that everything that goes up comes down, on account of gravity. She wasn't sure how satellites and so forth disobeyed the law of gravity. The government was keeping it all a secret. It didn't matter. On Judgment Day, God would fix things so that all the bodies—sinners and saints alike—would rise up from their graves and float up to Heaven. God would transform the resurrected bodies into a lightweight substance, so they could easily get to where they were going. She suspected that merciful Jesus would send only a very few—the truly wicked—back down to Hell.

Mrs. Woodbine opened the window a crack and called out to Marcus that it was getting dark and that it was time to come in and do some homework before Adrian got home and they all went out to eat at the King and Queen.

THE END

More Fiction from EnvelopeBooks

www.envelopebooks.co.uk

Frances Creighton: Found and Lost

KIRBY PORTER

Love demands trust but trust is a lot to ask, for victims of abuse. Having been bullied by two teachers in Belfast as a boy, Michael Roberts suppresses his childhood pains until the death of a girlfriend years later forces him to revisit lost memories and question his emotional inertia. EB7

Belle Nash and the Bath Soufflé

WILLIAM KEELING ESQ.

In the first volume of *The Gay Street Chronicles*, bachelor Belle Nash attempts to navigate bigotry and corruption in Regency Bath without compromising his boyfriend, the nephew of Immanuel Kant, or the legal talents of Gaia Champion. EB9

Lagos, Life and Sexual Distraction

TUNDE OSOSANYA

Twelve short stories, mostly focused on the struggle to survive in Lagos, Nigeria's commercial capital, and illustrating tensions that exist between the generations, the sexes and the country's different social classes and ethnicities. Written by an award-winning reporter with the BBC's West Africa bureau. EB13

The Attraction of Cuba

CHRIS HILTON

Chris Hilton went to Cuba to escape the boredom of everyday life and to make money, only to be entranced by the beauty of the country and of Yamilia, a street girl who brought meaning to his life but who could not help him from falling into an inevitable downward spiral. EB14

More fiction from EnvelopeBooks
www.envelopebooks.co.uk

Mustard Seed Itinerary
ROBERT MULLEN

When Po Cheng falls into a dream, he finds himself on the road to the imperial Chinese capital. Once there he rises to the heights of the civil service before discovering that there are snakes as well as ladders. Carrollian satire at its best. EB5

Belle Nash and the Bath Circus
WILLIAM KEELING ESQ.

In Volume Two of *The Gay Street Chronicles*, bachelor Belle Nash returns to Regency Bath from Grenada, inspired by a new love that leads him into various pretences that may compromise the ambitions of black circus impresario Pablo Fanque. EB16

The Train House on Lobengula Street
FATIMA KARA

An anguished but life-affirming novel, set within the Indian community in Bulawayo in Rhodesia of the 1950s and 1960s, about the capacity of women to gain the same advantages as men in the modern world while remaining faithful to traditional Muslim values. Affectionate and passionate. EB12

A Sin of Omission
MARGUERITE POLAND

An emotionally intense novel, set in 1870s South Africa at a time of rising anti-colonial resistance. The book examines the tragedy of a promising black preacher, hand-picked for training in England as a missionary, then returned to a mission station and neglected by the Church he loves. *Winner of the 2021 Sunday Times CNA 'Book of the Year' Award in South Africa.* EB6

Non-fiction from EnvelopeBooks

www.envelopebooks.co.uk

A Road to Extinction

JONATHAN LAWLEY

When Britain colonised the Andamans in 1857, the welfare of its African pygmy inhabitants was of no concern. Nine tribes died out. Dr Lawley now assesses survival prospects for the three remaining tribes and weighs up the legacy of his grandfather, who ran the colony in the early 1900s. EB2

Artist Spy Prisoner

GEORGE TOMAZIU

Artist George Tomaziu half-expected to be imprisoned and tortured for monitoring Nazi troop movements through Bucharest during the Second World War but thought that his heroism would be recognised when Socialism came to Romania in 1950. He was terribly mistaken. EB36

Postmark Africa

MICHAEL HOLMAN

Made an Amnesty Prisoner of Conscience while he was under house arrest as a student in Southern Rhodesia, the author went on to document Africa's emergence from colonialism as Africa Editor of the *Financial Times*. EB1

Why My Wife Had To Die

BRIAN VERITY

There is no known cure for Huntington's disease, a wasting condition that sufferers acquire from a parent. In this painful account, the author vents his rage at society, lawmakers, health services and the church for not grasping the need, as he sees it, to legalise compulsory sterilisation and assisted dying. EB11

Other titles from EnvelopeBooks

www.envelopebooks.co.uk

Princess Brainy
STEPHEN GAMES

She couldn't help being clever and couldn't help being hated for it but it didn't help that her mother was modern and that her father had banned the fairies. But what was she meant to do when disaster came to Rainland and the rivers dried up? Accept her deadly fate or get sacrificed to the revolution? EB37

From Bedales to the Boche
ROBERT BEST

Bedales, the progressive boarding school founded by J.H. Badley in 1893, instilled values that sustained many of its pupils through the rest of their lives. Robert Best recalls its influence on him as an enthusiastic army recruit in 1914 and, from 1916, in the Royal Flying Corps. EB3

My Modern Movement
ROBERT BEST

London's Festival of Britain in 1951 marked the belief that Modern design was visually, morally and commercially superior. Robert Best, the UK's leading lighting manufacturer, thinks the dice were loaded. This is his memoir. EB8

The Hopeful Traveller
JANINA DAVID

A collection of short stories about—and told by—single women who have put the past behind them but are still looking for their anchor in the present. It includes bitter-sweet accounts of the freedoms of postwar life, of foreign travel, of the rekindling of old friendships and of the search for new ones. EB4